Death Before Dishonor

By Kenny Hyman

A Black Magic ImagiNation Creation

By Kenny Hyman

A Black Magic ImagiNation Original.

Death Before Dishonor is a work of fiction. Names, places, characters, and incidents are products of the imagination of the author or are used fictitiously. Any resemblance to actual persons, events, or locations is entirely coincidental.

ISBN 978-0-9997359-0-9

Foreword

So, I came up with the idea for this book when I was seventeen. It took me years to write, though. You see, I had the content, but I simply lacked the know-how. The know-how came on the coattails of college. My two biggest struggles with writing came in the form of organization and narration. I learned that my brainstorming needed to be more organized and I had to write *scene* separate from *dialogue*. I also had to learn to throttle back on my descriptions. I'm verbose...in case you haven't met me before...and I'm even more so in my writing. That said, I had to chop a tremendous amount out of the story to keep it flowing. It's been a journey.

This is actually my second writing endeavor. My first was a vampire story that caused too many problems in writing (I wrote the first two chapters about fourteen years ago...and they were AWFUL), so I put it on the backburner until I could go back to the drawing board. At that point, my brother-friend Dorjan approached me saying that he had taken my idea for *Death Before Dishonor* (which I had devised initially with him) and developed it into a movie treatment. He was very excited about his development of the material, but I shot it down. It, too, was awful. He had taken the characters in a direction that I had never intended. In his mind, he saw a high-flying, Michael Bay-esque summer blockbuster trilogy. Not that there is a problem with Dorjan's style of writing—in fact, I quite admire it, and it makes us a good team. But I had always intended for the story to be gritty, violent, emotional, and finite. So, here we are today.

This story is fiction, but it's based on historical events. You'll see many names, titles, and locations that are true historical figures and places (i.e. famed ninja Hattori Hanzo and the Shogun Oda Nobunaga). I did extensive research into Japanese history to write it. Unfortunately, I haven't visited Japan yet (a trip that would have allowed me to write scenes from experience). So, my Japanese vistas are mostly written from pictures or my mind's eye. Also, my characters often speak Japanese throughout the book. Since I don't speak Japanese myself, I thought it prudent to signify when Japanese was spoken in-text. I initially narrated when the language was being spoken, but it became terribly cumbersome when my main characters would bounce back and forth between languages like so many bilingual people do. To remedy this, I've made the dialogue bold when Japanese is being spoken.

It is my greatest hope that you enjoy *Death Before Dishonor* as much as I do. I have grown up with the main characters, and they are like my family members. I also hope, too, that you can immerse yourself in the world of the shinobi—the famed ninja.

Special thanks go out to the following people:

Robert Wright for all the years of conversation and support that have gone into writing this story, acting as a sounding board and critic.

Dorjan Jones and William Smyth for being there at the very beginning, knowing in secret that the main characters are based loosely on you. Dorjan, the good news is: unlike the character Cortez, Terry has not changed.

Joseph Smyth for offering constructive feedback through my short story phase, aiding in my growth.

Adam Karaoguz for being my treehouse writers club teammate, NaNoWriMo partner, and a source of tactical ideas and feedback for my different writing projects.

Chelsea Leyden for being bubbly and excited to read whatever I sent her direction and to offer thoughtful and insightful analysis, feedback, criticism, and ideas.

Joseph Swindell for keeping me motivated when I had practically given up on a story that I had sworn I was beginning to despise.

Jessica Phenning for saying, "Dude, I hate deus ex machina"; wiser words have never been spoken, and that phrase taught me to be more accountable to my reader.

Kirsten Crase for being the best professor anyone could ever ask for and for finding time to be a thoughtful critic of my work even while grinding out a doctorate.

Frankie Bonner for bringing practicality, motivation, and ingenuity throughout the years that I was growing from a possible future novelist into a novelist.

And, finally, William Jones for dedicating time in making the cover.

Prologue

Honor is the soul of the Shinobi. Shadow is their blood.
The Shinobi Incantation, translated from Ninpo.

Damascus, Syria. Five Years Ago.

The air of the safe house was as thick and moist as bathwater, but at the very least, it was fifteen degrees cooler inside. Air conditioning wasn't something that Muhammad Ibn al-Aziz, employer of the Ciccone brothers—Terry and Yuri—factored into berthing mercenaries. The ability to fight and remain beneath notice were chief requirements, not comfort.

Terry didn't need comfort in the truest sense—after all, mercenary work wasn't glorious nor fabulous—but a more pleasant climate wouldn't have been asking too much. Out of the all the places on the planet, he wasn't fond of the Middle East. The heat was oppressive, and the air was muddy and miserable. To be honest, Terry didn't like any weather that wasn't temperate; had he been in Alaska, he'd have been just as irritable. Hot extremes and cold extremes were anything but enjoyable. His younger brother, Yuri, didn't so much mind it. He was never one to pay much attention to details as minor as atmosphere when his life didn't depend on it. Where weather irritated Terry, the culture of the Middle East irked Yuri. He lacked much in the way of cultural sensitivity. Consequently, the brothers were inclined to stay indoors. There, they were shielded from the weather and culture they didn't find endearing. Terry often chastised Yuri's reason for remaining inside, and of course, Yuri would counter Terry's criticism by highlighting Terry's lack of manhood for fussing about the weather.

Remaining indoors as often as possible had utility. It allowed Terry and Yuri to avoid the scrutiny of locals and authorities, which minimized the chance of operations being compromised, especially during planning and preparation phases. A dozen and a half foreigners congregating and brandishing weapons tended to raise suspicion in an area that was mostly ethnically homogenous. Like Terry and Yuri, most of the mercenaries weren't of Middle Eastern descent. A few were

1

racially black like Terry, several were white like Yuri, and the rest were a collage of Middle Eastern and Asian. Most of them—except for the brothers and two others—were Muslim, which allowed them to blend in during day-to-day routines. The two Orthodox Catholics had to be a little more cautious. Terry and Yuri made a concerted effort to stay out of any religious entanglements; the silence of Ninpo afforded them that.

The team had been in the employ of Ibn al-Aziz for nearly six months now. The Ciccone brothers and three others were the only original members remaining. Vacancies were a result of employees terminating their contracts voluntarily or involuntarily during operations. The current payroll consisted mostly of recruits brought aboard within the past month.

While the rest of the team handled soldiering, artillery, and frontal assault, Terry and Yuri specialized in the assassination of high-value targets, organic intelligence, and ambush. Operating with a group with a mixture of skills allowed for cross-training. Terry and Yuri took keenly to the demolitions aspect as well as the employment of small arms and long-range rifles. These skills complimented their profound abilities of stealth and stalking.

The team had recently returned from an operation into the Gaza Strip, making raids against the Israeli Defense Force, and was enjoying some time off before they prepared for another operation funded by Ibn al-Aziz, an operation that would never be seen to completion by the current team.

BOOM!

BRAKA-BRAKA-BRAKA!

Terry barreled out of the bathroom and down the hall towards the bedroom, screaming to his brother, "Yuri!" Terry was trying to pull on a stocking cap that matched his faded black collared shirt over his half-complete cornrows.

Yuri threw the bedroom door open and shuffled down the hall, trying to pull his body armor on over a brown T-shirt and jeans with both hands filled, an assault rifle in one and a small sword—a ninjatō—in the other.

BRAKA-BRAKA-BRAKA!

A firefight going on in the hallway downstairs and a hail of suppressive burst-fire splintered the walls and floor around them.

Yuri met Terry halfway up the hallway between the bathroom and the bedroom and tossed him the rifle. He then pulled another assault rifle from a nearby closet. "I'll take point going out the stairs. Shoot over my head; I'll lay suppressive fire."

"No, we have to get outta here," Terry hissed, barring his brother with an outstretched arm.

"What do you mean? We gotta stop them from taking this safe house."

BOOM!

BRAKA-BRAKA-BRAKA!

"Screw this place, Yuri! It isn't our loss!"

Yuri's face twisted as his eyes searched his brother's face. Yuri didn't like backing down from fights, but Terry was right: the safe house wasn't their responsibility—nor was the team. Still, today wasn't the day that Yuri was planning on turning tail.

"We can take these assholes, Terry!" He pushed Terry's arm out of his way. "We're not dishonoring ourselves by being cowards! If we die today, so be it!"

"No! It's not dishonorable! We're Shinobi, Yuri, and this is an ambush! When Oda Nobunaga attacked, the Shinobi retreated! There's no dishonor in retreat!"

"Are you—"

"Yuri, we don't know their number! We have to go!"

Terry was right; they had to move.

"You win," Yuri growled.

BRAKA-BRAKA-BRAKA!

The gunfire and screaming were getting closer.

Terry swam over the top of his brother. "Follow me!" he yelled, slinging his assault rifle across his back as he made a beeline for the window of the bedroom. He climbed out onto the ledge of the building, pressing himself against the wall. Terry's foot barely fit; the ledge was perhaps six inches. Yuri came out right behind him. Good thing neither of them were scared of heights considering they were nine stories up and the building was barren of handholds.

Terry sidled right towards a drain-pipe, inching forward around the windowsills that urged him off the ledge. He looked back. Yuri was still next to the exit, waiting to see what his brother had planned.

Terry wanted to get to a balcony. The nearest one on their floor was around the corner of the building and attached to an apartment that was on the same floor as the firefight. There was, however, a balcony right beneath them. He had originally considered dropping down to it but then realized that the balcony recessed beneath the ledge, and he didn't think he could produce the radial velocity to make it onto its platform.

Terry latched onto a pipe and dropped from the ledge, using his hands and feet to control his decent to the ledge right beneath. He sidled to the target balcony and rolled over the rail. Terry leaned out to see what progress Yuri had made. The ledge overhung the balcony with a foot of extra progress.

Yuri had stalled one window from the pipe, directly above Terry. The firefight erupted into the room that owned that window; he wasn't sure that he could skirt by without being seen.

BRAKA-BRAKA-BRAKA!

Bullets riddled the wall and the window.

Yuri couldn't stay on the ledge any longer without being shot. He'd have to jump.

"Terry," Yuri yelled, "take the gun!"

Terry reached up, leaning out over the rail. Yuri slipped the sling off his shoulder and lowered it his brother. Terry stretched, trying to grab hold, but was missing it by mere inches.

"Drop it," he said.

Yuri did.

Terry caught it—barely. "Hurry up!" Terry said.

"I'm not going make it. I got to jump!"

"Whatever, just make it quick! I'll catch you." Just then, Terry saw motion behind the curtain of the door to the balcony. He didn't have time to worry about it; he put the assault rifle on the floor and anchored his feet into the rail.

BRAKA-BRAKA-BRAKA!

Yuri didn't think. He dropped off the ledge, turning sharply. His hands impacted the ledge, slowing his momentum before he let go and continued his fall.

Terry saw his brother coming down feet first, and he had to time it just right—just like they had been taught. Terry rolled forward, using his feet as leverage. Yuri dropped one arm, making himself as long as possible. Terry preloaded his shoulder to keep it from jumping loose of its socket when the weight came on. Yuri reached in for his brother; Terry reached out.

SMACK! Their forearms made contact, and their hands slammed shut like vices. Yuri came to an abrupt halt, dangling six stories above the urban desert street below.

Yuri swayed back and forth slightly as Terry negotiated his anchor points, hoping that the rail didn't give out. He strained and pulled Yuri high enough for Yuri to sling his free arm up to the lip of the balcony floor. From there, Yuri dug his fingers into the rail and began climbing with Terry's aid. Once he was over the rail, Yuri and Terry breathed a sigh of relief.

Terry hopped up and went to the door with his rifle raised. Yuri snatched up his rifle and followed.

"There's someone in this apartment," Terry said without looking at his brother.

"I don't hear gunfire on this floor."

"On three…"

Three, two, one…

Terry swung the door open and zipped in low and right through the curtains, Yuri went high and left. A chorus of screams boomed as a room full of women draped head to toe in black robes scattered to the walls. Terry and Yuri fanned out, Terry going to check the kitchen, Yuri the bedroom.

The kitchen and its scarce pantry were clear. "It's clear over here!"

Yuri barged through the door of the bedroom and found a portly Arab man having intercourse with an equally portly Arab woman; they began hollering. Yuri's brow raised behind his assault rifle's sight. Then there was a clatter of something falling behind a closed door leading away from the bedroom.

Yuri slung his gun and drew out the matte-black ninjatō from the sheath on his back, pointing at the couple to remain on the bed. He approached the door cautiously and positioned himself against the wall opposite the hinges. He turned the knob and pushed the door open, retracting quickly behind the wall.

"Yuri, talk to me!"

Yuri ignored his brother and waited. Seconds later, a slender male emerged with a metal pipe in his hand. Yuri struck, disarming the man first with his sword and then driving a sidekick into his gut, knocking the slender man into the wall. Yuri was on top of him with the blade point in his face.

The slender man registered Yuri's savage eyes burning icy blue and his viper-like grimace. The man began whimpering in a strange Arabic dialect. Yuri could roughly make out what he was saying, but it was difficult. The man was begging for his life; that much, Yuri did know.

"Yuri?" Terry hollered again.

"It's clear!"

Yuri backed away from the man and jerked the blade tip into the air several times, indicating to the man to get up. The man's face was sheepish.

"Go," Yuri said in Arabic, pointing to the door to the common room. "Hurry." He looked over to the bed that the couple occupied, this time under the covers and ashen. "You two—out. Go."

All three jumped up and ran out quickly.

Yuri wasn't far behind. He came out and saw his brother on the other side of the common room eyeing the door.

"**We have to get out of here. We're no better here than we were upstairs**," Terry said to him in Japanese. Terry and Yuri used Japanese intermittently with English when speaking to one another, sometimes switching back and forth unconsciously, other times doing it tactically. They had spent their more impressionable years speaking Japanese and were just as comfortable communicating in it as they were in English.

"**The fighting sounds like it's stopped**," Yuri responded, noting that he didn't hear gunfire. He picked his way through the dozen or so people over to the front door and pressed his ear to it. He didn't hear any voices or footsteps in the hallway.

He took up the same position near the door as he had at the bathroom door, except this time he was on the same side as the hinges. Yuri pulled the door open slowly and looked through the space that opened on the hinge side. The hallway looked clear. He shut it, swapped sides, and opened it again.

"**Hallway's clear**," he said and closed it again, locking it this time and sheathing his blade. "**Maybe we can make it down the stairs without being seen.**"

Terry eyed the occupants diligently. "**I doubt it. Those blasts were flashbangs. This is a professional assault.**"

"**Let's find some rope so we can climb down.**"

"**You think they have seventy feet of rope in here?**"

"**Nope, I'm just being optimistic,**" Yuri deadpanned.

Terry's head swung left and right. Then he went into the bedroom. "**Maybe we can tie these sheets together,**" he yelled back.

"**That only works in movies.**"

Terry came back out and shrugged. "**What happened to being optimistic?**"

"**They're going to start going door to door. We don't have much time. We've got to figure something out.**"

Thump-thump-thump. There was a knock at the door.

Terry and Yuri glanced at it and then each other. One of the women sitting on the nearby couch squeaked. Yuri instantly became intense and raised the barrel of his assault rifle to her forehead, crassly mouthing that she should be silent.

BAM-BAM-BAM! The knock was much harder this time. Then the door knob rattled. Someone yelled in Arabic for the occupants to open the door.

Terry swiftly went for the bedroom to find a hiding place. He noticed a pile of laundry on the floor and drew out a hijab and an abaya—a veil and a robe. It was about Yuri's size, and Yuri's sun-bronzed complexion could pass for Arab at a glance—albeit, a fair one. Terry tossed the garments to Yuri and then posted inside the door.

Yuri pulled the hijab over his head and flopped down onto the couch facing the door, straightening the veil on his face and hiding his rifle beneath the material.

BAM-BAM-BAM! From outside the door, the person shouted that they could hear the occupants and they were going to kick the door down if whoever was there didn't answer.

Yuri pointed at the portly, sheet-wrapped man and then indicated the door. The portly man had the same sheepish look as he had in the bedroom. Yuri lifted his rifle from beneath the abaya. The man jumped up and stumbled to the door, pulling the sheet clear of his partner. She let out a startled, embarrassed sound that made Yuri wave vigorously at her to be silent. The portly man unlocked the door and backed up as he opened it. His eyes and mouth opened wide; all the women began to fuss again. Yuri mimicked the reactions of the women as he watched the barrel of a carbine materialize and level against the portly man as the door swung open. Terry could see two shooters through the space adjacent to the hinges from his hiding place behind the bedroom door. They were clad in urban battle gear with western carbines—Israeli Mossad.

The first one stepped into the room, and the second stacked in the doorway. The operators asked the portly man who lived in the residence. The portly man replied that he and his family did.

Yuri held his breath. He hoped that he could get his rifle up fast enough if the portly man cracked.

The first shooter scanned the cramped parlor of ten or so people. He locked Yuri's eyes when the operator's scan reached him. Yuri's eyes burned, betraying his body language—Yuri's sweaty grip constricted the handle of the rifle harder beneath the abaya—but the shooter dismissed him and moved on. The second shooter demanded that everyone take a seat while they looked around.

Sweat pooled inside the veil. It was going to be a fight, then. While Yuri could fool them by wearing a hijab, there was no way Israeli counter-terrorist operatives wouldn't check behind the door and find Terry. Yuri readied himself as he watched them cross the parlor to the bedroom. Terry did the same as he watched them approach through the crack of the door. They both just hoped that they could get the drop on the Israelis. Yuri would jump up and fire as much of his

8

magazine into their backs as he could manage, which would hopefully give Terry enough time to come out from behind the door and catch them in a crossfire.

Just then, more gunfire broke out on the floor above; there was screaming over the Israelis' radios. The Israelis immediately turned and sprinted from the apartment, telling the occupants to remain where they were.

Terry and Yuri got lucky. They used that as their opportunity to escape. Terry left $400 on the table for the occupants' trouble.

Payback was going to be a bitch.

*　　*　　*

Yuri sat in the driver's seat of a geriatric hatchback coupe that had long since outlived its existence. He was accompanied by a cache of weapons in the passenger seat covered by a gray wool blanket, and he entertained himself with an application on his smartphone, occasionally glancing into the rearview.

A phone call interrupted him. "What?" he answered in Arabic.

"The convoy is coming," a surviving mercenary also replied in Arabic. "I can see the helicopter over the buildings."

"Take it out when you see the signal," Yuri said in his rudimentary Arabic—he was more literate than conversational—before hanging up.

Yuri looked in the rearview again and saw the convoy of modern black SUVs turn down the southbound street and roll past, numbering eight in all. It was the Mossad director's executive motorcade, and it was practically on-time; one minute late to be exact.

Terry watched from a third-story window fifty yards to the south of his brother. He timed the lead vehicle's movement, and when it was in prime position, he hit the *send* button on a burnout cellphone.

A nondescript sedan parked along the southbound side of the road erupted in a deafening fireball, blowing out windows of cars and buildings for fifty feet. It pulverized the lead vehicle, stripping it of panels and doors and mangling the left side of the frame. The vehicle behind it was shredded by shrapnel but left mostly intact. The lightweight helicopter rattled from the shock. The pilot stirred the controls to keep the aircraft under saddle.

How much reactant did Yuri use? Terry thought. The shockwave was more intense than he had expected. Yuri, for his part, had wanted to make sure that the bomb did its job and stopped the convoy in its tracks.

The helicopter banked hard to loop around and try to get on top of the convoy to provide support. Terry watched it turn and then saw the contrail of a stinger missile rocket from the artificial horizon that the roofs across the street created. The helicopter didn't stand a chance; its tail was blown clean off, and huge pieces of its fuselage were launched through the main rotor, tearing it apart and causing the aircraft to smack into the side of a low-rise building about two hundred yards to the north and then tumble catastrophically to the street below.

Each vehicle in the motorcade began to react to the attack. The rearmost vehicle slammed its gearshift into reverse and squealed its tires backing up. The other vehicles began to follow.

Yuri threw back the blanket, drew up an RPG from a pile of assault weapons, and climbed out of the car. He watched the rearmost SUV weave through uninvolved cars towards him as fast as the driver could manage in reverse. Yuri took aim over the roof of his car and fired. The grenade struck the SUV broadside on the left and practically capsized it.

The road was now blocked; the trap was set.

Yuri tossed the launcher to the ground, grabbed an assault rifle and a satchel-style backpack, and circled around the back of his vehicle. He raised the barrel once he was onto the road and began unloading the magazine downrange into the trapped convoy.

Terry watched his brother obliterate the last vehicle and then return to the vehicle for another weapon. Terry stabilized his machine gun against a windowsill in which he perched and racked the charging handle, chambering a round. Once Yuri began opening fire, so did Terry, raining slugs onto the convoy from the second story.

Yuri moved south along the road, hugging the vehicles to his left in the event he needed cover, and continued to fire his rifle in bursts while Terry riddled the vehicles with armor-piercing shells. Terry laid the fire on heavy as his brother approached the seventh SUV in the line. Terry backed his coverage off and laid into the fifth and sixth vehicles before starting a reload.

Yuri came up to the vehicle and slammed the butt of his rifle into its machine-gun-riddled window, puncturing a hole in the bullet-resistant glass big enough for him to toss in the grenade that he had pulled from his backpack. He rounded the back of the SUV and ducked beneath its tailgate; the grenade went off just as someone on the right side opened the door to escape. The blast slung the man ten feet clear of the car and bowed all the windows outward. Smoke billowed out in a cone to the west.

Terry spotted three occupants from the second vehicle trying to escape to the west of the street and trained his muzzle on them, opening up on them with several short bursts. Two of them fell instantly. The third returned fire. Terry took cover but kept the man in sight the best he could. When the man turned to run again, Terry resumed firing, dropping the man just before he reached the sidewalk. Terry then began hammering the third vehicle. His ammunition was getting low, so he would need to dismount soon.

Yuri pushed down the southbound side of the road now. He stayed low, going through a cloud of smoke. As he emerged, he caught a man climbing from a sixth porous vehicle rubbing smoke-irritated eyes; he couldn't see Yuri coming. Yuri drew his ninjatō from its sheath, came in close, and slammed the blade into the man's back, the tip punching through the other side.

Another Israeli stumbled out of the thick smoke at the back end. Yuri snatched his ninjatō back and swung it in a swift arc, lacerating the man from hip to shoulder, and then Yuri plunged the blade into the man's chest. The man retched, and then he toppled.

Terry saw several flashes out of the corner of his eye from the cars that lined the street to the west of Yuri; someone was firing at him. Yuri disappeared behind the back end. Terry focused through the smoke and saw a shooter firing on Yuri from the cover of a parked car. Terry lined him up with the machine gun and emptied the last of his ammunition into the shooter, killing him and destroying the car in the hail.

Yuri pulled a grenade from the bag and lobbed it over the SUV he was using as cover. Seconds later, the blast rained dirt. It was a waste of a grenade, but Yuri's eyes were beginning to burn from the smoke. He was just trying to make sure that he was clear when he decided to move again. He needed to take a moment to clear his eyes.

Terry dismounted, jumping from the window down to the back of a mid-sized truck, then down to the roof of its cab, the hood, and then the ground. He made his way onto the street with his assault rifle readied. The director was in the third, fourth, or fifth vehicle, and Terry wanted to confirm that he was dead. He came onto the street near the third SUV and hammered its left side windows with half of the contents of his magazine just to be prudent. He didn't slow his stride and kept moving north towards his brother.

An injured man fired at Terry with a submachine gun from the backseat of the fourth vehicle. Terry took cover behind a car and pulled a grenade from his bag. He pulled its pin, allowed it to cook for a couple of seconds, and then beamed it like a baseball. The grenade exploded as it went through the window, fragging everything in a five-foot sphere.

Terry popped up and made a beeline for the fifth SUV, firing three short bursts into its mangled windshield as he approached. He drew another grenade, rolled it under the vehicle, and sprinted for cover again. The grenade click-clacked to a stop, and then the explosion lifted the front end of the SUV off the ground about six inches. Smoke billowed out of the shattered window. Terry emptied his magazine into the left side, reloaded, and then laid into it some more.

He ran up and slammed the butt of his rifle through the window several times until he could see into the vehicle—until he could see the most horrible sight he had ever seen. Terry froze.

12

Yuri cleared his eyes the best that he could. They burned, but he'd manage. He checked his rifle; the magazine was empty. He slung it around to his back and pulled his pistol from its holster. With it and his ninjatō still in his hand, he rounded the driver's side of the SUV. He could see his brother standing at the driver's side passenger door of the fifth vehicle. Yuri looked into the windows of the SUV that was next to him. Everyone was dead, and not a single corpse was the director.

Why is Terry standing there like a goddamn idiot? Yuri wondered.

Yuri sprinted towards his brother. "Terry!" Yuri yelled. "**Terry, what're you doing**?" Yuri came up next to his brother, panting. Terry was sheet white, and his eyes were unfocused as he stared blankly into the fifth SUV. Yuri looked in—a wave of disappointment washed over his body. They hadn't hit the director—they had hit his family. They were all slumped in the back seats of the SUV, hemorrhaging, gasping, or dead.

Their intelligence had been wrong. The director was supposed to be in this motorcade, but he wasn't. Terry overflowed with regret. How could this have happened? How could they have done this?

"Terry," Yuri said, trying to get his brother's attention.

Terry stared into the cab of the SUV.

Yuri lifted his pistol and euthanized them one at a time. The last one was a bit difficult—those eyes were so innocent. But he put that away.

"**Terry, snap out of it! We got to go!**" Yuri yanked his brother by the nape of his jacket. Terry came to, and the two brothers sprinted away from the burning scene.

Chapter One: Fortunately Born

Medical. Camp Zama. Tokyo, Japan. Twenty-seven years ago.

The feeling had returned, that feeling of desperation that preceded hopelessness. It was overtaking Francesca again.

She felt nauseous and miserable, sitting there in an office chair that felt more like a boat caught in the middle of a hurricane.

For the third time in a week, her husband, Pat, and she were meeting with their obstetrician to discuss fertility further. With each meeting, however, the possibility of pregnancy seemed more and more bleak.

Francesca was frustrated and queasy. She tore her attention away from her husband and the doctor, trying desperately to train her focus elsewhere to calm her nerves, if just for a moment. The doctor's nameplate, which read: *MAJOR IMRAN A. YUSEF, MD,* caught her eye, and she focused on it, attempting to find a moment of solace away from the hopelessness of pregnancy.

She couldn't afford the luxury of comfort in a hospital; she hated hospitals. Their smells, their bleach-white walls, and the colors of the staff's bland clothing were creepy and unsettling. She couldn't escape her personal torment here, try as she may.

Why was this so difficult? The human body had been giving birth since the dawn of time. Why did her body have to be the exception?

Considered to have a perfect bill of health, Francesca was the ideal specimen of Italian lineage. She stood an easy five feet nine inches, with raven hair, olive skin, and a pair of icy blue eyes. She kept her body fit by attending the military base's gym five days a week and by participating on the military dependents' intramural volleyball and softball teams. Francesca was the furthest thing from a struggling twenty-something-year-old, but rather a very healthy thirty-five-year-old woman with a body more than capable of handling pregnancy.

Francesca also wasn't some *young* military wife trying to get her life together while attached to the hip of her overworked husband. No, she had been married to Pat, the newly promoted Lieutenant Colonel

Patrizio Ciccone, for fifteen years; they had been together since grade school, minus a few adolescent arguments.

Pat was Francesca's opposite. He was of average height, standing five feet ten inches and of average build. Although born of hardy Italian stock, he didn't maintain the definitive characteristics that his wife did. He had close-cut, dirty blonde hair, fair skin, and dark brown eyes. Despite his lack of pedigree, Pat's grandfather, father, and uncles swore that they were descended from Roman Gladiators.

Before attending college at Rutgers in New Jersey, and its Army Reserve Officer Training Corps, he had competed in the amateur boxing circuit in Jersey City at the urging of his grandfather Estefano.

Estefano had assured Pat that he could be a champion boxer because of his legendary Italian ancestry and encouraged him to fight often. For all the hard work, Pat eventually decided that life in Jersey City may have fulfilled the older Ciccone men, but it didn't fulfill him. For Pat, boxing wasn't healthy anymore and wasn't the honorable exit that he needed. In spite of his retirement from boxing, Pat maintained his classic cruiserweight physique but placed his energy in other venues—namely, the Army.

Francesca and Pat were a perfect union; they would make beautiful, intelligent children. Why, indeed, was this so difficult?

"Francesca?"

She snapped back to reality when she heard her name. Dr. Yusef had been trying to get her attention for several seconds before Pat said something.

Dr. Yusef was a short, stiff, balding male of mixed-Arabic descent who spoke superbly with the faintest hint of a British accent. According to the accolades present on his shelves and walls, he had graduated from the University of Oxford in Britain, received his doctorate from Johns Hopkins, specializing in obstetrics, and then conducted his residency at Baylor Hospital in Dallas, all before receiving a commission as a medical practitioner in the United States Army.

"Honey, are you okay?" Pat asked tenderly.

"Yeah—yeah, I'm fine. I was drifting."

"Mrs. Ciccone," said Dr. Yusef, "I can assure you that we are doing everything within our power to find a solution. I do need you, however, to be as patient as possible. This may take some time."

Frustration boiled in her blue eyes. She was sure Dr. Yusef could see it—how she was feeling was never a surprise to anyone; she wore her emotions on her sleeve. *If one more person tells me to be patient, I'm going to scream,* Francesca thought to herself. *Ugh, my mother tells me that constantly.*

Her mother, Marcella, always advised patience. Marcella's advice drove Francesca up the wall. Now she had to hear it from the doctor too? How could the doctor caution patience, anyway? He wasn't having the slightest problem with fertility, judging by the pictures that decorated his office. He had a ton of rowdy children equipped with missing teeth, drooling fits, and T-Ball games. And his wife was pregnant again.

Francesca didn't want to hear it.

Dr. Yusef continued, "There is quite an extensive build-up that must be undergone to determine the best course of action. Perish the thought that we act impulsively and the effects are anything short of stellar."

"We understand, Doc," Pat said.

Francesca nodded feebly.

Pat sat back in his chair, feigning concern to give his wife peace of mind. He wanted a child of his own just as bad as Francesca, but he wasn't willing to sacrifice his wife's health in the process. In fact, he was willing to forgo children altogether if it meant keeping his wife healthy. He had loved her as far back as he could remember and didn't want to jeopardize that.

Honestly, Pat was against seeing the obstetrician. They came because Francesca wanted to, even if she showed no interest every time.

Francesca's agitation was growing visibly, so Pat decided that it would be best to conclude the day's appointment. She was already stressed. He didn't want to make it worse. Although they technically weren't done with the appointment, he had the perfect excuse; they needed to pick up Terry, their adopted son, from daycare.

16

"We thank you for your time, Doc," Pat said, interrupting the doctor and rising to his feet with a hand extended.

"Oh, uh, right then. I suppose we're complete for the day." Dr. Yusef stood to his feet and gripped Pat's hand. "You have a spectacular day, sir. And you too, Mrs. Ciccone. We'll all see each other soon enough, I'm sure. I apologize if this isn't the quick fix that you were hoping for. We will find a solution, though. You have my word."

"No apology needed, Major. After all, you're only looking out for our best interests."

*　　*　　*

"You were awfully quiet back there," Pat said, sounding matter-of-fact as he started the engine to their minivan. "Something wrong?"

"I can't seem to make my uterus work—but no, Pat, there's nothing wrong at all," she said as she situated herself in the passenger seat.

"Well, I appreciate you being diplomatic."

Her head turned towards him. "What's that supposed to mean?"

"It means I appreciate you being diplomatic."

"Something tells me that you're being a sarcastic dickhead." Francesca's voice became instantly venomous with her deep Jersey accent. "Are you being a sarcastic dickhead right now, Patrizio?"

"Baby, no. I was legitimately saying thank you."

"I bet you were."

"Okay, why are you being a psycho hose-beast right now? I didn't do anything to you?"

Her temperature climbed through the roof. "Now I'm a hoe?"

"No, babe. I said hose—hose, baby. Like a water hose."

"Mm-hmm. Don't backpedal now, sweetheart. You'll find all your stuff on the lawn when you come home from work tomorrow," she threatened as she began fixing rogue strands of hair in the mirror of the visor.

"Alright, you sit here. I'm going to run back inside."

"For what?" Her tone hadn't improved.

"To see if the doc will give you a prescription for an anti-psychotic, because this pregnancy thing has got you acting clinical."

Francesca exploded. "You know what? *Screw* you, Pat! I'm sorry that I don't take this as well as you do. You have *no* idea how humiliating this is—how upsetting. But you don't care about how I feel. You just want to try to act cute." She mocked her husband, "I appreciate you being diplomatic, babe," with a terrible imitation of his voice. "Psht—please."

"Whoa, whoa, whoa. Calm down, honey." Pat signaled with his hand for his wife to slow down. "I was just saying that I'm glad you didn't light off in the doctor's office—just like this."

Francesca exhaled disgust.

"Better out here than in there, I suppose," Pat said. "Temper-tantrums solve all problems, after all."

"Don't get all righteous with me. Remember, I know where you came from."

"What does that have to do with anything?"

"You think you're so righteous, but you came from the same place I did," she said sharply, her accent going into overdrive.

"What?" His face pruned. "Look, mafia princess, I'm sorry that I'm not living up to my impoverished ethnic roots, but my 'self-righteousness' got you out of Jersey City and feeds you currently."

Francesca's mouth dropped open. Mafia princess? Who did he think he was? "You must have bumped your head, asshole! Your family is no better. Don't think I don't know about your brother Alfonzo and your cousin Larry! Everyone else around here may think that you're God's gift to mankind, but I know where the real Patrizio Ciccone comes from. So try that diplomatic crap elsewhere!"

Pat looked at her blankly. "Are you done?"

She threw her hands up in a fit and turned to look out of the passenger window.

"Francesca—"

She cut him off. "Whatever, Pat."

"No, baby, for real. Listen, I was saying that—"

She cut him off again. "I just think it's funny how—!"

Pat slammed his fist against the steering wheel. "Would you be quiet long enough for me to get a word in?"

Francesca's lip curled.

"I'm not quite sure where this whole fiasco turned into a throat-cutting session—"

Francesca cut-in again. "How about when—"

"Francesca!" Pat raised his voice this time.

"Awright," she said, sounding surprised that he was getting upset. "G'head."

"I understand how stressful this is for you and sometimes it's going to make you act irrational, but you have to remember that I'm on your team here, baby. We're doing this together."

"How could you understand? You're not a woman."

Why did women always resort to semantics? Pat was just trying to be sensitive towards his wife, and she was crucifying him for it.

"Fine, forget that I said *understand*. Substitute *empathize* instead."

"This is easy for you."

"How do you figure?"

"You get to come home after work to a hot meal and an inviting wife. Then, after you've had your fun, you get to sit and spectate while I deal with my argumentative lady parts." Francesca folded her arms across her chest. "Must be nice."

Have his *fun*? Really? That's what this was about? "How did this become my fault."

"Everything is your fault. You're a husband."

Pat—at that very moment—realized that he was fighting an uphill battle, and he was losing it miserably. Francesca was not in the mood to have a rational, objective conversation, and Pat should've allowed her to have her time of melancholy and grief. She would have talked to him about how she felt when she was ready, and the blast radius wouldn't have been as large. He accepted that he had brought this on himself. But that didn't mean he was going to go out like a punk either.

"Observe," he said out of nowhere.

"What?"

"Observe."

A puzzled sneer crossed her face. "Observe what? What the hell are you talking about?"

19

"*Spectate* isn't a word. Use the word *observe* instead."

"Christ, save me," Francesca groaned. "I can't believe I said *until death do we part.*"

Pat smiled. "Baby, you make dying with me sound bad."

Francesca's face was stone. "Only if it's slow."

"Francesca," he said and then paused for effect, "any death with you will surely be quick."

"Keep pushing me, Pat, and your children are going to be fatherless." She pointed out the windshield. "Drive."

"I love you, baby. Even if you're the angriest woman on earth."

"Ugh, drive."

*   *   *

Pierside Market. Tokyo, Japan. Twenty-five and a half years ago.

Francesca passed through the open door of the pierside market, wiping the rebel strands of hair that blew into her face as she passed under the blower situated above the entrance. Her sundress waved violently in the rushing air, accentuating the disproportionate bulge of her abdomen; she and Pat were finally expecting a child of their own. They were due to have a boy in three short months.

The couple still hadn't decided on a name. They often spent hours going through baby books looking for the perfect one, something unique and enchanting, and befitting a first born.

There is power in a name. A name defines an individual in one short sequence. It's like a first impression except that a first impression requires face time; that's not so with a name. A name can invoke feeling by simply saying it aloud, or invoke a completely different one by writing it. Therein was the difficulty that Pat and Francesca were having with agreeing on a name: their expectations of their long-anticipated son were high beyond measure and different for each of them.

Pat wanted a son that was stocky and solid, that had his broad shoulders and his wife's mesmerizing eyes. Beyond that, outward appearance didn't matter. What mattered was what was inside.

He wanted his son to have heart and motivation. He wanted him to be a *man's man* with unparalleled athleticism and a high pain threshold. He wanted an athlete and a scholar. He couldn't wait to teach his son to fight, even though Pat had no intention of permitting his son to box, considering Pat's past.

Francesca's wishes for her son were more complex than those of her husband's. She wanted a son bestowed with her husband's brilliance and patience but hoped that he also maintained her side of the family's business and streetwise savvy—without the criminal element, of course. His physical appearance was also very important to her. Although Pat was an amazing athlete, she rationalized that her brother, Julius, was the ideal physical template for her son. Julius fit the description of *tall, dark, and handsome* one-hundred and ten percent. He was a mountain of a human being, with a full head of black hair—even at the ripe age of forty-two. He also had olive-toned skin that didn't burn in the summer and a square, chiseled jaw that made him look intimidating even when he smiled.

Like Julius, her son would be a heartbreaker with a warm smile and a loving heart. Unlike Julius, however, she would teach her son a woman's worth and raise him to be a true gentleman who would be the envy of all men—a feat that her mother, Marcella, hadn't been able to achieve with Julius. All of that coupled with her husband's patience, ambition, and perseverance would make her son a model husband and a successful professional. If she raised him as she intended, her son would provide her with grandchildren that Pat and she could dote on.

Francesca felt that Pat's expectations were too simple and too vague, but she respected that men are inherently different than women and Pat didn't love the same as she; that was okay with her. Pat was going to be an excellent father. Hell, he already was. He showed that daily with their adopted son, Terry.

Francesca loved Pat more and more every day as she watched him father a boy that was not of his making. Pat was the most amazing man she had ever met, and to think that she was going to give him a child—a child that she carried for him—made her feel tremendous pride.

How lucky was she? Francesca had known the minute that she'd met him in the seventh grade that their lives would come to this point, this fine moment; she had known that she'd be Mrs. Patrizio Ciccone with two beautiful sons. It was an amazing feeling indeed.

Her two-way pager buzzed.

"Please, don't be Pat," she begged beneath her breath as she chased after her pager inside her purse. She found it buried beneath a ton of miscellaneous accessories.

It was him. Pat had sent her a messaged that read: Baby where r u? Sent 10:11 AM

He was checking up on her.

Francesca Ciccone: In bed where im supposed to be hun. Sent 10:11 AM

Francesca wasn't supposed to be out of the house; the obstetrician had prescribed her bed rest for the final phase of the pregnancy. She was high-risk pregnancy, and the doctor wanted to ensure the greatest margin of success; still, Francesca had become stir-crazy. She couldn't watch enough terrible Japanese soap operas and couldn't shop through enough catalogues to pass the day. She had been cooped up for days on end and needed some fresh air. Going to the market, she'd decided, could not be so stressful on the pregnancy—not any more stressful than her lying idly in the house all day, watching soap operas one after the bloody other. Besides, she wanted to pick up something special for Pat and Terry.

Pat Ciccone: Where r u really? Sent 10:12 AM

Francesca Ciccone: In bed. Sent 10:12 AM

Pat Ciccone: R u lying to me? Sent 10:12 AM

Francesca Ciccone: No. R u spying on me or something? Sent 10:13 AM

Pat Ciccone: ;) I have my agents everywhere. Sent 10:13 AM

"Whatever," she snorted, tossing her phone back into her purse.

Francesca, realizing that she was holding up traffic at the door, moved clear, pulling Terry by the shoulder to allow a handful of elderly Japanese women to pass. Then she moved over more, noticing that a non-pregnant Francesca would have been clear, not an as-pregnant-as-a-house Francesca.

"I'm sorry." She waved to them. "I forget that I'm bigger than I remember."

22

The ladies, not understanding English, all nodded vigorously and smiled as they scooted past.

As if being in the way wasn't enough, her clothes were riding up; this never happened before. She situated her maternity clothing, thinking that maternity styles were cold hideous. She looked like a vintage car with a cover over it. She envisioned her husband at work conversing with his contemporaries about their restored muscle cars except that Pat wasn't talking about his car but rather his wife. That made her growl.

She supposed maternity clothing was low on a fashion designer's list of priorities. How does one make a horse not look like a horse, after all? Not to mention that pregnant women didn't need to look attractive since they didn't make great prospects. Francesca was sure that fashion designers just glued and stapled fabrics together and tossed them on the shelves at retail prices. Criminals...

Adding injury to insult, her back hurt on a regular basis, her feet swelled without notice, her usually smooth face constantly broke out, and her moods swung from one extreme to the next. Any *romantic* who romanticized pregnancy needed to get hit by a bus or a train or an aircraft carrier; Francesca didn't much care what a *romantic* was hit by as long as the object was very big and very painful.

Francesca waddled up and down the aisles in the market, looking at clothing, jewelry, and other miscellanea, not quite sure what it was that she was looking for.

"Mommy, can I get this?" Terry asked in his usual soft voice.

"I'm sorry, baby," she said, looking down at him. "What did you say?"

He regarded her with his big, dark orbs.

Terry was a tall-for-his-age four-and-a-half-year-old boy who had coffee-brown skin and a long, distinguished face. He was cleanly cut like Pat, who took Terry to the barbershop every week. Pat and Francesca did not know who Terry's biological parents were, but they had divined that his paternal donor was probably a prime candidate for the NBA based on the attributes passed to Terry.

Pat and Francesca had adopted their once-nameless son when he was six-months old and had named him Terenzio Gianni Ciccone after Pat's and Francesca's grandfathers; they called him Terry for short.

Terry was credited with being the most well-mannered child on the planet. He had rarely cried when he was an infant, reserving such behavior for the most extreme situations, and he had begun talking early. During Terry's terrible toddler years, he had only thrown a handful of temper tantrums and, on most occasions, had chosen instead to stare intensely when he hadn't gotten his way.

Terry was a curious child and an avid daydreamer. He loved to draw and read and especially loved helping out his dad around the house. He was meticulous for his age, keeping his room clean with little guidance, and he tended to catch on to new things quickly. Francesca's only worry was that he wasn't very social and didn't talk much. Pat assured her that he'd grow out of it and that he'd probably acquire Pat's biting sarcasm.

Terry held up a coloring book. "Can I get this?"

"Sure, honey. We can color together when we get home, okay?"

Terry smiled brightly, his dark cheeks swelling with pleasure.

"Okay, Terry, mommy needs to get herself together because I'm not even supposed to be here, and daddy's going to be really mad if he finds out that I've been gone long, so help me find something for him. Okay?"

"Okay," Terry said, nodding one distinct time.

Francesca moved about the market as swiftly as she could, knocking things over and then apologizing to people for cursing aloud. Eventually, she realized that her search had turned into aimless wandering and that she had somehow landed in the seafood section of the market when she last remembered being in a clothing section—weird. Now, where was Terry?

"Terry?" she said loudly. "Where are you?"

Panic began to pool in her stomach when she spun and saw him on the other side of the seafood section, fascinated by the live lobsters rattling around in their tank.

"Terenzio Gianni!" she yelled, rushing up to him and snatching him by his arm. "What are you doing over here?"

Terry's eyes and mouth were wide open, suddenly realizing that he was in trouble. He hadn't meant to make her mad; there was some really ground-breaking stuff going on in the lobster tank, and he pointed at them, trying to show her. Francesca wasn't buying that. Clearly, the lobsters were the most important thing going on in the world of little people.

She practically pressed her nose to his. "Terenzio Gianni, don't you ever walk away from mommy like that! What if someone had grabbed you and taken you away?"

He blinked twice.

Francesca heard laughing.

She stood up straight, pressing her hand into her lower back, and looked over her shoulder. There was an elderly Japanese woman behind the nearest counter giggling at her with a smile that stretched from ear to ear.

"Children funny," the woman said with a thick accent, struggling with the "L."

"I suppose they are, huh? They're especially funny when you can't find them."

"You pregnant."

Francesca couldn't tell if the lady was asking or stating the obvious. Francesca went with the former. "Yes—yes, I am. My husband and I are expecting in a few months."

"First children?" the woman asked.

"Yes—well, no. Terry is actually my first child." Francesca rubbed his head with her hand. "My husband and I adopted him when he was only six months. But this is the first time I've been pregnant. We've had some complications."

"Have name?"

"Oh, no. Not yet."

"You beautiful woman. Like flower. You have beautiful children."

"Oh my goodness," Francesca said, her eyes filling with tears. "Thank you so much, ma'am."

The woman pointed at Francesca's belly. "You name Yuri. Yuri mean flower, like you. Beautiful."

"Yuri?"

The lady's eyes opened up with excitement. "Yes. Yuri. Beautiful like you."

"Yuri," Francesca said to herself thoughtfully. Pregnancy was the most amazingly intimate thing that Pat and she had ever done together. In a literal fashion, their lives were blossoming in a very new and incredible way.

"Are you a Yuri?" Francesca asked as she rubbed her stomach.

The baby kicked.

Chapter Two: A Prom to Die For

The Shinobi are creatures of shadow. A Shinobi must remain concealed, and if exposed, a Shinobi must remove all traces of his presence or be dishonored.
The First Mandate, translated from Ninpo.

Greenwich, Connecticut. Today.

Terry and Yuri were in a busy suburb of Connecticut under the employ of a powerful Colombian figurehead based out of Newark, New Jersey, to eliminate an associate to his operation for undisclosed reasons.

Far from naïve to the nature of organized crime, Terry and Yuri assumed that the hit was a result of a failure in black market deals on the side of the associate and, for one reason or another, the employer could not eliminate the associate by more conventional means. So, the employer called in the big guns: a team of assassins that specialized in hitting deeply entrenched targets. The employer needed the associate, Constantine Levarity, to meet a silent end that would send a message to other associates but would not cause a huge commotion.

The silent treatment, as it was, Terry and Yuri could oblige: enter Levarity's house, corner him, and complete the task without anyone knowing they were there.

In spite of the layers of insulation usually attributed to powerful drug lords, the brothers hardly considered such men to be "deeply entrenched" and merely had to work around the paranoia that made them adept at spotting attempts on their lives. In planning the job, Terry and Yuri assessed the patterns, strengths, and weaknesses of the Levarity Cartel's security and then decided what approach to use.

The surveillance of Levarity's residence ended up being a tedious three-week process that included noting the security measures utilized, the guards on the payroll, and data harvesting of electronic correspondence. On the positive side of things, Terry and Yuri made three new female friends that Terry tended to spend extensive periods of time in the hot-tub with—for ease of surveillance, of course.

Eventually, the decision of how to execute the job needed to be determined.

After careful risk analysis, they concluded that sniping would be ineffective because either the windows presented poor angles or obstructions. Car bombing was obnoxiously loud. Poison was a potentially viable option but was thrown out because its administration required a margin of error they could ill afford. Finally, they decided on an up-close-and-personal approach to the execution of the job. The only problem was how to manage the hit without instigating a Wild-West shootout with the Levarity's employees.

Fortune smiled on the brothers, however, when an option emerged: Levarity's daughter's prom was on the horizon and inside the completion window of the job. Terry intercepted correspondence between one of Levarity's lieutenants and a limousine company.

Then he and Yuri went to open a contract with the company.

*   *   *

"Why the hell are you speeding?" Yuri boomed in Terry's Bluetooth through the thrum of engines and the gurgle of exhaust in the background. "You trying to kill me?"

Terry yanked the vehicle hard around a turn. "We're a bit behind schedule. Calm down." He was driving uncomfortably fast for Yuri, but Terry couldn't allow the job to go sour because they couldn't manage their time well. Granted, traffic wasn't their fault, but missing their mark because they didn't plan accordingly definitely was. Ninpo had no time for traffic nor poor planning. If Ninpo had no time for either, Terry had no time for either. Yuri, angry or not, had to suck it up while Terry decompressed the timeline.

"Are you hearing me?"

"Everyone hears you, Yuri. You're screaming."

"You're gonna fucking kill me!"

"I'm not going to kill you. Calm down."

"You're not the one who's about to have your face plastered all over the fucking highway!"

"I'm not going to kill you. Trust me. Now, stop screaming."

"Don't tell me to stop screaming!"

Terry jerked the wheel right, then left, then back to center, getting around traffic.

"What the fuck, Terry?"

"I can't concentrate on driving with you screaming at me. Stop it."

Yuri unloaded every explicative in his multilingual repertoire. Terry smirked but otherwise ignored his brother's vulgar dissertation. If not to keep them on schedule, this at least repaid Yuri in full for his smartass mouth. Brotherly payback—Terry wasn't better than that.

Yuri's hot temper made him an easy target when Terry wanted to irritate him. Irritation was the best way to fight Yuri. Sure, Terry could haul off and slap his little brother, but what would that prove? What did a thirty-year-old look like slapping his twenty-five-year-old brother? Not much like a thirty-year-old, that's what. Besides, slapping his brother was a useless gesture, Terry concluded. Yuri was too stupid to feel pain anyway. Mental abuse was way more effective.

"Terry, for God's sake!"

Terry listened this time and depressed the brake, slowing the vehicle to match the speed limit of the residential boulevard that led to Levarity's residence. Admittedly, he didn't like the way the limo handled at higher speeds. Driving slow was preferable, but sacrifices had to be made to keep a professional schedule. Yuri was mad now, but he'd be over it soon enough when he realized the time that Terry had bought them. For that, Terry could deal with his brother's volcanic mood.

Several minutes and several intersections later, Yuri's voice interrupted Terry's thoughts. "Time?" Yuri asked.

Terry glanced at his watch and then returned his attention to the road and to the sedan making a right turn ahead of him. "Five minutes. How you holding up?"

"Aside from the fact that—"

"Never mind, I decided that I don't care," Terry deadpanned as Yuri began to rant. Not that it stopped him. In fact, it had the opposite effect. Yuri opened his levies and began to pour anger through the Bluetooth. Terry let him vent until they reached Levarity's street and then informed Yuri to stow it so that he didn't blow their cover. Yuri did begrudgingly.

Terry eased the vehicle off the street and up to the gate, easing the brake on until the vehicle came to a halt. Terry scanned in an arc, noting a guard house posted by two of Levarity's security to the left of the gate and a security camera and lamp attached to the right. The guards approached the limo, and Terry rolled the window down, obliging the guards with a porcelain smile.

During the planning phase, Yuri had spent countless hours recording and reviewing video of gate security. He claimed that there were usually two goons standing guard at any one time, and they were relieved every few hours. Tonight was no different; two bruisers dressed in blazers, jeans, work boots, and fitted ball caps approached the vehicle.

Terry subtly sized them up. Each was carrying a handgun; the nearest had a weapon tucked into his belt and did a very poor job of hiding it, while the furthest had his holstered underneath his jacket.

"And you are?" the nearest guard asked, resting his forearm on the car's window.

"The..." Terry swished his answer around in his mouth and shot the guard a puzzled look, "limo driver?" It was a question and an answer all at the same time.

"You got jokes?" the second guard, clearly more bright than the first, retorted defensively.

"No, no jokes out of me." Terry put on the most non-confrontational voice he could muster and left both hands on the steering wheel. "I was just a bit confused about what you were asking. You know, whether you wanted my actual name or a description of my business here."

"Yeah, well, this ain't no comedy," the first guard said. "I'd hate to have to hurt a clown."

"**Stab the sonuvabitch, Terry,**" Yuri said into the Bluetooth. "**And I don't mean that as a euphemism.**"

Terry nodded vaguely and answered the guard and Yuri at the same time: "I don't want any trouble, sir."

The second guard asked to see the contract. Terry opened the glove compartment, pulled out a clipboard with the contract attached, and passed it through the window. The first guard reached for it, but

Terry pulled it away and pushed it past him to the second, brighter guard.

The first goon, still leaning into the window, frowned. "Do you really want to push me?"

"Absolutely not," Terry replied sharply, placing a hand against his face to smooth rogue hairs from his goatee. "I wouldn't dream of pushing a man your size."

The second guard pointed at Terry with the clipboard. "You got one more tonight, chump."

Terry raised his hands agreeably.

Both guards circled the vehicle, opening the doors, the trunk, and the hood, lifting up the seats, checking the compartments, and inspecting the massive wheel wells. Then they asked Terry to exit the vehicle so they could inspect him for weapons. Once they were satisfied, the second guard drew his radio and told someone in the house that the limousine had arrived.

Alright," he said, returning the clipboard to Terry, "pull through. The driveway snakes up to the rotary. The party will meet you there."

Terry nodded and pulled ahead, easing up the driveway to the house.

The initial portion of the driveway that led from the road to the house was relatively short, measuring perhaps thirty yards, and the backyard and pool with contemporary design were visible from it through the breaks in the shrubbery that bordered either side. The French chateau-style house had hints of Greco architecture and was composed entirely of brick. The house sported a splendid arrangement of colonnades along its portico and a massive fountain at the base of its granite staircase. Large patches of ivy climbed the front of the house to the second story, and several large, coniferous trees grew in front of and around most of the large windows. An awning attached to the northern wing stretched across the end of the driveway to connect a patio to the four-door garage. The driveway bowed around the front of the house in a circular shape to that turned back on itself at the southern wing, where a cylindrical breakfast room jutted from the southwestern corner.

Terry stopped the Hummer just past the edge of the bushes so that only the front end was visible to the prom entourage congregating in front of the patio to take pictures and carry on obnoxiously. Terry drew a cigar from his jacket and lit it. Then he pulled a rag from the glove compartment, slid out of the driver seat, and began wiping the brake dust from the driver's side rims—and started a silent sixty-count.

Terry rose and walked around the hood to the other side, scanning the small crowd: ten family-friendly goons, seven unknown females, an uncle, the mother, sixteen wired adolescents, and—*bingo*—the target. Otherwise, the immediate area was clear.

...fifty-eight...fifty-nine...sixty.

He took one last pull from the cigar and then regarded the ember. He didn't smoke often, but today was one of those exceptions. He gave a dignified exhale, let the cigar fall from his fingers, walked back to the driver's seat, climbed in, and situated himself before pulling forward.

Yuri watched his brother snake up the driveway to a stop, exit the vehicle, move to the front to reconnoiter, and give the *execute* signal. The signal was a cigar with a burning ember; if Terry had extinguished the ember, Yuri would have maintained his position.

Yuri tensed his muscles, pulling himself closer to the undercarriage of the vehicle to relieve the pressure on the retaining straps that attached his load-bearing harness to the vehicle's body and hit the quick-release buckles until he was free. With the faintest rustle, Yuri dropped from the limo, rolled clear, climbed to his hands and feet, and scuttled into the bushes. "**I'm clear,**" he said just a hair above a whisper into the microphone that pressed into his larynx.

"Happy hunting," Terry bubbled as he pulled away.

Yuri gave his gear a quick check. He hooked his thumbs into the harness to reposition it over his torso armor after both had moved roughshod while had been Yuri suspended beneath the Hummer for the better part of an hour. His matte-black sneaking suit, composed of lightweight shoes, sweatsuit-material cargo pants, and a fleece vest over a form-fitting, long-sleeve insulation shirt that hooked around the thumbs, was in place and situated. His balaclava was in place over the black camouflage paint surrounding his eyes. And his reinforced gloves, elbow and knee pads, and shin guards were sufficiently snug.

Yuri checked the security of his *ninjatō*—a shorter, straight-bladed version of the katana whose diminutive size facilitated stealth even when drawn and used in close quarters—attached to the webbing of his harness and holstered in a quick-release sheath; he aimed the handle down to ease its drawing. Strapped to his left forearm was his *tanto*—a ceremonial katana-shaped knife—encased in a matte-black sheath. He had a silenced handgun securely fastened in a holster against his right thigh and had two extra magazines holstered against the left.

All was in place.

"**The target's on the west side of the house with ten bystanders**," Terry said into his Bluetooth. "**Others are in and out of the house at random intervals. Lights out in the breakfast room and foyer.**"

Yuri scanned the yard and pool area for activity and then glanced at his watch. He had forty-five minutes to complete the operation: thirty minutes to infiltrate, make the kill, and exfiltrate. Fifteen minutes to cover the two miles in between the house and the rendezvous point. Now he had only forty-four minutes.

"**Hey**," Yuri whispered into the throat mic, "**Prince called and said he wants his goatee back.**" Terry didn't reply. Yuri supposed that Terry was currently in the company of others and couldn't blow his cover to return fire. Terry would just have to marinate; that satisfied Yuri.

Yuri hugged the shadows and the side of the house as he crept through the yard, sprinting through lighted areas and inching through the darkness. Levarity had two overweight Rottweilers that ruled the backyard, and Yuri needed to be mindful not to alert them.

The dogs were visible, sleeping in a drooling heap on the far side of the pool deck nearest the northeast corner of the house. Yuri looked for signs of wind direction and noted that he was downwind, so they wouldn't pick up his scent. He just needed to make sure that he didn't make any sounds that would draw their attention. At one point, he saw an ear perk up, but it settled shortly after.

He crawled under a bay window, noting that the lights were off in the living room. Ascending to eye level, he peered into the room, scanning it for occupants: it was empty. Entering through the back door was a good option, although he didn't have time to pick the lock if the door was locked; a drug lord's paranoia didn't often leave doors unlocked. Yuri had a glass cutter in one of his pouches. However, he didn't want to leave evidence of forced entry, and he was concerned that the glasscutters would emit a sound that could alert the dogs.

He looked for alternatives.

Luck was on his side. There was a doggy door on the door proper for an animal much smaller than the Rottweilers.

Yuri slithered up to the door and double-checked that the room was still clear. He checked the handle, noting that it was locked. He drew his ninjatō and pushed it through the doggy door, reaching up to compel the deadbolt open. With a muffled *click*, the catch disengaged. Yuri drew his arm back and froze; he had heard the dogs' collars rattle. The dogs lifted their heads and scanned the backyard but showed no sign of alarm. Unconvinced, the dogs licked each other affectionately and laid their heads back down.

Yuri recognized a drumming in his ears—the adrenaline. He delayed for a thirty-count to calm his nerves. There was also the bonus of ensuring the dogs were asleep again. At thirty, he hopped to his feet, opened the door, and entered the house, ensuring that he closed the door and locked it behind him. The alarm system let out a short chime, signaling that a door in the house had opened. No one paid it any attention—everyone was preoccupied with the procession.

Returning his *ninjatō* to the sheath in a choreographed motion, Yuri crept through a dark, theater-style living room into an equally dark kitchen. The refrigerator and the majority of the appliances sat on Yuri's right, an enormous table on the left, and a huge island situated in between. He slinked through the archway, simultaneously checking the corners for ambush and hiding spots. Then he heard movement coming towards the kitchen.

Repetitive rises and falls.

Footsteps.

Louder and louder.

Yuri dove for cover behind the island and pressed his body into it. He couldn't risk looking at the intruder. If Yuri did, he could alert the intruder to his presence. The human eye had mediocre night vision, but it had an incredible ability to detect motion; periscoping his head to look would draw the intruder's attention. Instead, Yuri engaged other senses he had been trained to use in darkness. He concentrated on sounds and smells: the footfalls were light and sounded like the patter of bare feet; there was an aroma of fruit, perfume, and shampoo. He concluded that the intruder was female.

He slowed his breathing—ensuring not to fill is lungs to full capacity, which would trigger a perceptibly forceful exhale—and remained in place, waiting to see the intruder's next move. He assumed that the intruder was either seeking a snack or passing through to the living room. If the intruder were just passing through, Yuri would linger until the intruder was out of sight, and then he would bolt into the foyer. However, if the intruder were planning an extended stay—which would surely include a light coming on—Yuri would rapidly find a better hiding spot.

The pitter-patter stopped short of the refrigerator, and then there was faint illumination, dancing shadows, and jingling condiments. Yuri dove from the island, timing it with the refrigerator door to use the noise to mask his own, slid on his side between the dining room chairs, and disappeared beneath the low-hanging table cloth.

"Pumpkin?" a young girl's voice squeaked in the twilight. "Pumpkin, is that you?"

Yuri gloated to himself about the accuracy of his guess.

The girl called, "Pumpkin?" whom Yuri thought may have been an animal. Apparently, she thought the noise he had produced had been made by Pumpkin—the likely proprietor of the doggy door—since he had made mostly no sound at all. As long as she didn't come snooping under the table in search of a furry companion, she was welcome to assume whatever she wished. If she did come under the table...well, Yuri would cross that bridge when the time came.

The girl rummaged through the refrigerator longer than Yuri felt was necessary. How long did it take to grab some jello or yogurt and go back to bed? She had to have been having withdrawal from being away from her cellphone and social media this long. Yuri's veins ran hot with aggravation—things tended to break when he became aggravated enough.

Then a cat's growl broke the silence.

The girl stopped what she was doing, and Yuri heard the squeak of feet as she spun around. "Pumpkin, what are you doing?"

Yuri looked to his left and saw Pumpkin: s plump, orange cat who was occupying the majority of a nearby chair. Pumpkin arched its back defensively, the hair on its spine standing up. It growled again.

"Pumpkin!" the girl demanded.

The damn cat was going to give away Yuri's position if it didn't shut up. Pumpkin wasn't going to give ground; it didn't give ground to Rottweilers, so why would it for humans? Yuri struck like a viper, grabbing the cat by its scruff and yanking it off the chair. Pumpkin writhed and bucked, digging its claws and teeth into Yuri's hand and arm. While his gloves and sneaking suit protected him from the cat's furious attempts to escape, it wasn't going to give up the struggle, and eventually the girl would come looking.

Just then, Yuri's receiver crackled to life. "Status?" Terry demanded.

Yuri pressed Pumpkin into the floor and shifted his weight so that he could free a hand to key the transmitter. "**Now is *so* not a good time**," he whispered finally.

Terry replied, "Give me an update as soon as you can."

Pumpkin shook violently and yowled. Yuri clamped down on the cat's head with his free hand to muffle the cat's vocalizations. This wasn't going to end well: the cat was either going to stay and fight or bolt and make a tremendous amount of noise. Either situation spelled disaster for his operation. There was only one other option. The muscles in Yuri's arm went solid. With a wet *pop*, the cat's head jerked free of the spinal column. Pumpkin twitched silently in Yuri's hands for a brief time and then went limp. After several seconds of silence, the girl lost interest in the cat and when back to the refrigerator.

There was the hollow *splash* of pouring liquid filling a cup followed by glassy *clinking* as a container was returned to the refrigerator's door. Yuri heard the rustle from a plastic container, which he assumed was the snack she was finally retrieving, before she approached the table and climbed into a chair to eat in the dark.

Yuri checked his watch: four precious minutes had gone by; he couldn't give up more time. The temperature in Yuri's veins climbed to dangerous levels. The girl was slowing him down in a major way. He began taking slow breaths in through his nose, trying to ease the tension so that he could keep a clear head and sit patiently with his eyes closed.

He heard the alarm chime several times as people entered and exited the house through the patio door. There was no telling where his target was now, whether he was upstairs or elsewhere in the house. The little girl was seriously cramping Yuri's style.

"Chastity," said a voice in a deep Jamaican accent that Yuri instantly attributed to the target, Levarity, after having heard him speak countless times over tapped phone lines, "what are you doing sitting in the dark?"

"I'm eating a snack, Daddy."

"In the dark?"

Two more minutes wasted.

"It only takes a second to eat a cookie, Daddy."

Yuri couldn't see the look on Levarity's face, but he was sure that it reflected the thoughts in Yuri's head—that was the most hare-brained answer he had ever heard. Being eleven must have been horrible. To be completely incapable of formulating anything logical was possibly the worst punishment he could think of. He never wanted to go back.

"Well, make sure you clean up after yourself, baby," instructed a woman's voice—Levarity's wife.

Yuri heard them leave; he focused on the sound of their footfalls. He was sure they had ascended the stairs. Since he knew his target's position, all he needed to do was get out from underneath the table. But apparently, it took longer than a second to eat a cookie. He was going to be sitting there for a while, he guessed, unless he was as decisive with the girl as he was with Pumpkin.

Yuri checked his watch again: three more minutes had passed. He couldn't sacrifice more time, not to mention that the girl's persistent drumming of the chair with her feet was driving him insane.

Screw it, Yuri thought to himself, *you know what they say about drastic situations.* He grabbed an ankle in each hand and yanked her out of the chair. Chastity disappeared beneath the table with a squeak. Yuri coiled around her to muffle her cries, and he constricted her throat with his arm; soon she went unconscious.

Yuri relaxed the pressure against her jugular and allowed her to roll gently onto the floor. He positioned her on her side, raised his balaclava to his nose, and hovered over Chastity's mouth. He could feel humid pulses hit his cheek; she was breathing but definitely unconscious. Terry would be terribly disappointed, but whatever, he could get trapped by a child underneath a table next and blow the operation by trying to play the part of the good-natured ninja. That wasn't Yuri's style, and Ninpo made no explicit argument against him—even though Terry would say something like, "*The ancestors would never have condoned killing children,*" to which Yuri would reply that she wasn't dead. When Chastity awoke, all she'd remember was being dragged under the table by a monster that lurked in the darkness. Ninpo's code of silence hadn't been violated, so there was no point in debating.

Yuri reset his balaclava and combat crawled out from under the table. He scanned the kitchen and the foyer through the next arch. When he was sure it was clear, he proceeded into the foyer, checking the two doorways and a hallway that led away. Satisfied that he still maintained the element of surprise, he drew his *tanto* from its sheath and crept up the curving marble steps.

A *tanto* was a traditionally ornate dagger that was used primarily for stabbing but could be used for slicing if the edges were sharpened. Yuri's tanto was unique, and he held it in high esteem, a status symbol of his battle prowess. The handle, which fit securely in one hand, was wrapped in black silk in a crisscross pattern that formed diamonds at the intersection points. The handguard was particularly ornate, sporting two matte-black coiled snakes that overlapped head to tail to form a polygonal shape. The blade measured six inches in length, with an extremely fine double edge. Etched on the blade was a viper with its fanged maw touching the tip and the tail touching the handguard. Unlike a ninjatō, a tanto was more than a tool. If the ninjatō needed to be left behind, Terry and Yuri—as with all Shinobi—felt no heartburn. The ninjatō was not considered the soul of the warrior to Shinobi like the katana was to the Samurai of old. Losing one's tanto, however, was seen as shameful, although not grievous enough to warrant seppuku—honorable suicide.

38

Yuri slithered down the hallway of the second floor, keeping the blade pressed into his leg to squelch any chance of reflecting ambient light and drawing attention. There was a television playing in a room as he crept past. The more white noise present, the better. White noise drowned out any noise he made.

Before he could press on to the master bedroom, he needed to make sure his exit was prepared. All the windows and doors were rigged with sensors that would trip the alarm system if opened. That is, all the windows and doors except Levarity's eldest daughter's window.

During their surveillance, Terry and Yuri had witnessed the daughter's rebellious streak as she'd sneaked out of the window of her room and crawled along the awning to the garage. Of course, she'd had friends waiting for her at the bottom. Terry and Yuri often joked about the irony of the situation. Parents often said that their children would be the death of them. Indirectly, Levarity's daughter was going to be responsible for his death. Her rebelliousness was going to afford Yuri the perfect means of escape.

Yuri pressed his ear against the door of the daughter's bedroom. He didn't hear anyone, nor should he have since the daughter had left for the prom, but there was never anything wrong with being thorough.

Staying low, he pushed the door open: the room was empty. Yuri slinked in, closing the door behind him, and skulked up to the window. He pulled the curtain back to introduce enough light for him to see. Then he searched the window's frame for the alarm's sensor. It was positioned in the upper-left corner of the window and required Yuri to climb on the sill to examine it. He realized how Levarity's daughter had managed to escape without being noticed; she'd tricked the sensor into thinking the connection wasn't broke by using another piece of metal whenever she opened the window. *Sneaky little beast,* Yuri thought. If it isn't broke, don't try to fix it; Yuri was going to leave through the window in the same manner as the daughter. If she hadn't been caught yet, no one would spot him.

With his exit strategy set, Yuri advanced into the hallway again in the direction of the master bedroom. He could hear a faint conversation as he stalked to the door. He pressed his ear against it and listened for any clues that would tell the position of his prey. There was the muffled echo of the wife's voice, the splashing of running water, the patter of bare feet against a linoleum floor, and Levarity's unfettered accent.

Yuri guessed that the wife was in the bathroom preparing to shower and was conversing with the target through the door. What was the target doing? Was he facing the door? Was he around the corner? Was he on the bed? Was the bathroom door open? Would the wife see Yuri enter? Would he have to kill the wife too?

Yuri pulled a fiber-optic camera from a pouch and pushed it under the door. Levarity was directly across the room from the door, lounging in a recliner and watching highlights of sporting events—his back was to the door. The wife was showering with the door open.

Yuri withdrew the camera and stowed it. He wouldn't have much time if he wanted the wife to live. He took a deep breath and then tightened his grip on the handle of his tanto as he reached for the doorknob.

*　　*　　*

"Honey," Levarity's wife said as she crossed the bedroom from the closet to the bathroom, "Mercy looked so beautiful and so *grown* in her dress tonight, didn't she?" She disappeared in the cloud of steam. "Our baby is really growing up, isn't she?"

Levarity never looked away from the massive TV. "I can't believe you bought her that dress. I wanted to choke you when I saw her half-naked."

"Don't be silly; she wasn't half-naked. That dress merely reveals the midriff. It's very classy."

"I don't like my daughter looking like a whore, Paulina. I shouldn't have let her go."

"Constantine!" Paulina yelled from the bathroom. "You should be ashamed of yourself, saying such a terrible thing about our daughter!"

"It's the truth!" he yelled back. "Never again. I'll send Chastity to an all-girls boarding school." His volume returned to normal as he said to himself rather than his wife, "I'll kill anyone who puts their hands on her. I don't care how old they are. Lemme catch one of them little boys

40

even look at her wrong. The next person who sees one of them will be a fisherman."

Suddenly, a gloved hand seized Levarity's face and slammed his head against the headrest. Startled, Levarity struggled to get up, grabbing at his assailant, but the assailant wrapped an arm around him, pinning him to the chair. Out of the corner of one eye, he could see a viciously pointed knife. Out of the corner of the other eye, he could see a shadow with two icy-blue, hateful eyes.

"I can't guarantee any *fishermen* will find you," the shadow whispered. It whipped the edge of its knife across the front of Levarity's throat, leaving a line of pink and red. Then the shadow plunged the blade into the space where the neck met the shoulder and jerked it. Blood coughed volcanically from the wounds, drowning the chair in crimson. The shadow held Levarity still by his face, muffling Levarity's death-throes with its hand until he gasped his final breath. The shadow reached down and drew the blanket that was in the target's lap up to Levarity's neck and tucked him in cozily. The shadow patted the top of Levarity's head and then stroked both of the blade's broadsides along the material of the upper cushion.

"Constantine," Paulina said as she exited the bathroom, tying her robe, "I was thinking..." She looked to her right because she swore she'd seen the bedroom door closing; must have been her imagination, though. She continued, "I think that we should enroll Chastity in an all-girls boarding school. I was thinking it would be safer for her. You never know what could happen. What do you think?" She approached the dresser and began applying a face cream to her aging wrinkles. "Constantine?" There was no answer. "Constantine, are you listening to me?"

Aggravated that he was not answering her because he was sleeping, she walked over to the TV and turned it off. She turned to look at her husband...

Her shriek would have left banshees envious.

*   *   *

Terry wove circles through the neighborhoods surrounding the Levarity estate. The teenagers took no notice; they were too engrossed in their festivities. The prom procession carried on with anarchic abandon. They were so loud that they probably woke people on the other side of the planet. Between the music and their screaming, it was miraculous that the police hadn't pulled the limo over. Terry didn't much care. He rolled all the windows up in the cab and pretended they weren't even in the vehicle.

He checked his watch—Yuri should have been wrapping up the operation by now. He had tried to get a status report from Yuri earlier, but he wasn't obliging. Terry assumed that Yuri had encountered a bit of resistance, and Terry was a little worried. His first instinct was to turn around and go in after Yuri, but Terry did not have the gear to do so, nor did he want to take the chance of blowing Yuri's cover. All Terry could do was his part and have faith that the ancestor spirits would guide his brother. Yuri wasn't nearly as pious as Terry, but that wouldn't deter the spirits. Yuri was, after all, a massively talented Shinobi who never betrayed Ninpo. Patience and faith were all Terry could concern himself with for now.

Once he suppressed his anxiety, Terry realized that he had a craving for potato chips and pulled the limo into a gas station. He exited the vehicle and approached the vendor, grabbed his bag of chips, and paid the clerk. He opened the bag and popped a handful into his mouth as he watched the teenagers festively behave like wild animals. Terry thought about what he had been doing at their age—not partying in limos, that much was for sure. Ninpo never allowed such luxury. Instead, it advocated a harsh, spartan, and pious lifestyle based on honor and fighting prowess.

It was by no means any way to raise children, according to Western societal norms. Children needed to be raised in a loving household with two well-off parents and taught the formula for financial success. Terry and Yuri hadn't gotten that for most of their childhood.

Whoever decided on this standard of normalcy apparently hadn't taken into account a family like the Levaritys. On the surface, they met all the criteria of a normal family: two well-off parents that raised their offspring in a safe, neighborly residence surrounded by loving family. One could suppose that it did not matter to the authorities on normalcy whether the parents were church deacons or murderous drug lords as long as they met the vague criteria. Clearly, Terry and Yuri were raised improperly because they did not grow up in such a commercialized household.

Above all else, Terry and Yuri had honor—Constantine Levarity didn't. That was why he had been marked for death. That was why Terry and Yuri had taken the contract against him. With any luck, his children wouldn't follow in his footsteps with their luxurious living and savage behavior.

Terry realized that he had drifted away in thought. He stuffed another handful of chips into his mouth, turned left, and walked around the corner towards the restrooms. Drawing another set of keys from his pocket, he walked up to a money-green luxury sedan sitting in a parking space under a burnt-out street lamp. He depressed a button on the remote, and the car's alarm disengaged, and the doors unlocked. Terry climbed into the driver's side, situated himself, buckled the seatbelt, and continued to eat his chips.

After several moments, Yuri swung himself over the top of the grimy cinderblock wall that divided the main road from the nearest neighborhood. Yuri sped over to the rear passenger door and dove in, closing the door behind him.

Terry munched more chips and turned to look over the driver's seat. "You're late, dumbass," he said sardonically.

"Shut the hell up," Yuri gasped trying to catch his breath. "I got hung up."

"Clearly."

"And you have no idea how fast I had to run."

Terry continued to chew, unconvinced. "What happened?"

"I was having milk and cookies with Levarity's youngest daughter." Yuri's eyes found the top of their sockets while he totaled the time that he'd spent trapped beneath the table. "Did you know that it takes an eleven-year-old nine minutes to eat a fucking cookie?"

Chapter Three: The Ties That Bind

Ciccone Residence. Tokyo, Japan. Twenty-three years ago.

"Daddy, why do I look different?" Terry asked, derailing their one-on-one basketball game. The question had been lurking in Terry's mind for weeks, but he finally decided that right now was as good a time as any.

Pat, who had readied himself to receive his son's check of the ball from their makeshift three-point line, didn't react at first. He merely pursed his lips and nodded as if nothing had happened. It was the type of hollow nod and expression that campaigning politicians gave inquiring constituents when the politician didn't want to make a polarizing answer.

"I'm sorry, what?"

"Why do I look different?" Terry stood there, holding the ball as if he were holding the weight of the world between his delicate hands.

Pat scrutinized his son, peering deeply into him with puzzled, squinted eyes. "Like...different...than what?" he asked. Was Terry asking Pat what he thought Terry was asking, or was he referring to something completely different? Had Pat's seven-year-old just asked him a deep, meaningful question that had no easy answer, or was Pat overthinking this? Was Terry asking why he looked different *when he was shooting the ball as compared to the way Pat shot the ball* or was he stirring up something *else*?

"Why do I look different than you and mommy?"

Oh boy.

"Well," Pat started as he searched his mental Rolodex for canned answers, "that's actually a good question, slick." Pat laughed awkwardly, wiping sweat from his brow. "Why do you look different? I mean, there's a lot of reasons."

"There are?"

"Sure!"

"Like what?"

"Well, you're really an alien, and you've come to earth in human form to devour—*brains*!" Pat playfully waved his hands and fingers.

Terry laughed. "No, I'm not! You're making that up!"

"You're right—I am." Pat looked across the yard to where Francesca was entertaining Yuri and his friend in the sandbox. She locked eyes with him. Then Pat took a knee, cuffed a hand to Terry's ear, and threw a thumb in Francesca's direction. "Want to know what really happened?" he whispered.

Terry nodded enthusiastically and whispered back, "Yeah."

"You see Mommy over there? Well, she used to be a real putz and dropped you head first into a can of brown paint when you were a baby, so you had a dark brown head and a different color body. We didn't want you to feel like a freak, so we painted the rest of you the same color. What do you think?"

Terry giggled, "No, you didn't."

"Yes, we did."

"No, you didn't."

"What kind of secrets are you telling my son about me, Patrizio?" Francesca said.

Pat rapped Terry's chest with his knuckles and then tossed his thumb at Francesca again. "Tell her 'only the good kind,' sport."

"Only the good kind, sport!" Terry shouted to his mother.

"No, no—you're sport, not her," Pat said, waving his hands vigorously. Terry giggled more. "You're supposed to call her Mommy. Say, 'only the good kind, Mommy.'"

"Only the good kind, Mommy!"

"Smile."

Terry did.

"Not at me, at her."

Terry did that too. Pat did as well.

*   *   *

Pat came into the kitchen from the living room, where he'd left the boys. Terry was coloring while a movie played, and Yuri slept soundly on the couch.

"Babe," he said, "Yuri's out. He's taking up the entire couch. Whatever you did to him wore him out."

"Why don't you put him in his bed?" she asked as she placed a sandwich that she had made Pat at his favorite place at the table.

Pat shook his head. "And chance waking him? No, thank you. It'll be endless civil war. I'm not dealing with that beast all night." He sat in front of his plate and scooped up the sandwich. "On another note: Terry's got one hell of a fade away. He might really have a future in basketball; might even get himself into college with it. I wonder if they have any good youth leagues around here. Doubt it, though. The Japanese aren't basketball fanatics like Americans."

"Maybe the base has club teams?"

"Worth looking into, I suppose."

"Otherwise, you're just going to have to go outside and shoot hoops with him until we get back to the states."

"Yeah—because I'm a *champion* basketball player," Pat replied as he bit into his food, and then he set it down to chew thoughtfully.

Francesca rounded the table, waved a hand that prompted Pat to put some distance between him and the table, and then she sat in his lap. Pat welcomed her with a warm smile and nuzzled her arm when she sat down.

"Ya know—I hate it when you call Yuri that," Francesca said, tracing the veins on his arm with her nails.

"Call Yuri what? What I do?"

"You called him a beast."

"Babe, I call him a lot of things. Beast is the mildest of them. Well, except for devil-spawn."

Francesca's mouth fell open, and she swatted Pat's chest with the back of her hand.

Pat laughed. "I don't mean anything by it."

"You don't call Terry any of those names."

"That's because Terry's different. He's not a rampaging lunatic like Yuri."

"He's not a rampaging lunatic, Pat. He's two. Two-year-olds act that way."

"I've seen a lot of two-year-olds, and none of them act like that. Terry definitely didn't. Yuri gets that whole rampaging lunatic thing from you."

Francesca swatted him again. "You can make your *own* sandwich next time."

46

He laughed, enveloped her with his arms, and pressed his cheek into her arm. "Baby, you know I love you."

"Let go of me."

Pat squeezed her. "Not until you tell me you love me."

"Let go of me."

And tighter still. "Tell me you love me."

"Okay, I love you."

"That's my girl. Can you make me another sandwich?"

Her lips became a thin line. "You've barely touched this one."

"That's because you've been in my way the whole time, but when you get up, I won't even taste it."

"You're lucky I love you," Francesca said, standing and making her way back to the pantry.

Pat swatted Francesca's buttocks. "I am that!"

She gave him a dirty look.

"Pat, I don't want Yuri and Terry feeling different."

"Funny you say that," Pat said, picking up his sandwich and taking a huge mouthful out of it. "Terry actually asked me today why he looked different."

"He asked you that?"

"Mm-hmm" was all he could manage with his mouth full. Only about a third of the sandwich was left.

"Oh God." Her voice poured concern, and her eyes softened in a way no one could expect her normally icy-blue eyes to soften. "What did he say?"

Pat swallowed hard. "He asked me why he looks different than me and you."

"When did he do that?"

"While we were playing basketball."

"What'd you say?"

"I joked a little and changed the subject."

"Why on earth would you do that?"

"I didn't want to jump the gun and answer a question that he wasn't asking."

"Pat, he was asking you a question that he deserves an answer to."

"But what if he wasn't? What if he was asking a more superficial question that required a superficial answer? I didn't want to hurl difficult-to-understand answers at him and open a can of worms that didn't need to be opened yet."

"He has a right to know, Pat."

"I never said that he didn't. I just don't think now is the time. I don't think he's ready."

"I think he is."

"Fine. I don't think I'm ready. I don't think I'm ready to tell my son that the world isn't impartial and that his identity will never be his own, that he will always be judged by somebody else's rules."

"Pat, if we don't talk to him about it, he'll come to his own twisted conclusions. You said to me once that you believed that prejudice was created when a kid asks a difficult question that isn't answered by an adult and instead the kid uses child logic to come up with their own answer."

"I did say that. But I don't think seven-year-olds have enough awareness to draw us into this conversation. I think he was asking an insubstantial question that we instinctively approach with an adult's logic."

"I would buy that if this wasn't Terry we were talking about. He's not your average seven-year-old. I just need him to know that he's a part of this family and that color and DNA doesn't change that."

"I—I don't want to do this, Francesca. I really don't think I'm ready to shatter his view of the world."

"Honey, I know this is difficult, but we have to do this. If we do it now while it's still fresh in Terry's head, we can address it early—not waiting until it becomes a serious issue." She pressed her hands into her chest. "Do it for me."

"I'll stand behind you on this, but I think we're making a mistake."

*　　*　　*

Pat, in his discomfort, convinced Francesca to wait until the next day to discuss Terry's past—it felt wrong. He supposed it was a function of him having no concept of what emotional tumult an adopted child goes through as they try to decide who they are in life. How does an adoptee decide the boundaries of family: along rearing-lines or bloodlines? Obviously, Terry was too young to make that distinction today, but the time would come when he'd have to. The thought of burdening this once-motherless and fatherless child felt abjectly immoral. Terry was a boy without his own history. He'd always have to substitute Pat and Francesca's for his own; but at least Terry had something. Pat felt like this conversation was going to take even that from him.

Francesca called Terry to her room, where Pat and she sat under the covers and leaned against the headboard. Terry strode in coolly and stood to her side of the bed. "Yes, Mommy?" he said appreciatively, his big, dark eyes glittering with trust. Pat couldn't hold his son's stare.

"Come up on the bed, baby," she said to him. "Mommy wants to hold you."

Terry did as he was told and climbed up to settle between his parents.

"Terry, Mommy and Daddy want to talk to you about something important. If you have questions, I want you to ask them, okay?"

"Yes, ma'am."

"Well," Francesca started but realized that she didn't know what to say. She swore she'd had this entire conversation suitcased last night, but now that it was time to put all the cards on the table, she had stage fright. After all, how was she supposed to start the conversation? Terry just stared deep into her eyes. She exhaled audibly when she noticed that she had been holding her breath.

Pat peeked at his wife when he heard her stall and not recover. Francesca chewed her lip as she tried to on-the-spot-engineer a kick-off statement. Terry watched her intently, surely noticing her embarrassment but not knowing from what.

Pat wasn't going to let his wife flounder, so he spoke up in spite of his reservations: "Son." Terry's head swung to look at him; so did Francesca's. "Do you know where Yuri came from?"

"Yes, sir."

"Where?"

"Mommy's tummy."

"That's right. He's Mommy's son, right?"

"Yes, sir."

"He's Daddy's son too, right?"

"Yes, sir."

"What else is Yuri?"

"My brother."

"That's right—Yuri is your brother," Pat affirmed mildly. "But Terry, you didn't come from Mommy's tummy like Yuri did."

Terry's eyebrows crinkled.

Pat didn't let it faze him and continued, "You came from another woman's tummy."

"Another woman? So, I'm not Mommy's son?"

"No," Francesca forced out even though it felt as though she had been punched in the gut and left breathless, "you're definitely Mommy's son, Terry. Mommy was just never pregnant with you like I was with Yuri."

"So, I have another mommy?"

"No—"

Pat interrupted with a hand in the air, "Yes, son, you have another mommy, but *Mommy* and *Daddy* are your family. Yuri is your brother. The people that you live with and grow up with are your family, and you must always accept them. One day, when you're an adult, you may decide you want to find your other mommy—that's okay. But remember that *we* are your family."

"Does Mommy love me like Yuri?"

Francesca gasped and fought back the tears that instantly filled her eyes. She couldn't make words come out. Pat did it for her, saying, "Of course, she does, Terry. Even though you didn't come from Mommy's tummy, you are her first son and always will be. You're Yuri's big brother, and we expect you always to take care of him like a big brother should. And remember: no one will ever love you like Mommy."

"Does my other mommy love me?"

"I'm sure she does," Francesca managed shakily, "wherever she is."

"Why didn't I come from Mommy's tummy like Yuri?"

Pat continued to speak for his wife while she composed herself more: "For a long time, Mommy and Daddy wanted to have a baby, but

50

we couldn't because Mommy and Daddy had difficulty getting pregnant."

"Why?"

"Because that wasn't God's plan," Francesca declared humbly. Pat met her icy eyes with his own, and he instantly knew the whole team was back in play.

"Another woman was pregnant with you but couldn't take care of you when you were a baby, so she gave you to us to take care of—to be our son." Francesca made an effort to make the statement as positive and lighthearted as possible; she didn't want Terry to feel abandoned.

"Why couldn't she take care of me?"

"Mommy and Daddy don't know." Pat rubbed the back of his own hand idly. "And I don't think it really matters. I guess it wasn't God's plan."

"So...what is God's plan?"

Both parents chuckled.

"That's between you and Him, son. But you have faith that God will take care of you," Pat said with a smile.

"I'm glad this was God's plan."

Francesca gasped again and snatched Terry into her arms; tears spilled from her eyes and were soaked up by his coarse hair.

"Mommy, I can't breathe," Terry squeaked.

She released him and stroked the side of his face. "I'll smother you with my love, and you'll like it," Francesca sniffled in her Jersey accent.

"Why are you crying?"

Francesca expelled something between a laugh and a sob. "It's because I love you so much, and I'm so thankful for you. I just want you to be happy." More tears rolled down her face.

"I'm happy, Mommy."

And yet more tears. Francesca was a pistol to most, but with her children, she was docile, loving, and unconditional.

"Mommy!" came the savage roar of a toddler from somewhere in the house.

"The beast is awake and ready to crush souls," Pat said blandly.

"Patrizio Ciccone!" Francesca demanded, launching daggers from her eyes.

Pat rested his arm on Terry's shoulder and shot a smirk at Francesca. "What?"

"You know what," she said sourly, wiping tears from her face.

Pat chuckled. "Terry, go get your brother and bring him here. We're gonna watch a movie as a family. Then we'll get up and make breakfast."

Chapter Four: Death from a Distance

Loyalty is the blood that runs in the veins of Shinobi. Never shall Shinobi commit any vile act against a clansman, elder, or ancestor, nor shall Shinobi allow such treason to go unpunished or be dishonored.
The Second Mandate, translated from Ninpo.

Rio de Janeiro, Brasil. Today.

High noon in Rio de Janeiro was a mesmerizing flood of tourist activity and native commercial business, but it was blisteringly hot and miserable for Terry and Yuri. Far above the masses, they were huddled on a rampart of a commercial tower, stalking their target—a Brazilian pirate that operated in the Somali Basin.

The contract required them to kill the target by any means necessary, but there was a catch. The intelligence provided by the employer regarding the target was sparse, and they had to do a tremendous amount of research to find her. The employer provided the brothers with a name, a profession, a geographic location, and three pictures. From the information, the brothers uncovered her background: The target's name was Fatima Terceira, a plain-looking fifty-year-old former Merchant Marine who was currently in the employ of a pirate collective that operated off of the east coast of Africa. She was an experienced ship handler that had been persuaded into maritime crime by a significant pay increase. In an incursion with a naval combatant, while she and her crew were in control of a hijacked vessel, she had dumped millions of dollars of stolen goods into the ocean as she'd made her getaway. As punishment for her actions, Terry and Yuri's employer wanted her eliminated. The brothers obliged.

They tracked Fatima to a residence in Rio de Janeiro, where she maintained a charming penthouse overlooking a beach in Leblon. There she stayed with her daughter and aunt during brief periods ashore: a prime location to set an ambush for when she returned from sea. There was no telling how long she would be ashore or how long her next at-sea period would be, so the brothers had to be ready to move against her as soon as the opportunity presented itself.

Fatima finally popped up one sleepy morning while Yuri was watching her flat. He went instantly from torpid consciousness to live-wire when he realized it was her through his binoculars, and he immediately put in a call to Terry for support. Yuri then moved to higher ground to ready their attack. Terry arrived shortly after with his rifle. From their new perch, they could see straight through Fatima's living room and kitchen windows. They simply had to wait for the right moment to pull the trigger. Five hours had passed since sunrise and since the two brothers had been able to move about actively—Yuri's patience was visibly wearing thin.

Terry lay prone on the parapet, clad in his marble-colored ghillie suit and gripping a small sandbag that supported the barrel of his weapon, focusing his attention through the scope of his 7.62mm cartridge-fed sniper rifle. He breathed slowly and deliberately so as not to affect the aim of his weapon adversely if he had to rapidly squeeze a shot off. He maintained constant pressure on the sandbag with his left hand to maintain the constant elevation of the barrel.

Yuri, also prone to Terry's left and equally dressed for the occasion, spied the penthouse through his binoculars. He swiftly noted atmospheric conditions and referenced them against the waterproof chart he had attached to his left forearm. After prompt calculation, Yuri explained the factors to Terry, who adjusted his aim accordingly.

Yuri reached into one of the pouches on his right hip and pulled out a pack of cigarettes, drawing a lone cigarette with his lips and lighting it with one fluid motion. Terry's left eye shot in Yuri's direction, his attention drawn by the grinding *click* of the flint and the raspy inhale that followed. Terry stared hard from the corner of his eyes before returning his attention downrange.

Yuri scanned the rooftops before lifting his head when he noticed something suspicious. "You need to check this out."

"What is it?"

"Just look."

Terry broke away from the scope and rolled slightly. Yuri placed the binoculars to Terry's eyes and pointed.

"Dude," Terry said venomously when he saw a woman sunbathing nude on a balcony, "are you freaking serious?"

"That's how Brazilians prevent tan lines."

"Can you fucking take this seriously?" Terry returned his face to the scope.

Well, that escalated quickly, thought Yuri. "Man, who pissed in your Cheerios today?" he asked, throwing Terry a sidelong glance.

"Got some things on my mind, and you're not helping acting like you're fucking twelve."

"Why don't you pump your goddamn brakes, Tinkerbell. I'm on your team, remember?"

Terry was silent for a moment. "I'm sorry. I overreacted."

"Want to talk about it?"

"Not particularly, no."

"Fine, suffer on your own then." Then there was silence between them for the better part of fifteen minutes. In that time, Yuri smoked two more cigarettes and sent intermittent text messages. Finally, he spoke again: "Hey, when we get done, I really want to go see that big-ass statue." Yuri threw a thumb over his shoulder.

"*That big-ass statue*? Mind narrowing it down a little more for me? That is, of course, assuming that *That Big-Ass Statue* has a name other than *That Big-Ass Statue*."

"Hell, I don't know." Yuri pointed at Corcovado Mountain. "The big-ass statue on top of that peak over there. You know, the one that you see on all the postcards of Rio."

"Oh, you mean the *Christ the Redeemer* statue?"

"Yeah—sure."

"You don't even know its name. Why would you want to go see it?"

"Do I need to know its name to want to go see it?"

Terry glanced in Yuri's direction with his left eye. "Usually, knowing a landmark's name is a requisite for going to see it. I mean, how can you appreciate something when you don't even know something as simple as its name?"

"What fucking difference does it make?"

"It makes a lot of *fucking* difference as a matter of fact."

"You scrutinize everything I do, Terry. You're such a *woman* about everything. I almost don't pay you any attention anymore."

"I don't scrutinize everything you do."

"The fuck you don't. You scrutinize everything."

Terry snapped his head in Yuri's direction. "No, I don't. I only scrutinize the stupid things that you do—which just happens to constitute ninety percent of everything you do. So yeah," Terry said with a shrug, "I guess I can see how that could be mistaken as constant scrutiny. Which brings me to my next point: Why do I have to bring up smoking on ops?"

Yuri rolled his eyes. "Oh, here we go with this shit again."

"Yeah—here we go again. I don't know why I have to keep repeating myself constantly, you simple-minded piss-ant."

"What'd you just call me?"

"Don't play deaf now," Terry said acidly, returning his attention to the scope again.

Yuri's eyes burned a hole in the side of Terry's face. He wanted desperately to crush Terry's cheekbone with the binoculars, but through the swelling anger, he doubted that he could make this shot alone. They were approximately five hundred meters from the target, and a shot from that distance was hard enough with two people—having only one would greatly decrease the margin of success. He would get Terry back later. In the meantime, Yuri lit another cigarette and bellowed smoke like a steam engine.

Terry focused through the lens, trying to ignore his brother's habit, noticing several rebel strands of ghillie suit had settled between his eye and the diopter. He forcibly exhaled upwards through puckered lips, trying to blow them clear. After several failed attempts, he realized that he would surely hyperventilate before he managed to get his suit to cooperate. Yuri reached across and moved the strands away from his brother's eyes and smoothed them back onto the suit.

"Better?"

"Yeah," Terry replied curtly, "thanks."

Another forty-five minutes had passed, and Terry was still agitated about his brother's continuous smoking. Yuri's rebellious streak used to get them in trouble when they were kids. Their headmaster, Kintake, had possessed an abusive penchant for punishing everyone when Yuri chose to be defiant; Terry had the scars to prove it. One day, Yuri's rebelliousness would get them killed if Terry couldn't convince him otherwise. He would continue to try. "You know, one of these days, they're going to see the smoke," he said.

"What?" Yuri's head jerked up from the binoculars, with his cigarette pressed in between his lips. "What the hell are you babbling about? Who's going to see smoke?"

"Fatima's security detail. They're going to see the smoke from your cigarette. We're supposed to be doing this thing called *stealth*."

"Get out of here with that." Yuri's expression was sour. "We're nearly five hundred meters away. How are they going to see the smoke?"

"They're a security detail, Yuri. They're employed to spot things that appear abnormal."

"There is nothing abnormal about cigarette smoke."

"Maybe not. But from the perspective of a bodyguard, there sure as hell is something pretty abnormal about two guys lying on a rooftop, dressed in Halloween costumes, pointing a rifle at your employer while taking the time out for a smoke break. They are going to see and probably smell the smoke."

"That's fucking impossible...and stupid."

"Oh—it's possible."

"Fine—it's fucking improbable, just like it's improbable that you're going to shut up."

"And it's a terrible habit."

"So is nagging, but you don't see me bitching at *you* constantly," Yuri said with an unsympathetic tone.

"I don't know how Veronica puts up with it. Hell, I don't know how I've put up with it."

Yuri flicked his cigarette over the side. "How about you leave Veronica out of this?"

"How about you stop smoking while we're operating?"

"How about you leave Veronica out of this before I kick that rifle up your ass?"

"I'm shivering, little brother."

"I respect your opinion on most topics. You'd do well to consider where your opinion isn't wanted."

"You're right." Terry nodded. "On second thought...smoke...drop dead."

"I hate talking to you, Terry."

"Feeling is mutual."

The stifling atmosphere of the ghillie suit and the tension between him and his brother caused sweat to pool beneath Yuri, and he drew closer to the edge to relieve some discomfort. The faint grinding of gravel between Yuri's suit and the concrete of the building drew Terry's attention. He instinctively lifted his head away from the scope to inspect Yuri's gear to ensure that Yuri's movement wouldn't expose their position.

Stealth and ambush were the foundations of Ninpo. All Shinobi were trained from a very young age to mind themselves, their fellows, and their surroundings to ensure they weren't exposing themselves to an enemy. While Shinobi weren't sympathetic to discomfort, they reasonably understood that discomfort decreased the endurance of a Shinobi's stealth and taught their initiates—Kodomos—to supervise their comrades for inconsistencies that might betray camouflage.

Yuri had none that Terry noticed, but what he did notice caused his ears to flatten against his head like an angry canine. Running the length of Yuri's back beneath the suit was a subtle, incongruous bulge—Yuri's ninjatō. Terry resigned himself to dismiss it but opted not to when he remembered that he'd noticed Yuri carrying it in an eatery earlier this week. He carried it, Terry reasoned, not for utility—since he couldn't find a single use for a ninjatō in an eatery—but rather as an ego-booster; and, Terry had had enough of Yuri's ego.

"You always bring your ninjatō on rooftop excursions?" Terry asked sardonically. "Plan on getting in a sword fight?"

"Bloody Christ!" Yuri peeled his face away from the rangefinder and looked skyward. "You're worse than a menstruating woman!" If the suit hadn't covered his head, he would have pulled his hair out. "What could you possibly be bitching about now?"

"Why would you carry a sword on a job like this? Unless, of course, you were planning on getting swept up into a sword-drawn romp with a cadre of evil ninjas."

Yuri frowned. "You're supposed to be finding a place to land a bullet on Fatima's spindly frame. Instead, you're wasting time worrying about what the fuck I'm carrying."

"Apparently, I have to babysit you. What happened to the tenet: **Shinobi carry no burden—the earth is like air to them**?"

"You going to tutor me in Ninjitsu-101?"

"I guess I'll have to since being Shinobi is brand new to you."

"I think I have enough experience in this profession to determine the necessity and utility of my gear, Terenzio," Yuri growled venomously.

"Then surely you realize that there's neither a *necessity* nor any *utility* for your *ninjatō* up here. I mean, I don't claim to know much—"

"Bullshit," Yuri interjected.

Terry continued, "—but I don't suspect you'll end up clashing swords any time soon. You're just carrying excess weight."

"Are you done?"

"Hell no, I'm not done," Terry said ardently.

Yuri let out an audible groan.

"You're not even going to try to justify it?"

"Just so you can listen to yourself talk?" Yuri shook his head. "No."

"Here—take the rifle. I'll be back in a moment; I'm going to find you some fireball-hurling ninjas to fight."

"Dude"—the energy seemed to drain out of Yuri's voice—"get off the evil ninja thing. It's getting old."

Terry agreed; the evil ninja comments had gone stale even if they were true. "You know what you did?" Terry asked, but it didn't sound like a question.

"I'm sure you're going to tell me..."

"You basically brought a knife to a gunfight. Flat-out poor decision-making. Rookie move if you ask me."

Yuri's head jerked in Terry's direction. "That's just it; I didn't *ask* you. And how is a fan of the *naginata* going to tell me about my poor weapon choice?"

"Don't be mad that you don't understand it."

"It's a freaking *spear*. And it was made for *women*."

"Exactly—it was a spear used in ancient times as a distance weapon. Know what I carry now when I need reach? A fucking rifle." Terry paused. "Which brings us full circle to the original question: Why are you carrying a sword on a sniping mission?"

"I'd rather have it and not need it than need it and not have it."

Terry chortled. "I would have bet money that you would have started in with the ninjatō-is-more-than-just-a-blade nonsense, where you repeat all the propaganda about it 'being a tool, a makeshift hammer, or makeshift ladder' and all that jazz."

"Terry"—Yuri paused to blow a piece of his suit away from his eyes—"*you're* a tool."

"It would honor me greatly if you and your ninjatō jumped from this ledge, Yuri."

*　　*　　*

The brothers tacitly engaged in a competition for first place in a smoldering game of silent treatment, not speaking to each other for nearly two hours—not even to talk about their current operation. Yuri, still spotting his brother, refused to give Terry any environmentals or advice. Terry, still needing spotting, refused to ask for any help. Terry refused to talk to Yuri until he admitted that he was unnecessarily carrying the ninjatō. Yuri simply wanted Terry to go to hell. More than anything, they wanted to terminate Fatima so they could dismount, go about their business, and take some quality time away from each other. Their target wasn't playing nicely, though.

Through the yawning windows of the penthouse, the brothers watched Fatima go about her day but were unable to fire. Even though a round would have little trouble passing through the glass, they didn't want to risk giving away their position by firing through a closed window and having the round deviate half a degree and wound Fatima or miss her altogether. Inside of a couple of hundred meters, glass wasn't much of a factor. But at the distance they were going to shoot, firing through glass had a margin of error they didn't want to accept.

"What if we don't get a clean shot?" Terry said finally, deciding that he wasn't going to continue to be petty.

Yuri didn't lift his head from the binoculars. "Then we'll have to shoot the bitch through the window and call it good. Sacrifices..."

"I was afraid you'd say that."

"Why'd you ask then?"

"I was wondering if you had put together a close-quarters backup plan while you were sitting up here spying on her."

"Do I ever have a backup plan?"

Terry nodded subtly. "Let's start considering our options."

"Here's an option: Shoot the bitch through the glass. We'll cross the *backup plan* bridge when we get there."

"If we give away our position on a bogus shot, we'll break the First Mandate. I'm not in the mood to commit seppuku."

"We only break the mandate if we don't remove all traces of our presence."

"That's going to prove challenging."

"Not if we knife everyone in the penthouse."

Terry sighed. Then, just as he was planning to reply to Yuri, Fatima, flustered by the conversation she was having with a colleague, stormed onto the balcony, right into Terry's crosshairs.

Yuri struggled to contain his elation. He quickly noted atmospheric conditions, did some calculations in his head, and blurted data to Terry. "End her!" Yuri demanded and then watched intently through the binoculars.

There was no *click*.

No thunderous belch.

No carbon on the breeze.

Not even the metal *clink* of the shell ejecting.

There was just an eerie silence followed by an exhale from Terry.

Yuri gritted his teeth and gave Terry another sidelong glance. "Why didn't I hear a boom?"

Terry didn't respond.

Yuri raised his voice. "Terry, why didn't I hear a boom?"

"I haven't fired?" Terry's tone was low and calculating.

"Get the fuck out!" Yuri exclaimed, his voice soaked with ridicule. "Why the hell not?"

"There's a child in the living room."

"Who cares?!"

"I care."

"The damn kid has been in the house the entire time! Why is it a problem right this second?"

Terry kept his attention trained down the scope. "I'm not going to kill Fatima in front of her daughter."

"Terry, you were just talking about not wanting to take the shot through the glass not even thirty seconds ago! Now that we have a clean shot, you're hesitating? If you thought the glass on a window was a problem, just wait until the *window* of opportunity closes. Then we'll have no choice but to shift to a new plan. And what if she skips town before we can attack again? We don't get paid!"

"Is that all you care about—the money?"

"On normal days—yeah."

"You forgotten why we stopped being mercenaries?"

"I don't remember money having anything to do with the reason."

"I wasn't trained to kill indiscriminately, and neither were you."

"This isn't indiscriminate killing, Terry. We took this assignment because it met all of the tenants of Ninpo. We debated it and then meditated on it for hours, and you know how much I *hate* meditating."

"That might be part of your problem."

Yuri flashed frustration but didn't let it slow him down. "This is as deliberate as it gets. If there's some collateral, that goes with the territory. Won't be the first target we've hit in front of children."

"I won't allow any red on my honor."

"How is honor in question here? We've already been over this."

"Because, Yuri, there is no honor in killing a target in front of his or her child. Ethics, remember?

"There isn't a single mandate that says anything about dishonor in making a hit in front of children."

"I'm not doing it regardless of what your skewed understanding tells you about honor. Wrong is wrong no matter what the price tag says."

Yuri watched Terry for a moment and then reached over and began to brush Terry's shoulder repeatedly with his hand. After about twenty wipes, Terry became annoyed.

"What the hell are you doing?" Terry snapped, lifting his head up from the scope.

"I'm trying to wipe that angel off your shoulder."

"Get the fuck off me. I told you that I'm not going to do it, money or no," Terry said before burying his face again.

Yuri inched closer to his brother. "Terry, we're assassins. We kill people for a living. That's how we make our money. Besides, whether you kill Fatima now or at a more *morally* opportune time, her daughter is going to find out."

"Shut up."

"I need a new partner." Yuri shook his head. "Mine's broke."

"We're not monsters, Yuri—"

"I am."

"Yes, *you* are. But we still have a code that we are obligated to follow. The ancestor spirits wrote the code to guide Shinobi through moments of moral strife. We are now at a moral crossroad, and I've decided to hold the shot. I'm absolutely positive that the ancestor spirits would stand behind my decision."

"Of course they would support your decision, Terry. The ancestor spirits had no concept of two million dollars. Back then, two million dollars didn't even exist on a single continent. But had they understood the concept, those dead-ass *bushi*-killers would have made a mandate telling you to stop being a bitch and take the damn shot."

"I highly doubt that."

"I'm not hearing the same confidence as before. Shadow of doubt?"

"Hardly. Like I said, the ancestor spirits would stand behind me—"

"And make fun of you for being stupid right now."

"Yuri, need I remind you that the *Shinobi* stood for something greater than crude, worldly things like money? They didn't need money."

"Again, they didn't know what two million dollars were. So of course *they* didn't need it. But *we* need it; otherwise, we can't afford to work in our profession nor live our lifestyle. We'll have to sell our condo in the National Harbor and get a townhouse in District Heights or something. Or worse, we'll have to go back to milking goats and harvesting small crops. Stop being so selfish and take the shot already!"

"We can't let greed dictate our ethics, Yuri."

"Terry, it was poor people that created codes, ethics, and anecdotes. Poor people made them to feel better about being poor."

"If you were poor, you'd have a different tone."

"If I were poor, I'd take the shot. You know why?

"Because you have no moral compass."

"That—and I wouldn't be poor after I got my two million dollars."

"You know what? I'm finished debating with you."

"Fuck!" Yuri screamed at a whisper's octave. "I want to dismount! Take the damn shot!"

"Why don't you cry about it? Maybe I can find some money to comfort you."

Yuri let out an indignant sound.

"I wonder if Veronica realizes how much of an undisciplined, greedy little beast you are."

"Why are you bringing up Veronica again?" Yuri snapped.

"Because I'm trying to figure out who has the problem: you or her."

"Terry," said Yuri pausing, "don't go there."

"Is she stupid or naïve?"

Terry finally hit the right button. The control rods that prevented Yuri's emotions from reaching supercritical levels were pulled out entirely, and Yuri exploded in a rage, screaming and shouting obscenities and threats. Terry allowed his brother to vent for a couple of seconds before he reminded Yuri over and over again that if he didn't get a hold of his emotions, they could blow it. Yuri, however, was beyond the point of rationality as he overflowed with frustration, caring little at that point about the mission.

Despite the blinding cloud of chaos Yuri produced with gouts of fury, Terry keenly watched Fatima, her daughter, and her guests as he had for the duration over the debate-turned-screaming-match. Fatima, still standing on the balcony, spoke to several associates before directing them and her daughter inside. The daughter sped through the opening of the sliding glass door, and Terry watched her sprint down the hallway and disappear deep into the residence. Fatima also made her way to the door, stepping through the threshold and spinning to shut the door behind her.

Time suddenly dilated, slowing everything to a crawl as Terry zeroed in. The muscles in his finger flexed, and he depressed the trigger. With a blast of carbon and an earthquake-like shudder, the rifle unleashed a thunderous howl and spat a flaming projectile at hypersonic speed.

The world was locked in perpetual stillness as the slug sliced through the air, momentarily agitating and heating the air molecules as it closed the distance. In mid-flight, it cut through the tips of the feathers of a very lucky bird that coincidentally moved into the slug's flight path; one-half of a centimeter to the left, and the bird would have disintegrated into a mist of feathers and gore.

The round spiraled across the balcony and through the rapidly closing space between the sliding door and the jam with only inches to spare, striking true just below Fatima's right eye. With a wet *crack*, Fatima's head jerked back as the bullet exited near the neck joint, painting an abstract mural on the floor as the contents of her skull emptied through the hole.

The gunshot snapped Yuri out of his fury, absorbing it like a sponge soaking up spilled water. He looked at Terry blankly.

Terry withdrew the weapon from its perch, grabbed a firm hold of the sandbag, rolled over, and sat up. "When you're done, let's dismount."

Chapter Five: Forest For The Trees

Ciccone Residence. Tokyo, Japan. Twenty-one years ago

Motherhood was the greatest blessing Francesca could have ever experienced. She had two beautiful and intelligent sons and a greatly talented husband to help her raise them. That was more, to say the least, than many women had. In the grand scheme of things, she had little to complain about—the operative word being *little.* Motherhood did present some exceptional *challenges* that Francesca had come to recognize over the years. Every day proved to be a learning experience.

Children were not easily raised. Francesca's mother, Marcella, always said that childrearing was no simple task because children did not come with an instruction manual; childrearing was a trial-and-error process. And because children grew, their needs changed often. In fact, their needs changed so often that the child being raised one year was hardly the same child the following year.

As each day passed, Francesca saw the wisdom in her mother's words. Marcella often said that there would be great days with her children, good days with them, fair days, bad days, and flat-out terrible days. Today was one of those flat-out terrible days. She was in a harrowed mood, and it showed in everything she did. Everything that could go wrong surely did, and she swore that she would kill someone before sundown.

The day started horribly. To begin with, she slept on her shoulder wrong, and she was now being plagued by sharp pain every time she moved it. Next in her line of gripes was the need to run errands—how she hated running errands. She then realized that her preplanned day of very-necessary errand running was going to be a very wet and very irritating day, as it seemed that the weather had its own agenda. Mother Nature, exhibiting how profoundly malicious her disposition could be, decided Francesca's errand-day was a great time to batter the entire western portion of Honshu with torrential rain and hurricane-like wind. And like the weather, Yuri too stirred a tempest by flying into a wild tantrum when he decided that Francesca's breakfast choice was not to his liking, which, of course, left Francesca none too happy. Cursing—loudly—was the only thing she could do to give herself a measure of comfort as she trekked through the torrent with an aching shoulder and stomped through pools in her stilettos. She also cursed her mother's voice in her head saying, in her nasal voice, "Fran, I can't wait till you have children of your own so you can see what you've put me through."

As if nothing else could go wrong, Francesca received a distressing phone call from Terry's school: Terry had been involved in a fight, and Francesca needed to attend a conference with the principal and the guidance counselor as soon as she could arrange herself and show up.

The conference didn't go as well as she would have hoped. When she arrived, she found Terry sitting in a room alone, covered in dirt and scratches. The faculty apparently hadn't found it necessary, or befitting, to either get him cleaned up or comfort him. They simply found it justifiable to isolate a nine-year-old in a room after he had been attacked. Furthermore, the faculty had yet to identify the assailants. Francesca made it a point to express her unhappiness with the manner in which the school was handling the problem with as much profane language as she could muster.

She knew that her husband would surely disapprove of the way she'd handled the conference and the faculty's actions—a small price to pay to defend her son's honor. She would just chalk it up to maternal instinct if Pat queried her actions; he always refused to argue that.

As she drove home through the thunderous gloom, she debated whether to call Pat at work and explain the situation and tell him to come straight home to handle this crisis. Francesca chose to wait until Pat arrived to explain the situation. It would have only been a couple more hours until he was off, and she didn't want him rushing home in this insanity.

*   *   *

Pat checked his watch; he had made it home in decent time despite the weather. Pat eased the van to a halt, trying not to hydroplane across the river that his driveway had become. The rain was coming down so hard that he could barely make out his wife's car only fifteen feet in front of the van's hood.

Pat craned his neck over the steering wheel, looking at sky's fury. Despite the myriad times that Pat had witnessed the Japanese monsoons, they still fascinated him. He was not quite sure what it was exactly about the storms that piqued his interest: the power, the indiscriminate fury, the torrents of precipitation, or the colossal surf it stirred. What he was sure of, however, was that the weather always seemed to reflect his wife's mood. And based on the day's forecast, Pat was sure that his wife had a terrible disposition. That was okay in his mind, though. He loved his hot-blooded Italian wife, and her attitude was one of the things that he found most attractive. He described her as having a really big personality in a really small body.

Pat tossed the door open, hopped out, slammed the door shut as he spun, and sprinted to the front door, practically diving into the cover of the patio. Drenched, he regarded the sky once more before opening the door and going inside.

"Hey, gorgeous," Pat said over the sound of squeaking dress shoes and the door closing behind him. He could hear Francesca moving about in the kitchen and the TV babbling in the living room. There was no answer, so he hung his keys on the rack and tried to get her attention. "How was your day?" Still nothing. He left the foyer, following the short hall that led into the kitchen. There, he found Francesca hovering over the sink—still in her stilettos—peeling potatoes.

"Babe?" he said tenderly.

"We got a problem," she said, swinging around, her voice all business.

"How do you do it?" Pat chortled.

"Do what?"

"Slave the weather to your mood. How do you do it?"

"Pat, I'm serious. We have a problem. A serious one."

"Okay—how serious?"

"Like stab-you-with-this-knife serious," she said, waving a cleaver in the air.

"Damn, you're hostile. How can something so beautiful be so hostile?"

"You asked."

Even roses had thorns.

"I did." He nodded. "Well, honey, you're in luck because I'm excellent at tackling serious problems and making those problems a whole lot less serious. So, what do you got?"

"Pat!" Francesca said through clenched teeth. She was not in the mood for her husband's problem-minimizing optimism. Instead, she needed his problem-solving abilities.

"Relax. I'm just joking, baby."

"I'm not laughing."

"That bad, huh?"

Francesca nodded.

"Okay, what's up?"

She pointed in the direction of the living room. "Go look at your son."

"Which one? We have two."

"Terry."

"Why? What's wrong with him?"

"Go look at him."

"You can't just *tell* me what the problem is?"

"Pat, go look at your son."

"What should I be looking for?"

"Pat. Your son. Go look at him!"

Pat bit back his pride and put his briefcase on the table along with his blazer. "Alright, alright. Where's he at?"

"I already said that he's in the living room."

The nearest Pat could tell, Francesca was already operating in fifth gear regarding being agitated. To that end, Pat was going to need a little backup. So he stopped at the refrigerator for a post-work beverage. "Want a beer, babe?"

Francesca's scrutiny was hot and burned a hole into the back of his neck. He supposed that he wasn't moving fast enough for her to be pleased. But even if he had magically teleported into the living room, she wouldn't have been any less angry. So Pat didn't allow himself to feel pressured; the best way to deal with crisis was to do so calmly. Pat looked over his shoulder and met the icy-blue stare of the woman he loved as he took a sip of his beer and left the kitchen.

"Hey, buddy. Mom told me to have a look at you. What's going on?"

Terry sat in the recliner on the far side of the sectional, focused on a sheet of paper that he repeatedly whipped a pencil across in even strokes. "Hi, Dad."

Pat walked up behind him and for a moment watched Yuri do somersaults in front of the TV. He considered telling Yuri to give it a rest but opted to give him the opportunity to come to that conclusion of his own volition—children needed to learn to make their own decisions—even four-year-olds. Pat returned his attention to Terry. "You watching that bonsai show again?"

"Yes, sir."

"How do you do it?"

"Do what?"

"How do you watch this channel? I mean, what nine-year-old really has the attention span to watch gardening?"

"It's not gardening, Dad—it's bonsai. And it's soothing."

"Oh, is it now?" Pat's head jerked in Yuri's direction when his swan dive from the coffee table to the couch drew Pat's attention.

Yuri spun and sat briskly onto the cushion, panting and smiling. Pat hoped Yuri had come to the realization that monkey business should cease now that Pat had walked in, but he doubted it. He was sure that Yuri was just resting in between spasms. Pat resigned himself to the fact that he would have to speak to Yuri sternly if his behavior continued.

In the meantime, Pat returned his attention to Terry and his art. "Soothing, huh? Didn't know that word was in your vocabulary. What other words you got in your repertoire that I don't know about? *Repertoire*, got that word?"

"No, sir."

"Well, make sure you do because that word will surely win you your next spelling bee, stud." Pat patted Terry's shoulder.

Terry didn't look up.

Pat continued, "That's great stuff you're drawing there, son." Pat leaned over the back of the couch for a better look. "What is it?"

"Mechatron Supremus."

"You don't say? What's he do for a living?"

70

"He's the defender of the multiverse and champion of all battle bot warrior-scions," Terry replied matter-of-factly.

"He must work some serious hours to make all that happen. Is he married? What's his wife think about his work schedule?"

"He's not married."

"No kidding. I'd be able to defend the universe too if your mother didn't expect me to be home by dinner."

"It's the multiverse, Dad."

"Sure—you know," Pat said, cocking his head thoughtfully as he scrutinized his son's artwork, "I don't claim to know much about art nor defenders of the mechnoverses and stuff—"

Terry cut in abruptly, "Dad, it's the multiverse."

"That too," Pat insisted, not missing a beat. "But I think you might be missing some necessary shading over in this section." Pat tapped the page with his finger. "What do you think? Where's the light originating from?"

Terry stopped and considered his father's question. Then, for a moment, he studied his sketch hard before replying, "Over here."

"Well, do you see that? Dad just might know what he's talking about after all, huh?"

"Yes, sir."

Pat swelled with pride. Terry was every bit as brilliant as he was artistic and capable of abstract thinking years ahead of what was expected of a nine-year-old. And although Terry's penchant for art did not require it, Pat sought to encourage him further and to teach him to scrutinize his own work.

Yuri was the athlete at four years of age that Terry wasn't. Yuri bounced and trounced all over the place and destroyed everything in the house. Pat and Francesca were resigned to putting anything valuable at a height that Yuri couldn't reach or to putting such things into storage until Yuri had reached a less destructive age. Pat wasn't sure there was such an age for him. Yuri was all instinct and impulse. He was a whirling ball of entropy that tended to wreak havoc all over the house. He was great to play with outside—the boy had limitless endurance—but damn it, he was annoying when the Ciccone's were trying to keep the house clean.

Terry was their artist; Yuri was their athlete.

Yuri was also in trouble now.

He leaped from the armrest onto the end table, readying an assault on Francesca's cabinet. "Yuri—son!" Pat asserted. "You want to stop acting like a savage and sit down quietly for Daddy? You're acting like a monkey with a hyperactivity disorder, climbing all over Mommy's furniture like that. She'll kill us all if she finds out."

Yuri paid Pat no attention—they weren't even on the same planet. Right this second, Yuri had a fight to win. He coiled like a spring, preparing to leap across the danger-filled chasm that separated Mommy's couch-fortress and the cabinet-mountain that he desperately needed to climb.

"Hey, monkey-boy!"

Yuri returned to earth and looked at his father.

Pat continued, "You want to give it a rest? We don't jump on furniture. I was giving you the opportunity to realize that yourself."

Yuri didn't hear the last part; all he heard was the first part: monkey-boy. "Don't call me that, Daddy!"

"Call you what, kiddo? I call you a lot of things."

"A monkey!"

"Why? Did I hurt your feelings, princess?"

Yuri's nose crinkled. "Don't call me that, Daddy!"

"I didn't call you a monkey this time."

"Princess, Daddy! Don't call me that!"

Pat neared Yuri and lifted him clear of the table and tossed him back onto the couch. Yuri laughed and began to rise. Pat's hand shot up. "Sit your behind down on the couch and calm down. I'm not going to say it nicely again, monkey-boy."

"Daddy, don't call me that!"

"Toughen up, kid. It's a harsh world out there," Pat said, changing the TV to something more kid friendly. "How about you watch this?"

"Okay," Yuri squeaked as he flopped back onto the cushion and lounged with his feet in the air.

"So, um "—Pat returned his attention to Terry—"your mom told me to come have a look at you. You wouldn't happen to know what she's talking about, would you?"

Terry was still scraping his pencil across the paper. "I don't know."

"Terenzio Gianni Ciccone!" Francesca's voice thundered from the kitchen. Terry's head popped to attention—when his mother said his whole name, the world was on the brink of destruction. Francesca continued, "You know damn well what Daddy's talking about!"

Pat gave Francesca a disapproving look. "Baby, can you give us a moment please?"

"Pat, he—"

Pat pumped the palms of his hands at her slowly and repeatedly. "I got this."

"But—"

"Babe, I got this."

Francesca growled, recalcitrant.

Pat returned his attention to Terry again. "Alright, son, I'd really appreciate it if you told me what Mom's all wound up about before we all end up on punishment."

Terry's drawing hand came to a halt. He inhaled deeply and then exhaled with a sigh. He looked up at Pat, revealing a swollen and bruised eye and a cut lip to match.

"That's a nice shiner you got there. I bet I don't want to look at the other guy." Pat nodded approvingly. "I had a couple of those in my day. Does it hurt?"

"Not really." Terry resumed his artwork.

"Tough guy—I gotcha, I gotcha. So, uh, how'd you get it?"

Terry shrugged.

"You don't want to tell me? Fair enough." Pat shrugged too. "Finish your picture. We can always talk later."

Suddenly, Yuri launched towards Terry, but Pat caught Yuri in mid-flight with both hands. Yuri squirmed and bucked.

"Someone's about to be out back with the dogs in the monsoon if they don't start listening." Pat placed him down again. "Now, sit down. Do I make myself clear?" Pat's face was stern.

Yuri batted his icy blues. "Yes, Daddy."

*　　　*　　　*

Francesca, temper still burning white hot, threw dinner into the oven and slammed the door. She realized that this wasn't Pat's fault—or Terry's for that matter—but she was afraid that Pat would dismiss it as part of growing up. This wasn't a part of growing up; no child deserved to grow up in a school that refused to provide fairness and justice because the child wasn't of similar race. Worst of all, she knew what she wanted from Pat but also knew that he was going to oppose *it*. She needed to find a way to say *it*...diplomatically, as Pat would say. Fat chance of that. She'd slam something else to vent her frustration instead.

"Slamming the oven isn't going to change things, hun," said Pat sardonically as he reentered the kitchen. "Why don't you sit down for a moment?"

"I can't."

"Why not?"

"How are people going to eat if I sit down, Pat?"

Pat managed to get a hand on her arm and stop her. "You know I'm perfectly capable of cooking. Why don't you let me take over?"

"No," she said, taking her arm back and resuming. "Cooking and grilling are not the same things. You're not feeding my babies burnt food."

Pat shrugged and then aimed himself for the nearest chair and let gravity do its job. He plopped his chin to his hand and watched his wife shuffle from one area of the counter to another without pause. "Babe," he said, "of all the traits you could have passed to Yuri, why'd it have to be your hyperactivity?"

"Don't test my twelve steps today," she growled. "I'm not in the mood. I'm not hyperactive and never have been."

Pat raised a brow. "Not according to Marcella."

Francesca grunted. "You believe everything my mother tells you."

"Not true," Pat hummed. "I didn't believe her when she told me that you were going to be an incredibly angry wife who would crush the souls of non-believers everywhere." He flashed a grin.

Her eyes cursed him over her shoulder before she whipped around with a knife in her hand, pointing it at him. "That's your last one tonight."

74

"C'mon, Fran." Pat threw his hands in the air. "This situation isn't bad enough that we can't share a laugh."

"I'm not in the mood to laugh."

"Okay—fine." Pat's grin crumpled. "We don't have to do the *loving-couple* thing today. Just tell me what happened, because Terry doesn't seem to want to talk about it."

At the very least, she could have given him a hug and welcomed him home before dumping the "we got a serious problem" into his lap—she realized that. It was moot now, though. She'd make it up to him later. Right now, she needed to keep her focus on Terry.

"That's what's really bothering me," she started. "He's so bottled up. It takes forever for me to get anything out of him. And it's been getting worse lately. I feel like I'm doing something wrong."

"You're not doing anything wrong. You show that boy more love than he probably needs. That's just the way he is. For the same reason, we can't get Yuri to stop climbing the walls. It's in Terry's makeup. We just have to keep hammering it home that communication is crucial."

"I know. I just...I just...I don't even know how to feel."

"Do you plan on telling me what happened?"

"Thanks a helluva lot, Mr. Sensitivity!" On second thought, she wasn't going to make it up to him later. "No, that's fine. I didn't need you to care and listen to how I'm feeling!"

"Whoa, pump your brakes, turbo. I never said I didn't care how you felt, but I thought we were talking about Terry."

Francesca sneered.

He continued, "You going to tell me what happened?"

"He got in a fight."

Pat blinked. "That much I've gathered."

"You asked—"

Pat raised a calming hand in the air. "Let me be more specific with my question: What happened? Who was involved? Where did it occur?"

Francesca planted her hands on her hips. "Supposedly, Terry was in the courtyard after school and was approached by some Japanese kids, and they attacked him."

"Did he fight back?"

"The principal didn't say." Francesca pointed into the living room. "He sure as hell doesn't look like it, though. And you know how passive Terry is, Pat. He doesn't have much of a killer instinct."

"What did the school say they were going to do about it?"

"They didn't say they were going to do anything. That's what's got me all pissed off. Terry's suffering, and nobody wants to do anything to help him."

"We'll go to the school tomorrow and interrogate the principal about his plans regarding the fight."

"That's not going to solve anything."

Pat rubbed his forehead with the back of his hand. "How you figure?"

"Because they don't care. It's not going to get any better like that."

"Honey, be positive about this. Kids get into fights all the time. It's part of growing up." He rolled his eyes. "I can't count how many I got into it with. We just need to make sure that the school is holding all kids equally accountable."

"Well, they're not. In their minds, he's just some stupid *American* kid."

Pat's expression became paternal. "Francesca, positivity, please. Do that for me?"

All right, she had reached her wits' end with diplomacy. There was no diplomatic way of saying it. She'd spent this entire time trying to point out that there was no high road out of this situation. So she decided to come right out and ask *it*. "Why don't you teach Terry to fight?"

Pat's face slacked until gravity turned his mouth into a frown and made furrows of his brow. He returned his face to his hand and stared at her suspiciously.

"Patrizio?"

Then he said, "Not going to happen," finally.

"Why not?"

"You already know the answer to that question."

"No, I don't."

Pat's voice came down an octave. "We've talked about this before. Neither of my sons is going to learn how to fight. I will not

76

encourage them to feed their egos with violence. Nor will I give them an avenue to be exploited by some unscrupulous bastard who sees them as a means to an end that only unfolds to their disadvantage." He repositioned himself in the chair and sat back defiantly. "Not going to happen."

Francesca approached and scooped his face up with both hands. "My love, I didn't say turn him into a boxer. I said teach him how to fight so he can defend himself."

Pat's mind was instantly drawn back to the past:

His father Dominic and his Uncle Isaac are tired of Pat being jumped by local street thugs. They teach him the sweet science and encourage him to show no fear, fight back, prove to the street that he can't be pushed around. Pat fights back for the first time and loses. But he gains self-respect. He fights back again and again and loses. One day, he fights back, and he wins. The rush is incredible. He keeps fighting back, and he keeps winning. There's a bloodlust that draws him into more fights. He is arrested one night. Dominic and Isaac bail him out. Pat is sternly berated by both men for being caught. They take him to a boxing gym called Cousin Geno's Slaughter House. Pat trains and fights with amazing talent. The men praise him for it. The rush is incredible. Pat fights and fights and fights. He fights in the gym, in the ring, in the street. He fights. He draws blood. They praise him. They don't praise his school work. They don't guide him in his relationship with the girl he's dating. They don't guide him in his future. They guide his bloodlust.

"Defending myself was how I got started," he replied, pulling his face away. "My answer is still no."

"But you can teach Terry control—control you never learned."

"Already am. I'm teaching him control by teaching him how to think his way out of situations—not by fighting. There is no such thing as restraint in a fight. To fight, you have to be willing to deal with escalation; you have to be willing to take somebody else's head off before they take yours. I'm going to teach my sons to be men, not animals."

"This isn't going to get better; it's only going to get worse. Pretty soon these kids will start using knives and guns, and if no one is stopping them now when they're pushing and shoving, no one is going to stop them when they bring real weapons. I want our sons to know how to defend themselves." She offered Pat her hands. "Can we at least teach Terry to defend himself so that we don't have to bury him early?"

"My answer is still no."

"What good are you?" She threw her hands up and let out a frustrated sigh. "You know what, Pat?" Her hands found her hips.

"What, Francesca?"

"All you've given me is more problems. I don't need more problems; I need solutions."

Pat rolled his eyes. He said *that* to her all the time. Now she was using it against him. Clever girl. It wasn't changing anything, though. "I'm not going to teach him. That's my final answer."

"If you won't teach him, would you agree to self-defense classes? Like karate or judo or something? I mean, we're in Japan. Somebody here has got to be a kung fu master."

Karate wasn't out of the question. It wasn't gladiatorial like boxing was, but it still could be used for fighting. He wasn't sure if he was opposed to it or not. "I don't know."

"Pat, something has to be done."

"I don't know, Francesca."

"Pat, please. For me."

Anxiety was starting to collect in his gut, and he clenched his teeth, trying to relieve the feeling. *Maybe martial arts is an option*, he thought to himself, but the doubt was still winning. "I'll look into it."

*   *   *

"This is the place," Pat said as he eased the brake in and brought the van to a halt just past a fire hydrant and a pile of garbage.

"Charming." Francesca swiveled her head, examining the congested street. The buildings seemed to have been built right on top of each other without regard practicality or appearance. The street was in disrepair and flooded with sewage from the recent monsoon. "Looks like the street you grew up on."

"True—but based on recommendations from one of the locals at the embassy, this place has a great reputation."

She gave Pat a sidelong glance. "For what? Racketeering?"

"Looks like it, huh?"

"Who exactly is this local?"

"One of the national officiates. He used to be a local representative here in Tokyo."

"Omigod! Is that a chicken?" Francesca screamed, startling everyone—Pat jerked in her direction, Terry bucked, and Yuri squealed. She covered her mouth with her hand and pointed out of the window with the other at an elderly Tokyo native carrying a thrashing bird and butcher knife.

"Goddamn, Francesca, you almost gave me an aneurysm," Pat replied.

"You scared me, Mommy," Yuri said, giggling.

"Omigod, Pat"—Francesca gripped Pat's arm, mortified—"she's going to kill it on the street!"

"You have to kill a chicken to eat, baby."

"Okay, asshole, thank you! I'm not stupid! I just have never seen anything like that. Who the hell kills chickens on the street?"

"First time for every—"

Francesca squeaked when the blade came down and separated the bird's head from its body, cutting Pat off.

"Mommy, look!" Yuri yelled with his face pressed against the passenger-side window, mesmerized by the decapitating spectacle.

"Yuri, stop yelling." Terry grabbed his younger brother by the back of his shirt and peeled him away from the glass. "Sit down."

"Let me go!" Yuri yelled as he struggled beneath Terry's grip. He lost his balance and fell back into his car seat when Terry overpowered him. Frustrated, Yuri bucked and kicked the back of the seat.

Pat whipped around. "Hey—hey!" he barked. "What the hell is wrong with you two?"

"Dad, Yuri was standing up in his car seat," Terry said. "I was—"

Pat cut him off. "Who calls shots in this family?"

"But, Dad—"

"But, Dad nothing. Who calls shots in this family?"

"You do."

"That's right, *I do*." Pat indicated himself with his thumb and then pointed towards Francesca. "If I need help, I have Mommy."

"Baby," Francesca chimed in, watching the woman carry the chicken back to her shop and seemingly oblivious to the interaction between Pat and the boys, "that was so disgusting." She searched for her husband's leg with her hand and patted it several times when she found it, never taking her eyes off of the chicken. "Why would she do that on the street?"

Pat ignored her. "Yuri," he said, glaring at his son, "you want to explain why you're out of your seat?"

Yuri's eyebrows were as high on his forehead as he could lift them as he pointed out of the window. "I wanted to see the chicken too, Daddy."

"How about you do what I tell you to do?"

"Okay," Yuri replied plaintively.

"When are you allowed to get out of your seat?"

"When Mommy tells me to."

Pat squinted his eyes. How had he just been left out of that equation? "Or when Daddy tells you, right?"

"Yes."

That made Pat feel a little better. It was the small things in life sometimes that mattered most—like manners, for example. "Yes, sir?" Pat asserted. If nothing, his sons were going to be polite.

"Yes, sir," Yuri repeated obediently with a puffy face belying his hurt feelings.

Pat signaled each son with a nod. "Both of you better get it together."

"Dad, I—" Terry began, mounting a defense, but Pat wasn't having it.

He snapped his fingers at Terry. "Shut it," Pat commanded and then spun back around. Terry's face crumpled, and he turned to the window, crossing his arms.

"Everything okay?" Francesca asked, losing interest in the dead chicken finally.

"Oh, nice of you to show up," Pat said.

80

Francesca cocked her head and smiled sourly. "Where's this place at?"

Pat pointed to one o'clock. "Right there."

"What's this place's M-O?"

"Not sure. This is my first time here too."

Francesca's face became frosty. Pat didn't pay any attention as he opened the center console and grabbed his wallet. He opened the door and climbed out. "Let's go, team."

Francesca exited the vehicle and opened the passenger door to let Yuri out. She commented that Terry shouldn't take his time. Then she shut the door and moved to the front of the vehicle, where Pat was waiting.

"What's gotten into that boy today?" Pat was referring to Terry. "I need you and *your* attitude to get out of the car, Terenzio. We don't have all day."

"The question that should be asked," Francesca said, straightening Pat's collar, "is what has gotten into you?"

Pat shook his head. "Nothing. Why?"

She looked into his face, unconvinced. "You seem a little edgier than usual."

"Nope—I'm good, hun." Pat watched Terry's feet finally hit the ground, and he was turning to shut the door. "For crying out loud, Terry, c'mon." Terry slammed the door and hurried to his parents. Pat was none too happy. "Do we slam doors?" Pat asked. It wasn't a question.

"Pat?"

He acknowledged her.

"Give it a rest. He didn't mean it."

Pat nodded. "Let's go."

Francesca gripped Terry's shoulder. "Walk, honey," she said tenderly. "Mind your father and watch your manners, okay?"

"Yes, ma'am," Terry said before starting off after Pat.

Francesca held Yuri's hand as they approached. She mimicked Pat's scrutiny of the building and the area that it occupied, looking for the things that were drawing his interest. The edifice that Pat claimed was their destination had no sign nor street address, and it looked weary and run-down.

The toe of Yuri's shoe became lodged in a crack of the unkept sidewalk, and *splat*, he was on his chest, face down and crying. Francesca cursed and demanded that Pat pick him up.

"C'mere, fireplug," Pat grunted, scooping Yuri off the ground and wiping the dirt from the raspberry spot that had appeared on his cheek. "It's all good, son," Pat said, trying to settle Yuri with a hug. "Falls happen. You're okay." Pat heaved Yuri onto his shoulder and pulled the door open, gesturing for his wife and Terry to go first. Francesca stopped to wipe tears from Yuri's face, but Pat urged her to leave Yuri be and go inside.

Just then, a middle-aged Japanese man dressed in an exquisite suit and mirrored shades and flanked on both sides by two young, brash-looking Japanese males who were equally dressed to kill but in a more urban fashion that showed off their heavily tattooed arms, forced his way out of the door, nearly knocking Francesca and Terry over. Francesca was outraged and let the men know it animatedly. The two younger men moved threateningly in between Francesca and the older Japanese man. She didn't appear the least bit intimidated as she continued to curse them loudly—her brothers were twice the size of these punks.

Pat put Yuri down and rushed in between the men and his wife. Then Pat recognized the man. "Mr. Oharu?"

"Patrizio! How unexpected!" Oharu said.

"Well, I came to check out the karate school you recommended."

"I see you have taken my advice, then. Splendid!" Oharu then barked at the younger men in Japanese, and their postures slackened. "I think you will find something special here. I assume this beauty is your wife?"

"Yes, sir, it—I mean, she is."

"It is a grand pleasure to meet your acquaintance, Mrs. Ciccone," Oharu said, bowing his head slightly.

"The pleasure is all mine," she replied hostilely.

There was loud *"hai!"* from the door, and all heads snapped in the direction. Another middle-aged Japanese man, perhaps in his late forties with a full head of hair, dressed in modest robes and bare feet, stood in the doorway. He had a ruddy, harsh face with a jagged scar running the length of the right side, his neck sloped to his shoulder, and he was broad across the chest. The man stood there in the doorway with his hands clasped behind his back. He barked something else.

The younger men eyed him knowingly. One spoke as if defending his position. The man in doorway cut him off with a grave tone. Then he looked towards the exquisitely dressed older man and barked something else. The exquisitely dressed man spoke in a tone that had little regard. The man in the door barked some more, and the younger men swaggered away.

"Well, this is indeed awkward. I really must go. Patrizio—warm regards." Oharu said, scurrying off behind the younger men.

Pat and Francesca watched them leave and then turned to the man in the doorway.

"Konichiwa," the man said with a nod, his eyes searching the Ciccones suspiciously.

"Konichiwa," Pat replied, alternatingly watching Oharu depart and looking at the man in the doorway.

The man asked Pat a question; his voice was soft but exacting. Pat's expression flattened, and he looked back at Francesca, who simply shrugged. Pat returned his attention to the man and smiled weakly. The man's brow rose as if to say he were unimpressed.

Then Pat remembered that Terry spoke Japanese. "Terry, what did this gentleman just say?"

Terry peeked out from behind his mother. "He asked if we were lost, Dad."

Pat shook his head. "No—tell him no. We're not lost; we're looking for a school."

Terry translated his father's words into Japanese for the man. The man looked intrigued. He spoke to Terry, who responded to the man's words rather quickly.

"He says *this* is a school and wants to know if you're looking for it," Terry relayed.

"Tell him that I was referred to a school here."

"Dad, I don't know how to say *referred*."

"For Christ's sake, just tell him that someone told us to come here," Pat said impatiently.

Terry did, and then he said, "He wants to know who told you to come here."

"Tell him the man that just left, Mr. Oharu from the embassy, recommended us."

"Dad, I don't know how to say *embassy* either."

"Oh, for crying out loud—"

"Try not to be too hard on the boy, sir," the man recommended in crisp English with a hint of a British drawl. "His Japanese is quite impressive for an American."

The whole family was shocked—except Yuri; he was too busy stomping on ants.

"You were able to speak English this whole time?" Pat said, feeling a little misled.

"Quite aptly, yes."

"Why didn't you just speak in English in the first place?"

"Americans don't frequent this area. You'll have to excuse my apprehension."

What could Pat say? He glanced over his shoulder at Francesca. She was at a loss too.

"So, you are acquainted with Oharu Shinji?" the man asked.

"Yeah—he's a colleague." Pat rub the back of his neck. "I take it you know him as well?"

"He is a...colleague as well." The man shook his head. "Where are my manners? My name is Omiyoshu Kintake, and this is my school." He stepped through the door and gestured through its opening. "Please, come in."

Pat glanced at Francesca. She made the words, "Well, go on," with her mouth. Pat turned and made for the door, and the rest of the family followed. The family filed into a ten-by-ten-foot waiting-area sporting a single rusting chair, a faded portrait, and a damaged wooden floor. There was a door opposite the entrance, and through it, the Ciccones could see a group of people moving about to a cadence.

Pat passed through the door that opened up into the much larger, partially carpeted, windowless room, where a class consisting of twenty students, ranging in age from child to teenager, conducted drills in unison. At the commands of two more young adult males who walked the rows that the students formed, the students threw a kick

84

followed by a punch, then a dip, a spin-kick, followed immediately by a sweep. Then the two instructors commanded the students to reset so the drill could begin again. The two young men—one tall, lanky, and awkward, the other one lean and chiseled—corrected the hand and the foot positions of the students and provided momentary one-on-one instruction where needed before moving on to the next student in need. Both had noticed the Ciccone family but continued instructing despite them.

The Ciccones watched the class sweat and pant through each drill, their movements crisp and controlled. The youths' precision and focus were impressive. Besides heavy breathing, they made no sound and were chastised by the two instructors when their feet made a sound louder than a light *swish.* For the Ciccones, once the initial mystique faded, they began to notice the furnishings in the chamber beyond the students hard at work.

The walls were lined with weapon racks stacked full of swords, training blades, spears, staves, different chain weapons, and knives. Hanging above them, and not in any sort of discernable pattern, were scrolls inscribed with tons of kanji or depicting scenes of traditional Japanese warriors in action.

"I am sorry," Kintake said, coming in between Pat and Francesca, interrupting their musing. "You have me at a bit of a disadvantage. I do not believe that I got your names."

Pat and Francesca both looked inward towards Kintake, but no one said a thing. Pat let out a nudging cough to motivate his wife—after all, it was her idea come. Francesca sprang to life. "Oh God, how rude of us. We're so sorry." She pressed her hand into her chest. "I'm Francesca Ciccone. This is my husband, Patrizio," she said, gesturing in his direction, "and our two sons, Terenzio and Yuri."

"It is a pleasure to make your acquaintances," Kintake said, bowing his head at each of them, and then he bent over and placed a tender hand on Yuri's head. "Hello, little one. You honor me with your presence."

Yuri curled around his mother's leg and managed a shy smile.

"Yuri," Pat said, flabbergasted, "when did you become shy?"

Francesca nodded, agreeing with Pat's question.

"Delightful, that one."

"Yeah, you wouldn't say that if you saw him at home," said Pat wryly.

"Very well," Kintake chuckled. "Now, how may I be of service, Mr. and Mrs. Ciccone? You mentioned that Mr. Oharu recommended my school."

"Well—yeah—at least, that's what my husband said." She indicated Pat, and he nodded in response.

"My husband and I are looking to put our son, Terry, in a self-defense class. He's been getting into fights at school, and we just want him to be able to defend himself."

"I see," Kintake replied.

Francesca continued, "I also want Terry to learn discipline."

"Very good."

"Do you think you can help us, Mr. um...?"

"Omiyoshu. Omiyoshu Kintake."

Francesca made several attempts at Kintake's name, butchering it every time. He repeated it several times to help, but she still couldn't make the name properly. Terry, embarrassed by his mother's lack of culture, even chimed in a few times to help. Francesca struggled in spite of him. Kintake laughed and eventually resorted to comically breaking his surname into syllables. Finally, she got it.

"I'm so sorry, Mr. Omiyoshu." Francesca's faced flushed visibly. "How embarrassing." It wasn't anything personal. She was just terrible with names, especially Japanese ones.

"It is quite alright, Mrs. Ciccone. Now," he said, approaching the line where the hard floor ended and where the carpet began, "this is, as you have already noticed, the main training area. Here, the school is instructed as a group. In the rear of the room"—he pointed beyond the students, toward the back wall—"you can see some weapons that we teach. Those wooden boxes that you see stacked sporadically along the walls are obstacles that we use to train and hone our agility."

"You don't use punching bags?" Francesca asked, looking at him.

"No, Mrs. Ciccone, we do not."

She turned to Pat and said, "They don't use punching bags..." Pat just shrugged.

"If I may request that you remove your shoes, I would like you all to follow me, please." Kintake gave them a moment to kick off their footwear and then crossed the training floor toward a door on the opposite wall that led outside, pointing as he went. "Over there are two individual training rooms where smaller groups can be taught. Through here is the garden."

The group emerged into a lush, abstractly-designed nursery with thoughtfully placed rocks and umbrella-shaped trees that leaned at impossible angles. It was a huge departure, to the say the least, from the urban grit and decay that surrounded the school. Suffice it to say that the garden was better maintained than the school itself.

"Wow, Mr. Omiyoshu," Francesca aspirated. "This is beautiful. Baby, this is amazing, huh?"

"Grand," Pat said, unconvinced.

Kintake continued, "I know it is small, but it affords students the opportunity to meditate and reflect on the world around them."

Terry lit up like a Christmas tree. "Sir, who prunes the trees?"

"Why, the students do, Terry. Bonsai is one of the arts we teach."

"Really?" Terry asked excitedly.

"Yes, Terry, really." Kintake pointed at a lonely tree nearest the corner of the garden. "That one is called—"

"*Han Kengai!*" Terry exclaimed before his hands found his mouth when he realized that he'd interrupted and adult.

Kintake raised a brow. "You are familiar with bonsai, Terry?"

"Yes, sir."

Kintake was impressed. Children lacked the patience and the appreciation for the transcendental art of bonsai, the art that commanded nature to redefine its laws to match the will of an artist. But not this child.

Francesca bristled with pride. "Terry watches the bonsai channel all the time."

"At such a young age, too?" Kintake noted in a humbled tone. "Remarkable."

"Mr. Omi…uh…" Francesca struggled to remember Kintake's name yet again.

"Omiyoshu, Mom."

"Mr. Omiyoshu. Thank you, Terry." Her face flushed again. "Mr. Omiyoshu, does your school award belts or—like—break boards and stuff?"

"No, madam." An amused grin stretched across Kintake's face. "In contrast with the more *cosmopolitan* schools that teach the arts internationally, this school and the art that we teach has not been altered by commerce."

Francesca feigned understanding, but Kintake knew otherwise; he could also sense Pat's apprehension. Kintake's expression became rock solid with conviction. He could sense that there was something special about these people—these boys—otherwise, Oharu wouldn't have recommended they come to Kintake's school. Kintake clasped his hands behind his back and whipped around, barking a command through the door in Japanese.

The two instructors looked up immediately. The class ceased their individual movements, shot up as stiff as boards, and bellowed an intimidating *ki-ai* in response to their sensei's beckon. The instructor of average height hastily approached Kintake, bowed, and exchanged remarks, repeatedly nodding as Kintake spoke. After a moment, the instructor bowed deeply to Kintake and returned to the class.

Kintake turned back to Francesca and Pat and spread his arms. "Would your children care to join in this drill?"

"What drill?" Francesca asked as she, Pat, and the boys watched curiously through the doorway as the class spread into a rough circle that began whirling around counterclockwise faster and faster and faster. As their speed increased, so did their laughter. Then one student leaped into the center of the circle and spun slowly while eyeing the other children hungrily as they passed him on the outside of the ring.

"Essentially, it is a game of tag. It really is quite simple: One student is chosen as the demon—he's the one in the middle—and all other participants are lotus flowers. Each lotus flower must remain as close to the demon as possible without being tagged. If the demon should manage to tag a lotus flower, that individual has been captured and must remain still just inside the spinning arc with his feet shoulder-width apart while the game continues."

"Why shoulder-width apart?" Francesca asked.

In a display of youthful athleticism, a lotus flower went on his belly through the legs of a captive, the demon just missing him. The captive sprinted to the outside of the circle to join his fellows.

"As you can see, Mrs. Ciccone, when lotus flowers pass between the legs of one of the demon's captives, the captive is freed. Eventually, we assign more than one demon to increase the difficulty."

Yuri let out a gleeful squeal and pointed at the other children having the time of their lives.

"The game is quite pleasing to watch," Kintake said, his voice becoming less grave, "and most of all, the children find it quite amusing. Plus, it's great for their fitness and nominal for team building."

Yuri spasmed. "Mommy, can I play?" He spasmed more.

"Sure, honey."

Yuri chirped with excitement as he raced through the door and sprinted to the circle to join the larger children.

Kintake looked in Terry's direction. "Terry, would you care to participate?"

Terry shook his head. Pat signaled to him to move inside—*Go.* Terry lowered his eyes and reluctantly headed for the training room. The adults weren't far behind; Francesca and Pat followed Kintake.

As they crossed the training floor again, Francesca spoke up: "Mr. Omiyoshu, I have to ask: Where are you from?"

"I am from a very remote village in the countryside of Iga."

"I'm not sure I know where that's at."

"Iga is in the Mie Province, southwest of here."

"Is that a tourist area?"

"There are parts of Iga, such as Iga-Ueno Castle, which sees a large contingent of tourists annually. My village, however, is not a place that tourists would frequent."

"Why? Is it dangerous?"

"Not particularly, no. However, my ancestors founded the village over five centuries ago, and my people have maintained it since. Jealously so. Why do you ask, Mrs. Ciccone?" Kintake asked.

"Honestly, I was wondering why your English is so great, almost like you've been speaking it all your life."

"I *have* been speaking it all my life, Mrs. Ciccone."

"Where did you learn it?"

"Oh, a little here, a little there. Mostly television, really."

"Really?"

He grinned. "No, Mrs. Ciccone. Not really."

Francesca laughed. "So where did you learn it? In school?"

Kintake looked away and shook his head.

"Oh," Francesca said, her face displaying confusion. "Did I offend you by asking?"

He shook his head. "No, Mrs. Ciccone. I—I'm just not at liberty to disclose that information because"—he lowered his head and his voice—"I am a spy."

Francesca burst into laughter. Kintake was charming for a man his age. Pat wasn't charmed at all, and his face showed it.

"Well, I really must say, I like what you have here," Francesca said with her hands. "It's rather spartan and quaint all at the same time."

"Why, thank you, Mrs. Ciccone." Kintake looked at Pat, who was vigilantly watching Yuri roughhouse with the older children. "What is your opinion, Mr. Ciccone?"

Pat exhaled but never took his eyes off of his youngest son. "You'll have to excuse me if I'm not as easily convinced as my wife—games and gardens won't sell me." Pat glanced at Kintake for a split second before returning his attention to Yuri. "I'll level with you. I used—"

Kintake interrupted with his hand. "I beg your pardon, Mr. Ciccone, but I did not quite understand you. You are going to *level* with me?"

Pat's mouth became a straight line. "That was a colloquial statement—sorry. What I meant was: I'm going to be honest with you."

"Oh. I'd prefer that, Mr. Ciccone. Thank you," Kintake interjected.

"I was a fighter—a boxer specifically. And like every fighter, I was fed lies, and I was sold dreams about championing a legacy. Those lies were for the express purpose of furthering someone else's agenda. I spent years getting my head beat in so someone else could make a buck or achieve some goal."

90

"I understand your apprehension, sir. But perhaps I can alleviate some anxiety." Kintake clasped his hands behind his back again. "You see, at this *Ryu*—or school in English—I teach *taijutsu*, which is the unarmed fighting tradition of the *Shinobi*—the *ninja*. It is a special discipline that has been passed down for generations to only the most exclusive group—only the most serious, focused minds."

Francesca's smile stretched from ear to ear. She was very pleased with the uniqueness.

Pat cracked a half-smile. "Ninja, huh?"

"That is correct, Mr. Ciccone."

"Does that mean my son is going to be running around my house dressed in black and swinging *nunchucks*?"

"I would hope not, Mr. Ciccone," Kintake responded dryly. "You see, taijutsu is divided into two subsystems: *daken-taijutsu* and *ju-taijutsu*—fundamentally, striking and grappling. These two facets, combined with subtlety—"

"Alright—alright, I've heard enough," Pat professed, interrupting Kintake, whose face darkened. "I'm not impressed, not in the least bit," Pat continued. "Fighting is fighting. I'm not okay with my son learning to hurt people. Thank you for your time, Mr. Omiyoshu, but no thanks."

Francesca's eyes poured embarrassment. Her gazed bounced between Pat and Kintake.

"I'll get the boys," Pat said to her as he started walking towards the twirling circle of giggling children.

Francesca called to him, and he stopped to look over his shoulder.

"Why are we leaving?" she asked.

"Because, Francesca, I'm over this."

"Is this—" She stopped, realizing she'd said that loudly and angrily; she lowered her voice. "Is this about you?" she asked in a more fitting tone, just above a whisper. "I thought we were here for Terry."

"Fighting is about ego and violence. There is no control to it despite what anyone will have you think."

"But look at this place. Look at the children. Look at how much fun they're having. That doesn't please you?"

"There's nothing pleasing about violence. When children find it fun, they live by it. They grow with it. Then they abuse others when they're men because violence is the only thing they know; it's the only thing that brings them pleasure. This place is *no* different than any other fighting establishment. These people are just wowing you with karate kicks, gardens, and children's games."

"What if you're wrong?" She pointed over his shoulder at the children. "Look at Terry over there. He's having the time of his life—Yuri is too. Terry is playing with children his age right now. He's not keeping to himself like normal. Can't you see that?"

He could see it, but his son was still going to learn to fight in the process. "If this trip is about finding him playmates, we can put him in soccer or something."

"Pat!" Francesca snapped angrily. She lowered her voice again. "Terry's the one with the black eye, remember?" she said, her head snaking side to side with each syllable. "I'm supposed to watch my son get bullied and beaten? As his father, if you won't teach him to protect himself, then I have to find someone who will."

Pat's face flashed red, sweat suddenly beading on his forehead. Just as he pointed an accusing finger at his wife and opened his mouth to speak, Kintake burst into the disagreement, trying to prevent it from disturbing the class.

"My apologies, Mr. and Mrs. Ciccone," he said, showing them the palms of his hands. "I think we are at a supreme misunderstanding. Perhaps a demonstration of why *taijutsu* was developed would be advantageous? If I may demonstrate." Kintake steepled his fingers and barked something in Japanese, and an instructor—the skinny one this time—again approached with the same ardor that his colleague had displayed earlier. "Mr. Ciccone, you said you are a boxer, no?"

"Was," Pat corrected.

"Very good," Kintake replied with a mild smile. "I assume, like most western boxers, you are adept at throwing punches?"

Pat's expression hardened. "Get to the point, Mr. Omiyoshu. My patience is running low."

Kintake bid the young man to come close and then spoke into his ear. The young man nodded as Kintake spoke and then stood, spun, and approached Pat. The young man bowed when he made eye contact with Pat. Kintake presented the young man with a hand. "Mr. Ciccone, please throw a punch at Ichiro."

Pat instead threw Kintake a perplexed, doubtful look.

Kintake gestured again towards Ichiro's direction. "Please, throw a punch at Ichiro."

Ichiro locked Pat's gaze and bowed again. Pat looked anxiously at his family, Kintake, and then Ichiro. He had mixed feelings. How was challenging him going to change his mind? Admittedly, though, Pat's pride was compelling him to lay the kid out on principal. Pat nearly felt obligated, and that made him angry.

Kintake raised his brow.

Pat rolled his eyes and scoffed, throwing a half-hearted, apathetic jab, which Ichiro dodged with barely a movement of his head. Ichiro glanced back at Kintake.

"I don't have time for this shit or your ridiculous games," Pat said.

Kintake nodded at Ichiro, and Ichiro returned his attention to Pat.

"Come now, Mr. Ciccone," Kintake said with a hint of disappointment, "I am sure you are far more capable than that. I assure you that Ichiro will not be so easily broken that you must hold back."

Pat didn't want to do this, but his wife was watching, and his sons were probably watching too. He couldn't just walk out of here; what would they think? He shook his head, loosening the muscles in his neck and shoulders, and then exhaled audibly as he settled into a fighting stance. He sneered at Francesca before he raised his hands. "I doubt that, but if you want a broken ninja, I'll give you one."

Pat locked Ichiro's eyes once more and clenched his fists. He focused his mind on the location that he planned to land a punch against Ichiro's face. Then he chose a different location, a location on the young man's chest, not wanting to allow his pride to influence him to hurt the young man too badly. When Pat was ready, his breathing shallowed, and with blinding speed and a *snap-hiss*, he struck.

Ichiro's eyes flickered to Pat's shoulder, then elbow, and then his hand. He displaced his head outside of the punch and reset as the punch withdrew.

Pat, visibly irritated, looked at Kintake.

"A combination now, Mr. Ciccone," Kintake said coolly. "Go on."

By now, the children were slowing as they noticed the adults squaring off. Pat could feel their eyes: Francesca's eyes, Terry's eyes, and Yuri's eyes. A bead of sweat rolled down the side of his face, and he readied a combo in his mind. He envisioned Ichiro's stance and saw his strikes leaving his guard for Ichiro's body. He saw Ichiro's movements and saw where his own fists could land. He considered where his arms and body would be when he threw, trying to anticipate from where the counters would come, if at all. Then he loosed his hands, launching strikes in a combo of six: two jabs, a straight, a hook, another straight and hook. Ichiro weaved outside the first two; then he drove the straight away with a hand before jamming the hook by wedging his elbow into the crook of Pat's. At that point, Pat's guard was spread so far apart that the last two punches were sloppy and desperate. Ichiro's crowding had rendered them ineffective.

Ichiro grappled Pat, pinning his arm, at the elbow, between his own body and arm. Ichiro pressed his fingers into a nerve cluster at the base of Pat's neck, suspending him at arm's length. Pat grimaced.

Francesca's mouth dropped open. She had seen her husband fight many times in his youth, but never had she seen anyone intercept his punches so deftly or surgically. It almost seemed unreal.

Kintake grunted, "Hai!" and Ichiro kindly released Pat, who took a few steps backward, and whipped around to face his teacher. Pat cradled his numb arm and did his best to hide the creeping feeling of humiliation. Kintake sharply gestured to Ichiro, who immediately lowered his eyes, faced Pat, and honored him with a deep bow before backing away with a low head.

"As you can see, Mr. Ciccone," Kintake noted, "our students are more than mere *nunchuck-swinging* athletes. Each student is taught that control, respect, and obedience are values held above all others. Early in their training, they learn that just because one has the ability to destroy, doesn't mean one has the right, despite the ability. This, Mr. Ciccone, stands in stark contrast to your assessments of fighters. While most fighters may thrive on violence, we do not. We thrive on enlightenment and self-actualization. I will note, however, a component of self-actualization is understanding the rights with which we are inherently born. One right that is relevant to your son's condition is the right of self-defense and prosperity. I can teach him this."

"I'm sold," Francesca said without hesitation.

Pat shot her a frigid look and then returned his eyes to Kintake. "So that what's this whole thing was about: You were just trying to prove that you were better?"

"No, Mr. Ciccone," Kintake said, shaking his head, "it was simply a means to get your attention. You're a fighter by trade. Therefore, you speak the language of combat. And now the words that were once falling on deaf ears are ringing loudly. I can help your son if you will allow me."

"How much will it cost?" asked Francesca, clapping her hands together beneath a brimming smile.

"Prices are negotiable, madam, but not a concern at this point. Would Yuri attend as well?"

Yuri leaped into the discussion to present his own counsel, "Please, Mommy, can I do it too? Please! I want to go with Terry!"

"You don't think Yuri is too young, Mr. Omiyoshu?"

"Heavens no—not at all, Mrs. Ciccone. Yuri is of perfect age. He is like fresh bamboo in a strong wind. Before the early adolescent years, most drills and exercises are cognitive at the core or based on agility and self-improvement."

"Perfect!" she exclaimed. She was so excited one would think that she was starting the class and not her boys. "What's the schedule? When can they start?"

"They already have, madam."

"Well, can I bring them tomorrow?"

"Yes, bring them at a time that is most convenient for you."

"Great! I'll bring them after school."

"Splendid," he said, bowing his head humbly.

"Well, I guess we should get going. *Let's go, honey,*" she said satirically, punching Pat in the shoulder. It was still numb, so he just looked at her sourly before turning to make his way toward the front door. Francesca waved to the boys and told them to follow their dad.

The Ciccones were filing toward the door when Kintake stopped them one last time. "Mr. and Mrs. Ciccone, would it be inconvenient if I gave Terry his first lesson—it will only take a moment."

Francesca looked at Pat, who shrugged his shoulder in defeat, and then nodded.

Kintake drew a wicker basket from a nearby shelf, squatted to eye level with Terry, and bid him to approach and remove the cover. Terry did as he was asked and looked in to find the contents to be an assortment of colored stones. Then Kintake returned the cover to the basket. Terry lifted his eyes and met Kintake's gaze.

"What is it that you observed within, Terry?" Kintake asked.

"Um, beads," Terry replied, rubbing his forehead with the back of his hand.

"Very good," Kintake affirmed, inclining his head. "What kind of beads?"

"Colored beads."

Kintake nodded, encouraging Terry to continue with his assessment. "Mm-hmm."

"Red ones, blue ones, yellow ones, and purple ones."

"How many red beads were there?"

"I don't know." Terry's eyes darted up to the right corner of their sockets as if he were searching through a catalog for an answer. "Seven or eight maybe."

"Maybe?"

"Yes, sir."

"You may call me Sensei, Terry."

"Yes, Sensei."

"Let's have a look." Kintake removed the cover again and picked out all the red stones, holding them up in his hand. "You see, Terry, there are eleven red beads, are there not?"

Terry simply nodded in agreement. "Yes, Sensei."

Kintake shook his head. "Terry, count them."

Terry did. There were nine, not eleven. "Nine, Sensei," he admitted.

Kintake poured them back into the basket. "You must always observe precisely and *never* accept hearsay. You should always confirm information with your own senses. Do you understand?"

"Yes, Sensei."

"Very good," Kintake said genially, returning the basket to the shelf. "One last question: Will you describe the basket for me?"

96

"It's made of wood."

"What type of wood?"

Terry's eyes and mouth took on u-shapes. "I don't know."

"How was the wood bound?"

"I don't know."

"Well, what did you think of the engravings on the side? Did you like them?"

"I didn't see any." Terry wasn't going to fall for the same thing twice.

"Very good," Kintake applauded, climbing to his feet. "He is a remarkable boy. You should be proud."

Francesca bristled again. "Oh, we are."

"Can I be of any further service, Mr. and Mrs. Ciccone?"

"Nope," Pat said sharply, resuming his exit. "Let's go."

"Thank you, Mr. Omiyoshu," said Francesca, guiding her boys to the door.

Kintake raised a welcoming hand.

Once they were through the door, Francesca stopped to straighten Yuri's disheveled clothes. "What was that about?" Francesca asked.

"How should I know?" Pat said, clearly still irritated.

Then they heard Kintake's voice from the door one last time: "Terry."

Terry turned to look when he heard his name.

Kintake continued, "You have learned a valuable lesson today: Never forsake the forest for the trees." Then he disappeared back inside the door.

The Ciccones all looked at each other. Pat shook his head and started for the car. Francesca picked Yuri up and followed.

"I liked him!" she said.

Pat wasn't amused. "I just want silence the entire drive home."

Chapter Six: What Goes Around Comes Around

A Shinobi's greatest weapon is silence. Let not the anonymity nor the sanctity of the ways be violated.
The Third Mandate, translated from Ninpo.

Houston, Texas. Today.

Finally, Yuri thought to himself, *a job without ethics or morals*. The last handful of jobs had included too many ethical variables that had stifled Terry's objectivity during operations and made him wishy-washy when the time to kill came. Yuri followed the code as strictly as the next person, but Terry's need for higher understanding was cumbersome, and it made Terry difficult to work with at times. Make no mistake that Yuri loved his brother, but Terry's strict adherence to his personal interpretations of Ninpo made jobs more taxing than Yuri liked. This job, however, was hardly going to prove as taxing since there wasn't going to be any collateral to make Terry squishy.

The entire executive board from a multi-billion-dollar energy conglomerate called Energy Solutions International had been arrested and indicted for accounting fraud, money laundering, and criminal business and were due to be tried in the coming weeks. If convicted, each person could look forward to a hefty prison sentence as well as all their assets being seized. As Terry and Yuri saw it, the prosecution was not batting a thousand in its attempt to pitch a conviction. The attorneys needed someone close to the executive board that would turn state's evidence and testify against the tight-lipped defendants; that person was the financial planner and chief of accounting, Carlos Irizarry.

Carlos was an avid gambler who'd accrued sizeable debts. That made him easy prey to the machinations of the ESI executives, who'd felt it necessary to involve him in the scandal if they were going to keep him from raising the alarm at the tremendous annual losses the company had been sustaining. He'd been coaxed into purchasing a large portion of shares of ESI at their true value and selling them at their inflated, fraudulent price, thus making a fortune in the process.

In comparison to the executives, Carlos was not as deeply involved in the scandal as the members of the board, and the prosecution, therefore, offered him leniency if he testified against his colleagues and relinquished the profit that he had hustled.

To protect their interests, realizing that they would surely be convicted if Carlos released ESI's fiscal reports and testified, the executives pooled their resources and hired Terry and Yuri to assassinate Carlos and make the fiscal reports vanish. As payment, Terry and Yuri were offered one hundred and fifty thousand dollars up front and Carlos's share-sale profit as a completion bonus provided they could extract it from his bank account.

Carlos was a creature of habit, Terry and Yuri noticed; the DA had made him more so. The Harris County District Attorney's Office kept a tight leash on Carlos, and that made surveillance easy for them. He went to work at the same time every day, stopped at the same coffee shop every morning, left work at the same time, walked the same path from the front door of the ESI satellite to the parking garage, and stopped for happy hour twice a week at the same restaurant.

After a week of surveillance, the plan was to ambush Carlos in a secluded location, force from him the information on the fiscal reports and the location of his profits, and ensure that he was unable to testify on schedule. A simple-to-execute plan, they just had to ensure that the linchpin of their plan was in place: Antwon Coates.

*   *   *

The bass peaked on Antwon's computer's subwoofer as he ditty-bopped from the bedroom to the bathroom to the beat of the song and strode up to the mirror, grabbing the tube of toothpaste from the sink and holding it to his mouth like a microphone, mouthing the lyrics. Antwon enjoyed escaping the constant grind—a grind of living from paycheck to paycheck, doing odd jobs for additional income, and enduring the persistent nagging of his daughter's mother. In the mirror, he was a rap superstar clad head to toe in designer clothing, performing on stage in front of a mass of screaming fans. To add to his mystique, he obscured his face beneath a fitted baseball cap, and he dazzled onlookers with the light reflected from the precious stones that covered an outrageously ornate charm that swayed from side to side at waist level on an equally ornate chain.

Suddenly, in mid-verse, an offbeat whine rang through the stadium. Puzzled, he and his adoring public looked skyward in search of its source. Despite it, though, Antwon managed to stay in the zone and continue his performance; the show must go on. The fans forgot the impromptu sound and returned their attention to the rhymes that Antwon created. Again, the whine's out-of-phase chime reverberated through the rafters; as it did, the entire right side of the stadium, from pit to rampart, dematerialized into nothingness, revealing a bleach-white bathroom wall.

Antwon stopped, lowering the toothpaste from his mouth. He listened closely for the whine again, and the portions of the stadium that had not faded began to. The whine rang once more, and Antwon left the bathroom for the front door, realizing that it was the doorbell he kept hearing; the concert faded into oblivion as he departed.

Through the peephole, he saw a white male with dirty blonde hair and icy-blue eyes, dressed in a purple polo and purple shorts, with a package under his arm. Antwon cracked the door and peered through. "Who are you?"

A pleasant smile stretched across Yuri's face as he pointed at the sigil on his shirt. "Federal Express."

Antwon opened the door fully, revealing his outfit: socks, boxer shorts, a midriff-revealing wife beater, fitted ball cap, and a dog's choke chain with an identity tag that read *Lacey* hanging from his neck. "What do you want?" he asked.

Yuri, caught momentarily off guard, fought back laughter with a cough but managed to maintain his pleasant smile. "Delivery?" he asked and declared simultaneously.

"Oh." Antwon scratched at his groin and leaned in to look at the package. "Who's it from?"

One of Yuri's eyebrows rose sharply, and then he tapped at the return address with his index finger. He then pushed the package into Antwon's arms and pulled his tablet, signaling for Antwon to sign electronically. "Nice chain, the by the way—bet the *bitches* drool over it."

Antwon looked down at the dog chain, not realizing until now that he had answered the door in costume. Feeling embarrassed, Antwon lifted his eyes, but Yuri had already disappeared into the stairwell. Antwon could hear Yuri's laughter echoing back up the steps.

Antwon closed the door and was looking the package over when the phone rang. He moseyed over to it and glanced at the screen to see who was calling. It wasn't a number he recognized, so he ignored it and went to the kitchen for a knife to open the packaging tape.

The phone rang again. And again, he didn't answer it.

It rang three more times, and he answered it finally, annoyed. "Who *dis*?" he said menacingly into the receiver.

"May I speak with Mr. Antwon Coates?" Terry asked in an affable tone.

"Whatchu want?"

"Is this Mr. Coates?"

Antwon's lips twisted. "Whatchu want?"

"It is Mr. Coates! Hello, Mr. Coates. How are you today?"

"Do I know you?"

"Oh, I'm well, Mr. Coates. Thank you for *politely* asking."

"I'm only gon' ask you one more time." Antwon lifted the phone and spoke directly into the receiver. "*Who dis*?" He returned the phone to his ear.

"Fine," Terry said, "I'll depose with the formalities then, Antwon. I can call you Antwon, right?"

"Yeah, dis conversation's over with."

Terry's pitch climbed patronizingly as he said, "I wouldn't hang the phone up, Antwon. Not with how much you have riding on this call, anyway."

"What?"

"Antwon"—Terry paused—"I'm a businessman—cut and dry. Now, whether I'm a good businessman or a bad one is entirely up to you."

"You...you threatening me?"

"Oh no, Antwon. I would never threaten a man of your social status, especially not with a chain that authentic." Antwon looked down at the dog chain again and then shot the receiver a puzzled look before returning it to his ear. "But enough with the small talk; let's get right down to the matter at hand. I think I may have a proposition that you'll find rather profitable."

"Really?" Antwon was unconvinced.

"Really."

"I'm listening."

"The package you have in your hand, open it."

Antwon turned the package over in his hand, opened it, and peeked into it as suspiciously as he'd answered the door. What he saw, however, robbed his mouth of its moisture. "Holy shit!"

"What you're looking at, Antwon, is ten grand in twenty dollar bills for you to use at your leisure."

"Holy shit!"

"You said that already."

"Holy shit! Are you for real?"

"Do I sound like I'm joking?"

"I mean...is this shit real?"

"Don't insult me, Antwon. It hurts my feelings."

"Alright, wait a minute." Antwon's mind was racing. "What's the catch?"

"No *real* catch."

"So there is one?"

"Well, nothing comes free, now, does it?"

"What do you want?"

"Only a small favor."

"Which is what exactly?"

"For you to simply keep your mouth shut and follow my instructions precisely."

Antwon hunkered his head down into his shoulder has if he were trying to hide the conversation from eavesdroppers. "About what?"

"Two unfamiliar men are going to visit your job after hours. I want you to let them pass without question. And you won't speak of them afterward."

"You want me to do what?"

"Antwon, don't play dumb. You heard me just fine."

"So if I do, I get to keep the money?"

"Precisely."

Antwon flipped through a stack of bills with his thumb in thoughtful silence as he contemplated the reality of the conversation and the money. "What happens if I just keep it?"

"I was so hoping you'd ask me that question. Arrogance brightens my day. Antwon, open the package back up, and you'll see a manila folder." He opened it again and pulled the folder free from its bindings. "Yes, that one. Please open it."

A confused look washed over Antwon's face. Could the person he was talking to see him? He approached his glass balcony door and scanned outside at the other balconies, windows, and roofs. Nothing— Nobody. Resigned, he pulled open the adhesive and removed its contents: several eight-by-ten photos that caused his body to seize briefly with astonishment and fear.

"Antwon, believe me when I tell you that your daughter, Takara, is more beautiful in person that she appears in pictures. How old is she—eight, nine maybe?" Antwon shook his head, hardly able to believe what he was seeing or hearing, and Terry's voice became saturated with menace. "In any case, I'd hate for something unfortunately brutal to happen to her. She seems so happy and serene sitting on the swing at the daycare right now. Don't let your ego put her in a body bag."

Fear transformed into rage, and Antwon slung the pictures across his small living room and howled into the phone, "You better not touch my daughter, motherfucker! I will fucking kill you!"

Terry laughed, and Antwon could hear him clapping his hands in amusement in the background. "Antwon, you are hardly in a position to make threats. After all, you can't see me, but I can see your daughter. Think about that. Remember our deal. I'll call you later if I have more tasking. Ta-ta," Terry said.

*   *   *

"Mr. Irizarry, the District Attorney's Office called to reschedule this week's appointment," Carlos's secretary said, charging into his office. "They also faxed these documents for review."

Carlos slouched in his chair with his back to the door and his desk, gazing out of the windows of his office with the phone pressed to his ear. "Okay, Miss McGuiness. Thank you," he replied over his phone conversation and then returned to it. "You were saying?"

"Oh, and your wife called—"

"Mm-hmm just put them in the inbox," he said absently, pointing in the relative direction of the box at the corner of his desk in his distinct Mexican-American accent.

"—twice. The movers said they need your written consent to move the statue."

"Hold on for me a second," he said into the phone and then spun to face her. "Sign those documents for me and notarize them. I have to get going."

"How about the orphans' charity luncheon?"

After a couple of seconds more of the conversation, he placed the phone on the base. "I'm not sure what time I'll be in tomorrow. Forward all my calls to my cellphone."

"Fine. But what about the luncheon?"

"And put that memo you typed on letterhead and tell the D.A. that Wednesday is fine."

"Yes, sir. What about the luncheon?"

"I heard you the first time, Aileen."

"Can I get an answer?"

"If I cared about the orphans, they would have been first on my list of priorities to address. And considering my current legal entanglements, I'm not letting go of any money that's not going to land me in prison."

"Fair enough. Luncheon is off the list. Anything else?"

Suddenly his attention returned to the office. "Now that you mention it, Aileen...fishnets and stilettos would really spice this place up."

"I'll get right on that, Mr. Irizarry."

"In fact, something low-cut too."

Aileen extracted some documents from Carlos's desk and pretended to pay him little attention. "Sexual harassment is a crime, Mr. Irizarry."

"What's the worst thing that could happen?" Carlos laughed deviously. "One more litigation to add to my résumé. Besides, I'm so much better looking than that thing you call a boyfriend."

104

Aileen turned and stalked out as swiftly as she'd entered. "Good night, Mr. Irizarry."

"Let's get a drink."

"Go home to your wife, Mr. Irizarry."

"You don't know my wife," Carlos said as he watched his secretary walk back to her desk.

His mind drifted to the legal muddle that enveloped him and how badly it was firebombing his life. His wife was planning to leave him, and his daughters would hardly speak to him unless they were calling to scream. He was losing the house, his children's college funding was evaporating, and his debt was soaring. What was he to do? Life was at an all-time low. Why couldn't he do something to make himself feel better? Hell, his wife wasn't helping.

No—this wasn't her fault; this was his. He knew that he just wanted it to go away. Why had he allowed himself to get involved with the scandal? He knew better. He was no criminal; they were. They were the individuals who'd plotted this whole ménage of greed. He'd simply given in to temptation like every human does from time to time and found himself trafficking with white-collar criminals.

To be honest, he didn't want to testify against them; many had become his friends. But he had to look after his own interests as well as those of his family. He had no time to help others when his own life was unraveling.

Carlos looked over at the clock and realized that he had drifted off in thought for longer than he had meant and needed to gather his effects and leave for home.

*   *   *

Antwon looked up from the security monitor of the lobby's security node and noticed Carlos stepping off of the elevator. "Hey, Mr. Irizarry! When you gonna hook me up with that big-paying job?"

Carlos's face was sullen as he passed, heading for the door. "When I'm not on the chopping block, Antwon."

"I feel you," Antwon replied, clapping his hands together. "You just gotta maintain. The world is yours if you want it to be. You just gotta decide if you a king or you a peasant."

Carlos backed through the glass door as he nodded at Antwon. "I'll keep that in mind. You have a nice evening, Antwon."

"Stay up, Mr. Irizarry."

*   *   *

Terry sat on the back of a bench of the bus stop outside of ESI, dressed in unassuming clothes that camouflaged him against the other patrons waiting for mass transit. He keyed the dial function of his mobile, ensured that his earpiece was properly seated with a tap, and dropped the phone into his coat pocket as the call was answered. **"Yuri, the target is moving your direction,"** he said. Only one person in the bored crowd paid him any attention when they heard his Japanese. No one else seemed to care.

"**Understood. He's coming directly to me?**"

"**Looks that way. He's entering the parking garage now.**"

"**Engaging.**"

*   *   *

Carlos was on autopilot as he walked down the sidewalk to the parking garage. His life was coming unglued, although, in spite of it all, life was greatly more relaxed than he had assumed it would be on the cusp of a prison sentence. Try as he might, though, he could not shake the sickening feeling that his testimony would make his situation worse. He assumed the relative calm was before the coming storm. Only time would tell, though.

"Hey, mister, you—you got a dollar?" The suddenness of the strained, raspy voice in the seemingly empty parking garage startled Carlos, and he leaped away from the stanchion from which the voice came. A beggar with a dirt-caked, graying beard and draped in tattered, filthy rags peered around the concrete cylinder with an outreached hand. "I—I gotta eat."

Carlos's alarm drained away, and disdain filled the space it left. "What you need to do is go away."

"I don't mean you no harm, mister," the man said. "I just want a dollar so I can eat."

"Get a job, because I don't have any money to give." Carlos continued to his car. "Now, go away."

"Aw c'mon, mister. I—"

"I will pepper spray you," Carlos warned calmly.

Yuri's receiver crackled to life with Terry's voice as Yuri stalked his prey. "**The area is clear on this side**," said Terry. "**I'm circling the garage to look for other intruders. Confirm that you have the target in sight.**"

"**I have him**," Yuri whispered into his throat microphone.

Carlos opened the door to his luxury vehicle and climbed in, cursing the homeless man venomously. As he was getting situated and buckling his seatbelt, his mobile phone rang; it was muffled, and Carlos didn't remember where he had put it. He foraged through the pockets of his coat and then his pants before he dove into his briefcase, finally finding it at the bottom. He pulled it out, managing to see only the glowing screen before he fumbled it and dropped it in between the seat and the center console.

Carlos aspirated a combination of frustrated curses and then groaned aloud as he stuffed his hand into the tight space. By the time he reached the phone, however, he had missed the call, and his hand ached from forcing it into a space too small for it.

The phone evaded Carlos's grip for several seconds until he was able to manage a solid grip with his fingers around the case. He extracted it slowly, trying not to catch the lip of the center console as he drew his hand and the phone through the space that his hand only struggled to pass through. At least the pull was easier than the push—though it didn't hurt any less.

Phone in hand and sitting back against the seat, Carlos breathed an indignant sigh and looked at the screen. The call was from his oldest daughter, who was probably calling to harass him for the tragic mess that he'd made of her life. He was relieved that he'd missed it—aching hand notwithstanding—and stuffed the phone into his coat, opting to wait until he had arrived at home to call her, and pulled out his car keys. He glanced around the garage as he turned the key in the ignition, noting that the beggar was nowhere to be seen. *Good riddance*, he thought to himself.

Crash! The driver's window imploded, splashing glass all over Carlos. It was a blur at first, but once he recovered from the initial start and persuaded his heart out of his throat and back into his chest, Carlos realized that he was staring down the barrel of a pistol with the bearded and marred face of a beggar behind it.

"You're one hell of a philanthropist! You know that?" the beggar barked.

Once the adrenaline haze cleared completely, Carlos became acutely aware that not only was he at the receiving end of a gun but it was so close to his face that he could make out the rifling that spiraled the length of the barrel interior. He lurched backward but was yanked to a stop by the seatbelt like a sprinting dog reaching the limit of its leash.

"Stop moving," the beggar demanded, more quietly this time. "Otherwise, I'll consider you a threat and blow your head clean off."

"Okay—okay!" Carlos yelled with his hands up. "I won't move. I swear I won't move!" Puddles of desperation began to pool in his eyes. "Please don't kill me! Please—I'm begging you! I have a family, a wife, and daughters. They need me! I'll give you anything you want. You just name it! You want money, my wallet, my car keys?"

The beggar inclined his head. "You'll give me anything?"

"Anything!"

He leaned into the window, looking Carlos straight in the eye, and licked away matted strands of mustache from his own lips. "First off, I want you to stop screaming, because you're hurting my ears. Second"— his mouth became a hateful grimace—"I want you to stop crying, because it's just flat-out embarrassing, Carlos. Pull yourself together."

Carlos swallowed hard and tried to straighten himself despite the fact that the barrel of the pistol tracked his every movement. "How—how do you know my name?"

The beggar pressed the barrel into the soft tissue of Carlos's left temple. "I'm the one with the gun, Carlos. I'm going to ask the questions."

"I'm sorry! I'm sorry!"

"Stop screaming. That's the last time I'm going to tell you. Next time, I'm going to ventilate the side of your fucking face." The beggar rested his free arm in the window and leaned on it. "Now, if you *must* know, you're all over the news, Carlos. Who doesn't know your name?"

"Are you going to kill me? I don't want to die." It all came out practically as a single word.

The beggar chuckled, "What kind of monster do you take me for, Carlos?"

Terry's disembodied voice rang in Yuri's ear again: "**Stop playing with your food and wrap it up. We don't want to draw attention.**"

"**You can't rush perfection,**" Yuri whispered.

"We're going to play a game," the beggar rasped. "Here's the rules: I'm going to point this gun at you while I ask you some questions. If you tell me *exactly* what I want to know, this will go quickly. If this doesn't go quickly, it's because you decided to toy with me. People who toy with me have a liaison with my gun. You understand what I'm saying?"

"So you're not going to kill me?"

"I just told you that we were going to play a game, Carlos."

Carlos whimpered as he exhaled relief. "Oh, thank the Lord."

"Don't thank God just yet, Carlos," the beggar said condescendingly. "I'm still holding a gun to your head. Now, when I say *exactly*, I mean *exactly*. No holding back. Am I making myself abundantly clear, or do I need to say it in Spanish?"

"Yes—yes, of course," Carlos said immediately, but then he realized he was being ambiguous. "I mean, *yes I understand* and *no, you don't have to say it in Spanish*."

The beggar smiled hard beneath all his facial hair. "Good." Then his mouth became a straight line. "How much money did you make off the illegal sale of your shares?"

"Almost three and a half million dollars."

The beggar scowled and pressed the barrel into Carlos's temple. "I said *exactly*."

Carlos yelped, "I don't know!"

The beggar rolled his eyes. "How many shares did you sell?" he sighed.

"Forty-eight thousand."

"At what price?"

109

"Seventy-two dollars per share."

"Okay," the beggar said sharply, pressing harder with a gun, "do the fucking math, Carlos! Didn't you get a degree in accounting?"

Carlos mewled but nodded his head.

The beggar roared in his ear, "Do the fucking math, then!"

"Three million four hundred fifty-six thousand!"

"How much of that was profit? Be exact."

Carlos closed his eyes as he counted to himself. "Two million eight hundred forty thousand."

"Where's the money now?"

"In an overseas account..."

The beggar's mouth twisted with insult beneath his beard. "Obviously—the feds haven't seized it yet. What account?"

"Swedish Trust."

"What are the account and personal identification numbers?"

"Wh—what?" Carlos asked, his eyes flickering between the pistol and the beggar.

"Did I stutter? Account number and PIN, what are they?"

"I have to release those funds, or I go to prison."

"Prison or the afterlife, Carlos? Your choice."

"But..." Carlos decided to play dumb; he had to protect that money if he intended to survive the litigations. "I don't know them by heart."

"Bullshit," the beggar snarled. "I watched you type them into your cellphone yesterday."

"You've been watching me?"

The barrel thumped the bone between Carlos's eyebrow and eye socket. "I'm asking the questions. But since you asked, I was paid handsomely to watch you. I've been doing it for weeks. I've been watching your family too. Maybe they'll be more cooperative with a gun to their heads than their obstinate man of the house."

Carlos heard the creak of the trigger and blurted out the account number and the PIN.

"Now we're getting somewhere."

"Where are the fiscal reports that miraculously went missing?" the beggar asked.

"On ESI's GEEKS database, but I had it destroyed."

"Information is never destroyed. Where is the database?"

"It was on an external drive that I hid at my house."

"No wonder you were caught." The beggar shook his head. "Where at your house?"

"In the safe in the floor under my office desk."

"What's the combination?"

"There isn't one. I have to use my identification card to access it."

"Where's your ID card?"

"Locked in my desk drawer at ESI."

"Where's the key?"

"Right here on my key chain."

"Tell me, Carlos"—the beggar's face softened beneath the dirt and grime that caked his face—"are you a God-fearing man?"

"Yes—of course."

"Do you read the Bible?"

"Yes."

"Remember Isaiah 54:17?"

Carlos searched the beggar with his eyes. He didn't recall that verse.

The beggar reminded him. "No weapon formed against thee shall prosper and all that jazz?"

Carlos nodded vigorously.

"That verse doesn't apply to you."

Carlos's face became sheepish, but then he realized what the beggar was saying: the beggar had planned to kill him the whole time. Carlos pleaded and yowled, but the beggar ended Carlos's pathetic falsetto with a cascade of carbon gas, bloody mist, gray matter, and skull fragments. Carlos's body slumped over the center console, twitching and pouring blood into the passenger seat.

The beggar unleashed two more bullets into Carlos's corpse for good measure. Then he leaned into the window, reached across the steering column, turned off the car, and pulled the keys out. The beggar dropped the keys into his overcoat pocket and then pulled the sleeve down to cover his own blood-splattered arm.

Yuri surveyed the hit and smiled with satisfaction. "**It's done. I'm on my way to meet you**," he said over the net.

From the corner of an adjacent street, Terry spotted the beggar exiting the garage and waved him over.

"Oh, hello," the beggar said as he approached, situating his tarnished overcoat.

"**Took long enough**," Terry said, adjusting his sunglasses and starting in the direction of ESI.

The beggar followed. "Theatrics are a necessary evil. Got to keep the job interesting, you know."

"Your disguise looks great, by the way. Almost don't recognize you. I'd swear you've been doing this your whole life."

"I'm an artist in my own right. How else am I supposed to work in broad daylight?"

"Yeah," Terry chortled, unconvinced, "whatever."

"I am—don't hate."

"If you say so, Yuri."

"This job was easy as hell. They made it sound like it was going to be difficult."

"They always do."

"I suppose." Yuri stroked his matted, fake beard thoughtfully as he walked. "The security measures here stink too. How is he going to leave his ID card in the desk?"

"That's why he and our employer got busted for shady business. They're not very good at what they do."

"Clearly."

Terry and Yuri looked over at the security node as they walked in the direction of the elevators. The security guard stood to his feet, preparing to query the two strangers, but Terry beat him to the jump. "Good evening, Antwon."

Antwon's lungs froze—he didn't even want to watch them get on the elevator. Once the men were out of sight, he took a deep breath, looked around the lobby, and then returned to his chair, trembling—ten thousand dollars richer.

Chapter Seven: The Coming Storm

Suzuka Mountains. Mie Prefecture, Japan. Eighteen years ago.

Terry was not happy.

Of all the things he could think of doing during the summer, being volunteered by his parents for a camping trip into humid Japanese backcountry was not one of them. Yuri did not mind—he mostly loved anything that irked his brother.

Pat and Francesca had been called away to a diplomatic conference on the southernmost Japanese island, *Kyūshū*. Not wanting to bring their children along for the week-long festivities, the couple had opted to leave their boys in the care of Kintake, who was planning to return to his village nestled deep in the Suzuka mountain range in the Mie Prefecture. Kintake's village was hosting a summer camp for his martial arts students so they could live and learn the history and tradition of the rural Japanese as well as continue the study of martial arts in an immersive environment.

Pat and Francesca had jumped at the opportunity. A summer camp was an excellent opportunity for the boys to make friends and experience something other than the fast-paced lifestyle of Tokyo. Terry didn't share his parents' enthusiasm—no summer camp was worth hiking through the mountains and humidity. Not to mention the car ride was long and uncomfortable.

Kintake had picked the boys up in his cramped and venerable, once silver but now rusting four-by-four truck and driven three hours from the heart of Tokyo into the mountains. He departed a lonely paved road about two hours into the trip for an equally lonely winding dirt road. The dirt road weaved through the terrain, ending in a small clearing blanketed by a canopy of trees near a sleepy, remote farm, where Kintake parked the vehicle.

"Omiyoshu Sensei, where are we?" Terry asked suspiciously.

"Northeast of Iga, near *Togakure Ryu*—my village. Come, boys, we still have some walking to do."

Still sitting in the cab, Terry's head followed Kintake as he exited the vehicle and walked to the bed of the truck. "How far do we have to walk?" Terry asked.

"About two hours."

Terry groaned audibly. "Two hours?!"

"Give or take, depending on the pace you two keep. Make haste, please. We are limited on daylight, and I would prefer not to make this walk in the dark."

Terry groaned again, pushing the passenger door open. Yuri rushed over him and leaped from the vehicle. Terry groaned more, slid from the passenger seat, and closed the door behind him.

"Boys, make haste." Kintake rapped the bed with his knuckles. "Take from your suitcases *only* the belongings that you will need and place them in your backpacks. Also, ensure that your shoes are well tied. The ground's angle changes regularly, and a loose shoe can lead to an injured ankle. Traversing the mountains with an injured leg or foot could be challenging at best or torturous at worst."

Terry and Yuri did as they were instructed and then set off with their sensei.

*   *   *

In his humble, matter-of-fact tone, Kintake spent the rest of the trip educating the boys on the history of his village, the Shinobi—the creators of taijutsu—the mountains and their utility to the Shinobi, and how the politics of feudal Japan had shaped the Shinobi. The boys listened distantly as they followed—Yuri ballistically so and Terry sulking even further back. Kintake paid their idiosyncrasies little attention. After nearly three years of teaching them, he was accustomed to these sorts of behaviors.

Kintake continued his exposition of Iga, suggesting that *Togakure Ryu* had been founded by his ancestors, the Fujibayashi clan, over four hundred years ago when they'd left a war-torn region of Iga, which, he added, was one of the two birthplaces of the famed ninja—or *Shinobi,* as he referred to them. The terrain had played a key role in site selection, he noted, when the Fujibayashi—and the many other now-defunct clans—had sought to lay the foundation for a new home

114

hidden from the whirlwind politics of belligerent Shogunates—feudal dictatorships that Kintake referred to as *bakufu*. He claimed that the village had been established on the banks of a divine river that was created when the spirits began to weep over the slaying of the first Shinobi. Legend had it that the slain Shinobi were reborn from the river as *Mamushi*—the Japanese viper that was revered as their corporeal spirit. This, he asserted, was the reason that the river snaked through the basins of the range. The river, of course, provided water and industry to *Togakure Ryu* and acted as a natural border to the village. But most importantly, it provided a rapid, tactical egress if *Togakure Ryu* were to be overrun.

He directed their attention to the many peaks and crests with his hands. Kintake claimed that the Fujibayashi used them as listening posts for invaders and other threats. However, if their enemies managed to control one or several of the peaks, the Fujibayashi had nestled *Togakure Ryu* beneath a thick canopy of trees, all but eliminating an enemy's ability to locate their village.

Additionally, he explained that the boulders that dotted the wooded mountain faces and basins—numbering perhaps in the thousands—were not natural to the terrain. The Fujibayashi had placed them about to slow the advance of invading armies, to break up their ranks, and to place cavalry at a disadvantage.

After nearly two hours at a slow jog's pace, the three travelers crested the final ridge and began their descent into the *Togakure Ryu* basin. The village was situated in a flat area littered with trees, resting against the bank of the river that divided two tower escarpments and a lazy crown. The ear-shaped basin in which *Togakure Ryu* was established broke the otherwise uniform makeup of the terrain much like swirling eddies broke the flows of streams.

Kintake stopped near a cluster of trees to take a swig from his water bottle. The boys joined him seconds later, Yuri singing "One Hundred Bottles of Beer" with conviction as he approached and Terry grinding his teeth with frustration.

"That is quite enough singing, Yuri."

Terry threw his arms up. "Thank you, God! He has been driving me crazy! I swear I'm never going to drink beer when I grow up now!"

"Why, Terry? Daddy drinks beer."

"He wouldn't if he had listened to you sing that song three times in a row."

"Daddy loves that song."

"Don't know why," Terry snapped.

"Terry, Yuri, that is enough from both of you." Kintake's voice became stone. "Now, pay attention, please. *Togakure Ryu* does not often receive visitors. Therefore, you will be under tremendous scrutiny. I expect that both of you will be on your best behavior. You will not dishonor yourselves, me, the Fujibayashi, or *Togakure Ryu*. Do I make myself clear?"

"Yes, Sensei," they said in stereo.

"Most importantly, you will bow to everyone you meet, especially the Shinobi-no-mono, Hattori Hanzo. He is our grandmaster. You must not make eye contact with him unless he commands it. He does not take kindly to outsiders."

Terry was instantly apprehensive. "He won't like us? Is he mean?" Terry asked, remembering the feeling of being ostracized by Japanese boys in school.

"I will leave you with no illusion, Terry. Shinobi-no-mono will not favor your presence. He will be rancorous and petulant towards you."

Yuri sheepishly raised his hand. "What does that mean?"

"It means he's not going to like us, Yuri," claimed Terry.

Yuri's face pruned with distress.

Kintake waved a dismissive hand. "Hattori Hanzo is similar to a priest in church. He is closest to our ancestor spirits. He does not command the Togakure Ryu—I do. He commands me and all other *kōchō*—Shinobi headmasters. The *kōchō* command all other Shinobi. You will be safe."

Terry's interest was piqued. "There are other headmasters?"

"*Kōchō*," Kintake corrected. "There is only one other today. The Momochi kōchō. The other clans died in the 1800s."

"What happened?"

"Not relevant right at the moment." Kintake finished his water and stuffed the bottle into his bag. "While you are here, you will be required to learn the mandates of the code that governs *taijutsu*—Ninpo. We are strict regarding it, and you will have to learn it quickly if you are to be accepted. Are we clear?"

"Yes, Sensei," they said again in stereo.

"Very good. I'm going to recite the First Mandate, and I want you to repeat it. Once you've grasped it, you will repeat it aloud until we reach the village. Clear?"

They acknowledged again.

"Very good. The First Mandate reads: *The Shinobi are creatures of shadow and must remain concealed. A Shinobi must remove all traces of his presence or be dishonored.*"

After Kintake's first recital, he gave it to them in pieces, sentence by sentence, and demanded that they repeat it back. Once they had grasped it, he set out again with them, repeating it and following again.

*   *   *

Kintake and the boys came down the final brae into the village's basin, nearing a fence surrounding grain crops. A modestly dressed man directing a passel of hogs spotted them, showing at first alarm and then surprise. He left the passel and quickly ran up to Kintake, bowing deeply when he came close. Kintake nodded his head vaguely and waved for the boys to hurry. Terry and Yuri smiled at the man as they trotted by, following Kintake into the village's first cluster of cottages. The man reciprocated the boys' greeting—albeit with mortified suspicion.

Togakure Ryu was a geriatric thing, practically misplaced in time, not at all what one would find in travel brochures, but rather in history books. The construction and the architecture of the village lacked any panache or vitality in modern terms—being composed mostly of wood and colored muted browns. At the center of the village was a large cabin that was orbited by satellite clusters of cottages. Crops and livestock pens were further out.

The central cabin sported a starkly different design than its satellites. It had a pyramid-shaped roof that was supported at its four corners by carved wooden stanchions whose *kanji* translated to read: *Allow Not Dishonor To Go Silently*. The cabin's front porch faced the river, which was approximately one hundred yards to the west, and opened through a rice paper sliding door. The other three walls exhibited windows with angled panels similar to blinds that offered a view from the inside but not the outside. The exterior was encircled by gardens—floral, food-bearing, and rock. Unlike the rest of the buildings, this one was powered by electricity, identifiable by the thrum of a generator in a covered area to the rear.

The cottages were simply built, more for utility rather than aesthetics. They were plain and unexceptional and faced every which direction, with front doors facing the rear of one cottage and the side of another. Each one was built nearly on top of the others in their cluster. The clusters, however, were spaced out, situated perhaps twenty yards apart.

The residents of the little rural village were going about their daily routines and chores but stopped dead in their tracks to honor Kintake as he passed through the clusters—then their eyes followed Terry and Yuri jealously. Kintake and the boys weaved through clusters and villagers along the gravel walkways.

Nearing the center, Kintake signaled the boys towards a gathering of curious children standing beneath the canopy of a massive, impossibly shaped tree. "Please, wait over there with the other children," Kintake requested as he stalked off. "I must greet Shinobi-no-mono."

"Yes, Sensei," Yuri replied obediently and sprinted towards the other children.

Terry watched apprehensively as Kintake made his way across a rock garden towards a group of adults on the porch. Kintake signaled him towards the children once again. This time, Terry followed directions.

"Hi!" Yuri exclaimed to a boy slightly shorter than Terry. The boy's hair was cut in a bowl shape that hung to his eyes, and he was dressed in a worn, faded plaid shirt and denim jeans, with a pair of tattered tennis shoes. "My name's Yuri!"

The boy wiped his hair from his eyes and angled an empty look at Yuri.

Terry caught up with his brother. "Yuri, speak Japanese. Not everyone speaks English."

"Oh, um…" Yuri tried Japanese. "**My name is Yuri.**"

The boy's face reacted. "**I'm Takejiro Saki.**"

"And this is my brother," Yuri said, exaggerating every word. "His name is Terry. He is older than me. He is twelve. I am seven."

"Nice to meet you," Saki said, looking at Terry and nodding.

"Nice to meet you too."

"How old are you?" Terry asked Saki in a more dialectic—and less proper—Japanese than Yuri used.

"I'm thirteen."

"Cool."

There was a moment of awkward silence as the children regarded the two new boys. Then Saki spoke up, "Where are you from?"

"Well"—Terry searched for the right answer—"I'm from America, but we live in Tokyo now."

The eyes of a girl standing nearby, wearing a cotton shirt with a lacy collar and a knee-length skirt with a pair of tattered saddle shoes, illuminated, and her mouth dropped open to speak. But before she could get a word out, Yuri jumped in: "Terry, we've never lived in America!"

"Shut up, dummy," Terry retorted, dismissing his brother.

"You're from America?" the girl asked finally.

"No!" Yuri blurted out, trying to beat his brother to the punch.

"Well, kind of." Terry mooshed Yuri's face with the palm of his hand, forcing Yuri back a step. "My mom and dad are from New Jersey."

"Where's New Jersey?" the girl asked.

"Uh, close to New York, I think."

"You've been to New York before?"

Terry opened his mouth to reply, but only the sound of Yuri's words came out: "No, but my mommy and daddy took us to the president's house before."

Terry shook his head. "That's in Washington, DC."

"Really?" She clasped her hands together just below her chin. "I want to go to New York one day and meet the president. I think my father knows him. Father says that the president is an imbecile."

"My dad says the same thing, but I don't think he knows the president."

Yuri derailed the topic. "**You're pretty**!" he exclaimed, getting awkwardly close to the girl. "**What's your name**?"

The girl put space in between them.

Terry threw his hands up. "God, Yuri, stay out of people's personal space. Dad tells you that all the time."

Yuri's face flushed. "Leave me alone, Terry!"

"**It's okay. We're not allowed to stand so close to boys**," she said. "**My name is Akiko**."

"**Are you here for the camp**?" Terry asked.

Saki, Akiko, and the other children exchanged looks. "**What camp**?" Saki replied.

"**You're not here for camp**?"

"**No**," Akiko said. "**We live here**."

"**You're from Omiyoshu Sensei's village**?"

"**Yes**," Saki replied.

"**He's my father**," Akiko interjected.

Terry's eyes squinted. "**You're Omiyoshu Sensei's daughter**?"

"**Yes**."

"**I didn't know he had a daughter. How old are you**?"

"**Ten**."

Terry considered it. He wondered who else from their class was coming for the camp.

"**Have you come to train with us**?" asked Akiko.

"**I don't know**." Terry rubbed the back of his head gingerly. "**What are you training to do? We came to do taijutsu for the summer**."

"**Akiko, be quiet**," Saki demanded. "**The Jonin are watching us**."

"**We came for the summer camp**," Yuri said, disregarding Saki's and Akiko's growing uneasiness. "**Omiyoshu Sensei is going to teach us karate in the mountains and how to farm. We learn taijutsu. Do you know any karate**?"

The native children became instantly silent and focused their attention on the adults that were suddenly regarding them from the porch. After another moment, Kintake and the *Jonin*—elder, high-ranking Shinobi—departed the porch and walked briskly across the rock garden towards the children. Saki, Akiko, and the other children bowed deeply, and Terry followed their lead. Yuri, who had his back to the cabin, was clueless and kept talking.

"Yuri, bow."

Yuri cut Terry off, yelling "No, you shut up!"

"Yuri!" Terry's face hardened. "Stop being stupid! Here comes Omiyoshu Sensei. *Bow!*"

Yuri did.

"**Daughter**," Kintake called to Akiko as he came near, backed by his entourage of adults, "**how are you**?"

She bowed again. "**I am with honor, father**."

"**I expected no less, daughter**," Kintake replied, acknowledging her, and then he signaled to Terry and Yuri. "**Terry, Yuri, come**. The brothers did as they were told and approached their sensei.

The three of them were surrounded on three sides by villagers Kintake's age and older, perhaps twenty in all. They were a sea of disdain and contempt, resembling an eerie display of gargoyle statues grimacing and growling silently from their perches. The brothers suddenly felt unwelcome.

Kintake addressed the oldest and most infirm of the group. He was in his eighties and hunched shorter than an average man was tall. His head was wrapped in a line of ragged gray hair, and his face sported a long goatee. He was draped in dark blue robes, and he was missing an arm.

"**Shinobi-no-mono**," Kintake said, "**if I may, these are the two youths of whom I spoke**." Kintake placed a confident grip on Terry's shoulder. "**This fine young man is Terry. Terry has a sharp mind and an artist's dedication**."

"**Hello, sir**," Terry said sheepishly.

"**And this young man is Yuri. Yuri has unparalleled tenacity and a fortitude rarely found in a child**."

Yuri parroted his brother.

"**Terry and Yuri**," said Kintake, scooping the air with his hand in the elder man's direction, "**I present to you our Shinobi-no-mono—his most holy Hattori Hanzo. Please show our Shinobi-no-mono deepest honors**."

The boys bowed deeply and resumed.

Hanzo was staring hard, his eyes all ice, entertaining a cold silence. "**Omiyoshu Sensei,**" he rasped finally, "**you do too much. Do not think that the ancestors and I are blind to your maneuvering.**" Hanzo disappeared into the cabin.

Kintake swished his mouth thoughtfully and then managed a smile as turned towards Saki and Akiko. "**Saki-san, daughter, return to your duties and then see Takenaka Sensei. He is near the well; he will instruct you. And please allow Terry to accompany you,**" he said, extending an inviting hand.

Akiko and Saki both acknowledged and bowed in unison and then signaled to Terry to follow before sprinting in the direction of the well.

"**Hey, wait for me**!" Yuri yelled. He was beginning to accelerate to follow his brother and the two older children when Kintake grabbed hold of Yuri's shoulder.

"Yuri, let them go." Yuri protested, but Kintake was not fazed. "You will come with me," he said. "We have much to do before sunset."

*   *   *

"**I love it out here, away from the grown-ups!**" Saki exclaimed, stopping to catch his breath.

Terry was bent over next to him with his hands on his knees, gasping for air. They had run quite an extensive distance up an adjacent precipice and down into a neighboring valley. Saki was clearly in much better shape, as he'd managed to outdistance Terry by several body lengths for the entire duration of their run. That was to be expected, however, of a boy who lived in a remote village surrounded by steep terrain. At the very least, the pain of running made Terry forget that he hadn't wanted to go on this *stupid* mountain exploit in the first place.

"**Where are we going, Saki?**" Terry panted.

"**To get firewood.**"

Terry stood up and used his shirt to wipe the sweat from his face. "**What's wrong with all *these* trees?**" Terry looked around at the hundreds of equally spaced trees that seemed to be aligned in perfect rows.

"Nothing. These trees are sacred; we cannot cut them. Besides, we're going somewhere special first."

"Where?"

"You'll see," Saki said, tapping Terry's shoulder as he breezed by, accelerating deeper into the valley. "You're gonna love it too!"

Terry sighed as he watched Saki bound over several fallen trees and then angle around a rocky outcropping. Terry shook his head and then started off in pursuit of his new friend.

As Terry slid through the turn about the same outcropping, his shoes lost their grip on the wet forest bed, and he tumbled end over end down the hill. Ten revolutions later, Terry came to rest on some rather uncomfortable rocks and sticks. He didn't move.

He welcomed the excuse to catch his breath, this time, inhaling the humid air through his nose and exhaling via his mouth. Saki barely gave him anytime at all when they stopped last; his lungs were burning. But yet Saki was still not content with resting. He approached Terry with an extended hand and pulled Terry to his feet.

That is when Terry saw that which Saki was excitedly trying to reach.

The two boys stood just ahead of a great wooden Shinto gate— a *torii*—faintly etched with kanji that was fading after centuries of wear. To either side were two ailing stone lantern-shaped statues— *tōrō*. Leading beyond the archway were withered stone steps ascending to a derelict path—the *sandō*—that led to several obscure buildings. To one side of the sandō, about twenty yards or more, were three small tool-shed-sized structures—*chōzuya*—that were at one time dedicated to physical purification and worshipful expression. Just inside that were tombs numbering thirty or so that lined either side of the sandō. And, directly following those, to the right of the sandō, was the *shamuso*; in the shrine's heyday, the shamuso was its administrative node. Just beyond, and obscured by the shamuso, were the *haiden* and the *honden*—an oratory hall and the house of the kami spirit respectively.

"What is this place?" Terry asked.

"It's a shrine."

"For what?"

"To honor our Jonin and our greatest warriors," Saki said rigidly.

Terry turned his head in Saki's direction.

"**In the old days,**" Saki continued, "**the mightiest warriors fought here. Then the dead were buried along the path. My father says that when the winds blow from the northern pass**"—Saki pointed to a saddle that separated to mountainous crests—"**you can still hear their swords clashing in an epic battle.**"

"**Have you ever heard it?**" Terry murmured.

"**No. My father said the wind only blows when someone with great honor approaches the shrine.**" Saki's shoulders relaxed. "**I guess I am not with great honor—but one day, I will be.**"

"Oh." Terry was slightly confused. He was not sure exactly where Saki was going with his idea of *great honor*. "**How are you going to do that?**"

"**I'm not sure yet. Perhaps in battle.**"

"*Battle*?" Terry snickered dubiously at the thought as he wiped his nose with his forearm. "**That's kind of like a movie.**"

Saki eyes were fixated deep into the shrine. He shot Terry a faraway look and then managed a smile. The smile made Terry feel somewhat accepted. He was rather hesitant to engage other Japanese children and adults. He felt like an outsider in most circumstances and tended to keep his thoughts and opinions to himself. Questioning Saki's reference to battles and honor felt as if Terry was crawling out on a very thin limb, but much to his reassurance, Saki's reaction appeared favoring.

The small surge of confidence urged Terry to ask another question that had been bouncing around in this head. "**Why didn't Akiko come with us?**"

"**Girls don't get firewood. She had to get water from the well for dinner and then help cook.**"

"Oh." Terry shrugged. "**My mom cooks dinner for us, although Yuri helps her a lot.**"

Silence fell between the boys again. Both were natural introverts, feeling no need to fill the silence with unnecessary conversation. They both remained at the archway and took in the scenery at the shrine, archiving it for later.

Finally, Saki felt compelled to inquire into Terry's life. "**So, where are your parents?**"

124

"They had to fly to Kyūshū."

Saki suddenly came to life. "In a plane?"

Terry kicked a stick that laid at his feet. "How else would they fly?"

"I don't know. I've never been on a plane."

"Seriously?" Terry blurted in English instinctively, but he translated it to Japanese when he noticed Saki's reaction.

"Yes. But I see them in the sky sometimes. Have you ever been on a plane?"

"Plenty of times. We go see my grandparents in New Jersey every Christmas."

"My grandparents are dead," Saki said, derailing the conversation.

"Oh." Terry ran his hand through his hair. "Where are your parents?"

"My mother is preparing for dinner and instructing Akiko and the other girls."

"Where's your dad?"

"My father is dead."

Terry's mouth became a straight, solemn line. "How did he die?"

"The elder council demanded his life."

"Huh?" Terry's face pruned.

Saki lowered his eyes and then looked towards the shrine. "We better start getting the firewood. We shouldn't be out here after dark."

"Why?" Terry asked, picking up the stick and flinging it. "What happens after dark?"

"I can't say—but if we're found out here after dark, we'll be punished—badly."

Terry started to ask another question, but just as it was starting, Saki bolted off in the direction they'd come, beckoning Terry to follow.

*   *   *

"Hi, Mommy!" Yuri bubbled into the phone in the center hall.

The sound of Yuri's voice warmed Francesca's heart. "Hi, angel," she said lovingly. She hated being away from him and Terry. They needed her; no one could care for them and love them the way she could, and it made her feel guilty anytime she wasn't present for them. But she was more than just a mother—she was also a wife. And sometimes her duties as a wife had to take priority, like accompanying her husband to a diplomatic congress to negotiate a peaceful resolution on the world stage.

Francesca mashed the power button on the TV's remote until the video and audio winked out of existence—she didn't want any distractions while she talked to the boys—and then called upstairs to Pat that his children were on the phone.

"How are you?" she asked, returning her full attention to Yuri.

"Mommy, this place is so cool. It's really old, and I learned how to milk goats! Maybe we can get some, and I can milk them for you." Yuri sat Indian-style on a mat, beaming an angelic smile from ear to ear. Terry sat on a mat to Yuri's right, wiping the mud from his tennis shoes.

"Oh, is that what we should do?" she asked with a faint smile.

"Yeah! And I met some other kids, Mommy! But they're all younger than me, well, except for Saki and Akiko, but they were with Terry the whole time."

"That's wonderful, honey."

"And our beds are the on the floor, and we have to take our shoes off when we come inside..."

Pat hustled into the living room and leaned over the couch, coming to rest with his ear pressed to the backside of the phone. Francesca yanked her head and the phone away, shooting Pat a wretched look. He responded with a brash expression and mouthed, "I want to listen."

Yuri didn't miss a beat. He talked and talked, recounting his entire day in no specific order. He described the mountains, the village, the strangely dressed people, and the new friends that he and Terry had met. He was especially excited about all he had learned about farming and romping through the mud chasing a goat's kid. Francesca only managed to chime in with the occasional acknowledgment, but she doubted Yuri even took notice; he never responded when she asked him to repeat himself.

126

Pat practically begged Francesca to pass him the phone. She told him that Yuri was still explaining his first day at camp. Pat affirmed to her that Yuri wasn't going to stop anytime soon; he'd talk until the battery died. Agreeing, Francesca handed her husband the phone. Yuri's voice squeaked in between them until it reached Pat's ear.

He listened for a moment but then interrupted. "Damn, fireplug, can I get a word in edgewise?" Pat asked half a monologue later.

"Hi, Daddy!" Yuri said excitedly, barely pausing.

"Wait, whoa, son."

Yuri stopped fully this time. "Yes, Daddy?"

"Hey!" Pat said gleefully. "How are you, spud?"

"I'm fine!"

Pat put on his stern military voice. "Are you behaving?

"Yes, sir!"

"What have you learned since you've been there?"

Yuri erupted with enthusiasm, recounting the story he had told Francesca but even less organized this time around. In fact, Pat had difficulty understanding Yuri through his excitement and even had to peel his head away from the receiver as Yuri's volume peaked.

"Son," Pat asserted, interrupting again, "I can't understand you when you yell. Why don't you bring it down a couple of notches?"

"Sorry, Daddy. Is this better?"

"Much." Pat nodded even though Yuri couldn't see him. "Tell me *one* thing you learned today. Just one thing."

Yuri hummed as he thought about which one thing he should respond with. When he decided, he replied eagerly, "I learned how to milk goats and get eggs from chickens!"

"Well, I'll be damned." Pat flashed an impressed smile at his wife, and she reciprocated with an inquiring look. "They're turning you into a regular Old McDonald. Maybe I'll drop you on a farm, and you can make me some money. What do you say?"

"Okay, Daddy!"

Pat laughed. Yuri was so agreeable…now. That was sure to change in a couple of years as his mother's tenacity and intensity grew inside him. Pat knew that Yuri was going to grow into an obstinate epicenter of defiance just like her. Francesca's mother and father—Marcela and Nico—had never been more relieved than when Francesca had married Pat and moved away. They had effectively pawned off their only daughter's impossibility on him. Fortunately, she had mellowed a little bit over the past decade. Yuri was going to be picking up the torch soon. In the meantime, Pat was going to take full advantage of Yuri's childlike affability. "I'm glad you see it my way, pal. Where's your brother?"

"Right here, Daddy. You want to talk to him?"

"May I, please?"

"Yes, sir. Here he is, Daddy."

There was childlike grumbling followed by the snap of an attitude. Then Terry's voice came on the phone. "Hello?"

"Hey, stud."

"Hi, Dad," Terry replied in a monotone.

Pat huffed, "Don't sound so happy to hear from me. Did I *interrupt* marshmallow roasting or something?"

"No, sir."

There was a moment of awkward silence until Pat spoke up; Terry apparently was not in the mood to be forthright. "So...what do you think?" Pat asked.

"It's really pretty here. The village is in a valley, and woods surround it. Yuri's also getting a lot of practice talking in Japanese."

"That's excellent."

"It's also really humid, and there's no electricity either—except for here in the Shinobi-no-mono's hut."

"The shuh-who?" Pat laughed.

"The Shinobi-no-mono. He's basically the grandmaster of the village."

"Wow—okay. Why not?" Pat's brow arched, and he nodded in resignation.

Francesca inquired.

Pat told her that the boys had a grandmaster with a weird name. Then Pat returned his attention to Terry. "I guess they're making a man outta you, huh? I know how much you dislike humidity, and I'm sure you're going crazy without the internet."

"They said we have to get up two hours before sunrise tomorrow too."

"Really?" Memories of the many training exercises Pat had had to embark on with several different units over the duration of his career flooded into his surface thoughts.

"Yes, sir. I don't know why."

"Okay, well, I know how that is. That's what we had to do every time I had to go out in the field for training. And we had to eat stale, boxed food—"

Francesca tapped her husband on the shoulder, brandishing an open hand towards the phone.

"Hang on for me for a second, chief. Mom wants to talk to you," Pat said before pushing the phone into Francesca's hand. As her fingers began to close around the device, Pat snatched it away with eyes wide from a sudden revelation. "Hey, before I give Mom the phone, I want to tell you something, and I want you to *listen* closely. Do you understand?"

"Yes, sir."

"You know that when I'm not around, you're the man of the house, right?

"Yes, sir."

"Well, that responsibility extends beyond the house. That means you're responsible for taking care of your brother even when you're not at home. Do you understand?"

"Yes, sir."

Pat stabbed at the air with his finger. "You and Yuri are Ciccones—and Ciccones stick together. We take care of each other. Are you tracking?"

"Yes, sir," Terry affirmed, unamused.

"Let me hear you say it," Pat demanded.

"I'm tracking, Dad."

"Super." Pat turned his attention to an incredulous-looking Francesca, who repeatedly opened and closed the hand from which the phone was hastily withdrawn. "Okay, here's Mom. I love you, son. Tell Yuri I love him too and that you two are my world."

"Yuri, Dad says he loves you and that you're his world," Terry said aloud. Pat could hear her Yuri squeak in the background. Then Terry spoke into the phone again, "Love you too, Dad."

Pat handed the phone over, and Francesca rushed it to her ear. "Hi, my love," she said immediately.

"Hi, Mom."

"Are you having fun?"

"I guess..."

"Have you made any friends?" she said, watching Pat leave the living room through the garage door.

"Well, I met another boy named Saki. He's pretty cool. We had to get firewood, and we sat together at dinner. And I met a girl named Akiko. She's Sensei's daughter, and she also sat with us at dinner."

"A girl, huh?" Francesca said mischievously. "Pat, Terry met a girl!"

"That's my boy!" Pat yelled.

"Mom!" Terry replied disapprovingly, clearly embarrassed.

"I bet she's cute, huh, honey?"

Terry said his mother's name in a drawn-out, chastising manner.

Okay, that was enough embarrassment for now. She didn't want to overdo it; there would be plenty of time to embarrass him as he matured. "So, what do you think about summer camp?" Francesca asked, moving on.

"It's okay," Terry replied, unconvinced.

Francesca softened like any mother would when her child sounded less than absolutely certain. "What's wrong?"

"I don't think they like us."

"Who doesn't?"

"*Everyone*. They look at us weird and hardly talk to us. I don't think they like us because we're not Japanese—just like the kids in school."

"I doubt that, honey," Francesca asserted, trying to reassure him. "Why else would Mr. Omiyoshu bring you out there?"

"Mom..." Terry paused, and Francesca could feel his anxiety through the phone. It made her feel ashamed that she couldn't be there to console him. "The grandmaster," Terry started again, "just stared at us like he was mad. I don't think we're welcome here. I don't know why Sensei brought us."

Francesca tried to clear the apprehension in her by saying, "Well, Yuri doesn't seem to notice anything."

130

"Mom, Yuri wouldn't notice a marching band in the middle of the night…"

Francesca pursed her lips as she decided on what she should say next. "Where is Mr. Omiyoshu now?" Perhaps, she thought, she should call him and explain to him how Terry was feeling. Terry, after all, had been dealing with mistreatment from Japanese natives for years and tended to feel ostracized.

"I don't know. I haven't seen him for hours."

"Really?"

"Yes, ma'am."

"I don't know how I feel about that." She was definitely going to call Kintake. "Tell you what, get some sleep and call me in the morning, and we can see if things have improved. Okay?

"They're not going to get better, Mom."

"You don't know that, honey. Be positive."

Terry didn't say anything.

"Okay, get some sleep, and we'll talk in the morning before me and Dad leave."

"Yes, ma'am."

"I love you."

"I love you too, Mom."

Francesca pressed *end* and sat quietly staring at the phone for a moment before opening her contacts list and scrolling down to Kintake's name. She opened his profile, hit *call*, and placed the phone to her ear. The electronic operator asked her to wait while she was connected to her party. Then it began to ring. The sound of a phone ringing outside suddenly started. Her eyes flicked to the open windows near the front door. Then there was a knock.

She ended the call, stood to her feet, and made her way to the door; the phone outside chirped twice more and then went silent.

Pat came into the doorway from the garage. "Is there someone at the door?"

"Yeah," she replied suspiciously.

"Were you expecting someone?"

"Nope, but I'll get it," she said as she reached the front door. Pat lost interest and went back into the garage. Francesca looked through the peephole—it was Kintake and Mr. Oharu. What the hell was going on? Why was Kintake here and not at the summer camp with the boys?

She unlocked the door and pulled it open. Kintake, wearing a plaid shirt and denim pants, smiled at her warmly through the glass of the storm door. Mr. Oharu wore his usual jovial expression.

"Mr. Omiyoshu, Mr. Oharu, this is rather unexpected." Francesca unlocked the storm and pushed it open. "I thought you were at the summer camp with my sons," she said to Kintake

"Mrs. Ciccone, I have most urgent news for you. May we come in?"

"What's wrong?"

Kintake gestured through the door. "May we?"

"Yes, come in."

"Thank you," Kintake said, stepping out of his shoes and leaving them on the patio. Oharu did the same and passed through the door. Kintake turned and closed the door behind him.

"Who is it?" Pat called from the garage.

"It's Mr. Omiyoshu and Mr. Oharu!" She turned back to the men and folded her arms. Okay—what's this about? Why are you not with the boys?"

"You must understand, Mrs. Ciccone, what I am about to say to is sacred and must never be repeated."

Francesca shrugged and showed him her hands. "Repeat what? What're you talking about? You're scaring me."

"Promise me."

"Promise you what?"

"Promise me."

"Fine," she said in resignation, dropping her arms to her side. "I promise—"

Once Francesca's arms were down, Kintake moved with such speed that she didn't have time to flinch. He whipped his tanto out of his sleeve and jammed the blade through her breastbone. There was considerable resistance at first, but once he cracked the sternum enough, the blade went in easy and came out even easier. Blood erupted from the hole like a geyser under pressure. She croaked and called for Pat, but it came out as a gurgle. Then Kintake plunged the

132

knife in an arc into the side of her neck, giving it a yank once the knife settled to the hilt; blood spattered the wall in a fan.

*   *   *

Pat was through the door and into the kitchen with purpose, calling to Francesca. She had said that Kintake and Oharu were at the door, but that didn't make any sense since Kintake was in the middle of the island at a summer camp with the boys and Oharu was where Japanese diplomatic fat cats go during the summer months. Then he heard choking sounds. He came into the hall and found Francesca slumped against the wall, surrounded by an amoebic-creeping pool of blood and a fan of crimson on the wall next to her. He barely had a chance to react before he was attacked by swift movement from his flank—a freight train struck the side of his face, and then a wrecking ball sent him sprawling through the dining room.

Pat turned end over end, both physically and emotionally, as he crashed into the pantry. He looked up and saw Kintake bearing down on him—Oharu was even further back, watching. Pat ducked low and shot to the right, out of the way of Kintake's foot, but Kintake was already on him. Pat took a kick to the back of his leg, followed by several blows to the side of his head. He staggered, trying to clear his vision, and raised his guard. All he could see was a blurred apparition.

Pat slung several punches at Kintake, but Kintake was out of the way before the first one reached full extension. He backed up to the table, giving Pat a wide berth, and allowed Pat a moment to gather himself. Kintake wanted to savor this.

"What'd you do to my wife?" Pat roared.

"Remember, Mr. Ciccone, when you came to my school the first time? Well, I never expressed to you how you dishonored me in front of my students. I am here to take that honor back."

Pat stuttered. He didn't know what to say. The grief of seeing his wife's lifeless body, the pain in his face and side, the recounting of an event three years earlier, none of it made sense. None of it.

"I will take it back with your life."

Kintake smashed Pat's jaw with a thunderous roundhouse. The force of it crushed the socket and sent Pat to the floor. Then Kintake was on top of him. "Your wife's death was swift." He struck Pat with his fist. "But yours, Mr. Ciccone, will not be." He struck Pat again. "Honor cannot simply be returned; it must be harvested." He struck again. "I am Shinobi; I cannot live with dishonor."

He struck Pat again.

And again.

And again.

Until Pat's face was mangled and dented and blood flowed from every hole and orifice.

Chapter Eight: Watery Grave

A Shinobi bears true faith in the wisdom of the Jonin and strays not. Allow not doubt to break the bonds of the clans. Respect all Shinobi, for each carries with them the wisdom of the ancestors.
The Fourth Mandate, translated from Ninpo.

The Tarragona Bay. Five miles from the coast. Tarragona, Spain. Today.

Maintaining a watchful eye on a few faint, dancing lights on the horizon, Terry set the engine of his ten-foot craft to idle and turned it to port, placing the bow up-current and pointing out into the darkness of the Mediterranean.

Terry appreciated the silence of the open ocean; it made him feel light years away and gave him time to reflect. There was no hustle out here, no traffic, no email, no media. It was just Terry and Ninpo. Seemed like it had been forever since he'd had a quiet moment like this with his thoughts. When had the last time been? Perhaps while lying in a field well outside of the village border, taking time away from the strictness of the Fujibayashi.

Had it really been that long? That had been nearly fifteen years ago.

He also remembered the harsh punishment he'd received for being gone; had the scars on his shoulders from the lashes he took—it had been worth it, though. He'd had time to think then, and he had time to think now. And it was the past that was boiling in his thoughts, sins that plagued him with guilt. He had been brooding for months as he'd dealt with a fit of depression, and it was straining the paper-thin patience of his brother. But the dark, sleepy ocean took all that away from him and set it adrift to somewhere else—at least for the time being.

Terry searched Ninpo's mandates for wisdom into dealing with depression but found none. It was surprising—and a bit disappointing— that a culture that had been founded during a time of severe political strife and rebellion and that based its existence on the conduct of asymmetric warfare hadn't devised a technical means of coping with the emotional injury that came with the seriousness of being Shinobi. Perhaps Terry was missing something implicit to the mandates, though. Perhaps adherence to conviction was therapy in its own right. Perhaps he had begun to slip in his devotion and needed to realign and to reprioritize. Easier said than done. He'd need something prolific to shake him out of his melancholy.

Or was it dishonor that he felt rather than depression?

The mouse-like alarm on his watch chirped—1:13 AM local time—and shook him free of his drift. He set himself to purpose, checking his gear one last time, after he silenced it. He began with the mask and snorkel hanging from a carabineer attached to his shoulder, looking it over. Then he moved on to his wetsuit, flotation, oxygen tank, weighted harness, and dive fins. Everything on his body was in order, so he pulled out a waterproof bag that he had stowed underneath the bench. He unzipped it and drew out his night vision goggles, placing them over his eyes, pulling the strap over the back of his head, and toggling the power on.

Faint dancing lights on the horizon suddenly materialized into a grainy green-on-green feed of a towering mega-yacht backed by a green-black oceanic horizon. The yacht was a mobile mansion that sported decorative lights all around its waterline, a pool on the forecastle, and four weather decks dedicated to entertainment. There was even a helicopter pad on the afterdeck. Three lower decks were staterooms, maintenance, and engineering as well as a small boat dock—a convenient place for Yuri to swim up and board the vessel.

Terry keyed his microphone. "**I'm in position**," he said. He had been waiting for the yacht's course to stabilize.

"**Currently tailing the target**" was Yuri's reply and not what Terry wanted to hear.

"**Well, cut it out! You'll make him suspicious!**"

"**How about you let me work?**" Yuri bubbled into the mic. Certainly, it was imprudent to hover over a target, but he was just trying to add a little thrill. Could a guy want some thrill once in a while? Besides, the likelihood of the target realizing Yuri as a threat was about as likely as finding a one-night stand in a nunnery. After all, Yuri was a professional—a tiger skulking through tall grass, trying to close within a hair's breadth of its prey—and the target was inebriated and high by the look of it.

Yuri had boarded the vessel via its at-sea dock thirty minutes prior. Terry had dropped Yuri off in the no-wake segment of the channel, from where Yuri was able to swim—sprint, really—to the yacht and grab hold. From there, Yuri held on to an overboard drain pipe until the yacht was into the main thoroughfare and could make way. Once the vessel started to pick up speed, Yuri slid aft, hand over hand, until he reached the dock and pulled himself out of the water. Once he was onboard, he made his way to his *insider's* stateroom to change and suit up.

When he arrived, he stripped his wetsuit off and had to take a moment to rest; the forty minutes that he had spent hanging from the side was brutal with the wave action and speed. He didn't look forward to doing that again. How was it, though, that Yuri always ended up hanging from the bottom of cars or the side of boats? He was sure Terry had designed it that way. Then he noticed how messy the room was. One thing was for sure, his *insider* was a first-class slob, since she had only been onboard a couple of hours. No matter, he needed her to be good at what he had hired her for, not for cleanliness.

Once he had gotten his wind back, he climbed into the tuxedo that his *insider* had brought aboard for him—it was hanging in the closet. Once dressed, he ventured out into the party to track down their target and figure out how he was going to get him into the small boat with Terry.

The job required that Terry and Yuri make the hit look like an accident and leave no connection to any party involved. The agreed-upon payment was $500,000, with twenty percent of the total payment upfront.

The target was an ultra-partisan political-upstart Eurocrat named Vyasa Henchoz. He had built a reputation within the European Union's Parliament for leading aggressive campaigns and intimidating opposition. His constituency reflected his policies: they either loved him or hated him. He won elections by landslides, mustered support in areas where he had seemed to have none, and pushed legislation that was initially doomed to failure. It seemed that everything he touched turned to gold, and many Eurocrats rallied to his side in hopes of finding an ally in his political entrepreneurship.

Those that opposed his platform believed that his success was, in part, due to corruption, and they searched for information that they could use to shake his reputation as the next election approached. Months—and hundreds of thousands of dollars—later, the opposition found the information they *didn't* want: Vyasa Henchoz was actually a former banker as well as an information broker and financier for the Yugoslav Civil War who operated under the alias of Miloradovic and helped engineer the siege of Sarajevo and the extermination of the Kosovars. He'd allegedly severed his ties with the Serbian front and silenced anyone that could identify him once things took a downturn. He'd faded into the European public—hiding in plain sight—only to resurface on the new European political landscape. In short, the skeletons that Henchoz's opponents had found in his closet were quite literal, and they feared the backlash of exposing him.

In spite of their fear, political obligation required the opposition to remove Henchoz from office, if not because he'd conspired to commit genocide, at least to deliver retribution to those Europeans who'd been killed by his ideology. To that end, two Croatian Eurocrats sought to employ Terry and Yuri.

They—well, Terry—met with the Croatian officials at a coffee shop in Beirut, where they negotiated a contract and payment. Unbeknownst to them, Yuri sat at an adjacent table, with a concealed, albeit drawn, weapon in the event the meeting went awry and the brothers needed to kill the officials and beat a hasty retreat—one could never be too careful with powerbrokers. Fortunately, everything went according to plan.

Never the type to procrastinate, the brothers got to work immediately. Terry went to Strasbourg, France, to collect information at the EU Parliament, and Yuri went to Salou, Spain, to collect information at Henchoz's residence.

They sifted through truckloads of information until they were able to piece together a telling dossier about Henchoz that was relevant to their job. What they found was that Henchoz frequently threw lavish parties on his yacht, which consequently had a nightly operating overhead that could purchase enough food to feed starving populations of small countries for days. With all the alcohol and substance abuse, it was the perfect setting to stage an accidental death—drowning would be ideal. They could throw him overboard and drown him without leaving signs of a struggle. All Terry and Yuri needed to do was appropriate a copy of the invitation to the upcoming event, board the vessel once it got underway, and make the kill.

Additionally, the brothers noted that Henchoz had a weakness for blondes—the tall, busty, promiscuous type that lacked limits. Yuri recalled seeing a ton of just those types of professionals when he'd been in Dubai once. He made some phone calls and contracted a tall, Russian type named Sacha. Terry transferred half the money to her immediately, promising to complete the transaction once she had reached the terms of her employment, and flew her to Tarragona, Spain. Meanwhile, Yuri pulled some strings and pushed some extra money into the hands of one of the party staff to add Sacha to the guest list. She was told that the party was a celebration for Henchoz and that she was his gift; they also instructed her to carry a tuxedo onboard and keep it in the closet of her stateroom.

Once Yuri was dressed and moving about the decks, it didn't take him long to spot Sacha; she looked every bit as delicious as her pictures claimed. She was draped in a white evening gown with gold trimming and red stilettos and stood at the far end of the deck politely acknowledging everyone that addressed her, sometimes two or three at a time. Then Yuri spotted Henchoz at the other end of the deck tending to his guests. Yuri slithered through the sea of people in his direction. But as Yuri approached within striking distance, Henchoz broke off his conversation suddenly and angled towards the restroom. Well, Yuri couldn't kill the guy, even if the bathroom was a perfect place to make the hit, so he decided that he'd have a little fun and play a little cat and mouse to pass the time. He wasn't exactly sure how he was going to make the hit happen—perhaps he'd have to extract Henchoz from Sasha's bed before sunrise—but he'd make it happen soon enough.

There was an industrial *swoosh* of the toilet flushing followed by the *click* of a stall door's lock, and Henchoz exited a restroom stall wiping his nose vigorously. Yuri was standing at the sink opposite the stall, adjusting the bowtie of his tuxedo and watching Henchoz in the mirror as he'd finished recharging his narcotic fix in the stall. Henchoz approached the adjacent sink and started the flow.

"Beautiful night, no?" Henchoz said in French, politely acknowledging Yuri. Henchoz was a fifty-two-year-old balding man of Serbian descent who stood an easy six foot three inches and weighed in at an out-of-shape two hundred ten pounds. He wore a navy-blue suit and blood-red tie.

Yuri looked at Henchoz in the mirror—his icy-blue eyes overflowing with menace—and replied in French with a smile, "To die for."

Henchoz left the bathroom for the main floor, and Yuri dried his hands.

"**To die for**?" Terry's voice, dripping with sarcasm, crackled over the radio. "**What is this, an action-drama? Are you foreshadowing?**"

"Dude, drink Drāno."

Yuri exited the restroom to get eyes back on his target, but it seemed that Sacha was already doing that for him. Henchoz and Sacha made eye contact for the briefest of moments—eye contact that spoke volumes.

Game on, Yuri screamed inside his head. A wave of mirth rippled through his body, and his jaw muscles flexed with elation. Now he just had to bide his time, so he grabbed a spot at a standing table and enjoyed the show.

Henchoz made his way from the portside of the bar area to centerline as he greeted and exchanged formalities with his myriad guests: celebrities, politicians, undisclosed businessmen, etc. He attempted to be discreet, glancing at Sacha occasionally. Sacha, however, did not exercise the same subtlety. She barely paid any attention to any of her potential suitors, dedicating the whole of her attention to tracking Henchoz with her eyes. Finally, Sacha grew tired of waiting and approached Henchoz as he spoke to the leader of the Moroccan Action Party, saying something in Russian.

He excused himself from the conversation and then said in French, "I'm sorry, I don't speak Russian."

"Well, fortunately for you, darling, I do speak French."

"Splendid."

There was a moment of silence between them while Henchoz hung on the sound of her heavy Russian accent.

"Forgive me. I'm Vyasa Henchoz," he said, extending his hand.

She clasped it. "I know who you are."

"Is that so?"

She looked directly into him as she sipped her champagne. "You've been watching me all night, Monsieur Henchoz."

"You think so?" he countered.

"Tell me you weren't, and I'll walk away."

"Okay," he conceded. "I'm guilty."

"Do you like what you see, Monsieur Henchoz.

"So far. I don't believe I got your name."

"Sacha."

"Naturally." He paused. "I don't believe we've ever met. Are you someone's date?"

"I am, Monsieur Henchoz. I am your date."

He chortled. "Please, just call me Vyasa. What do you think of it?" he asked, gesturing to the yacht and the party.

"It's very big."

He smiled. "Yes, it is."

Sacha looked over her shoulder in the direction of the bar. "You should buy me a drink."

"Well, I don't have to buy anything—I own everything here. Just tell me what *you* want."

"No, Vyasa—not everything. Not yet."

"Perhaps we should get some fresh air, instead, yeah?"

Oh, this was perfect! Yuri couldn't have asked for this to play out better. Sacha's charms had hooked Henchoz in no time flat. She was every bit the consummate professional entertainer. Yuri did not exactly consider prostitution to be the most reputable profession, but who was he to judge? After all, he killed people for a living, and she had moved his target into the kill zone for some *alone time* without a struggle. Perhaps he and Terry should offer her a job when all was said and done. Now Yuri needed an approach.

"He took the bait," Yuri said, keying the mic. "**And the bait is goddamn good.**"

"**What are we looking like on time?**"

"**Not long if we're lucky. Brood or something. I'll let you know when we're good.**"

Yuri slinked his way through the gulf of tuxedos and evening gowns. His eyes fixed the bar lead, who was robotically filling orders and placing them on trays. Yuri swooped in to grab a tray, but the bar lead intercepted Yuri's hand. "Wrong one, mate. Pay attention," he demanded in a heavy Cockney accent, indicating a nearby tray.

Yuri set his tray down, picked up the one the man had pointed out, and then disappeared into the crowd, holding it in one hand and using the other to lead block. He passed through the door leading onto the dimly lit catwalk where Henchoz and Sacha were making nice.

"**The target's right where I want him,**" Yuri whispered. "**This couldn't have gone easier. Get ready.**"

"**Don't be premature. If the time isn't right—**"

"**Hey, I'm fucking this goat. *You* just hold its head.**"

"**Whatever. Don't mess this up.**"

"**Shut up, you. Get ready.**"

Henchoz was so completely enraptured by the exquisite rise and fall of Sacha's cleavage that he didn't notice Yuri creep up. Sacha hadn't noticed either.

"Wine for you and the lady, monsieur?" Yuri asked in French with a terribly American accent, watching both of them jump at the sound of his voice.

"You have the devil's timing, lad," Henchoz aspirated. Both he and Sacha placed their hands on their chests and laughed.

"I'm not sure if that's a good thing or a bad thing, monsieur."

"That would depend on how strong the liquor is on your tray."

"Only the best for you, Monsieur Henchoz," replied Yuri, passing him a champagne glass. He took the glass, sipped it, and then asked for something a little stronger to chase it. Yuri asked what he'd prefer and then whipped around to go back to the bar to fill the order, but he was stopped dead in his tracks when his abrupt movement caused the tray to teeter and spill all over Sacha. She was outraged! Freezing alcohol

142

stained her vestment and ran down her cleavage! Yuri apologized fervidly to the curse-spewing Sacha. Then she stormed off to the bathroom to attempt a rescue of her extremely expensive—albeit likely ruined—dress.

Yuri watched her leave and then looked back at an incensed Henchoz before dropping down to clean the glasses. "I'm terribly sorry, monsieur. It was only a mistake."

"I should have you thrown overboard." There was the real Vyasa Henchoz—Yuri knew he was in there somewhere. And how ironic that Henchoz considered *overboard* to be effective disposal.

Like lightning, Yuri found his feet and whipped a hand at Henchoz's throat, connecting just below the chin with the knife-edge. Henchoz lurched and grasped his neck. Yuri planted his palm against Henchoz's face and pushed him into the lifelines. Henchoz clawed at the cables to regain his balance and keep himself from falling overboard. He tried to yell but couldn't because his larynx was temporarily paralyzed from the strike. Yuri grabbed Henchoz, driving his arms outward first before grabbing hold of his suit, and heaved him over the side. Henchoz flopped against the side, holding onto the lifeline for dear life.

Yuri rolled his eyes and kicked Henchoz's hand, forcing him to let go.

Henchoz fell. Nearly three stories. Landing on his back in the water. Hard. Huffing all of his air.

Henchoz finally surfaced, undoubtedly stunned by both the impact and the temperature. He could scarcely cry out with the waves forcing themselves down his throat and the Venturi effect throttling him against the hull as the yacht steamed at ahead-quarter.

Yuri flung the tray overboard like a Frisbee and then gawked at his handiwork. *Man, this couldn't have gone any better*. He'd thought for sure that he was going to have to get creative and spirit Henchoz out of his stateroom, down the passageways, and over the side without anyone noticing. While not impossible, it wouldn't nearly have been as clean. Of course, having to be creative would have been better sport. Whatever, it was done, and that was all that mattered. Score one for Ninpo.

Yuri bent over and pulled a waterproof infrared strobe light from his sock. "**He's in the water. I'm marking him with a strobe**." Yuri ensured the infrared filter was secured tightly and tossed it in Henchoz's general direction.

"**I see it**," Terry replied.

Henchoz finally pulled himself together and realized that he was alone in sixty-something degree water in the middle of the Mediterranean with his yacht steaming away. To make matters worse, he was not a great swimmer, and it was taking a sizable amount of effort just to keep his head above the water. The frigid water made his breathing labored, and the anxiety of being up to his chin in blackness put him on the edge of panic. This couldn't be happening; he didn't want to drown! He had to get out of the water!

He screamed until he tasted blood mixed with salt water in his mouth. No one on the vessel could hear him over the festivities. How long would it be before they noticed he wasn't onboard? Would they search the boat for him? Would Sacha notice that he'd disappeared? He looked fearfully in all directions for perhaps another boat, but he saw nothing. He never thought it would end this way, never in a million years. He was going to die alone, adrift at sea, and nobody would find him. Nobody would have an answer for his wife and his children.

Then he heard the sputter of what sounded like an engine. He was sure of it! The ocean didn't sound like that—the distinct growl and mechanical thumping of pistons.

He kicked and pulled, wheeling himself around toward the sound, coughing up the water he ingested. Was it a boat? It had to be.

Out of the darkness drifted a small boat pitching casually on the aftershocks left by the yacht. Henchoz, revitalized by the possibility of rescue, screamed and splashed, trying to gain the attention of the boat's pilot. The pilot shined a brief light at Henchoz and then steered the boat alongside him. Henchoz seized the side of the boat and coughed his appreciation and relief. The pilot reached down and heaved Henchoz aboard by his jacket and pants.

Henchoz rolled onto his back, groaning and coughing to clear the seawater from his mouth and throat. "Oh God!" he wheezed.

"Thank you—thank you so much! I thought—I thought I was going to die! Thank you!"

"No problem," the pilot assured him, speaking English. "It's no problem."

Henchoz's faced wrinkled with confusion, not fully recovered from the fall, the fear, and the cold. He coughed some more before saying, "You understand French?"

"Yeah," the pilot replied in English again, "I just don't speak it well."

"You're American?" Henchoz spoke English now, recognizing the accent.

The pilot nodded and opened the throttle, starting off into the inky blackness.

Henchoz sat back, finally able to relax his body. His mind was still racing, though, wondering if the crew had realized that he had fallen overboard. He couldn't believe that had happened. Wait—that waiter had pushed him overboard—deliberately. The waiter had attacked him. Was it a hit? Was the waiter a hired killer? How had he gotten onboard? Never mind, he'd address all that once he got back to land. What mattered right this second was that he was alive. Retaliation would come later.

Henchoz noticed that the pilot was wearing a wetsuit and had an oxygen tank strapped to his back. "What're you doing out here?"

"Diving. What're you doing out here?"

"I fell off my yacht. I was pushed, actually."

"Pushed?"

"Yes, I think it was an assassination attempt."

Terry slammed the throttle closed. "An assassination attempt? Are you somebody important or something?"

"Yes—and you could say that."

"Well, it's a good thing I just happened to be out here."

"Yes, it is. I'm sorry, but I didn't get your name?"

"Mamushi."

"I'm sorry? What is it?"

"Mamushi. It's the name of the Japanese viper spirit."

"Well, Mamushi, I owe you a huge debt of gratitude," Henchoz replied, beginning to wonder why the boat had come to a halt. He hoped that it hadn't run out of gas. He just wanted to be on land.

"Is there something wrong?" asked Henchoz.

"Not at all."

"Why are you stopping, Mamushi?"

"Because," Terry said, fastening the Velcro on his neoprene gloves, "this is your stop." Terry lunged from his seat, barreling Henchoz over the side.

Henchoz felt the sudden rush of cold and the taste of salt again. He flailed wildly as Terry snaked his way around behind Henchoz and grabbed two handfuls of Henchoz's clothes. Terry, breathing from the regulator, kicked deeper and deeper into the water, dragging a thrashing Henchoz.

Henchoz spun, whirled, and kicked. His elbow struck Terry on the side of the head, cracking the seal of his mask. Cold water poured in, and Terry released Henchoz, disappearing into the murk and gloom of the sea.

Henchoz convulsed, his lungs burning for air. His vision had become a tunnel, the edges merging into the blackness of the ocean. Unconsciousness whispered in his ear, but Henchoz refused to listen. He clawed and kicked toward the surface, willing himself to remain conscious just a little longer.

Just as his fingertips broke the surface and his lungs were a half-second from taking in fresh air, Terry shot out of the darkness, struck Henchoz, getting his arms around Henchoz's waist and dragging him under. The force of the initial strike forced Henchoz to breach for a brief second, but he still couldn't manage to inhale air—only water. Terry rolled over the top of Henchoz and used their momentum to drive them downwards.

Terry was horribly annoyed and frustrated by Henchoz's escape and gripped his clothing like a vice this time. He tried not to be as ruthless as his brother, but that's what Terry got for being cordial. He was inclined to grab Henchoz by the neck but could ill afford to leave marks that could show signs of struggle; a struggle would only belie the truth of the situation. In any case, Terry was not going to afford Henchoz another chance at escape.

146

Henchoz tried to hold what breath remained, but his breathing impulse was beginning to override his command. He tried over and over to break free, but his strength was leaving, being replaced with lethargy. This was it. His vision was almost completely black, and his body was numb; even the fire in his lungs had gone out. This was the end; he knew it. Then his mouth shot open, and his diaphragm drew downwards, compelling his lungs open. His fingers became hooks, and his legs spasmed. With a sudden jerk, Henchoz stopped moving.

Terry shook him just to be sure that he was dead. Satisfied, Terry surfaced, spit out the regulator, and paddled to the boat, which hadn't drifted far. He pulled himself aboard and keyed the mic. "**It's done. Are you ready**?"

"**Yeah, let me know when you're five minutes away**," Yuri answered. "**I'll go overboard when you are. Don't take forever either; the water isn't exactly warm. No one has even noticed he's gone. The prostitute has been looking for him, but that's about it.**"

"**Perfect. I'm on my way.**"

Chapter Nine: Death Is The Only Certainty

Suzuka Mountains. Mie Prefecture, Japan. Eighteen years ago.

The rain was coming down hard, making the slopes of the mountains that cradled the village treacherous as Terry, Saki, and Akiko scaled them. Saki and Akiko were accustomed to the unforgiving rise and fall of the terrain as well as the weather at these altitudes. Terry, however, was not. He was, though, starting to adapt to the environment, and his ability to keep pace was improving day by day. Terry was hardly as athletic as Saki and Akiko. They could leap tremendous distances for their sizes and scuttle along thin outcroppings and ravines deftly like aspiring tightrope walkers. They had amazing upper-body strength, allowing them to hoist up to and around overhangs in no time, whereas Terry spent much of his time trying to negotiate shear surfaces with their disagreeable instruction or having to navigate a less treacherous secondary route. The handholds and footholds were harder to grasp firmly, and the sharp turns were harder to negotiate, but with youth came a daredevil spirit and limitless energy.

Daylight was fading rapidly—what daylight was available from behind the electricity-hurling monsters thundering and shaking the mountainsides—and they were trying to make it back to the village before sunset. They were not allowed to be outside the village periphery after dusk and did not want to violate their curfew if they could help it. The rain set them back a little, the persistent downpour obscuring their view, but it didn't slow their pace.

"**Guys, slow down**!" Terry panted.

"**We can't**!" Akiko yelled over her shoulder, "**If we get back after dark, we'll be punished**!"

Violating curfew meant, if they were lucky, a reprimand from any number of Jonin and a host of chores added to their already large daily list. If they were unlucky, they could expect that the kōchō would demand that they were punished. The kōchō didn't take keenly to dissonance nor disobedience and would punish severely for offenses. Punishment took various forms, but all of them involved pain. The last person to be punished had been made to hold hot coals in front of the entire village. The burns had been horrendous, and the smell had been even worse. The children didn't want to be punished, so they gave it everything they had to make it back in time.

They tore down the ridgeline that snaked its way along the river that bordered the village, but the ridge climbed again to even higher peaks that bordered a saddle. Climbing it, while necessary, was just going to add time to their return and would make them late. The best choice they had was to climb down the ridge and travel up the bank of the river, but they were unsure whether the face was stable enough to climb down. Saki decided that he would chance the ascent up the ridge. He reasoned that they could make up lost time on the descent and then pretend that they were playing in the goat pen until dusk.

Akiko didn't see it that way. "**Saki, we're not going to make it that way. Terry isn't fast enough.**"

Terry was still loping down the mountainside toward them.

"**What do we do?**" she asked

"**We're going to have to follow the river, then.**"

"**Saki, what if we fall?**"

"**We won't fall...**"

Just then, Terry arrived, struggling to breathe.

"**...because we're going to jump.**"

Akiko looked at Saki, mortified. Terry swung his head between them. Saki's face was determined.

"**That's a long way down.**" she said.

"**If we don't, we won't make it back on time, and we're going to be punished, Akiko.**"

"**Wait—you guys aren't really thinking about jumping are you?**" Terry's breathing was finally settling. "**What's the big deal, anyway? There's nothing out here.**"

"**No, Terry, we're not going to jump.**"

"**Good, because that's a long—**"

Saki shoved Terry, and he went over the side screaming "fall." He wasn't graceful, nor was his water entry. They'd never even asked him if he could swim. Saki and Akiko went over the side shortly after. Their fall was precise and elegant. The same couldn't be said for Terry.

The three pre-teens hustled along the bank toward the village. The way through the forest was darkening as daylight faded, but strobes of lightning lit their path towards an opening in the perimeter fence.

Through the waning light, Saki, in the lead, could make out a villager at the fence waving to them vigorously. Saki slowed as he approached, apprehensive as to whether the Jonin and the kōchō had sent the adult to retrieve them for sentencing.

Saki swore that they had made it back in time, but the kōchō was not given to leniency nor technicalities. Honestly, Saki was scared, and so was Akiko when she caught up seconds later; Terry, panting heavily, wasn't too far behind. The villager, an older man, perhaps in his mid- to late-sixties, dressed in stained overalls and a tattered plaid button-down, and with a gray, balding head, insisted that the children follow.

They all hurried single file through the mud of the rutted field to a far corner that opened into the village rim, where another villager, a lady this time, wearing a khaki-colored pants and tunic and with her hair in a saturated up-do, was waiting for the man. She bid the children follow her just the same and darted off towards the village center; the man returned to his post along the fence. As the woman and children rounded the corner of a cottage, they could make out a figure standing in the rain and masses of villagers huddled in a chaotic, half-moon shape behind him. As the children and the leader drew closer, they finally could identify the Shinobi-no-mon and several elders and villagers encircling a dirty blonde child—Yuri. The woman came to halt a short distance away, and then the children followed her lead as they arrived one at a time. Saki and Akiko stopped and regarded Terry while he puzzled over his brother.

Yuri clutched the grandmaster's leg, shaming the rain with hysterical tears and the thunder with grief.

Hanzo dropped to his knees, splattering mud all over his robe, and beckoned Terry with a hand and a weak nod. The woman softly instructed that he obey the grandmaster, and Akiko pushed him toward Hanzo by the shoulder.

Terry took several steps through the deepening mud before stopping again and hovering just out of reach. He heard a drawn-out plea from Yuri but could scarcely make out what he was saying through the hysterics and the rumbling storm. In between the thunder, more words became clear: *Please! Mom! No!* Terry edged even closer, glancing over his shoulder at Saki and Akiko, who watched him anxiously with equally confused looks.

Hanzo beckoned Terry more vigorously. Apprehension made Terry's feet heavy, but he compelled them forward anyway. Yuri howled that he wanted to see his mother, and the misery in his voice made Terry's stomach boil with anxiety. He'd never heard such unfettered anguish in his brother's voice.

Terry was close enough now that he could hear Hanzo say hoarsely, "**Terry, I am most sorry**." This was the first time Hanzo had spoken to him in the month that they had been in the village. "**It is with great regret that I must tell you that you will not be returning to your parents. I just received news from Omiyoshu Sensei that your parents are gone. Their plane crashed into the sea a couple of weeks ago.**"

Terry's face was awash with confusion, then disbelief. Then it became a mask of abject horror. His mouth moved, saying *what*, but nothing came out. He was in a tunnel suddenly, and the world was crammed inside with him. The walls of the tunnel were tightening—closing in. He could feel the pressure increasing. Hanzo was saying something else, but Terry couldn't hear him. Terry could only see Hanzo's lips moving. In fact, everyone's lips were moving. He was surrounded on all sides; they were closing in just like the tunnel. Terry didn't know what to do; he could barely breathe. Several villagers rushed over to console him. Their hands were on him, but he couldn't feel them. Yuri's screaming pulsed in Terry's ears, but he couldn't hear Yuri, he just felt Yuri's grief pounding against his eardrums. Yuri reached out for Terry—the walls closing in even more. Then he could make out Kintake standing beneath the awning of a cottage with a hardened, unsympathetic stare and apathetic, folded arms. And at that moment, Terry's world exploded—everything caught fire and burned—and Terry bolted out of the crowd. The Shinobi-no-mono reached out to stop Terry, but Terry slipped his grasp and ran for the fence and then out into the howling storm and the dark forest.

Saki and Akiko felt powerless, but they couldn't just let Terry run out into the forest by himself; he didn't know the area well enough. Akiko shot Saki a compelling look, and he nodded. Then both children sprinted off in Terry's direction. The villagers nearby tried to stop them, but they were no more successful than Hanzo had been with Terry. The villagers, however, gave chase, trying to stop the children from running out into the hazardous storm and the treacherous countryside.

Kintake, still standing at his dry perch amid a throng of elders and retainers, sucked his teeth contemptuously at the villagers ambling about in disarray. The old man—*Hanzo*—had once again showed his ineptitude at leadership, unable to even control children. He was the reason the Shinobi were falling apart. And Kintake wasn't sure, or comfortable, with Hanzo's sudden compassion toward the two American boys when just yesterday he had been vehemently opposed to them. Suddenly, when Kintake had brought him the news of the untimely death of the boys' parents, Hanzo had become sensitive to their needs. That didn't make sense. That wasn't what Kintake had anticipated. That was not part of the plan. And Kintake wouldn't abide Hanzo's new pets if that's what they were. They were Kintake's project, not Hanzo's. Hanzo had a profound way ruining everything for Kintake—he always had.

In a dark corner of his mind, Kintake hoped that being out in this rain would cause the Shinobi-no-mono to catch pneumonia and that he'd die from it. It wasn't likely considering it was summer, but a man could hope. Kintake contemplated killing Hanzo outright, but that wasn't in the cards since the Fujibayashi and the Momochi would assume foul play at the sudden death of their spiritual messiah, and they'd all be relentless in their investigation. Kintake couldn't afford dissension, and he'd have to consider his options. In the meantime, there was the pressing matter of his daughter and Saki chasing the older of the two Americans through the canyons in the dark of night and in a monstrous thunderstorm. He'd handle that first and then consider what he needed to do in the wake of *this* backfiring.

Kintake gestured to two young-adult males wearing robes and with swords protruding from their belts, and who were standing in the rain nearby, into the forest. They bowed deliberately, gathered several others, and promptly galloped off into the storm after the children.

Kintake regarded Hanzo, Yuri, and the Jonin and villagers in the courtyard. He rubbed the wretched scar on the side of his face thoughtfully before telling his entourage that he was going indoors and not to disturb him until the children were found.

*   *   *

Thunder bellowed, a deafening roar like an angry carnivore; in the sky directly above, lightning cut jagged lines. The storm threatened Terry with impunity. He felt no fear. He felt nothing, only emptiness. It was as if some part of him had disappeared or been destroyed altogether. There was a hole where that something had once been. Terry did not know where he was going; he was just letting his feet do the driving, with fate riding shotgun. He began to round a bend to a low area, thinking he recognized the terrain features. Not that it mattered; he just kept running. He slid down a berm into an area of perfectly aligned trees that materialized into walls of gray that whizzed past him as he sprinted through the torrential gloom. His feet carried him through the mountain forests independent of his mind. He was not sure if his mind was even working; his thoughts were a mess. He was a mess. *Everything* was a mess!

The rain was still coming down in torrents, and the lightning backlit a solemn montage of silhouetted mountains. The wind was howling through the valley, blowing the rain sideways and whipping the trees. Over the noise, Terry heard something faint and strange. It sounded like banging metal. It was rhythmic.

Then Terry's foot caught something, and he came down with a *splat* into the ankle-deep mud. He tried pulling his hand from the mud, but the mud pulled back. Terry overpowered the earth and climbed to his feet, wiping the mud and water from his face, finding himself at the base of the pi-shaped *torii* of the shrine. He waded through the mud towards the threshold of the arch.

Terry heard the sound again and looked over his shoulder, seeing the dark landscape through the static of pouring rain.

Terry started again, marching beneath the *torii*. Beyond it, he could just barely make out the weathered cemetery bisected by the *sandō*. He continued to follow the faint, strange sounds of clashing metal. The grounds around the cemetery and the shrine grabbed at his feet. Despite the wind resisting his movement, despite the rain's attempt at drowning him, the thunder's attempt to deafen him, and the lightning's attempt to terrify him, Terry pushed forward. He followed the distant sound to the *honden*, deep within the confines of the burial ground.

Terry stumbled along the *sandō*, passing the worn wood structures. Terry passed through the *haiden*, unable to take refuge there because of its lack of walls. Just on the other side were slippery stairs that he ascended to the door of the *honden*. He pulled the door open, and it groaned from its age. Over the groans and thunder, Terry could hear faint but sharp clashes of steel and flat war cries. Then they went instantly silent. Terry stood in the sideways rain and beckoned into the midnight antechamber of the honden. No one answered.

"Terry!" he heard several voices call to him over the storm from the opposite direction.

Terry pulled the rotting door shut and disappeared into the darkness to hide. He climbed atop a huge wooden slab etched with kanji off to the right of the stanchions in the middle and huddled into a ball. He could faintly hear them calling to him still, but he refused to answer; he had nothing to say.

Chapter Ten: Nuclear Winter

A Shinobi has power beyond imagination. This power can only be wielded by Shinobi with honor. Shinobi without honor are a cancer that must be incised either by their own hand or another's hand. Only in death can honor be regained. Be vigilant and merciless and bring death to the dishonorable.
The Fifth Mandate, translated from Ninpo.

Trans-Ili Ala-Tau Mountains. One hundred miles south of Uralsk, Kazakhstan. Today.

Terry and Yuri weren't fond of politics, but political contracts tended to be the most lucrative, the most challenging, and most akin to the entanglements for which Ninpo was designed. After all, the ancestor Shinobi were more often than not used as instruments against the political rivals of the Shoguns. Like their classical brethren, Terry and Yuri were called upon to act as political instruments.

The brothers were contacted by NATO authorities to assist in defusing conflict between Russia and Georgia. Specifically, the Ossetes had declared their intent to fully secede from the Georgian state. The government had chosen force instead of diplomacy this time and sought to quell rebellion decisively. In response, the Russian Federation had executed another invasion across Georgian borders to support the secessionists. In the ensuing violence, a radically partisan Georgian group named Rytsari Krasnoy Oseni—*The Knights of the Red Autumn*—or RKO for short, looking for an edge against the superior military might of the Russians, had located and seized a mothballed Soviet nuclear weapons facility buried deep in the remote mountains of the Altai and Trans-Ili Ala-Tau mountain ranges. Their intent was to make weapons out of the existing material to intimidate or attack the Russians and the Ossetes.

More than just the belligerents were fearful of the aggressive move by the RKO. NATO, worried about a non-sovereign, often terrorist-affiliated group entering the world political arena, dispatched special long-range operatives to depose the RKO leadership.

Unfortunately, all but one of the operatives had had their dental remains mailed back to their parent government. The RKO then had claimed that they would detonate a nuclear weapon in an undisclosed location in Europe if the West involved itself again. Seeking a less invasive means to accomplish their desperate goal, at which NATO had failed, authorities contacted Terry and Yuri.

The brothers received a dossier containing intelligence they would need to execute the job and agreed to commence once they received half of the payment.

Their employer required that the acknowledged leader of the RKO and the munitions expert that the RKO employed both be eliminated, as well as the operative's body be located to confirm his status change from MIA to KIA. Terry and Yuri knew that the parent government was trying to tie up loose ends by disassociating its involvement in the Russo-Georgian conflict, which meant that if they found the commando alive, he needed to be eliminated.

After careful review of the intelligence, the imagery, the terrain, and the topography, Terry and Yuri decided to infiltrate by crossing the Kazakhstan border aboard a plane piloted by Tajik smugglers out of Karachi, Pakistan, and parachuting into a drop zone twenty miles north of the facility under the cover of night.

From there, the brothers would hike over the mountain and descend into the valley where the facility was hidden. Besides the infiltration, every phase of the operation had a primary execution tree and a backup execution tree in case the situation did not proceed ideally.

The plan was to gain entry to the facility through the sewage spillway. To that end, Terry and Yuri would have to cut through the ice of the frozen lake, situated to the immediate west of the principal buildings, which was used in the cooling of the facility's nuclear elements. From beneath the ice, they would ascend into the spillway and then proceed through the maintenance access into the facility. Once inside, they'd split so that they could complete multiple objectives simultaneously. That said, Yuri would find any supplies that had been smuggled into the facility by train and destroy them. After which, he would exfiltrate out of the main yard by going over the wall. Terry, for his part, would track down the operative and the high-value targets and eliminate them. Terry would then exfiltrate behind his brother, following his brother's lead.

If things went south, they had devised a solid backup plan. If their entry through the ice was compromised, they would switch gears and low-crawl through the snow to the helicopter pad—a plan they hoped to avoid. Crawling through snow increased the chance of hypothermia and frostbite. Moreover, that area of the facility had shorter walls than other parts, which, if the RKO leaders were worth their salt, meant that that area was more heavily guarded. The backup entry plan, at the very least, would give direct access to the facility even if it would be a bigger pain.

If the spillway entry plan went off without a hitch but the maintenance access was blocked, Terry and Yuri planned to proceed through the ventilation. The shafts were anything but sophisticated, made up entirely of brick and mortar. They snaked throughout the facility like tunnels in a termite mound and were covered at the access points by metal grates.

The exfiltration backup was to go out the way they came in, a situation they wanted to avoid at all costs. Simply put, swimming in was advantageous because they had time to dry off in the spillway. If they swam out, however, they would have no reprieve from the bitter subzero Kazakh winter.

*   *   *

To protect themselves from the elements and to hide from scouts, airborne or otherwise, Terry and Yuri camped on the leeward side of the mountains in a shelter they had erected in less than an hour. They built a fire inside their shelter for warmth, knowing that the smoke would be barely visible since they were downwind of the facility with rising terrain in between. They planned to begin their attack after dusk. Until then, they rested and placed the finishing touches on their plan. Terry massaged his shins while he rehearsed it aloud, allowing Yuri to participate while he busied himself with checking their gear.

"Once we get through the ice," said Terry, "I'm first into the water. I'll find the entrance to the mainline of the spillway. You anchor our cable and follow with the gear."

Yuri moved on in no specific pattern to the rebreathers of their dive equipment.

Terry continued, "If the mainline grate is still in place, we'll set the cutting pylons. When you're ready to arm them, you give the signal."

Yuri's middle finger shot up.

"Real mature."

Yuri cracked a smile; it was the little things that mattered.

Their plan outlined that when they were into the mainline, they'd make their ascent to the spillway. They'd need to be efficient and couldn't afford mistakes. They were using rebreathers and didn't want to bust their submerge time with taking forever to find the mainline or in rigging the cutting materials if the grate was still present. Once they were into the spillway, they'd strip off and hide their wet gear. Then they'd file through the maintenance access into the facility proper with Yuri on point and Terry bringing up the rear. When they were at a safe staging point, they'd make any final adjustments before splitting up.

Terry tapped his finger against the blueprint. "It looks like we can use this point here as the staging point. What is that, a loft?"

Yuri peeled his attention away, limped over to his brother, and leaned over the chart. "Nope—that looks like a catwalk or an observation platform. See?" He brushed Terry's hand aside and tapped it with his finger. "There are the ladders."

"Oh yeah. Alright."

"Might not be worth it. If there are sentries on the roofs nearby, they may spot us. If nothing else, it'll be a pain to haul the rest of the explosives up there."

"Suggestions, then?"

"Audible." Meaning that they'd play it by ear and make a decision once they were planning to exit the vents.

"I knew you'd say that."

Yuri limped back to his inspections. "Then why'd you ask?"

Terry raised a concerned brow. "You okay?" he asked.

"Yeah—why?"

"You're limping. Is the cold bothering your foot?"

"Screw this foot." Yuri's reply came out menacing.

"You know you might want to see a podiatrist."

"Why? I'm not a kid."

Terry glanced around the shelter, confused. "W-what? Kid?" Then confusion turned into disappointment. "Not a pediatrician, numbnuts—a podiatrist—a foot doctor."

"I'm *messing* with you. I know what a podiatrist is. And fuck that, I don't have time for doctors."

Terry laughed. For a moment there, he'd really thought his brother was mildly retarded. "Your foot isn't going to get any better if you don't. Kintake did some pretty serious damage. You've been limping for years when it gets cold."

Yuri didn't look up from his work. "I might just put this foot in Kintake's ass."

"Yeah, because that worked the last time you tried..."

"I might just put this foot and a podiatrist in Kintake's ass."

Terry laughed and went back to planning.

From the staging point, they'd start the clock and go their separate ways. Terry would track and eliminate all three of the targets, which they estimated should take forty-five minutes. Then he'd exit the facility by the time sixty minutes elapsed. Meanwhile, Yuri would find the RKO's supplies and rig them with explosives. They predicted that ten minutes would be sufficient since the satellite imagery showed the supplies imported by and stored in train cars. He'd be complete with setting the explosives once fifty minutes had elapsed, he'd escape by sixty minutes, and detonate by sixty-five.

"Wait," said Yuri, "what happens if you get hung up trying to exit a building?"

Terry's hand went to his chin. "Good point. Tell you what, if I need extra time, I'll chirp you twice on the phone." The *chirp* would instruct Yuri to add five minutes, detonating instead at seventy minutes. After which, the brothers would find a place to bed down before making the three-week hike south out of the mountains.

Terry stuffed the charts and diagrams into his pack and climbed over Yuri to help with the inspection. Yuri grimaced as his brother pushed over his back while using him for support. Terry settled on the other side and started with their snow shoes.

"Let me ask you a question," Yuri demanded without even looking up.

"Shoot," replied Terry.

"You going to tell me what's been going on?"

Terry's head was troubled by something he had been dealing with for months, and Yuri could see it. Terry was irritable and depressed but refused to talk about, not that that was anything new. Getting Terry to talk about his feelings was about as fruitful as finding an undiscovered bikini model in a senior citizen home. But Yuri was going to need to get to the bottom of his brother's malaise if they were going to be successful with their current contract.

"With what?" Terry asked.

"You've been acting real testy."

Terry lifted his head. "Pot. Kettle. The color black. Does any of that ring a bell?"

"I'm supposed to be petulant. I get it from our mother."

"At least you admit it."

"I do admit it. Now I need you to admit that you've been acting real volatile over the past six months."

"Get out of here with that noise."

"Terry, I'm your brother. I can't keep operating like this. Please, talk to me."

"What's there to talk about?"

"Well, for starters, you've been a real bitch to work with lately. Figured we could talk about what's going on?"

"Nothing's going on."

Yuri stopped what he was doing. "C'mon, Ter, that's bullshit, and you know it. Stop being such a little girl and talk to me."

"I've just been dealing with a lot of guilt lately."

"Guilt? Guilt over what? That job in Rio?"

Terry wanted to talk about it but *didn't* want to talk about it at the same time. He needed to get it off of his chest but didn't want to let it go. Unable to make the choice as to which way to go, he chose the status quo—not talking.

"Terry?"

If Terry couldn't talk to his brother, who could he talk to? Being bottled up wasn't only punishing himself, but it was punishing Yuri too.

He was taking the brunt of Terry's torment, and Yuri, at the very least, deserved an explanation. He decided to open up. "I feel really guilt about our retaliation in Israel."

"Are you serious? Terry, it's been like five years."

"See? That's why I didn't say anything." Terry's voice became venomous, regretting being open and wanting to bottle up again.

"Whoa, easy, slick. I was just stating a fact. I wasn't judging you."

"I know. I'm sorry."

"You don't have to apologize. Just talk to me."

"Okay—I know this happened like five years ago, but I just can't let go of the scene." Terry swallowed, trying to dilute the pool of embarrassment in his stomach. "I still see the expression on that girl's face as she looked at me through the window of the burning car—looked into me. Her eyes haunt me; they have ever since."

"Shinobi don't hang onto death, Terry. Death comes for us all."

"True enough, but that doesn't take away the guilt. What we did was wrong. What we did was motivated by revenge, not ethics."

"They attacked us first, Terry. We just returned the favor."

"No. We were foreigners in a foreign war that we had no business being involved in. We were killing not in the name of honor but in the name of an ideal that wasn't our own. We were used, and we let ourselves be used. Surely, you felt it."

"What I feel is that we were young and didn't know exactly what we were doing. We thought that's where we needed to be. We thought the code implied we needed to be there. So, we were wrong." Yuri shrugged. "I'm sure the ancestor Shinobi made mistakes along the way. Ninpo just didn't appear to them overnight. It had to be developed."

"That doesn't make what we did right."

"I'm not saying it is. What I'm saying is that we need to leave it in the past and move forward."

Terry wasn't convinced.

Yuri continued, *"The Shinobi are ministers of justice; their duty is a righteous one. A Shinobi must execute his duty swiftly and precisely at all costs or be dishonored. At all costs, Terry."*

"What we administered wasn't justice; it was vengeance. We were driven by pride, not duty. We wanted to satisfy ourselves, not the universe. I think our honor is in question." Terry stared at his hands. "The result: dead children and crippling guilt."

Yuri went over and sat next to his brother. "I got news for you, bro, we aren't the first Shinobi to let our pride get the best of us. And we—"

Terry cut in: "Yuri—"

"Let me finish," Yuri said, blocking Terry just the same. "We'll find a way to make it right. I don't feel any guilt towards it. I feel like that's just the way the chips fell. The code doesn't say vengeance is wrong."

"You're playing technicalities. And it's that sort of ambiguity that made Shinobi detestable in the eyes of the Samurai."

"Call it what you want, Ter. The undersecretary got what he had coming to him. Dishonor kills indiscriminately. His dishonor killed those closest to him. We were the instruments of death, not the architects. We didn't design any of that; we carried it out. Whatever your personal feelings were, they were coincidental—nothing more. Ninpo taught us that. And you're not Samurai. And I don't care what the Samurai thought. I wouldn't care what they think if they still existed today. I follow Ninpo, not Bushido."

"I thought you didn't care much for Ninpo."

"Terry, do we have to do this now? I don't want to debate my feelings on Ninpo."

"No. I guess not. Now's really not a good time."

"Thank you." Yuri poked his brother in the meat of his shoulder. "Hey, no stutter-stepping. I need you on your *A-game* for this one. None of that half-ass moral-high-ground shit. We're in enemy territory, and they'll kill us if we don't kill them first. Think about the SAS clowns."

"Yeah."

"Are you good?"

"I'm good."

"You sure?"

"Yeah—let's go over the plan one more time."

Terry and Yuri made use of snow shoes over the frigid wastes, dragging a rake behind them as they trekked through the waist-deep snow blanketing the topography separating them and their target. Terry was in the lead, navigating to their point of ingress. Meanwhile, Yuri brought up the rear, dragging the rake to scrub evidence of their passage.

The climbs were fairly benign—frozen wilderness notwithstanding—but the descents proved treacherous as the windward sides were less stable and the climbing, cutting, diving, and demolition gear were weighing them down heavily. Terry tried not to let discomfort frustrate him. Yuri, as usual, didn't seem to notice the weight or the weather.

Terry kept a close eye on his watch, wanting to keep them on schedule. They had built this operation with a large enough margin of time to deal with slowdowns, but they still needed the cover of darkness. He estimated that the current pace would put them at their final checkpoint within the target time. When they finally arrived, they fanned out to inspect the area. Then they met back up, and Terry remarked that they were twenty minutes behind schedule. Yuri didn't much care so long as they were in the water before the lookouts had sunlight on their side.

Yuri dropped his gear in the snow, organizing it all in a line. Terry followed suit, squeezing the releases on his buckles and the gates on his carabineers, dropping his mountain gear into the snow next to his brother's. Finally relieved of the weight, he stretched his arms above his head as far as his winter jacket would allow, arching his back to ease the stress.

"Hey, how'd the visit with Veronica's family go?" grunted Terry while he stretched.

"It went."

"That's it? *It went?*"

"Pretty much." Yuri started assembling the saws while Terry laid out his weapons in case they needed to defend themselves and beat a hasty escape.

"What'd you all do?" he asked.

"You know, the typical shit: dinner, boring conversation, politicking."

"Sounds glorious."

"It was for me."

"Why's that?"

"I tried to kill her father," Yuri deadpanned.

"Not in the *least* bit surprised by that. What stopped you?"

"The rest of her family when his face turned blue."

Terry chortled a steamy exhale.

"Hey, can you double-check our position, Ter?" Yuri requested, estimating about how far they appeared to be from where the shore should have been. "If the shore were visible through the snow, I'd be able to tell, but all I can do is guess right now."

Terry pulled his tablet from his pack and tapped an imagery icon that showed local temperature gradients. The area where they were standing was the warmest location situated closest to the spillway entrance. "Yeah—this is it. Dig in, bro."

"Splendid. Now *move*," Yuri demanded as he slammed the blade of a saw down at Terry's feet. Terry leaped backward the best he could with snow shoes on. The teeth of the saw bit into the wooden rim of the shoe, catching Terry's foot and causing him to fall into the snow.

"What the fuck is your problem?"

"Sorry—it slipped," Yuri said, smiling.

Yuri swept aside bushels of snow with the broadside, building a mountain of his own to either side of a small trench at the bottom of which he planned to cut the hole. Terry pulled off his snowshoes, unfolded his spade, and began assisting. By the time they struck ice, they were up to their shoulders. Once they had sufficient ice showing and a satisfying space cleared, Yuri began chipping away ice with the blunted tip until he was through to the water beneath. From there, the brothers could plunge the serrated portion through, and they sawed a three-foot wide by four-foot long block that was easily two-foot thick within thirty minutes, heaving it clear.

Terry wasted no time getting out of his winter gear and into his anti-exposure suit, pulling on his dive harness and rebreather. Yuri quickly ran his hands over the weak points, seams, and connections of Terry's gear. Everything checked out, so he connected the tether to a D-ring on Terry's shoulder and dragged the demolition gear up to the edge of the hole.

"Make sure you check the seals on the electronic equipment before you jump in," Terry reminded Yuri as he pulled on his mask. "A drowned tablet won't help us."

"Dude, I *got* this. This isn't my first rodeo." He gave Terry a firm smack on the backside. "Giddy-up."

Terry shook his head. "I'm just trying to make sure you don't forget anything."

"Why are you not gone yet?"

Terry stuffed the regulator of his rebreather in his mouth. He took a raspy, mechanical inhale; it gave him a positive indication of flow. All was in order nearest he could tell. He took a momentary sanity check as he neared the edge of the hole.

"Get going already," Yuri barked as he started pulling on his own anti-exposure suit.

Terry's middle finger shot up. He closed his eyes, readying himself for the opening shock of wet, frigid hatred, and plunged through the hole.

Thunk-ba-doom.

Terry struck the slush, his eyes slamming open and his muscles seizing despite the suit. It was so cold, in fact, that Terry's senses thought he was being burned. Then he willed his lungs to breathe; the hollow gurgle of inhalation through the rebreather rebooted his higher brain functions, giving him something else to hang on other than cold. His awareness, like a sonar pulse, instantly spread out in all directions.

The next thing his senses detected were the near imperceptible low-frequency waves that shifted him laterally in long periods. Next was the sloshing silence that cradled his head through the hood of his suit. There was, also, the high-pitch warbling of the ice creaking due to the dynamic motion of the water. Different portions of the ice sheet were impressed upwards while other areas were compelled down as the ice flexed with waves. Terry toggled on his headlamp, and it lit up a cone of frozen gloom when it hummed to life. He checked his compass and locked onto a heading, flattened himself out, and began kicking in the direction of their next checkpoint. Kicking forced blood back into his extremities and helped keep his body temperature manageable. After several minutes of busy flutter kicking, Terry noticed multiple vertical inconsistencies, which he bet were the bars of the grate covering the mainline to the facilities sewage. He kicked hard toward them until they came into view. He wrapped his fingers around two bars and gave them a solid tug, checking their integrity. Although they were old, rusted, and brittle, they still had enough resilience to shrug off human-grade force. They'd have to cut through. Terry and Yuri were prepared for that.

Thunk-ba-doom.

That was Yuri entering the water. And he sent a shock out that interrupted the death-like stillness in all directions. Terry felt it as his depth pulsed in response.

Yuri propelled himself in his brother's direction using the tether as a guide, towing his gear behind him and cursing the cold water with unholy expletives. Yuri kicked furiously, trying to produce a desperate level of warmth, not paying attention to how rapidly he was closing the distance between himself and his brother. He torpedoed Terry, slamming them both into the grate. Terry, for his part, felt the tether tug as Yuri approached but hadn't expected him to plow into his back. Startled, Terry spun and clipped Yuri with his elbow, breaking the seal of Yuri's mask, who immediately pulsed backward, releasing a mouthful of bubbles and curses that sounded like "Muh-moo-wow!"

Terry responded with "Muh-moo-moo-mwah!"

"Mwah," Yuri snapped, clearing his mask and toggling on his headlamp, and he shined it on Terry's tow pack. He unzipped it and pulled out the first of five cutting-pylons. With one hand, he grabbed the bar of the grate and then wedged the pylon between his shoulder and the bars, pressing into it to hold it; with the other hand, he adjusted his ballast. Satisfied, he gripped the pylon and secured it to one of the bars using zip ties, and then he reached for and drew another. Wash, rinse, repeat. Once Yuri was finished, Terry checked that each pylon was adequately secure, that their blades were unobstructed, and that the charges were securely fastened.

Everything checked out, so Terry and Yuri backed away, Yuri pushing his tow pack clear and Terry disconnecting from his pack and letting it sink.

166

Terry looked at Yuri and flickered his headlamp: *Ready to do this?*

Yuri's middle finger shot up.

Terry shook his head and hit the switch. The blades punched through the rusted metal with a squealing buzz and splash of sparks that bloomed in straight lines, never arcing like the streaks of phosphorous from an overhead fireworks detonation, and cooled a split second later into nothingness. The light from the sparks reflected off the icy ceiling and the murky floor, and in that split second, Terry and Yuri could make out their environment: above them was a grey-colored, frozen sky with dagger-like stalactites stabbing into the depths. Below was inky blackness that blanketed a floor that he couldn't see—despite its relatively shallow forty-foot depth. Between the ice and the floor, suspended in the water, were myriad particles of different sizes that reminded Terry of falling snow.

Terry checked the hole they had cut in the grate; it was big enough for them to swim through unhindered. He pulled himself through, giving one strong dolphin kick to drive him clear, and then turned to watch his brother come through. Yuri followed with no trouble, and they flutter kicked, with Terry in the lead, in the direction they estimated the opening of the spillway to be. Yuri aimed his headlamp above Terry's head, trying to aid him in locating the outlet that led into the spillway. Terry, now on his back and coasting in between kicks, scanned above them, looking for evidence. After several moments, he saw a patch of black that was blacker than the rest and made his ascent. As Terry neared the blackness, he slowed to look for more evidence. He didn't want to poke his head out in the wrong place—like, say, in front of two gun-toting guards.

Three rusted, derelict pipes came into view along his ascent, assuring Terry that they were ascending into the correct location. Terry figured the pipes were part of the supply lines used in cooling the apparatuses the Soviets had used nearly a century ago to enrich uranium as well as keep the munitions cool.

Now he was in a tube-like vein with walls made of brick and dark brown slime. Just ahead—well, above him, really—the shine of his headlamp didn't dissipate into nothingness as it had for the duration of their time in the water. Now the light shined as if onto a wall, a glassy, shiny one. It was the surface.

Terry strangled his headlamp and slowed his ascent so that he didn't breach like a startled whale. The top of his head broke the surface slowly, and he spun in a circle, looking for light—guards needed light. He saw none, turned his headlamp back on, and looked for a way to climb out.

*   *   *

The spillway, a sideways cylinder bisected lengthwise, one hundred feet in length and with a twenty-foot radius, constructed entirely of brick, slime, and algae, was painted in phantasmal green light from a bundle of glow sticks the brothers had hung from a spike that jutted from a wall. Corroded pipes ran the length of the walls and burrowed into the brick at the far end to make their way into the facility. There was also a door that serviced the spillway, and it was flanked by openings that led into narrower tunnels that doubled as ventilation and as overflow in the event of a spill.

"Does it bother you that we just did the backstroke in toxic waste?" Yuri asked.

"I always wanted kids with three eyes."

"That's the least of your concerns."

"What's that supposed to mean?"

"You lack this necessary element called *a woman*."

"Fine, I want a three-eyed niece."

Yuri chuckled

"I do. I want a niece that I can call Triclops."

They laughed as they stripped off their anti-exposure suits and stowed their gear. Then they toward the door. Yuri checked it. It was rusted shut. He pointed to the ventilation system, and Terry nodded.

Terry pulled the grate free and then positioned his night vision goggles on his head. "After you," he said, inclining his head.

"Thank you, sir," Yuri said, going on to his stomach into the tunnel, dragging the demolition gear behind him. Terry followed, pushing Yuri's pack from the other side.

168

The tunnel wasn't as claustrophobic as other vents they had crawled through, but it was perhaps the dirtiest with all its cobwebs, slime, and algae. At least their shoulders weren't rubbing against the walls, which added a measure of comfort since they didn't feel as though they were going to get stuck. They inched their way through the vent as it wormed through the facility.

Yuri hadn't had a cigarette in forever, and he was climbing the walls. The air was blowing on his face and back into the spillway. He was downwind, and now was as good of a time as any. Terry was going to bitch about it, but Yuri was used to it.

Terry heard the *snap-click* of what he swore sounded like a zippo. "Did you just light up?"

"Yup," Yuri replied, slithering through the pooled muck of the vents on his forearms.

"You've got to be shitting me," Terry rasped. "Are you trying to get us caught?"

"Yup."

Stupid questions required stupid answers.

"Yuri!"

"Screaming's only going to get us caught, princess. Being downwind *won't* stop your screaming from being heard."

"I'm not screaming," Terry said archly.

"Keep pushing. You're getting sensitive, and it's causing you to stop working."

"Goddammit, Yuri, you're impossible."

"I concur. But don't worry, everyone here is eastern European."

Terry lifted his head over the pack and burned a hole in his brother's back with his eyes. "What the hell does that have to do with anything?"

"Everyone in Europe smokes. Even if they could smell the smoke, they wouldn't know any different."

Terry hissed. "That's the stupidest logic of ever heard."

"But it's still logic." Yuri stopped because he felt Terry stop helping. "Talk and push, bro."

"I swear Mom must've dropped you."

"You leave the dead woman out of this."

"I thought you quit."

"I did."

"Well, what the hell happened?"

Yuri ground to a halt again, inhaled deeply, and then pulled the cigarette from his mouth. He exhaled in a steady, tight stream of fumes, and the ghostly red beam of an alarm installed into the vent became visible just ahead.

"Realized quitters never succeed."

*   *   *

Yuri found a grate that opened into the yard of the compound in an area that afforded the most natural cover. The brothers opened it, exited, and surveyed the area, putting the final touches on their plan before they split and went their separate ways.

Yuri crept towards the rail depot. He had assumed that much of the material was stored in the rail cars for two reasons: first, the facility lacked much storage space that didn't require heavy-lifting equipment, which couldn't be used in this kind of weather, and second, the roving security details were centrally located near them.

Meanwhile, Terry hustled across the facility courtyard and aimed for the central buildings of the facility. He slithered up to a door that led into the main compound and disappeared inside once he was sure that the coast was clear. The clock was running.

*   *   *

Yuri crept along the gray-brown snow trails carved by repeated patrols between the rusted hulks of train cars. The RKO, like any prudent para-military organization, had posted sporadic sentries along the walls and the guard towers—mostly in the guard towers, where they had the greatest view of the yard and the area surrounding the facility. Inside the compound, the RKO had posted rovers to walk about and ensure the internal security. While infiltration was highly unlikely this far into the winter wasteland, the RKO couldn't afford to slack on their security in light of the recent infiltration by a special operations unit and the possibility of a Georgian raid. A two-man team seeking to cut the head off of the proverbial serpent was at the bottom of their list of practical and probable threats. Most of all, the RKO were grossly unequipped to deal with Terry's and Yuri's skill and precision, and the brothers knew it.

Yuri froze and then disappeared into the shadow of a train car when he got a whiff of cigarette smoke followed by the sound of crunching snow. Yuri allowed an unsuspecting rover to pass him by, close enough that Yuri could make out the rover's facial hair.

The rover was dressed warmly in leathers, furs, and a wool cap, with a cigarette hanging from his lip and a carbine hanging from his shoulder. Yuri remembered that he and Terry had decided to minimize the casualties. They weren't against snapping a neck where necessary, but if the body count started to climb too high, the RKO would grow suspicious and initiate a messy manhunt and gunfight. Yuri and Terry wanted neither.

Once the rover turned a corner, Yuri went about inspecting the cars. He poked his head into them and shined in his infrared flashlight. The cars lit up like daytime in his night vision monocle. The first six hulks turned up nothing of interest, but the seventh, which was much closer to the inlet rail, bore fruit. Yuri climbed into the car and flooded it with IR light. Palletized equipment lined the bulkheads, covered in a tarp. He lifted a corner.

Bingo.

Yuri dropped his pack and started pulling out C4 charges and planting them to maximize the effect of their blast radius. Considering he was unsure as to how much material the RKO had brought in, he had to ration the explosives since his supply was limited.

Now just seven or so more cars were left to check. He looked at his watch: 00:09:26. He was well ahead of schedule.

*   *   *

Terry crept through a dark access hallway that led into the main ventricle of the mill that wrapped around the yard and the main facility in the shape of an "L." He had no clue where his targets were, but the mill, he figured, would be a great place to start since it looked to no longer be in operation and since its ventricle was open and surely dark.

The mill smelled damp and stale with the lingering sweet smell of rotting wood. Terry scanned the cavernous space. It was littered with antiquated hardware outdated by more than half a century and had the classic Depression-era administrative office at the end nearest him. The light was on too.

Well, it was worth a look.

Terry darted from cover to shadow and back to cover again as he approached the office. At one of the workstations, he noticed incongruous stains that were sticky as his feet stepped in them. That drew his attention—more like his intuition—and he hovered his head over the largest stain and sniffed it; its scent was metallic and aggressive. Blood. Dried no less. The aggressive scent, though, was that of flesh necrosis. He lifted his head and followed drips and spatter up the legs of the workstation onto the table, where a large rusted circular saw was suspended in its yoke. Terry could make out the concentric circles that blood had painted onto the rim of the blade. There was more blood spatter about the track. Leathery strips of flesh dangled from the teeth.

Terry's mind began flipping through possibilities. Extremists weren't above torture. Hell, their leader was reputed to have used it during his years as an Eastern Bloc general. That said, the RKO could have used a saw—this saw—as a means of punishment for dissenters or a captive. The thought that the RKO was using this hardware to butcher game popped into his head as a possibility, but he dismissed it. Considering the numbers of personnel that he had already seen around the facility, the amount of game that would be needed to feed the entire group would be quite vast, and the need to hunt would be quite frequent. Terry hadn't spotted any hunters or foragers outside of the compound, nor had he seen any signs of such. The RKO had to be transporting their food in. Furthermore, Terry had worked with extremist types before—this stank of their modus operandi. He was sure that someone had been run through the machine, most likely the operatives that were killed. He was close to a target.

He crept to the door of the office and peeked in through the window. The office was empty save for an old desk and a few chairs. On Terry's left, there was a table with a bloody sheet covering something.

Keeping low, Terry pulled the door open just enough for his body to fit and crawled in, staying beneath the windows. Once inside, he located the light switch and killed the lights. It wasn't completely black since the lights from the main ventricle afford some illumination, but it wasn't much. Terry stood to his feet and drew back the sheet. What he saw caused his moral center to scream.

There was a human head and torso with stubs for arms, an intact left leg, and three-quarters of the right, barely breathing. The human's face was mangled beyond recognition, missing a nose and an ear. The skin was frayed like useless newspaper and peeled away in some places. Its trunk was battered and bruised but didn't seem to have any major trauma. The human whimpered and gurgled once it realized Terry was there. It wasn't by sight, though, that the body had noticed Terry; its eyes had been gouged out. Terry gritted his teeth. He had seen this happen before. An organization he had been employed to work for in the Middle East had used heinous torture tactics and beheadings to intimidate their enemies. It was one of the reasons he and Yuri had left mercenary work behind. It angered him then, and it angered him even more now.

Terry was practically sure it was the operative, but he needed to confirm it. He scanned its wretched body for markings until he eventually found an identifying tattoo on the man's last remaining shin that matched the one depicted in the dossier. The first target was found.

Terry felt terrible. This man had been brutalized and tortured to further the political ends of criminals. They were all without honor and deserved to die, not this man. He was a scrupulous warrior like Terry, only separated by culture. Terry felt as though killing the man only added to the man's torment, but in reality, killing him, at this point, was the most merciful thing Terry could do. He figured that he'd numb the man's pain before proceeding, so Terry pulled two field syringes of morphine from his survival pack, unscrewed the caps, and plunged their needles into the meat of the man's thigh. Then Terry backed away and drew his pistol. Terry whispered a prayer to the ancestor Shinobi to guide the warrior to his resting place. He touched the barrel to the man's forehead and ended the operative's suffering with a silenced round. Death brought the operative honor.

Terry checked his watch: 00:13:42. He was still on schedule. He still had thirty-two minutes to find the other two targets.

*   *   *

Yuri cursed with disappointment when he climbed into the eighth car and noticed that it was full of equipment and he had only one charge left. He had been using them sparingly, trying his best to maximize their effectiveness, but even that hadn't been enough. He'd have to improvise. He searched the boxes and pallets until he found a pallet full of artillery shells. Suddenly, he wasn't so frustrated anymore! Yuri could rig an IED. The best part was the shells had a much larger explosive yield than C4, so when the shells blew, they would turn this car into the mother of all fragmentation weapons and pulverize everything within a considerable radius. Oh, the mayhem. Yuri liked that idea greatly.

He didn't waste any time; he got right to work building the IED. He unscrewed the casings and drew out their wiring, cutting and splicing them to meet his needs, and then connected a detonator to them that linked them to his cell phone signal. He estimated that one shell would easily level the rail car, so all eight would be the right amount of carnage. The RKO was in for a treat, that was for sure. Perhaps mercenary work hadn't been the most honorable living, but he sure had learned some invaluable skills, like building IEDs for example.

Yuri touched the light on his watch: 00:51:31.

Just then, he heard someone approach the door of the car. Yuri cursed under his breath; he hadn't finished rigging the explosives yet, and he still had to check two more cars. With any luck, the guard wouldn't force Yuri to make a messy scene.

Yuri pressed himself into the bulkhead and held his breath. He didn't want panicked breathing to give him away. He made himself flush with the corner of a stack of pallets, coiling to strike with his matte-black ninjatō. The guard hefted himself into the car, looked around, and then began walking towards the end of the car where Yuri was hiding. Yuri tightened his grip and waited for the guard to come close. When the guard was within arm's length, Yuri struck with the malice of a cornered viper. He grabbed ahold of the guard's face with

174

his left hand and, with his right, plunged half of the blade into the guard's gut just below the sternum. Yuri drove the man bodily against the corner of a pallet and muffled the man's cries with one hand while pressing the forearm of the other into the guard's jugular, trying to speed him into unconsciousness. The man tried to exhale forcibly but couldn't with the blade preventing his diaphragm from moving, and unconsciousness came quickly, followed closely by death.

The clamor had been louder than Yuri had meant. He hoped that no one else had heard it, but he darted to the opposite side of the car so he could ambush another rover in the event someone came to investigate the noise. Sure enough, another rover did.

The new guard came to the door, shined his flashlight, and made a query in a language that Yuri didn't know. Yuri burrowed between two pallets and waited for the guard to make a move: either the rover would get bored and leave or he'd get suspicious and enter the car. In the case of the former, the new rover would live to see the next day if he was lucky enough not to be caught in the blast. In the case of the latter, Yuri would kill him and leave him with his comrade. It didn't make a difference to Yuri which outcome was realized; he just needed to stay on the clock.

He checked his watch: 00:53:02.

The new rover queried again and then climbed into the car. He swung the flashlight in an arc, the beam missing the top of Yuri's head by several inches. The light caught the feet of his prostrate comrade, and the rover moved in deeper, trying to get his attention. He drew closer, and the circle of light cast by the flashlight crawled along the dead rover's legs until a pool of blood became visible. In seconds, confusion became disbelief and then became panic. A sound of alarm began to rumble in his throat, but Yuri was out of cover and on top of him before the sound could leave his mouth. Yuri grabbed him from behind with both hands, locking his fingers underneath his chin and, with a violent jerk, yanked the man's head back and buried his knee into the rover's spine. The rover's vertebrae crumpled audibly, and Yuri tossed him onto the deck next to the first rover, splashing his blood in a semicircle. Yuri stepped over the new rover and ran him through. Then Yuri went back to rigging the IED.

Yuri checked his watch again. He needed to hurry.

Terry crossed the bridge that passed over the main yard and connected the mill's second-story catwalks to the second story of the main facility. He looked out toward the rail depot, wondering how things were going for his brother. There hadn't been any gunfire, nor was the body count climbing, which meant that Yuri was keeping quiet—that was promising.

Terry checked that there was no movement on the other side of the entrance and skulked through. He stalked the halls of the complex, searching for the general and the minister. The security inside the facility was minimal, limited to personnel transiting the spaces. Terry was a ghost hiding inside doors, around corners, and in the shadows. He planted his ear against closed doors to listen for occupants, and if there were none, he'd open them and check for any trace of the minister and the general. For rooms that he determined to be occupied, he would stand to the side of the door and look in with a fiber-optic cable if the room was lit and the hallway was dark. However, if the room was dark and the hallway was backlit, he would hover over the crack of the door to block the light as he looked in so as not to alert someone to the presence of his silhouette.

Terry left the second story for the main deck, where the observation deck to the engineering space was situated. As he came into the hall that led from the stairwell to the "T" of the claustrophobic main passage, which was scarcely wide enough to fit two people side by side, he saw a portly man in his late fifties pass left to right. *That might have been the minister*, Terry thought to himself. The man was heavy enough. Terry just needed to get a better look to see if the man's face matched the picture in the dossier.

Terry sped up to follow him. When he reached the corner, he checked that both directions were clear and watched the portly man beeline for a door further down the hall to his right. Terry crept into the hallway and gave chase, following the suspect to the same door. From the smell of methane, Terry instantly identified the room as the latrine. Terry gave it a twenty-count and followed.

The portly man was standing near the sink. He turned when he heard Terry enter through the old, whiny door. They both paused; the man tried to place Terry's face, and Terry was confirming his. The man's face was a match; he was definitely the minister. Terry launched a roundhouse that connected hard with the minister's cheekbone. The minister shuddered and collapsed onto the sink with a grunt, and Terry leaped on him, grabbing a handful of what was left of the minister's thinning hair. Terry wrenched the minister's head back, wrapped a garrote wire around his neck, and pulled. The minister bucked wildly, but Terry was able to keep him pressed into the sink with his weight despite the minister's marked size advantage. The minister's eyes bulged and shot through with red lightning streaks until they filled with a passive orange and then auburn red. His tongue wagged violently as Terry cinched the wire tighter, cutting through the minister's skin and closing off his carotid, jugular, and trachea.

The struggle came to a bloody crescendo as the minister smashed his hands and arms into the ceramic of the sink, the tile of the walls, and the glass of the mirror, causing an infernal racket but to no avail. The minister relinquished control of all of his fluids and gasses before slumping lifeless against the counter. Terry yanked at the garrote one last time to be sure.

Now he had to hide the body. The best place to put it was in the exact place the minister had intended to go—the toilet. Terry let him fall to the floor, stowed his garrote, and dragged the minister's opulence to the door of the stall and sat him up. He grabbed beneath the minister's arms and hoisted him off the ground, cursing beneath the man's immense girth. Terry drove him back into the stall and dropped him onto the seat, wiping the sweat off of his own brow and checking his watch: 00:42:54. Only thirteen minutes left.

Terry checked the hall from the door. It was clear, so he made his way down to the door from which the minister had exited. Its position was congruent with the location of the observation room. Perhaps the general and minister were using the room as the command center for the facility while they returned it from mothball. He approached the door and pressed his ear to it. Inside, there were three distinct voices: two nearing the door and one deeper in the room. Someone was leaving. Terry scanned the passage for options. There was no way he'd make it to the bathroom before the person exited the observation room. Perhaps he could make it into an adjacent room in time—if the doors weren't locked.

Time was up. Terry had spent too much time deliberating, and the individual was opening the door.

Terry, giving testament to his athleticism, quickly bounded up the walls and suspended himself directly above the door by pressing against opposite walls with his hands and feet and his back against the ceiling. Two RKO exited the doorway and passed beneath Terry, never noticing him. They turned the corner without so much of a thought about the Shinobi hovering above the floor—claustrophobic hallways had their advantages. Terry waited just to be sure. After a few moments, Terry was confident that they weren't coming back and released his handholds and footholds, dropping to the floor with the same acrobatic grace he'd used to get up there.

Terry checked the doorknob—it was unlocked. He turned it and slowly pushed the door open—it groaned loudly. Terry winced, stopping before it was even cracked a half-inch. Then a voice beckoned from the inside, clearly alerted to the door's opening. Since the cat was out of the bag, he'd just use the direct approach: Terry drew his pistol, swung the door open, and swaggered in.

The general, a fit man of maybe sixty years with a bald spot on top of his head, stood to his feet when he saw a stranger waltz through the door. He was gripped with suspicion and barked something in a language that Terry wasn't familiar with. "I don't speak Russian, comrade," Terry said casually, slamming the door behind himself.

"You are American?" The general asked disdainfully in English.

Terry didn't reply.

"So, the Westerners believe they can still interfere? How many more of you do I have to kill?"

Terry slowly flanked the table, behind which the general was standing. "I'm not an agent of any government."

"Then you're a mercenary. Which means no one will miss you when I leave your body to rot in the snow."

"Mercenaries aren't creatures of honor, General. I'm no mercenary."

"So, you are just a common assassin. What do you hope to achieve here? You are horribly outnumbered."

"Surely your superior numbers have hindered my ability to be in this room with you. Superior numbers also apparently prevented me from choking the life out of the minister."

The general's face became indignant.

"I am the instrument of the consequence of your dishonor. Superior numbers can't prevent what you've brought on yourself."

"Dishonor?" the general laughed. "You are sorely mistaken, my boy. I am the vanguard of the Georgian Republic. No action for the honor of Georgia is dishonorable."

Terry eased around the corner of the table until he was standing in front of the general. "You know nothing of honor, then."

The general yanked a wretchedly angled bowie knife from his belt and rasped, "I'll have the honor of carving out your heart. I have survived many assassins; I will survive you."

The general lunged at Terry, bringing the knife down in a lethal arc. Terry reacted swiftly, taking a step back and catching the blade with the receiver of his pistol, grinding metal on metal. He pushed the general back effortlessly and returned the gun to his side. The general set a low center of gravity and circled. Terry seemed uninterested, standing there as if he had all day. The general came at him again with a sweeping motion. Terry slipped to the outside, allowing the blade to whistle past. The general lunged again, and Terry gave ground to remain just beyond range. The general growled in frustration. Then Terry flicked the safety on his pistol and tossed it onto the table.

"Are you truly stupid enough to discard your weapon when you had the upper hand?"

Terry shrugged. "I'm *stupid*, I suppose."

The general rushed Terry, swinging and stabbing wildly. Terry bobbed, weaved, and parried to keep the knife from making contact and zigzagged across the observation room, stringing the general with him.

The general was getting winded; he wasn't as young as he used to be. He couldn't let this assassin wear him out. Otherwise, the assassin would make short work of him. He gave into desperation and slung a Hail Mary at Terry, trying to jam the point between Terry's neck and clavicle. Terry intercepted the general's knife hand at the wrist and used his momentum to sling the general into the table. The general careened into it, knocking all of its contents to the floor. Terry maintained control of the general's arm and had it painfully locked behind his back. Terry torqued the general's arm until he bared his teeth and released the knife. Terry scooped the knife in midair and buried it into the general's free hand. The general's body quaked, and he let out a blood-curdling shriek.

"Only the vilest, soulless creatures use torture," Terry whispered into the general's ear.

"My men will kill you!" the general wailed. "They will kill you and rape your family!"

Terry tore the general's shirt, exposing his abdomen. "Torture is the weapon of the dishonorable. Anyone who uses it deserves a slow, excruciating death." Terry drew his tanto and flashed it in front of the general's face. "Are you ready?" taunted Terry, and then he scraped the blade across the general's stomach, slicing through the walls of skin, fat, and muscle. The flesh covering the abdominal cavity sprung open like curtains drawn open by their string, and his guts spat onto the floor with a sickening *plop*. Terry let the general fall to the ground and watched the doomed man mill about trying to gather his innards.

*   *   *

Yuri had rushed the final riggings of the IEDs. He hoped that he hadn't incorrectly wired them, but he didn't have time to inspect them thoroughly. He hoped that the combined blast and fragmentation would cause enough bedlam to render not only the rigged cars useless but also the cars that Yuri couldn't rig. At this stage in the game, he had to accept what he had managed to rig and leave as planned—no heroics.

He climbed the side of a rail car adjacent to a series of other cars that acted as an improvised high-road escape route over the wall of the compound. He bounded from car roof to car roof until he could scale the short distance up the perimeter wall and leap over the side, beneath the notice of a sentry tower. Once outside, Yuri raced through the snow to the hide point to wait for his brother.

Yuri tumbled down a snowy embankment, rolled to a halt at the designated location, and lay there panting. His lungs burned from the cold. He had bludgeoned his way through thigh-high precipitation because he hadn't had the time to put on his snowshoes. They wouldn't have afforded him the ability to sprint anyway.

For the first time during his entire time in Kazakhstan, the cold felt pleasant as Yuri looked up at the stars. In spite of the burning in his chest, the cold was calming and made the landscape serene—serene until Yuri initiated the apocalypse anyway.

Ba-deep ba-deep. His phone chirped. Terry needed five more minutes. That was fine with Yuri; he needed more time to lay there in the snow and decompress. Hell, at this rate, Terry could chirp a second time, and Yuri would grant him another five minutes if it meant that Yuri could lay there for a little while longer. Then his thoughts went to Veronica. Wow, he missed her. He hadn't thought about her in several hours, but—

Yuri's eyes slammed open. How long had he been lying there? He raised his watch to his face. He had to blow the charge in forty-five seconds. Phew, he felt like he'd been dozing forever. It had only been about seven minutes.

Just then, he heard someone coming. His hand went instinctively to his ninjatō. Then Terry flopped over the side of the same embankment, slid down the side, and came to rest against his brother. Terry panted just as Yuri had.

"If I weren't so tired, I'd say something sarcastic," Terry said.

"Meh—your jokes aren't that funny anyway."

"Well, at least my timing is great."

"You're like FedEx...you deliver."

"Ha!"

"Speaking of deliveries, look that direction," Yuri said, tossing a thumb toward the compound and mashing a combination of buttons on his cellphone.

There was a low rumble accompanied by several popping sounds. Then there was screaming, followed by an orange and yellow pressure wave and an ear-splitting roar. The blast was so big that an entire rail car crushed a portion of the perimeter wall when the car careened into it. The blast was more colossal than Yuri had anticipated, and the concussion forced them to cover their ears. Afterward, Terry asked Yuri to explain how he'd produced that much yield with C4. Yuri claimed that it was simply "ninja magic."

Chapter Eleven: The Crushing Blow

Suzuka Mountains. Mie Prefecture, Japan. 9 years ago.

The night was exceptionally dark—so dark, in fact, that Terry and his small team of Shinobi had to navigate the rustic ascent of the surrounding mountains more by feel than anything else as they moved toward their objective. The eighteen training Shinobi had been undergoing an intensive two months of instruction in preparation for this evening's exercise—or test. The past two months had come under the explicit scrutiny of the Shinobi-no-mono and the elder council, requiring Kintake to remain in the village long past his desire, and therefore he couldn't operate his school in Tokyo. That made him irritable and harsh—more so than usual. Making matters worse, he and the Shinobi-no-mono visibly weren't getting along. All the trainees found it better to avoid Kintake the best they could lest they become outlets for his frustration.

Terry and his Genin—low-ranked Shinobi—were scaling the sheer face of a cliff, trying to shave off time to their objective. Terry was the second Shinobi to reach the apex behind his scout. He spun around and sat down, dangling his feet over the edge as he used his climbing claws to pull a rock from between the toes of his tabi boots; the rock had been plaguing him the entire climb.

A Shinobi who was finishing the hundred-foot climb just below him called to him.

Terry tossed the rock over the side and reached down to grab a handful of the Shinobi's sword harness, hoisting his teammate the rest of the distance onto the ledge.

The Shinobi rolled on his side and looked Terry in the face. **"Terry, Masaharu has injured himself."**

"Okay, keep moving." Terry didn't seem concerned; injury was commonplace in their lifestyle. Shinobi simply bandaged themselves and kept moving—invisibility was hard to maintain, after all, if one didn't do so. **"We'll deal with it once we get to the objective."**

"No, Terry, you do not understand. Masaharu cannot walk. We believe his leg is broken."

Terry's eyes went up and to the right as he thought about how to handle the situation. Should he leave his teammate here with someone to care for him until they had completed the exercise? Could they carry Masaharu to the objective? Or was it just better to move him to someplace safe and call for help? Either way, Kintake wasn't going to be happy. It made Terry anxious just thinking about Kintake's response.

Terry looked down into the darkness and saw the silhouettes of his teammates. Some were preparing to make the climb; others were undoubtedly tending to Masaharu.

"Very well. Let's find a way down and check him out. If it's as bad as you say, then we'll move him back to our stage point. Omiyoshu Sensei won't be happy, but we'll just have to deal with that."

*   *   *

Kintake was counting down the minutes until it was over as he sat there against a boulder in the cool darkness. He had grown tired of Iga, of Togakure Ryu, of the Fujibayashi—these relics. Most of all, he was at his wits' end with the Shinobi-no-mono, and it was making him hate everyone—even his students. He just wanted them to be done so he could leave and distance himself from Togakure Ryu to recharge his batteries before he had to come back again…only to be reprimanded by Hanzo. Being away and running Togakure Ryu's day-to-day operations remotely through his Chunin and Jonin—middle-ranked seniors and high-ranked elders—and the elder council was worth the reprimand. He just needed to make it through the evening without strangling someone.

His students were stalking through the hills to their objective. They had to get past Kintake's Chunin undetected and simulate an assassination by killing a hog that was chained to a stake in a nearby glade without being spotted. Kintake just needed them to get it right so that he could leave at sunrise. He needed to attend a meeting in Tokyo that he had had to postpone repeatedly.

Then, over the ambient nighttime sounds, Kintake's thoughts were interrupted by the faint sound of whistles attenuating through the terrain. Something had happened.

"**Sensei!**" a Jonin with shoulder-length hair and receding hairline called as he approached.

"**I heard it,**" Kintake hissed, beginning to seethe. "**Go tell the others to meet me at the *yorishiro*.**" This was the sacred tree with a rock formation placed at its base five hundred years ago that sat just below the hills. "**Then you come back here and see to it that the hog is returned to the village.**"

Kintake stormed off.

*   *   *

When Terry and his Genin arrived, Kintake and the Jonin were there waiting. Saki's Genin, which included Yuri, even though he was technically a Chunin like Saki, and his brother, were fast approaching from the south.

Terry could feel Kintake staring a hole through him. Terry kept his focus on his Genin as they carried Masaharu to *yorishiro* and set him down. Masaharu winced as they made an earnest effort to settle him as gently as possible, positioning him so that he could sit with his back against a rock for support.

Terry stood and straightened his tunic beneath his harness before looking at the kōchō.

Kintake's eyes were serpentine. "**Explain yourself.**"

"**Sensei, Masaharu broke his thigh bone while we were climbing. A handhold came loose, and he fell to the rocks below.**"

"**Do you not realize how important this is? Why did you not leave him there?**"

Just then, Saki, Yuri, and Saki's Genin crested the hill and made their way towards the rest of the Fujibayashi.

"**I do realize how important this test is, Sensei, but leaving him there was too risky. What if something happened to him? I mean, he's badly injured and in tremendous pain. Leaving him there would only make it worse.**"

"**Chunin will not lecture me, Terry! There is nothing more important than this test!**"

"**Not even the life of a Shinobi, Sensei?**"

"No—all of your lives are forfeit! They are meaningless to Ninpo. You do what you are instructed and not what you desire! The outcome you desire is contrary to the demands of Ninpo!"

"With respect, Sensei, I disagree. Ninpo doesn't demand that we forfeit our lives."

Kintake's fists clenched. "I am the proprietor of Ninpo, Terry, not you! I make that determination, not you!"

"I understand that, Sensei, but you're wrong."

"How dare you!"

"Sensei, I don't mean to offend—"

Kintake struck Terry on the side of the face with blinding speed, and the force rocked Terry backward two steps. All the Shinobi backed away; Kintake's blast radius was notoriously large.

Terry managed to stay on his feet—barely. Kintake struck him again, feeling that Terry remaining standing was yet another act of defiance. Terry, however, didn't go down. Kintake hit him a third time, a fourth, a fifth, a sixth, and so on. Finally, Terry hit the ground, bleeding.

For a split second, Yuri was mentally paralyzed as his brain processed what he was seeing. Kintake had just reared back and struck Terry repeatedly.

Terry...

As in Yuri's brother, Terry.

Yuri heard his mother's voice in his ears saying, "Yuri, your brother is your responsibility."

Yuri's vision became a tunnel as he stalked with unfettered intent towards Kintake, weaving through the small crowd of Shinobi. They quite nearly didn't notice Yuri because they were so focused on Kintake's violent outburst and Terry dripping blood onto the grass.

Retribution pooled in Yuri's left hand; his fingers swelled with purpose. He clenched his fist, collecting every ounce of that purpose into it—his hand burned with anger.

Yuri swung as hard as he could, throwing every ounce of fury into his strike, and caught Kintake just above the jaw on his blindside, retribution exploding against Kintake's face and setting him stumbling. The impact shook the entire group, and they surged.

186

Kintake wobbled forward a few steps, trying to right himself, but couldn't maintain his balance. He fell onto his side and shook his head, trying to clear it. He looked up just in time to fix an airborne Yuri with his eyes. Decades of training and experience made Kintake a next-to-impossible target; his body reacted, and he rolled to the side. Yuri's foot landed thunderously where Kintake's face had been.

Kintake couldn't catch his breath; Yuri was on him, launching repeated kicks, firing low as he tried to punt Kintake's head off of his shoulders. Kintake blocked and rolled with the impact the best he could on his knees.

Yuri broke through and landed a kick that forced Kintake onto his back, but Kintake bounced back immediately. He let the momentum of his fall draw his legs over his body and recovered over his shoulder in a backward somersault.

Yuri snatched the ninjatō from a nearby Genin's sheath and pursued Kintake, who had righted himself. Before he could find his feet, Yuri slashed a silver ribbon in the air that missed the bridge of Kintake's nose by a breath. Yuri followed it with his foot, planting it in Kintake's chest and driving his back into a rock.

Yuri whipped the blade up in an arc, stopping it parallel to the ground. The point hummed mere inches from Kintake's right eye; a bead of sweat ran down the side of Kintake's face as he looked into Yuri's inhuman facial expression.

It all happened so fast. Saki and several other Chunin leaped to Kintake's aid with weapons drawn, threatening Yuri to get a grip. The rest of the Fujibayashi barked in protest; they couldn't believe what they were seeing. Never in their history had they ever heard of Shinobi attacking the kōchō. To do so was sacrilegious, defying Ninpo.

Yuri was unfazed, and he spat sulfuric curses and threats. He had finally reached his breaking point. His fury had burned off what reason he had left and twisted his features into something terrible. The years of abuse by Kintake had finally caught up as Yuri had watched him beat Terry. All Yuri cared about now was retribution.

Terry and Saki pleaded with Yuri to see reason. The Fujibayashi were chaos, a storm cloud of drawn weapons, yelling and floundering. Despite a sword being only a nanosecond from taking his life, Kintake barked a command, and the rumble ceased.

This wasn't the first time Kintake had found himself at the business end of a sword—or any blade for that matter—he had the terrible facial scar to prove it. He had learned every aspect of sword fighting, even the aspect of being unarmed against a sword wielder. As long as Yuri remained at his current distance or closer, Yuri couldn't use the reach advantage that the ninjatō gave him. Kintake could exploit that, but he'd have to act quickly if he was to survive; Yuri's killer instinct was not to be trifled. To that end, Kintake waved off the other Shinobi—*allow me to handle this*. They did as they were told.

Kintake needed to use Yuri's anger to coax him to commit. When he did, Kintake would even the playing field. He'd have to be quick and precise, though, knowing that Yuri would not back down even when stripped of his advantage. Yuri would surely press the attack immediately.

"Yuri, if you do not kill me, all of your brothers will know that you have the ego to begin a fight but that you lack the heart to finish one," Kintake said calmly in English. "They will finally know for certain that you are without honor."

"You don't think I'll kill you?" Yuri hissed.

"No—I know you will not. You don't have the soul for it. You are not worthy of Shinobi, and you will not survive into adulthood."

Yuri bared his fangs like an angered serpent; the ninjatō quaked as his muscles strained to hold back its thirst. "You really don't think I'll kill you, you old bastard?"

"No—you will not." Kintake finally spoke in Japanese, wanting the rest of the Fujibayashi to understand him. "**You are a coward and an actor, seeking only to intimidate me and to usurp that which are unworthy of ever having. But there's no weapon you can raise against me that will kill me. I was chosen. My honor shields me from your aggression. It was your lack of honor that killed your parents. You were the instrument of their death. And it is your lack of honor that will cause you to be realized a failure here.**"

Yuri's emotional levies buckled.

Kintake's eyes saw the instantaneous tightening of the individual muscle fibers in Yuri's jaw as he willed his arms to impale Kintake. The kōchō reacted, his hands shooting up to intercept the blade, clasping the blade between them. He pressed his palms together with all his might, the friction draining the sword of its force—just enough for him to displace his head and allow the blade only to ruffle his hair. Surprise caused Yuri's grip to loosen, and Kintake snatched the blade from Yuri's control and slung it to the ground.

The surprise was brief, as Yuri suddenly came to realize that Kintake could turn the ninjatō on him. Yuri pressed the attack.

Yuri led with his fists, hurling strike after strike. Kintake parried and redirected, trying to give as little ground as possible as he tried to climb to his feet. Yuri aggressively tried to tear down Kintake's guard. He fired low with his lead leg. Kintake snaked his foot out and intercepted it with his instep. Yuri immediately drew that knee to his chest and fired a side kick, planting it in Kintake's flank, driving him back.

Yuri ramped up his offense, spinning and whirling, fists high, kicks low. Kintake was forced to retreat despite his blocks. Yuri's aggression and instinct made him a force of nature in a hand-to-hand fight.

Kintake saw an opening in a flurry of strikes and countered, catching Yuri in the ear with a back-handed strike. Yuri rolled with it and gave ground. Kintake wheeled his leg around, arcing his heel at Yuri's head. Yuri caught the lightning strike in his peripheral vision and slid beneath it in the nick of time. He then coiled in advance of his own strike.

He lunged at Kintake at waist level, like a football player hungry to make a sack. Yuri was trying to crowd him, and Kintake was not going to take the bait. Kintake hopped backward, trying to open some space. Yuri excelled at fighting in a free-for-all, able to overwhelm multiple opponents with devastating precision. Yuri was every bit of the killer that Kintake had honed. To that end, Kintake knew that his chances of being seriously injured were too high if he continued to trade blows with the younger, hungrier Shinobi.

He was going to need to take away Yuri's ability to fight.

Yuri went airborne, coming down with bone-shattering force against Kintake's high block, driving him to a knee. The power of Yuri's blow reverberated throughout Kintake's body, causing his back teeth and joints to ring with pain. Yuri chained more attacks behind it.

Kintake slipped Yuri's blows and sneaked a fist through Yuri's guard towards his ribs. Yuri thrust his elbow down, intercepting the strike, and drilled his other hand into Kintake's mouth. Hard. Drawing blood.

Kintake again rolled backward and found his feet. Yuri, an opportunistic predator by nature, saw the haymaker's chance to finish the fight and launched a furious roundhouse aimed at Kintake's guard. If he could shatter Kintake's forearm, it would leave a wide-open hole for Yuri to drive a second spinning side kick through. If he could land it, he'd surely break all of Kintake's ribs.

The roundhouse finished its arc, battering Kintake's forearms and slinging them away from his trunk, leaving it open for the second half of Yuri's combo. He planted that foot and pooled all of the kinetic energy he could muster into his side kick.

The foot raked low through the air until it was vectored against Kintake, and Yuri launched the knife of his foot for the opening with every ounce of force he had.

Kintake tossed out his baited line, and the angry little fish bit.

Kintake had kept giving ground, denying Yuri's preferred rush tactics. Yuri had been forced to make large, extended strikes as his fury and desperation intensified. Kintake had feigned the strike to Yuri's ribs knowing that Yuri would counter and overcommit once he saw blood. Then he'd placed a weak guard up that Yuri would instantly take advantage of.

Yuri's spin slowed in Kintake's mind. He watched the concentric arcs that Yuri's knee and foot transcribed in the air and saw the path that led to the opening that Kintake presented. He could also see the arch of Yuri's foot—the delicate nexus of bones that made up its base. He timed it, held his breath, and then hooked his fist as hard as he could into Yuri's arch.

The closure between fist and foot was epic, and the thunderous impact even more so. Kintake's hand shot back from the impulse, and Yuri crumpled, howling.

He howled like an unsuspecting hound stepped on accidently, through gritted teeth, holding his mangled appendage in both hands. He rocked back and forth like a capsized turtle.

Terry, Saki, and the rest of the Fujibayashi were a sea of blank stares.

Kintake's forearm trembled from the combined impact of Yuri's sledgehammer-like foot and Kintake's rock-like fist. He'd feel it for days to come; he didn't recover as fast as he used to. **"Get this animal off of these sacred grounds,"** Kintake demanded of his disciples, looking at them hard, as if he had not just been in a fight with someone who'd had an intent to kill. **"He doesn't deserve to be here. None of you do. Only true Shinobi may walk these grounds. None of you are worthy. Begone!"**

Yuri yelled and cursed through the excruciating pain, trying to climb to his feet to continue the fight. The Fujibayashi hoisted him off the ground and began to carry him away. Yuri protested angrily.

Kintake watched his disciples cart Yuri away from yorishiro and decided to stop the group as they were leaving. **"Yuri, you are no longer worthy to be among the Fujibayashi. You are to leave Iga by first light."**

Terry's face twisted, and he turned towards Kintake. **"What?"** he asked. Kintake couldn't be serious. **"What do you mean?"**

Kintake's face became as dark as the nighttime sky. **"He has turned on his sensei and therefore has turned upon the clan. He will leave. He is no longer Shinobi, nor is he welcome here any longer."**

"Sensei, do you hear what you're suggesting?" Saki implored.

Kintake's head cut towards him. **"You will be silent!"**

"This makes no sense," Terry said, finally wiping the blood from his mouth. **"He was defending me. That's not against the code."**

"If you wish to defend him, then you will leave with him."

"Sensei, you're being unreasonable. Where are we supposed to go? You already won. What more do you want?"

"You *will* leave."

Terry swore he'd heard an ultimatum in Kintake's voice. **"Or what?"** Terry asked, just to be sure.

"You are but a single person, Terry," Kintake said deadpan. **"Our clan is many."**

"Why would you do this to us? We have nowhere to go."

"You will live with his dishonor, and you will not return until such a time when he has found honor or the code commands your

return. **Leave now if you cherish his life**"—Kintake paused for effect—"**and your own. You are no longer recognized as Fujibayashi so long as his dishonor exists.**"

Kintake turned and left with his entourage in tow. Terry watched him leave, not knowing what to say; he could still hear Yuri yelling. What were they going to do now?

Chapter Twelve: Ritual Revelation

The Shinobi are ministers of justice; their duty is a righteous one. A Shinobi must execute his duty swiftly and precisely at all cost or be dishonored.
The Sixth Mandate, translated from Ninpo.

The Ciccone Residence. National Harbor, Oxen Hill, Maryland. Today.

Yuri and Veronica stumbled out of the elevator inebriated, merged as one. The air around them was electric.

Yuri came up for air, scanning the hallway insincerely. "Is this my floor?"

She cradled his head in both hands and arched herself into him, her bottom lip touching his. "Does it matter?" she managed before devouring her lover again.

Yuri couldn't speak with his mouth overflowing with a mixture of his and her passion. He tried a look at condominium numbers adjacent the front doors, but the alcohol made it practically impossible. She was right, though, it didn't matter.

She peeled her face from his, holding his head with both hands. "These clothes are strangling my body. Get me home so you can get me out of them."

"I think it's this way. But I'm not really sure because the numbers keep moving." He staggered down the hallway towards the door he thought was his suite, trying to maintain his balance despite his intoxication. Veronica had convinced him to imbibe a little more alcohol than he had planned. She had been enticing him all evening, and he had been trying to play hard to get. The alcohol had allowed her to up the ante. Evil woman.

Not that she was easily ignored, with her full, hour-glass figure, her bright, amber eyes, waist-length, sandy hair, and tender veneer that masked the predator beneath with a voracious sexual appetite. A woman after his own heart.

Yuri hid from Veronica well. To her, he was not the fiery, tenacious hitman, but rather a calm, collected, and sometimes aloof man who authored fiction in Japanese and published his work abroad—or at least that's what he had been telling her for the past year and a half.

He had kept up the facade this long; he was not going to buckle anytime soon and show her his true face—the face that Ninpo forbade any *Shinobi* to show. Granted, he wanted to open up to her from time to time. Who would not want to? It was only natural, right? That a man wanted to be with a woman and just surrender? She made him feel different. He could not quite explain it. But he was not just simply a man. He was more than that. He didn't want to be, though. He wanted to be like everyone else. He wanted to be her truth. But he couldn't be. The alcohol tried to persuade him otherwise.

"You should have worn a tie," she said, her eyes piercing him deeply.

"Why?"

Veronica grabbed the collar of his jacket and jerked him forward, their mouths coming so close that their lips nearly touched. "Because it would be easier to make you do what I want." Then she licked his lips affectionately.

Yuri swallowed hard, trying to cool the conflagration in his chest. He could hear his pulse pounding in his ears. His hands were beginning to sweat too. This was *not* the first time he and Veronica had been intimate, but it sure felt that way. Hell, it felt like the first time he had ever been intimate. He was coming apart. It had to be the alcohol.

They arrived at his door. Well, at least, he thought it was his door. Perhaps it wasn't. He sure hoped it was, though. He squinted, trying to confirm the apartment number, and fumbled in and out of his pockets, searching for his card key—an otherwise unchallenging feat if not for his lover's persistent caressing.

Veronica pressed herself against his back and stroked her hands from his chest to his thighs and gripped handfuls of slacks in both hands. "Hurry," she purred.

Yuri was trying. It was just that the alcohol and the adrenaline were making his hands shake.

Veronica's fingers were climbing his trunk again, and she rubbed his leg with the inside of her thigh.

Yuri's hand dropped to his side, and he rubbed the exposed, smooth skin of her leg. The feeling made him grind his teeth.

Veronica ripped open his shirt, launching the buttons in all directions. "Hurry, baby," she whispered again, craning her neck to kiss his. Electricity shot through his body. Veronica wormed her way between her lover and the door, her cleavage visible over the top of her form-fitting—yet sophisticated—dress. "Am I all you want?"

"Sometimes," Yuri aspirated.

"You sure it's only *sometimes*?"

"You're right. I rarely want you around at all."

She giggled.

He tried to keep a certain amount of emotional distance between them, but perhaps she knew that he was lying. He thought that he'd made it sound sincere. Maybe she could see right through him. He doubted it. But perhaps he was losing focus. It had to be the alcohol.

"Hurry." Veronica kissed him deeply. "Or are you going to make me *take you* out here?"

Yuri resumed his search, probing the rest of his pockets for the elusive key. Veronica inched along his cheek, from his lips to his ear and then down his neck, leaving a trail of lipstick. She began a most sinister descent to her knees in spite of her four-inch heels, rubbing and kneading his exposed chest and abdominals as she went. She squatted on her haunches and began tugging at his snakeskin belt. He investigated his internal coat pocket—nothing. Veronica whipped Yuri's belt from his pants and tossed it across the hall. *Bam!*—the buckle slammed into a door of another suite. Yuri continued to search for the key, finally finding it in his wallet.

Veronica grabbed hold of Yuri's jacket, hoisted herself up, and snatched the key from his hand. She slid the card into the locking mechanism, and it hummed until its jam clicked open. Using her index finger, she depressed the handle, and the door creaked open, spilling light and lust into the otherwise dark great room.

Yuri stumbled through the threshold and caught himself on the statue standing immediately to the door's left. He blinked several times, trying to adapt his night vision, but resolved that in his drunken state, his eyes were going to be less than useful in the dark. All was not lost; he would just give his other senses time to come alive.

Within seconds, his hearing began to compensate for his eyes, and his ears picked up the sound of Veronica's stilettos tapping the ivory tiles as she moved about the room. Then a hollow metal-on-metal sound told him that she was opening the drapes. The light that poured in was intense. He raised a hand to shield his eyes.

"Somebody's a little drunk," she said devilishly, pushing him onto the sofa.

He rolled onto his side and tried to sit up, but she pushed him back.

"Relax," she said. Veronica pulled off both of his shoes and then stood back. "You know, Yuri," she said, wrapping her fingers around the bottom of her dress and pulling it up to her waist, "if we keep this up, you're never going to get rid of me."

"You're underestimating my ability to eliminate people."

She stood above him, with a leg to either side of him. "Is that so?" Then she descended slowly to straddle him.

"Yeah. I'm a professional."

"Mm-hmm," she said, unconvinced, kissing his chest. She dragged her lips to his neck. "Are you a professional at stalling too?"

Yuri hung onto her words and her touch. He found them euphoric; they penetrated him deeply. Veronica was surely the most beautiful thing he had ever laid eyes on. And it was not because she was almost naked; there was something else—something deep and intoxicating about her.

Perhaps it was just the alcohol. It had to be the alcohol. He should not have drunk that much. The alcohol was making him rethink his life. But maybe, just maybe, there was a life beyond what he had always known. Ninpo had always felt like an unscrupulous master—a prison. But Veronica gave him a view of a different life. An image of a life where he had a house and a yard and a loving wife.

This felt good.

This felt right.

This is what Ninpo could never give him.

Veronica grasped his face with both hands and kissed him. Deeply. Devouring him with gentle turns of her head. Passion poured from her lips. It washed over him. He consumed it. It became part of him. He was drowning, but he didn't want air.

Yuri felt as though, for the first time in his life, he had found real meaning. He'd found something that was able to fill the void that Ninpo had always left.

He had to tell her everything.

Everything.

Yuri came to life. Not the construct that he had created to deceive others. But rather, the real Yuri. His passion burst into fire, lighting them both ablaze. He rolled over, ripped his shirt from his body, and dove into Veronica. She cooed as they became one.

The temperature soared.

The volume increased.

Then the sound of someone clearing their throat sliced through the moment. Yuri and Veronica suddenly were drawn back into their separate bodies. Yuri lifted his head, and Veronica did too, arching her neck to see over the back of the sofa.

"Omigod! Terry!" Veronica shrieked, snatching a pillow to cover herself. She looked at Yuri and whispered, "What is he doing here?"

"I live here," Terry replied matter-of-factly. "Remember?"

Terry was supposed to be gathering intelligence on a potential target. Or as Veronica knew, Terry was on a date.

"Hey, Ter," Yuri said. "You're not creepy or anything. And no, you didn't just interrupt me having sex with my girlfriend. Maybe you could find some shrubbery to manicure?"

"I need you to listen to this voicemail." Terry sounded concerned.

"How about no?"

"This is important."

"How about no, Terry? I'm a little busy."

"This doesn't have time for busy."

"Are you serious right now?" Yuri growled.

"As a hole in the head. Yuri"—Terry paused and searched for the right words—"just listen."

"There's nothing more important than Veronica right this second! Especially not a goddamn voicemail. So, unless you're missing both legs, get out!" Yuri started kissing Veronica's neck, but she had gone cold and unresponsive.

"What?" Yuri demanded, stormily. "What's wrong with you?"

Terry keyed the voicemail application and turned on the speaker.

Discomfort pooled in her eyes. Frustration filled his.

"Omigod, Terry. I'm going to pull your head off your shoulders."

A man spoke solemnly in Japanese. The voice was stoic and familiar. It was a voice that they had not heard in over a decade. Yuri was instantly sober.

Veronica's face twisted, puzzled by the voice and the expression on Yuri's face—it was as if he had just seen a ghost.

"What?" Veronica asked. "What's he saying?"

Yuri raised a silencing hand. "Terry, run it back."

Terry did.

The voice began again. "**Terry, Yuri. Hattori Hanzo is dying. He may not survive the week. When his life expires, Ninpo requires that the ritual combat be undertaken. You must return to Togakure Ryu. We will be waiting.**"

It was Kintake. There was no mistaking his voice.

The muscles of Yuri's jaw flexed. He wanted this life, but it was impossible to have. He was chained to Ninpo. Ninpo was his reality. Veronica was just a dream. Yuri found his feet and gathered himself.

"Yuri!" Veronica said, indignant, scrambling behind the pillows. "Yuri, what's going on?"

He raised another silencing hand.

"No, don't tell me to shut up."

"I didn't tell you to shut up. I simply don't need to talk right now."

"Yuri."

"Not now," he said as he started toward his bedroom.

"Yuri! Wait a minute!"

"I said not now, dammit!"

*   *   *

198

"So, you don't know when you're coming back?"

"Nope." Yuri knew he was going to get yelled at. But what could he do? His better judgment told him that he should have ignored her and dealt with the backlash when he returned—if he returned.

"Nope?" she parroted.

But he couldn't do it.

"Nope," he repeated.

She burned a hole in Yuri's face with her eyes.

"So that's it?"

"Pretty much."

She threw her arms up. "When are you just going to be honest with me, Yuri? Why are we doing this?"

Yuri was a statue.

"Care to explain why you're rushing out of town?"

"It's complicated, Veronica."

"Try me," she snapped.

"No."

Veronica exhaled. "What makes this complicated is the fact that you refuse to tell me why."

"I just have some things I have to wrap up."

"In Japan?"

"Yes."

"*Nobody* flies seven thousand miles to *wrap* things up."

Yuri remained stoic, difficult as it was. He reviewed his options in his head. If he gave no ground, their relationship was done for; he didn't want that. If he gave in, he would violate Ninpo. There had to be a middle ground.

"Nothing to say?"

Maybe there *was* nothing to be said. Maybe it was over, and Yuri was in denial. His heart was overloading, but he kept up the visage of stoicism.

"Why are you playing games with me, Yuri?" she roared.

Yuri shook his head. "I'm not."

"Yes, you are!"

"Please, stop yelling at me."

"You need to stop playing games with me!"

Yuri's voice became stern. "You. Need. To stop. Yelling at me."

199

Her eyes filled with tears. "You're hurting me." She dropped onto the couch.

"I—I'm sorry, Veronica." Yuri's stomach suddenly ached. "I'm not trying to hurt you."

She buried her face in her hands to hide her tears.

Yuri felt a quake in his heart. He didn't want to go to Japan. He had unfinished business there, but he wasn't willing to hurt Veronica over it. His duty and his honor pulled him back. He was a reluctant piece of metal to Ninpo's magnet. Veronica's heart was the victim.

Terry warned him not to get too involved. The deeper Yuri dove into his relationship, the harder it would be for him to come up for air. Yuri didn't want to admit it, but Terry was right. Veronica, though, gave him something indescribable. Yuri couldn't let that go. Terry wouldn't approve. Then again, Terry had never been in a *real* relationship.

Yuri searched for the right thing to say. He really had to be careful with what he said. And giving up a sliver of the information would raise her suspicion. She was an attorney, and she was a professional at squeezing people for information. Yuri was under enough pressure and didn't need to be squeezed.

Being honest bounced around in his mind. How bad could it be? Who would know that he'd told her anything?

Yuri remembered one of his earliest lessons of Ninpo: *One cannot outrun dishonor. It is a contagion that will kill those one holds dear. Never believe that one can escape dishonor. Many have tried, only to realize that dishonor is a grave tax collector.*

He couldn't tell her. Besides, Veronica wouldn't understand—or perhaps even believe—the situation if he fully explained it

Yuri sat down next to hurt and wrapped her in his arms. "I know this is tough. It's tough for me too."

Veronica lifted her head and sobbed. "We can't go on like this. I can't continue to have you shut me out. It's like you're hiding from something or somebody."

"Okay—look, I have to handle some family issues—"

Veronica cut in, "I could have sworn you said that you don't talk to your family."

"It's complicated."

"Try me."

"No."

"Why not?"

"Because you wouldn't understand if I told you."

"How do you know until you try?"

What was he to say? *Honey, so I'm like a ninja, and I kill for a living? And now I have to go back to Japan and participate in a duel to the death with a rival ninja clan?* No. He couldn't say any of that. Never mind that he would have to kill her immediately and then take his own life.

Regardless, his silence was going to poison his relationship until it fell apart. He had to be honest with her about something. "There are things in my life—especially in my past—that I'm just *not* ready to disclose. There are some pretty terrible things. My family is not at all what it seems."

"I didn't mean—"

"It's nothing against you," he cut in. "Things...life takes time."

She looked at him now. "How long is it going to take us, Yuri? I have to know."

"I don't know." His eyes were soft for the first time.

"Yuri, I don't want this to destroy what we have, but you have to be two feet in with me. I can't be the only person in this relationship willing to devote time for us to develop as a couple. I can't just love who you are now. I have to be able to love who you were in the past as well. And if you can't trust me with your past, then you can't trust me with your future."

Once again, she was right. But the future was going to have to wait. He still had to handle his past.

"This isn't any easier on me than it is on you. Believe that," he said. "I have to go. I don't know when I'll be back. It totally depends on how long it takes for Terry and me to find a resolution." He smiled. "And you know that Terry doesn't do anything fast."

Veronica gave a weak smile.

Yuri kissed her on the side of her face, and then he found his feet and headed for the door.

"Yuri?"

He stopped.

"Can I at least drive you to the airport?"

Yuri shot her a smile over his shoulder and then left.

*   *   *

Paying no real attention to the passing scenery, Terry stared aimlessly through the back window of Veronica's SUV. Why on earth had he agreed to let Veronica chauffer them to Dulles International?

It was nice of her to do so, no doubt. It alleviated the need for long-term parking or having to pay the sizeable Uber fee for a ride from Oxen Hill, Maryland, all the way to Loudon County, Virginia. Now Terry regretted not paying the money, since he was presently a captive audience—and a hostage—to Veronica's final interrogation of Yuri.

Veronica was notoriously skilled at disrupting Yuri's focus. In fact, she was speaking to him in a playful voice, and Yuri was eating it up. Terry, however, was not the least bit fooled. He knew that Veronica was trying to mask her real intent: use Yuri's emotions as leverage to force him to reveal things that he otherwise would not.

Women had an uncanny ability to make men open up. Even the most resolved man could be reduced to a blathering idiot, spilling every secret he had—all in the name of love. In fact, the clan trained female Shinobi—*Kunoichi*—to exploit this ability, making them peerless infiltrators and interrogators. Veronica may not have been a disciplined Shinobi, but her training to notice the smallest technicalities as a legal professional made her quite formidable.

Terry laughed.

Veronica looked at him in the rearview mirror. "What's so funny?"

"I just fantasized about stabbing you," Terry said.

"What?" Her face pruned. "Why?"

"No particular reason, really. That's what made it funny."

Her mouth became a scalene triangle. "Okay, then."

"Okay, then," said Terry.

"Okay, then." Yuri decided he'd join in. He was tugging at his seatbelt to the rhythm of the song, the inertial reel locking—*thump*—with each pull.

"What are you boys going to do while you're there?"

"I told you. Wrap some things up."

"There is no way you two gorgeous boys are going overseas just to visit with family the entire time. I know you guys are going to go out."

Terry glanced at Veronica. She was going for the throat. *Cute* wasn't working, so now she was employing a different approach. Crafty little minx.

Thump. Thump. Thump. Yuri continued banging the seatbelt lock. "We really don't go out that much when we go home."

"Why do I find that hard to believe? Especially considering how flamboyant Terry is."

Terry became suddenly suspicious. "I'm not sure how I should take that last statement."

She laughed and glanced over her shoulder for a brief second. "I was implying that you're friendly and love crowds. I don't know how you could resist the urge to go out and hook up with all the Asian women."

Little did Veronica know, more often than not, when Terry was out indulging in the nightlife, he actually was meeting with clients or gathering intelligence on targets. Rarely did he go out to socialize these days. There was way too much work to be done and training to keep up with. When he was free, he did bonsai.

In fact, Terry and Yuri used to meet clients and conduct intelligence together; however, Yuri's relationship tended to cramp their espionage. Quite often, the responsibility fell on Terry when Yuri was busy tending to his relationship. In fact, on the evening Terry had interrupted Yuri and Veronica, Terry was supposed to have been on the Odyssey Cruise gathering intelligence on a foreign dignitary suspected of committing treason against his parent country.

To that end, Terry found a measure of satisfaction in Veronica's misinterpretation of his true personality. It meant that his version of Terry—the disguise as it were—that he portrayed to those not of the Fujibayashi was effective.

Yuri unfolded the sun visor and looked at himself in the mirror. "I'm telling you, babe; we don't really go out much when we go home. We grew up a good distance from the city. Hell, you have to pack a lunch just to go to the market." Satisfied, he stowed it and resumed his drumming of the seatbelt.

"So, where did you get your food?" she asked.

"We grew it."

Thump. Thump. Thump.

"That's *so* cool."

"Yeah—well, personally, I prefer the grocery store and microwaves."

Veronica's mouth dropped. "You didn't have microwaves?"

Thump. Thump. Thump.

"Naw, we had pigs and goats."

Veronica laughed. She imagined Yuri in a pair of overalls and a straw hat, tending a small herd of livestock, and Terry dressed the same, staring at him. Just believing that Yuri was an author of foreign literature and Terry was a Bonsai Artist was hard enough. But farmers? Now, that was almost far-fetched.

Thump. Thump. Thump.

"So," she said.

"So?"

"Are you going to call me while you're there?"

Terry clenched his teeth.

Thump. Thump. Thump.

"Yeah. I'll call—" Yuri's seatbelt cinched violently across his throat. Yuri coughed, startled.

Veronica glanced at Yuri.

The seatbelt loosened, and Yuri rubbed his neck gingerly, whipping his head around the headrest to look at Terry.

Terry's brow was furrowed. "Quit. That. Shit."

Quit what? Drumming the seatbelt or talking to Veronica?

Veronica was unaffected by the brothers' exchange. "Are you going to call me at all?"

Yuri turned back around in his seat. "Yeah—I'll have my satellite phone."

"Do you promise?"

"Yeah."

"Tell me you promise."

"What?" Yuri asked tersely.

Terry rolled his eyes and shifted his attention to his smartphone.

Veronica checked her blind spot and merged right. "Say, 'Veronica, I promise I will call you every chance I get.'"

"I said, 'I promise.'"

"No. You said, 'Yeah.'"

"I'll call you."

She looked at Terry in the rearview and called his name to get his attention. He looked up. "Make sure he calls me, please," she said.

A caustic grin stretched across Terry's face. "I'll do that."

"Promise?"

"Yeah—Veronica, I promise I will tell Yuri to call *you* every day."

Terry would say just about anything in exchange for silence the rest of the way to the airport. Much to his chagrin, however, their jousting persisted the remainder of the ride. Veronica threw inquisitive jabs, and Yuri ducked and countered with half-truths—which only spurned her need to ask more questions. She formulated four or five new questions for every answer Yuri made. She even repeated questions in different formats. Yuri was holding his own, though. Yuri was an expert at silence and espionage, after all. Terry just hoped that he stayed that way.

The *Departures* sign zoomed by and a feeling of relief rippled through Terry's body. Ten more minutes with the two lovebirds, and he may have killed them.

Veronica weaved the SUV around traffic, coming to a halt in front of the door. Terry wasted no time and leaped clear, angling for the trunk. Veronica asked Yuri again if he intended to call her.

By the time Yuri and Veronica meandered to the rear of the vehicle, Terry had already pulled the luggage out and arranged it on the street.

"Terry, are you going to take care of my man?"

"Sure, great care," he replied distantly, putting on his headphones and pulling the hood of his sweatshirt over his braids. "Well, I'd say it was a pleasure, but then I'd be lying." Terry smiled, heaved his bags up, and made for the door.

"What's eating him?"

"You'll have to excuse him. He's grumpy because he's sore. His anal beads got stuck last night."

Veronica laughed. "You two are something else."

Yuri shrugged.

"You're going to call me, right?"

"Only if you ask me a million more times."

Veronica looked past him, her facial expression betraying her uneasiness.

"Yes, I'm going to call you."

"Promise?"

"I promise—"

"**Talk while walking!**" Terry yelled from the door. "**We have a plane to catch! You two can talk about this over the** *phone!*"

"I don't have to speak Japanese to know that he wants you to hurry." Her stomach was in knots.

"Well." Yuri's stomach was in knots too. "I guess this is it."

"I guess so." She lowered her head, trying to hold back tears.

Yuri lifted her chin and kissed her. The floodgates opened, and tears fell relentlessly. He wiped her face and smiled. "I'll see you soon."

Yuri grabbed his bags and headed towards the doors.

"**Damn,** Prince Charming; **I was halfway to Japan.**"

Yuri walked past him. "Shut it."

With her arms wrapped around her for warmth, Veronica watched as the two brothers made their way into the terminal. A security guard approached her and informed her that she needed to move her vehicle. She exhaled an acknowledgment, her breath visible.

Suddenly Veronica was gripped by a measure of valor, and she ran towards the terminal door. "Yuri!"

Terry glanced over his shoulder but kept walking. Yuri stopped and turned at the sound of his name.

"I"—her lungs cramped—"I love you!" She held her breath, feeling suddenly vulnerable and insecure.

Yuri's eyes focused on her face, and it was as if, for a brief moment, everyone in the terminal except he and Veronica ceased to exist. He smiled. He waved. Then he turned and followed his brother.

She watched him go. Anxiously.

The security guard approached her again and told her that she needed to move her vehicle or it would be towed. Again, she acknowledged, and then she climbed in and drove off.

Terry and Yuri stood in the sea of travelers as they waited to board. They stood silently for a long while. Although not showing it, Terry was concerned about his brother's focus. He was afraid that Yuri was going to be too preoccupied with Veronica to be able to cope with the return to Togakure Ryu. Not that he thought that Yuri was soft; Terry was just worried that Yuri's frustration would manifest as belligerence and they would have a repeat of ten years ago. After all, they had left Japan with a considerable amount of unresolved business. Terry was concerned; he just wasn't sure how he should voice it. He'd think it over. He had a seventeen-hour flight to figure it out.

Yuri lifted his head after hitting send on a text message. "I really hate flying," he said.

"What?" Terry asked as he watched a group of women pass by.

"I hate flying."

"What are you talking about?" A puzzled, unconvinced expression painted Terry's face. "You fly all the time."

"Yeah, I know. I just never say anything."

"Whatever," Terry said. "It isn't flying that you hate."

Chapter Thirteen: Family Reunion

Shinobi are assets to the clan, never burdens. A Shinobi unable to lift his sword can no longer shoulder Ninpo.
The Seventh Mandate, translated from Ninpo.

Suzuka Mountains. Mie Prefecture, Japan. Today.

Terry and Yuri hadn't been in Japan for nearly a decade, and it seemed that not much had changed. From the moment they stepped off the plane, memories of their youth flooded their minds, brought on by the sounds, smells, and the atmosphere unique to the island nation of their childhood.

Terry didn't miss the trip to the village. He remembered the first time as if it was yesterday, except that he had made the original trek in the summer and now it was cold. Yuri, just like when he was a prepubescent boy, didn't seem the least bit fazed by it; his mind appeared adrift, somewhere other than their current location. Was his mind on Veronica or was it on Hattori Hanzo—or on Kintake?

Kintake. That name gave Terry a sore feeling. It invoked some pretty difficult memories. Kintake was a hardened teacher who expected perfection from his Shinobi and met anything short with harsh reinforcement. In light of their final, devastating encounter that had resulted in Terry and Yuri's departure, they rarely spoke Kintake's name. The anticipation of seeing Kintake was not welcomed, and both brothers were dealing with that anxiety quietly.

Honestly, neither of them were looking forward to returning to the village. The brothers had grown apart from their connection to the Fujibayashi, and this whole endeavor brought mixed feelings. In some way, Terry was excited about returning to the village in which they'd spent the better part of their childhood—the clansmen who had taken in him and his orphaned brother. On the other hand, Terry was extremely apprehensive. He wondered if the intervening decade had mended old wounds. He doubted that in the case of Yuri, and he was right in his thoughts. Yuri's feelings were mixed simply because he was concerned for his brother. Yuri was the commander of grudge holders everywhere, the emperor even. His fight with Kintake hadn't ended; it had only been interrupted. The problem with his desire to finish the fight with Kintake was that he was afraid of hurting his brother in the process. Terry had always been devastated by the sudden fissure that had opened up between the Ciccone brothers and the clan all at once. Yuri didn't care except that he wanted to settle things with Kintake once and for all. He'd debated with himself for the duration of the seventeen-hour flight to Japan as to whether he should pick a fight the moment they arrived in the village or if he should just let it go. The prudent thing to do was to let it go—the honorable thing, anyway. But he was starting to wonder if he truly cared about honor anymore. Or did he question his loyalty to honor because of Kintake—sort of as a means of rebellion? He decided that he wouldn't let his personal grudge get the better of him for now, but that could change once they arrived in Togakure Ryu. For Terry's sake, though, he would try his best to remain composed.

The feeling was numbing as they made the three-hour drive from the airport to the point where they parked their vehicle. Parked there also was Kintake's beat-up old pick-up truck. The feeling became sharp once they exited the vehicle and began walking the remainder of the distance; the closer they got, the more intense the feeling became. Finally, they made the final descent into the distinct ear-shaped river basin, and the first evidence of Togakure Ryu began to come into view.

As they neared the edge of the village, Terry focused on suppressing his discomfort and found himself looking over his shoulder at his brother for reassurance. Yuri returned his brother's occasional glances with conflicted, raised brows and a pursed expression.

By then, they had passed the perimeter fence of the pigpen and angled toward to the most direct path through the peripheral cottages to the meeting hall from which Hattori Hanzo conducted business as well as resided, the inorganic hum of its generator becoming discernable through the ambient sounds of the mountain fauna. When the brothers broke through the wall of cottages, they could make out the meeting hall's *kanji*-covered stanchions, its shrubbery, and a score of villagers congregating on and around the porch.

"Don't do anything crazy," Terry said, sounding more suggestive than demanding.

Yuri spat a mouthful of saliva before he replied, "Like what?"

"I don't know. Something crazy."

"Don't start with me. I'm not in the best mood."

"I know. That's exactly why I said, 'Don't do anything crazy.' I'm not trying to piss you off, little brother."

"I won't. I'm here for the family reunion just like you."

Terry rolled his eyes. "Right."

"I even brought presents."

"I'm sure they'll be appreciative."

"How's your Japanese?"

"Rusty by their standards, I'm sure. Why?"

"Because you're doing all the talking."

A teenage villager in a plaid shirt and worn corduroy trousers who was cleaning gardening tools on the side of a hut between it and the pen spotted them with surprise. Terry waved and shot a smile at the young man. The young man dropped the tool and waved both hands, nearly unable to contain himself.

"Who's that?" Yuri asked, leaning closer to Terry's ear.

"I don't remember."

Terry greeted the teenager in Japanese, and he responded to Terry with stuttering excitement, bidding that they follow. Terry and Yuri did. The youth explained that the Shinobi-no-mono had fallen ill and that Omiyoshu Sensei had been awaiting their arrival but was unsure whether they would show.

Terry assumed that the youth was too young to remember what had transpired between the brothers and Kintake so many years ago. Perhaps Kintake had forbidden any talk about the brothers, and as a result, those who hadn't been present had never been informed.

Curious, Terry thought.

As they made their way to the village center, those who weren't already outside came out to see the long-absent Shinobi. The brothers made eye contact and nodded toward each villager they passed; however, the villagers looked at the brothers like complete strangers. All the years they had spent in this village, and it felt foreign, as if they were unwelcome tourists walking aimlessly around Iga Ueno Castle looking for ninja memorabilia like those shown in western media. It made them even more uncomfortable.

They approached the door of the center hall, where three Jonin in their late seventies and dressed in muted browns greeted them with nods. Terry and Yuri came up the steps and bowed at the waist, and Terry readied his atrophied Japanese. No one said anything, however. The Jonin just looked at them awkwardly. Terry looked back at Yuri; he was giving a look that read, *Well, say something.*

Terry swallowed hard. "**Masters, my brother and I were recalled by the kōchō. We were ordered to return per the Ninth Mandate of Ninpo.**"

The eldest Shinobi, and the one furthest away in their huddle, said, "**Under terrible circumstances must you return, Terry, but the ancestors paved this path of righteousness so that we may be with honor.**"

Terry bowed deeply, and Yuri as nearly. "**Yes, Sensei**," Terry replied. "**May we see Shinobi-no-Mono?**"

"**Of course**," another said, gesturing the door.

Terry and Yuri bowed again and moved to the door, removing their shoes before entering.

The interior of the meeting hall was immaculate and seemingly untouched by the ages—despite being the only building in the village that had electricity—a relic of a bygone era that connected the Fujibayashi to their past.

The brothers walked lightly across the antechamber towards a room near the back. There, they found Hattori Hanzo closer to his end with each passing moment. He had changed tremendously in the better part of a decade. Age had not been friendly to him, decimating his virility and endurance. He couldn't walk or see. Age had robbed him of his ability to talk or teach. He was no longer capable of being Shinobi and by normal standards should have committed seppuku like Ninpo demanded of any lame or inept warrior. The Shinobi-no-mono, however, was forbidden seppuku, only being allowed a natural death at the hands of fate or of combat but not by his own hand. Unfortunate, Terry and Yuri thought, to be trapped in an infirm body, unable to interact with the world. It felt dishonorable, but the Shinobi-no-mono was a position only the most honorable could hold. He was the spiritual leader of all Shinobi clans, who communed with the ancestors regularly and communicated their wishes and demands to the clans. He was their medium—their *most holy*. And when he passed from the mortal world, the clans would have to sacrifice their most promising Shinobi to their ancestors so that a new Shinobi-no-mono might be granted the wisdom to ascend. The lives of those sacrificial Shinobi filled the Shinobi-no-mono with the power to command the clans.

The time for sacrifice was almost upon them. It only came once every couple of generations, and only the most capable Shinobi were honorable enough to participate and perhaps give their lives for their clan and Ninpo as a whole. It was a fatalistic system of beliefs, but it was adhered to religiously by the Shinobi and had been for millennia.

Terry knelt next to Hanzo's mat. "**Shinobi-no-mono, it's Terry. I...uh...I'm here with Yuri.**"

Yuri put his bags down and took up a position next to his brother.

"**We're here because Ninpo has demanded our return,**" Terry continued. "**It has been a long time. Yuri and I have accomplished much in our absence. You'd be proud. Yuri is right here next to me.**" Terry nudged his brother with his elbow. "**Say something.**"

"Hi."

Terry sighed, "**Yuri hasn't changed much.**"

"**Yuri. Terry,**" came a woman's voice from the doorway. "**You have arrived after all.**" It was a voice that they remembered. It reminded Terry of his childhood and made his heart flutter.

They turned and looked. There stood Akiko with her alabaster skin, her hair atop her head in a messy pile, and dressed in plain gray robes with a ninjatō suspended beneath her belt at the small of her back. The bulk of her robes made her look far less petite and delicate.

"**Akiko,**" Terry said, climbing to his feet, "**it's so good to see you—even under such compromising circumstances.**"

Yuri found his brother in the corner of his eyes, thinking that Terry's reaction was anything but subtle.

"**Likewise,**" Akiko said, unfazed, and then she turned her attention to Yuri. "**Yuri, you are well?**"

Yuri nodded, his bright blue eyes betraying his discomfort and suspicion.

"**How have you been?**" Terry asked her, bubbly and just a hair above a whisper.

212

Yuri's eyes shot back to his brother.

"**You look great,**" Terry continued. "**Haven't changed a bit, really. You're just a slight bit taller.**"

Akiko cracked a cornered smile. "**Father and Saki went to the shrine to meet with the Momochi to negotiate the terms of the ritual. They are due shortly. I should take you to your quarters in the meantime so that when he returns, we are all ready to speak with him.**"

"**Sounds good,**" Terry replied.

Akiko clasped her hands together and turned to leave. "**Come with me.**"

Terry followed.

Yuri watched them exit into the antechamber and head toward the door. His discomfort was growing; he didn't want to be here. He looked down at Hattori Hanzo and considered that he might not be feeling anything for the Fujibayashi.

"**Yuri,**" Terry yelled through the doorway, "**are you coming?**"

"**Sure.**"

*   *   *

Yuri was antsy, and Terry could visibly see it. He watched Yuri pace the interior of the cottage, sharpening the blade of his tanto and staring angrily into space. Terry didn't want to waste time inquiring into his brother's feelings since he already knew how Yuri would respond. Terry, however, was concerned about Yuri's reaction when they saw Kintake. Terry wasn't worried that Yuri had unfinished business with Kintake; Terry was worried that Yuri would aim to bring that business to a close. Yuri did, after all, have a nasty penchant for grudge holding. Terry just needed Yuri to keep his cool.

After nearly an hour had passed, Akiko returned. She knocked before she slipped through the rice paper door. "**Father has returned. He summons us all.**"

"This should be entertaining," Yuri said, tossing his rag onto the floor and sheathing the knife in the holster beneath his shirt.

Terry climbed to his feet and pulled on his jacket. "Nothing crazy, Yuri."

"Dude, get off my case."

Akiko interjected, "**Is there a problem?**"

Terry's eyes became furtive. Was Akiko joking or just playing dumb? Surely, she knew why Terry was addressing him. "**No. No problem. I'm just making sure my brother remembers protocol.**"

"I'll be sure not to pull the pins on any grenades," Yuri retorted, venom dripping from his mouth.

Akiko didn't pay any of it much attention. She knew Terry and Yuri to be a quirky, unorthodox duo and didn't stress over their oddness. She departed the cottage without so much as a word, Terry and Yuri followed. As they came out from between two cottages, they could see that a rather large contingent of villagers—Genin, Chunin, and Kunoichi—had gathered in the rock garden of the meeting hall, and the Jonin had collected into a huddle of twenty or so at the base of the steps. All were dressed in the robes similar to those worn by Akiko, colored gray or brown, with their ninjatōs stashed in their belts. Terry and Yuri felt out of place. It wasn't just the way they were dressed, though. In their adolescence, the villagers had paid them a monopoly of attention. Now it was as if they were invisible. Terry didn't know what to make of it, but it enhanced Yuri's desire to be elsewhere. Villagers continued to arrive even after Terry and Yuri.

Kintake and Saki exited the central cottage and approached the congregation; their faces were painted with the seriousness of a physician preparing for brain surgery. They came to the apex of the stairs, and Saki raised his arms above his head. The crowd went instantly silent, bowing deeply.

"**The time is nearly upon us,**" came a voice from the grouped Jonin. An indistinct, balding, gray head rose from the bowed assembly. "**This is a time when the honor of Shinobi is tried and weighed. This is a time where Shinobi meet on sacred ground in the audience of our ancestors and showcase their devotion to Ninpo. Only the most devout are called upon to approach the sacred ground with weapons drawn.**

"**Our blades are sharpened for generations until a time such as this. It is a time when selfishness is dissolved and sacrifice becomes the means by which we exist. This time will not be easy, nor will it bring us delight; sacrifice is never easy nor delightful. From it, though,**

214

our honor will be honed, and our existence will continue. We will persist as we always have. May the ancestors grant us wisdom and Ninpo guide our blades."

Everyone stood, moved by the elder's speech, inhaling deeply of conviction and dedication; Kintake didn't seem so affected, his eyes were like Yuri's—contemptuous.

Saki came forward. "**Our three Chunin seniors will take to the sacred ground carrying only the weapons of the ancestors. There, they will engage the Momochi in our most sanctified ritual and, hopefully, be bid to ascend to the halls of our ancestors being regarded among the greatest Shinobi to walk the earth. Terry, Akiko, and I will begin training tomorrow when the sun sets. We have much to revisit—**"

"No." Kintake placed a silencing hand in the air. "**Akiko will not fight; Yuri will take her place.**"

"**Father!**" Akiko's voice hummed with betrayal as she pushed through the small crowd to the front. "**I am third Chunin next to Saki and Terry! It is my duty to go onto the sacred ground!**"

Kintake's browed furrowed, and he shot her a look of ice. "**You will be silent. No Kunoichi will go.**"

"**Master, if I may—**" Saki jumped to her defense but was cut off by the blade of Kintake's tanto pressing into his throat, nearly lacerating him with the speed by which it was drawn.

Kintake locked Saki's startled gaze; the aging Shinobi's speed was easily forgotten until a sharp-edged reminder was applied. "**The next Shinobi that challenges my authority will die by my hand. Do I make myself clear**?" The group was silent. Their concurrence was silent too.

Kintake returned his knife to its sheath beneath the sleeve of his robe. "**Continue**," he urged Saki.

"**Yes, Omiyoshu Sensei,**" Saki replied obediently, resisting the urge to rub his throat. "**In the morning, we must honor Mamushi. We will meet on the bank of the river. All not involved with preparations shall attend.**"

Terry's stomach dropped. Yuri's nose flared, a sneer rising at one corner of his mouth. They weren't looking forward to being *poisoned*.

The villagers, composed of the Jonin and the more senior of the Genin and Chunin, numbering perhaps twenty in all, knelt in a half-moon-shaped cluster, shoulder to shoulder, near the edge of the river, with Terry, Yuri, and Saki at the center. In front of them was Kintake, flanked by a single elder holding in his hands the revered Mamushi—a pit viper native to the mountains in Iga.

To the Fujibayashi, Mamushi was a kami—a spirit inhabiting an animal body. It was regarded as a spirit-guide, and legends held that Mamushi, angered by an invasion of his territory by the Shogun Oda Nobunaga, divided himself into many parts, entered the bodies of vipers, and sneaked into the tents of Nobunaga's generals, killing them with venom. This legendary act allowed the Fujibayashi, the Momochi, and the other Iga clans to strike decisive blows against the Shogun's forces. In the chaos, the clans were able to escape into the mountains. In spite of Mamushi, the Shogun ultimately routed and wiped out the Iga clans. The Fujibayashi, however, attributed their survival to the efforts of Mamushi.

The ritual, thus, arose from the Fujibayashi paying homage to Mamushi by proving that only a true Shinobi could ingest Mamushi's venom and survive. Each neophyte, called *Kodomo*, who had reached the plateau of his or her initiate training, usually around age fifteen, partook in the ritual to become Genin—those that survived. Any who perished were deemed unworthy and never spoken of again. Following the ritual, all new Genin received a tattoo of Mamushi. The tattoo was unique to each Shinobi, and its placement on their body expressed their personal strength and their contribution to the clan. Terry's tattoo was etched along his spine. Yuri's snaked from his armpit to the top of his abdomen by way of his ribs. Saki's tattoo stretched from shoulder to shoulder.

Saki, Terry, and Yuri were not, however, imbibing today so that they could cross over; they had done that more than a decade earlier. They were imbibing because Mamushi required that Shinobi carrying out the Ninth Mandate of Ninpo must prove his or her worthiness by ingesting his poison once more.

Two Kunoichi approached the huddle of meditating Shinobi, carrying between them a hot cast of freshly brewed tea. They set it down in the gravel between Terry, Yuri, and Saki, and Kintake and his aide. They opened the cast and filled three small cups with the ladle.

"**To merely follow Ninpo is not, in and of itself, honorable,**" Kintake said in an intense, solemn tone. "**Any base creature could follow Ninpo's mandates, but to allow Ninpo to guide oneself like a honed blade in service of our ancestors is to be Shinobi. Ninpo's most genuine pupils have the most serious minds and unquestionable dedication. Not even the threat of death can sever a Shinobi's connection to Ninpo. Today, the three of you will prove that Ninpo and the Shinobi are indivisible.**" Kintake approached his three Chunin and placed a considerate hand on each of their heads. "**Are you ready**?"

They nodded in unison.

Kintake snaked his fingers through his aide's grip and grabbed the base of the viper's head; it writhed in his grip. The elder man looked to Kintake for assurance that he had positive control of the agitated serpent. Kintake gave him a stern, hardened look and nodded. The aide released the snake's body and backed away. The viper defiantly coiled itself around Kintake's arm and formed a hateful grimace with its mouth.

Kintake raised the viper's head level with his own eyes. "**Mamushi, I give you my best Shinobi. Their worthiness is yours to determine. If they be so worthy, let your venom empower them. If not, their lives are yours.**" Kintake lowered the viper's head to the first cup and squeezed. The viper's jaw came unhinged and opened, revealing its needle-like fangs. He pressed the viper's jaws to the top of the cup and expelled venom into the tea. Then he moved on to the other two.

"**My Chunin,**" he continued, "**Mamushi has made his decision. Now drink and see if he has deemed you worthy.**"

All three were reluctant. Deciding whether or not to drink the tea was like putting a single round in a revolver's cylinder, giving it a whirl, and then putting the barrel in your mouth. Chances were that you'd survive the first couple of pulls, but the more pulls you made, the worse your chances became. Terry, Yuri, and Saki had survived this ritual before, but doing it again was like pulling the trigger a second time. All they could hope for was that adulthood made them more resistant.

Saki was the first to reach for his cup. Terry and Yuri followed a half-second later. They all sat there momentarily, minds racing. Then they placed the cups to their lips and poured the tea into their mouths. Saki didn't let it linger; he let it flow down his throat immediately. Yuri swallowed hard and then exhaled his stress. Terry swallowed in pieces, watching Mamushi wriggle in Kintake's grip.

The tea tasted faintly of coconut, like they remembered, seemingly benign, but they knew the worst was yet to come.

*   *   *

The past week had been awful. Awful was an understatement. Terry, Yuri, and Saki weren't afforded much time to recover from the envenomation. Hell, they were lucky to be alive. The venom first induced a sustained burning sensation in their veins, followed by nausea and vomiting. It caused fevered chills and teeth-grinding cramps. The worst of it came in their sleep, however. It caused night terrors that left even the most stoic individuals sleepless. The clan showed little sympathy, waking them up shortly before sunset to eat and then begin training. Food only increased their nausea, and nausea made training cruel.

The Fujibayashi woke the three warriors for an assembly with the Jonin to meditate and to consult matters of spirit and prayer. Afterward came physical conditioning, sparring, stealth training, and weapons training, followed by more spiritual conditioning, sparring, and training, and then to bed before the sun rose.

Each evening, the three men had to run up the eastern ridge and then climb down the craggy cliffs into the adjacent valley only to have to return the long way up the river before the sun came up. They had lost count of the number of times they'd had to stop and vomit. Despite the venom's punishing effects, they managed to endure.

The Fujibayashi waited in the dark with prepared meals, fresh clothes, medical relief, and plans for follow-on phases of training and conditioning for the three warriors. When they returned, the

Fujibayashi swarmed over the warriors, tending to the men like prized race horses; Saki, Terry, and Yuri couldn't brush their hair or go to the bathroom without tenders assisting. This went on for weeks.

By the third day, Yuri was well enough to use the personal time he was given to sneak off to call Veronica on the satellite phone, standing on the edge of the village to talk in peace. Terry didn't approve, but he didn't say anything.

Yuri missed Veronica. She was on his mind during prayer and meditation. She was on his mind when he was conditioning, when he was fighting, when he was training, and when he was surrounded by the darkness and silence during stealth training.

Terry could see that Yuri was distracted. In fact, Yuri had almost lost a hand during a live sword drill when he hadn't moved as fast as normal. The Shinobi in charge of honing their atrophied skills with traditional weapons had chastised his complacency. Yuri's eyes had burned with disdain for the criticism. Terry had suggested that his brother remain focused. The suggestion had only elicited the same disdainful look from Yuri.

Within three weeks, their bodies had settled into the demands of retraining and the muscle memory of using of weapons they hadn't used in years. Saki was still familiar with many of the weapons, but Terry and Yuri had not dedicated attention to exercising their skills with staves, chain weapons, swords, and other traditional weapons. Such weapons just weren't necessary for their line of work. It didn't take them long to remember their katas and tactics, however.

While their bodies were beginning to operate like the well-oiled machines that they had been trained to be, their minds were not in sync. Saki and Terry were aligned, but Yuri was thousands of miles away. He put no energy into their work; he was simply going through the motions. Terry was coming to realize that Yuri wasn't exaggerating when he said he didn't care about *any of this anymore*, and it showed in his performance. Terry, however, did have to defuse an altercation between Yuri and two Jonin when Yuri grew tired of their treatment of him during training. Yuri told everyone aloud that he didn't care about Ninpo enough to give it any real energy. He truly was disconnected. He was paying too much attention to Veronica. Terry wasn't happy about that. He decided he was going to talk to Yuri about it.

*   *   *

Terry finished bathing and made his way back to the cottage that was solely dedicated to housing the Chunin seniors. They had been given several hours of free time to tend to themselves before they needed to get to bed. He came through the rice paper door to see Saki kneeling on the floor, meditating over a freshly cleaned ninjatō.

"**Where's my brother?**" Terry asked.

"**I have not seen him for some time,**" Saki replied without opening his eyes. "**He was not here when I came in.**"

Terry stalked out of the cottage, resisting the urge to slam the door behind him. This relationship with Veronica was becoming frustrating. Yuri's focus was strained, and he needed to remember his priorities.

Terry walked out to the pigpens, where Yuri usually went to have a peaceful conversation, but Terry didn't see him. Terry scanned the pens, the hillside, and the yards around the immediately visible cottages. There was only a boy in one of the pens to his left and a handful of livestock.

Terry asked the young Shinobi who was tending the goats if he had seen Yuri.

"**Earlier,**" the boy replied. "**He passed through the pigpens and went that way.**" The boy pointed up the incline of the pass that led up the western ridge.

"**What? Where was he going?**"

"**I'm not sure, Terry. But Yuri had a bag on his back when he left.**"

*   *   *

"**What do you mean *he is gone*?**" Kintake inquired from his place on the floor at the center of the room of his cottage. His legs were tucked beneath him, and his tanto was in its sheath on the floor in front of him. "**Who is gone?**"

Kintake was flanked by three Jonin: one bald, one balding, one blind and all dressed in midnight-blue robes. Their attention suddenly

220

focused on Saki, Terry, and Akiko. The Jonin's faces already displayed disapproval, even though Saki had only begun his explanation. Never before had he been under such scrutiny as he was now, and the Jonin were showing him no quarter despite Saki being the first senior and one of the most gifted Shinobi that the Fujibayashi had ever raised.

"**Yuri is gone**," Saki said humbly just inside the doorway, followed by Terry and Akiko.

"**Where has he gone to?**"

"**I am not sure, Omiyoshu Sensei.**"

The skin around Kintake's eyes tightened, and the contours of his face distorted. "**You are not sure, you say?**"

Saki swallowed hard and nodded.

"**Well, find him**," Kintake said delightfully, the lines in his face softening again. "**You are Shinobi, after all. Surely, finding one man on the grounds should not be too much trouble.**"

"**Therein is the problem, Sensei. We have searched the immediate grounds and the surrounding areas. We are unable to find him.**"

"**We have more training to complete before the ritual begins if we are to ensure success!**" the bald elder snapped. "**Yuri delays that!**"

Akiko, Terry, and Saki had agreed that Saki would handle all the talking when they entered the kōchō's quarters to show a unified front, but Akiko didn't agree with the unexpected ambivalence that Saki was displaying. She decided to speak up. "**He should have returned some time ago. I fear that Yuri has abandoned us.**"

Terry's eyes shifted to Akiko; she ignored him.

"**He violates our traditions by leaving!**" said the balding elder. His voice was gravelly and strained by wisdom, and he'd barely given Akiko a chance to complete her sentence.

The blind elder watched them blankly. "**He violates Ninpo! A grave crime indeed!**"

The bald Jonin opened his mouth to continue chastising when Kintake raised a silencing hand. "**Surely, there is a logical explanation for this.**" He pointed past Saki. "**Terry, what is the meaning of this?**"

Terry chewed his bottom lip. **"I don't have an answer, Sensei."**

"Don't you?" Kintake's voice was doubtful.

"He does," the bald Jonin interjected with an accusing finger. **"The second senior is closest to Yuri. He witnesses Yuri's behavior, but he does nothing."**

"What am I supposed to do?" Terry asked disdainfully; it wasn't a question.

"Many of the Jonin claim that Yuri lacks focus and dedication," the bald Jonin continued, **"that he has become a shell of a Shinobi. He no longer cares about our traditions or our code. His time away from the Fujibayashi has distanced him from Ninpo. He must be killed, or he'll bring dishonor upon us all."**

Terry's face hardened. **"Let's not get crazy."**

"You dare challenge a Jonin?" the blind Jonin demanded angrily. **"Have you forgotten your station?"**

"Terry, be calm," said Akiko, placing her hand on Terry's arm.

"Oh, I'm calm. Don't worry," Terry said dismissively, less to her and more to the Jonin. His stomach was in knots. Why had his brother put them—him—in this situation? It didn't make sense. Sure, Yuri had expressed some discomfort with returning, but Terry hadn't thought it was this serious. Had Yuri left to a place where he could just separate himself from the clan's constant grind, or had he truly abandoned them? The latter Terry doubted greatly. Yuri wouldn't abandon him above all things; betrayal wasn't in his nature. Still, Yuri's absence was causing outrage, not just with Kintake and the Jonin, but with Saki and Akiko as well. Saki was viewed as their leader, and the burden of disappointment fell upon his shoulders. Akiko, on the other hand, felt horribly slighted by her father preventing her participation in the ritual. Yuri's seeming disregard only added insult to injury. And worse yet, the outrage would only grow once the village at large found out. Terry didn't know what to do. He just needed time to talk some sense into his brother.

"Do you see?" Kintake asked.

"See what, Father?" Akiko asked. **"Do we see what?**

"Do you see what dishonor does to us? I told you all about this when you were children. Dishonor destroys those around us. Here we are, challenging each other and condemning our own to death on the doorstep of the eve of our finest moment." Kintake's stare penetrated the three seniors. "**Dishonor is a cancer. It sickens us all.**"

"**My brother is not without honor, Omiyoshu Sensei,**" Terry replied, leaping to Yuri's defense. "**He's a dedicated Shinobi and strong with Ninpo. If only you could have seen his performance and deeds over the past seven years. His skills are peerless.**"

Akiko was unconvinced. "**Then why would he have left?**"

The Jonin concurred aloud.

"**Yuri is dealing with his own demons, and let's not forget that we were forced to leave on unforgiving terms. Perhaps he's acting out as a result. Perhaps he feels unwelcome; I know that I do at times.**"

Kintake rolled his eyes. "**We would not want you to be** *uncomfortable*, **Terry.**"

"**And what is this** *forced* **nonsense you speak of?**" Akiko said, supporting her father. "**No one forced Yuri to leave. He—and you—left of your own accord, your own selfishness.**"

"**What are you talking about?**" A mixture of anger, disappointment, and surprise was bubbling up from Terry's stomach. He couldn't believe what he was hearing. "**We didn't choose to leave—**"

"**Hai!**" Kintake asserted loudly. Everyone stopped what they were doing and looked at him. "**Are we geisha or Shinobi? None of you are going to interrupt my meditation to bicker about your troubles with getting along. We are not going to argue this anymore. Terry, where do you believe Yuri has run off to?**"

"**I don't know, Sensei,**" Terry said sincerely. "**Tokyo, probably. He's definitely not anywhere near here; we looked everywhere. I would call him, but he took the satellite phone with him. And the nearest signal for my cell phone is easily a two-hour walk from here.**"

Kintake massaged the tension from the muscles on the back of his neck. Yuri was always impossible, and for that reason, Kintake did not miss him. Even in Yuri's absence, he was a catalyst for pandemonium. One thing was sure: Kintake was going to put Yuri's talent for disruption on the battlefield if it was the last thing he did.

"**Use the telephone in the center hall to see if you can reach Yuri. If not, Saki,**" Kintake said, "**you will take Terry and Akiko and find Yuri—by whatever means necessary. Allow me to be clear. Yuri has a penchant for disobedience and disruption. While I have been tolerant of such behavior in the past, my patience has thinned with age. I expect our most hallowed ritual to proceed without disruption. I expect that Yuri will be present…but I won't allow him to dishonor us either. Go find him and don't return until you do.**"

"**What happens when we find him, Master?**" Saki asked.

"**You are all Shinobi; you will do what is necessary. The ritual opens in two weeks, and it will proceed as planned. Be gone from my sight.**"

The three seniors filed out through the door single file. Her argument unfinished, Akiko was reluctant to leave, but she could see that the look in her father's eyes placed him near his wits' end, and she didn't want to push him further, so she did as she was told and followed Terry and Saki.

"**Omiyoshu Sensei, we must decide how we are to deal with Yuri's transgressions,**" the balding Jonin said. "**We must satisfy the ancestor Shinobi, for their anger is terrible.**"

These three old vultures were no better than his hot-headed seniors! Kintake had finally had enough. "**You three get out too, before I have your heads removed!**"

The Jonin scurried out as commanded. Kintake watched them go and regretted not being heavy-handed. There was a time when no one had trifled with his authority—except Yuri. Yuri had always been the thorn in his side. His daughter was right; Yuri should be killed. It would even make Kintake happy. But to do so would play havoc on what lay ahead. Kintake needed the ritual to go off without a hitch. He couldn't afford for it not to.

*　　*　　*

There was a knock at the door. Yuri heard it from the bedroom of his hotel room and became instantly suspicious. Most people would assume that unexpected knocks would come from housekeeping or the concierge, but the predator inside told him differently.

He listened for voices or perhaps the door opening from the doorway of the bedroom of the suite before checking over his shoulder to ensure that the bathroom door was shut completely. It was, and the shower was running, so any noise would be drowned out by it as he crept to the front door.

There was another series of raps on the door.

Yuri could wait it out and see if the visitor left, but what if his instincts were right? What if he really was in danger? Whether or not he wanted to take part in the Fujibayashi's activities, he was still subject to their consequences. That said, he wanted to know who was at the door. If he was in danger, he wanted to know a face.

By now, the Fujibayashi had to have realized that he was gone, and he was sure that they were swarming about like a disturbed hive of angry wasps. Leaving was not an easy decision, especially if it meant leaving his brother behind. Honestly, Yuri was terribly conflicted about leaving his brother, but what was he to do? Continue to blindly follow the directives of people he hadn't seen in the better part of a decade? Yuri had left the village without saying anything. He had quietly and unilaterally decided that he had reached his limit and was leaving. He hadn't talked to anyone, not even his brother. Yuri hadn't wanted to argue about it, especially in light of the ritual revering Mamushi; that had been the last straw. Yuri remembered the horrors of drinking the legendary venom of the viper that had killed the entire cadre of Oda Nobunaga's army. It had nearly killed him as a child, and he would have sworn that it was going to kill him as an adult. He was lucky to have survived again, he thought. But what if he hadn't survived? He'd have never seen Veronica again. Sure, he could perish in the ritual fight, but he, at least, was willing to die in combat; he had some control over that. He wasn't, however, willing to die participating in any other rituals that used his life as a mere offering.

Another series of knocks interrupted his thoughts.

Yuri left the bedroom and crept into the parlor. The shades were drawn, and the kitchen was clear. His ninjatō was underneath the cushions of the couch, and his tanto was in his jacket hanging just to the left of the door. He was more than willing to spill blood if he needed to, but it was going to be hell to clean up. The walls of the suite were painted red and were no trouble, but the plush carpet was pearl white. Blood would be next to impossible to eliminate. That was just a consequence he'd have to deal with if the situation arose. Even if he was through, it was doubtful that his brother and his fellow Shinobi were going to take no for an answer, especially after going through all the trouble to find him.

Yuri held his breath and looked through the peephole, and he saw a distorted image of Terry wearing an unassuming collared shirt and jeans backed by Saki and Akiko, both dressed like impoverished farmers. Their arrival wasn't joyous; they were no doubt armed, and he was unsure of their intent. If he weren't so uneasy, he'd have been impressed by their ability to track him.

Terry knocked again, harder this time.

Yuri looked over his shoulder, making sure that the parlor was clear. It was, so he unlocked the deadbolt and opened the door until the chain went taut. Yuri's eyes locked with Terry's eyes, then with Saki's, and then with Akiko's; their faces were all business. Nobody said anything at first. There was an ocean of tension boiling between them. Yuri hadn't figured out what he was going to do. He was rolling the dice. Then Terry broke the silence.

"**Yuri, what are you doing?**" he demanded just above a whisper.

Yuri didn't reply; he continued staring.

"**Yuri,**" Terry demanded again, "**what are you doing?**"

"What?" Yuri said finally.

Terry looked back at Saki and Akiko; their faces were as hard as stone, and their eyes were boring holes into the door. He returned to Yuri. "What do you mean what?"

Yuri chose to be evasive. "What're you all doing here?

"I was going to ask you the same thing," Terry retorted.

This time, Saki didn't have the patience to deal with Terry's and Yuri's secretive conversations in a language he didn't speak. "**Why have you abandoned the clan**?" he asked, the veins in his forehead made visible by his simmering anger.

Yuri wasn't a bit intimidated. "**Was I talking to you, Saki**?"

"**You forget who you are!**"

Terry put his hand up like Kintake tended to do to silence others. "**Stop.**"

Yuri didn't seem to care, though. He was a livewire and continued to engage Saki through the door. "**No, you forgot who I am.**"

"**Why would you leave at such a crucial time**?" Akiko asked in a stern voice, barely letting Yuri get out his reply. "**Have you no honor?**"

"**Stop**," Terry demanded, trying not to raise his voice, "**all of you. Arguing isn't going to get us anywhere.**"

"**You want some of this too?**" Again, Yuri wasn't trying to heed his brother's sensibility.

"Yuri?" came a woman's voice from the bedroom. "Who are you talking to?"

Terry's face fell apart; he knew that voice. It wasn't possible, though. There was no way on this green earth that Terry should have heard that voice. It wasn't possible that the voice could be in this hotel, in this city, in Japan, in this hemisphere. But it was her; Terry knew it.

Her.

How was this possible? How could this be happening? What was Veronica doing in Japan at such a crucial point in Ninpo?

The stone of Akiko's and Saki's faces turned from suspicion to betrayal.

"**What is the meaning of this, Yuri?**" Saki yelled.

Veronica was a couple of feet from Yuri now in her plush hotel robe and with a towel around her head, but his body blocked the door; she couldn't see who was outside. "Yuri, who's at the door? Her face was painted with concern. She'd never been to Japan before. Had she angered somebody by acting inappropriately? Had their credit not posted for the room? What was the problem?"

Yuri peeled his head away from the door and pointed past her. "Go back into the parlor. Now."

"Yuri?"

"Go!" he commanded finally.

She walked backward into the parlor, confused by what was happening, and sat down on a couch that allowed her to keep watch of what was happening at the door. She was starting to become scared.

"**I cannot believe what I am seeing**," said Akiko, not trying to hide her disappointment.

"**Stop**," Terry said, turning his head slightly in her direction. "**I'll handle this.**"

Akiko wasn't having it. "**Don't tell me to stop, Terry. We are here to find him, and here he is gallivanting with some harlot.**"

"You better watch your fucking mouth, bitch!" Yuri snapped. If they wanted to talk down to him, fine, but there was no way he was going to let them belittle Veronica. He grabbed his tanto out of his jacket pocket and began undoing the chain.

"**Stop.**" Terry was animated in trying to make them listen. He spun bodily towards Saki and Akiko. "**Let me talk to him in private.**" Then he turned his head back to his brother. "Yuri, let me in so I can talk to you in private, okay?"

Yuri's face was unconvinced.

"Yuri, it's me for God's sake. Let me in."

"**The two of you have changed**," Akiko said over Saki's shoulder. "**You are not the Shinobi you once were, the Shinobi that we knew. You disappoint me.**"

Terry was tired of not being heard. He felt like he was dealing with children, and his voice reflected that. "**Just give us a moment, please**."

"**We will wait downstairs. Do not take long; we must consider how to handle this**," Saki replied without ever taking his eyes off of Yuri.

Terry's hand shot out. "**Fine, I'll be down shortly**."

Saki and Akiko turned and walked away, disappearing into the stairwell instead of walking to the elevators. Terry watched them go; then there was tense silence. Terry finally turned back to Yuri. "Can I come in?

Yuri's eyes were burning with distrust, but he nodded and opened the door, checking the hallway behind his brother before closing the door behind him.

Terry made his way into the parlor, finding Veronica sitting up perfectly straight on the couch with an unmistakable look of fear and confusion on her face. She didn't know whether to be polite and say hello or just remain quiet, so she opted for the latter.

"See, Veronica? I told you we had family issues here in Japan," Yuri said sourly.

Terry decided not to involve her. It would only complicate things far more than they already were. He said nothing to her and just cut directly to the problem. "**What's she doing here?**"

"**I flew her out here**."

"**What for? What were you thinking?**"

"**I'm a grown man, Terry**," Yuri replied unapologetically. "**I don't have to explain myself to you or anyone else**."

"**Yuri, what's going on?**"

The hilt of Yuri's sheathed tanto came up between them. "**You know what's going on. I've told you**."

"**This is causing a tremendous amount of hate and discontent in the village**."

"Fuck them," Yuri said deadpan.

"**Where is this** *fuck-the-world* **attitude coming from?**" Terry's arms shot out to either side. "**This isn't like you.**"

"**I don't care about Ninpo anymore!**"

"**Yuri, stop it. I know this isn't easy. I mean, our lives are on the line here.**"

"**No, you stop it, Terry. I'm not doing this.**" Yuri stabbed the air between them with his finger. "**I don't care about the code. I'm through.**"

Terry didn't know what to say. Yuri had fallen far, and Terry didn't know what he could do to change it—to make it better. Yuri had truly chosen Veronica over honor, money over the Shinobi, luxury over Ninpo. And now here they stood at a crossroad with a weapon between them, an outsider watching, and two other Shinobi waiting in the lobby. The code was coming apart, it seemed, and Terry didn't know what to do. Well—he did know what to do, but he didn't know if he should do it—if he could do it.

"**You all came here to kill me, didn't you?**" Yuri asked softly.

This caught Terry off guard. "**What? No.**" So Terry lied even though he had considered it and he and Saki and Akiko had argued about it. "**No, Yuri, we need you.**"

"**I don't care what they want. I'm out. I'm done.**"

"**Not them—me. I need you. I can't do this without you.**"

"**Then don't do it,**" Yuri countered without hesitation. "**We don't owe them anything.**"

"**Yuri, they raised us.**"

"**They abandoned us, too.**" Yuri paused, searching his brother's eyes. He saw the same pain that was in Terry, but it was as if Terry didn't acknowledge it the same. "**Where were we supposed to go, Terry? What did we have?**"

"**Is that what this is about—about what we had?**"

Yuri aspirated frustration. "What—are you fucking stupid? **No, Terry, we had nowhere to go. You had to practically carry me as we walked out of the village back to civilization because my foot was broken. Did you forget that? Did you?**"

"No."

Now Yuri was animated. **"Because I was defending you, in case you forgot! And I had to walk out of Togakure Ryu on a broken foot!"**

"No, I haven't forgotten. I'm not saying that they've never been wrong. I am just saying that they're our family and—"

"I'm your family, Terry!" Yuri howled, his face flushing bright red. "I'm the only family you have left! I'm the only family you've ever had!"

"I don't know what to say." Terry was at a complete loss. What or who was he to betray: The good people who'd raised him, his beliefs and means of salvation, or his family?

"Then don't say anything. Just walk away"—Yuri indicated the door with his finger—"or leave me alone."

Terry stood silently for a moment with eyes unfocused. **"I—I can't just let the code go unfulfilled."** He didn't sound sure.

Yuri's thumb broke the seal of his tanto's sheath, preparing it to be drawn. **"Then you've made your choice."**

"Yeah...I guess I have," Terry said, turning for the door. He opened it and looked back, opening his mouth as if to say something else, but he swallowed and slipped out.

Yuri's convictions were at war in his head. Did he hate Ninpo, or did he hate the Fujibayashi? Or did he think that he hated the Fujibayashi because he hated Omiyoshu Kintake? Hell, he was beginning to think he hated Terry.

Yuri shook his head. He didn't hate Terry; Yuri's emotions were so distorted that he was having difficulty separating anger and hate. Anger was alive and white-hot and burned in the chest. Hate was a black, insidious ichor that burned somewhere beneath the stomach. Both burned, so they could be mistaken for one another.

"Yuri, what happened?" Veronica asked finally. She'd watch this drama unfold from the couch. Even though she couldn't understand what had been said except for the sporadic English curses, the intensity had been unmistakable. She was terribly worried about Yuri and his brother. Veronica had never seen them legitimately fight, argue and bicker perhaps, but not fight to such finality. "Baby?"

The anger and hate were growing in intensity, burning Yuri's internal organs. "Those bastards are driving a wedge between me and my brother."

"Who is, Yuri?"

"Goddammit!" Yuri wasn't going to let this happen. He wasn't going to let his family be torn apart like it was before; he wasn't going to let Terry put his life on the line without him. "I'll be back," he said before sprinting out of the door and jumping into the elevator.

Yuri pounded the "lobby" button repeatedly with his finger, cursing the elevator and demanding that it hurry. The doors closed finally, and Yuri paced hungrily as the elevator fell. Sixteen stories couldn't go fast enough, and the doors barely had time to open before Yuri squeezed through and sprinted into the polished-brass lobby, nearly knocking over a family of patrons checking in with their bags.

"Terry!" Yuri yelled. He could see them standing out on the curb of the valet. "Terry, wait!"

Terry spun, as did Saki and Akiko, who clandestinely readied themselves when the saw Yuri coming fast with his sheathed tanto still in his hand.

Yuri slowed through the automatic doors, standing up straight to give his lungs room to expand. He gulped in a tankful of air. "I'm not going to let you do the ritual by yourself."

"I won't be by myself. Saki and Akiko will be with me," Terry said with hurt in his throat.

Yuri gulped more air. "No. You're not going to do this without your family. It's not the way Mom would've wanted it."

"Okay."

"But after that, I'm out. I'm through."

"What if we don't survive it?"

Yuri shook his head. "Don't give me another reason to say no. I'm doing this for *you*, not for Ninpo or the Fujibayashi."

232

"Alright, then. I...uh..." Terry started looking over at the other two Shinobi. "We'll wait for you to get your things."

"Don't bother; I'll meet you there." Yuri threw a thumb over his shoulder. "I have some loose ends to tie up."

Chapter Fourteen: Uninvited Guest

Shinobi are supple warriors. The bakufu expects an opponent to stand and fight. Strike from behind and kill without being seen.
The Eighth Mandate, translated from Ninpo.

Suzuka Mountains. Mie Prefecture, Japan. Today.

The trek was *amazing*! Despite the overcast sky, the wind, and the cold, Veronica thought the vistas were to die for! Never had Veronica seen a countryside so unique and so beautiful. When she was in college, she had gone backpacking with a few friends, but it had been nothing like this. Yuri really amazed her with his savvy in the foreign wilderness. His understanding and comfort were so intriguing and attractive. He amazed her more and more since her arrival in Tokyo. He was so well versed in Japanese customs and the Japanese language, it was as if he had been doing it his whole life. Yuri never hid the fact that he had grown up in Japan, but he was never generous with his knowledge of it, and his command of it was deep and impressive.

Yuri and Veronica, dressed like backpackers on a Euro-vacation, completed the final descent into Togakure Ryu. Yuri took the long way down to accommodate Veronica—the less-treacherous path. The routes into the village didn't often trouble Shinobi, but the uninitiated didn't have the same athleticism.

"There's the village," Yuri said, pointing toward the collection of cottages through the canopy.

"Are you serious?" Veronica couldn't contain her excitement, waving her arms animatedly and grabbing Yuri's pack and shaking it. Her feet ached from the three-hour hike, but this was totally worth it, this unfettered piece of Japanese history that was nestled in a most divine pocket of a range of mountains boiling out of a white landscape. The village was quaint and charming in the cold, but Veronica bet that it was absolutely breathtaking in the spring, when the trees and flowers were in full bloom.

"Omigod, Yuri, this is magnificent! I can't believe you actually grew up here. You've got to be pulling my leg."

234

"No, I'm dead serious." He pointed deeper into the village. "I stayed in the house over there."

"So, where are your parents?"

"Come on," Yuri said, smiling and disregarding her question. "I'll show you around."

Veronica stopped when she noticed a group of villagers encircling two men fighting. "Who are they? Why are they fighting."

"Just some villagers I grew up with. And they're sparring, not fighting."

"Why are they sparring?"

"This is Japan, Veronica. Everyone in Japan does karate," Yuri replied sardonically.

Then she realized that she recognized one of their faces. "Oh, that's Terry."

Terry batted his opponent's fist away. The strike had aimed for his face, but Terry sent it over his shoulder and then closed the distance with a step. His opponent replied with a flurry. Terry parried and weaved.

Terry's guard was surrounded by an imaginary square; his blocks painted arcs and chords that touched the corners of the box. Every strike was driven outside of its borders. Terry moved, and the box changed aspect. Aspect changes zoned out Terry's opponent and forced him to move.

The men danced around each other, Terry acting as the focus of a circle and his opponent drawing the circumference. His opponent pressed the attack, delivering punches and kicks to the head and the body. Terry was unfazed, pushing the man's attacks outside of the square until Terry was close enough. Terry drove his knee through his opponent's gut, forcing a retreat. His opponent backed away, holding his stomach, puffing steam into the air. Terry circled to the right, watching his opponent intently. He reset and coaxed his opponent forward with a hand. His opponent fired a side kick and followed with several rapid-fire kicks. Terry parried and dodged, blocking left and right and dancing a figure eight. He planted his feet finally, and seemingly effortlessly penetrated his opponent's guard, catching him in the ribs. Terry's opponent wasn't interrupted; his attack remained energized as he switched from feet to hands.

Terry weaved lines in the air with his arms, intercepting the strikes and driving them outside of the imaginary box, spreading out his opponent's guard more and more with each strike.

Movement in Terry's peripheral vision captured his attention—more so than usual. His eyes leaped off of his opponent and fixed two people on the other side of the pigpens through the layer of spectators. Terry squinted his eyes, trying to be sure that he was really seeing what he thought he was seeing.

No.

It wasn't possible.

His mind had to be playing tricks on him.

Just then, Terry felt fire in his face. Terry couldn't keep his footing and toppled. His opponent had cracked off a shot and landed it against Terry's jaw, jamming the hinge against his skull, while he was momentarily distracted. The crowd couldn't believe it; neither could Terry's opponent. Terry was a far superior fighter, and pulling off a shot that managed to take him out of the fight was completely unexpected. They all were a sea of blinking eyeballs.

Terry shook his head to reboot himself. The pain in his jaw was the least of his concerns, and he hopped to his feet, wiped the mud from his hands, and pushed through the crowd. Their confused eyes followed.

"Why is everyone staring at us?" Veronica asked.

"They don't get visitors often," Yuri said, watching his brother approach. "Don't worry about it."

Terry thundered across the pigpens, outrage boiling in his stomach, to where his brother was standing with Veronica. "**What are you doing? Are you crazy?**" he asked once he reached them.

"Hey, Ter," Yuri said, smiling brightly. "What's up, buddy?"

Veronica's smile was equally bright. "Hi, Terry." She waved at him. "This place is amazing."

"Veronica," Terry replied tartly, returning his attention to his brother immediately. "**Do you not realize what you're doing? You just brought an outsider into Togakure Ryu. You know that's against the code.**"

"Terry, don't be rude. You know Veronica doesn't speak Japanese. Stop making fun of her." Yuri's smile didn't disperse, but his eyes told a different story; they overflowed with disdain.

"**What're we supposed to do now**?" Terry asked, taking the cue from his brother's eyes, not his smile.

"Yuri, is he really making fun of me?" Veronica had no clue what Terry was saying. His body language and tone, however, were unmistakable for a woman of her prowess.

"Sure is. Terry does that to you often, don't you, Terry? Make fun of people in a language they don't understand, I mean."

Terry placed his hands his on hips. "**Playing dumb isn't going to make this better**," he said venomously. "**You just made this far worse for all of us.**"

Yuri heard him, but Yuri just wasn't listening; he didn't care at all. The Fujibayashi weren't going to do anything to *him*. "Well, you're being Chatty Cathy today. It's going to be a long couple of weeks. Come on, babe, I'll show you where we'll be shacking up." Yuri grabbed her by the arm and dragged her off.

"Yuri, you want to explain to me what's going on?" Veronica whispered as they made their way along one of the paths that etched its way between the cottages. "I don't have to speak Japanese to know that there is some real tension after last night."

"Nope."

"Were you boys unable to work out whatever differences you had in the hotel?"

"No, we worked everything out—mostly everything, anyways. He's just being sensitive about something going on *here*." Yuri turned and looked at her with a smile that stretched from ear to ear. "You know how *family* can be."

"Yuri?"

"Don't worry about it. My entire family is well behaved. I'm the only one who has behavior issues."

"Imagine that," she laughed. "Which reminds me, we need to talk about you and my father."

"Can it wait until we get back to the States?" Yuri said, walking up the stairs of the porch to a cottage that bordered the river. "I don't want to deal with any dating politics while I'm on vacation."

"Yuri."

He stopped at the rice paper door and turned. "Hm?"

"You're hiding something?"

"Of course."

*　　*　　*

Akiko, Saki, and Terry had been looking all over for Kintake. They had found him returning to his suite after bathing in the river. There was no peace for a kōchō when he was in the village, especially this close to the ritual. Kintake's face was marred with frustration when he saw Chunin marching in his direction, especially during such a personal time. Akiko's gait moved with purpose, as did Saki's. Terry, however, just seemed along for the ride. Kintake paused to wait for them, removed a layer, and began drying his short salt-and-pepper hair. He nodded at them and waited.

Akiko was the first to reach him. She bowed swiftly and got right to business. "**Father, Yuri is completely out of control.**"

Kintake barely had time to return the bow. He raised a hand, trying to settle her. "**Calm down, daughter. That is a trait very typical of Yuri and not something to be alarmed about.**"

Saki and Terry came alongside her and bowed to the kōchō. He returned their respect with a nod.

"**Father, Yuri has brought an outsider into the village.**"

Kintake hung the damp garment across the back of his neck and rubbed his hand through his hair to see if it was still wet. "**I am aware. Sumimito Sensei informed me as soon as Yuri and his guest had arrived.**"

"**We have to do something.**" Akiko's face was beset with urgency; it even oozed from her pores.

"**Now is not the time for overreaction,**" Kintake replied, his voice full of caution.

"**How is righting this transgression *overreaction*?**"

"**Master,**" Saki interjected, "**Akiko is right. Yuri has blatantly violated the code, and it cannot be overlooked. The entire village is aware. Something must be done.**"

238

Kintake sighed loudly. **"We've been over this; Yuri is going to fight. End of discussion."**

Akiko couldn't contain her disappointment and anger any longer; this was outrageous! Never in a million years would she have thought that she'd be entangled in such a hypocritical situation that tore down every ethic that held their very existence together. But here she was, standing on the river's edge, listening to her father—the kōchō—disregard their very laws. **"Father, you can't be serious! Do you not see his blatant disregard for our traditions and laws—traditions and laws that have existed for centuries**?"

Saki couldn't understand either. Was Kintake blind? **"Why are you so adamant about Yuri fighting despite his behavior**?" Saki asked.

Kintake stroked his chin thoughtfully, noticing that the wind had picked up. **"Akiko, the selection of warriors for this ritual is based not on choice but rather on destiny. Saki, Terry, and Yuri are destined to do battle."** He looked deep into his daughter's eyes. **"You are not."**

Akiko's face twisted with anger. **"So, we are to let him continue to soil that which we hold most sacred and then allow him to carry dishonor onto our most sacred land unchecked? We are to do nothing?"**

Kintake didn't like his daughter's tone, but he understood her anger. For that, he let her words slide. **"Terry,"** Kintake said, turning his attention toward his silent Chunin, **"have you nothing to add."**

"I—I don't know what to say."

"Say that we should uphold Ninpo, Terry!" Akiko blurted out, forgetting her manners and her place.

Kintake gritted his teeth and exhaled frustration into the frigid air through his nose. **"Daughter, I will not tell you to control your outburst again."**

She huffed resentfully.

Kintake continued, **"Destiny is not always enjoyable, nor is it always agreeable. I do not condone Yuri's actions, but I cannot change what Hattori Hanzo divined decades ago."**

"Divined?"

"Yes, daughter—divined. Hattori Hanzo communed with our ancestors decades ago about these exact moments, and the ancestors destined six specific warriors: three Fujibayashi and three Momochi.

239

That is the reason I am so adamant. I cannot undo what the universe has written thus."

"Well, he divined wrong!" Akiko asserted just below a roar.

Terry's head snapped in her direction.

She continued, "Yuri deserves to die for violating our code. He has become an enemy of Ninpo." Akiko bowed and stormed off to seethe elsewhere.

Terry followed her. She had Yuri all wrong, and he was determined to set her straight.

"Akiko, Yuri's wrong, but he hasn't abandoned Ninpo. He has upheld it proudly for years; he's just terribly confused right now."

"Greater Shinobi than Yuri have been hunted and eliminated for their crimes. What makes Yuri different?"

"Are you hearing yourself? This isn't some story we're telling; this is my brother. We all grew up together. Think about that."

"Ninpo does not differentiate between confused disregard and blatant disregard, Terry. You would do well to remember where your allegiance lies."

Terry stopped in his tracks. "Are you threatening *me* now?"

Akiko stopped too and spun to face him. "No—I am saying that we dishonor ourselves by allowing him to do whatever he chooses and to leave us to pick up the pieces. Dishonor will see us all to our doom. We must act swiftly and without hesitation."

"We mustn't overreact. This *is* the twenty-first century, not the seventeenth. We don't execute our own because of what we perceive as a slight to our interpretations."

"Both of you have changed." Her voice echoed with spite. "Leaving Togakure Ryu damaged him—it has damaged you. Far from Ninpo, you have drifted."

"My brother is dealing with his own demons," Terry said, patting his heart with his hand, "but I haven't changed. I'm still the same person you knew."

Akiko raised her chin and stared Terry deep in his eyes as if he wasn't almost a full head taller. "No, Terry, you are not." And she turned and left.

240

Terry leaned up against an uprooted tree, wearing his gray tunic, trousers, and tabi shoes, staring at the sky. Saki, dressed the same but with his cowl over his head to keep warm, wasn't so serene; he paced in front of Terry. Yuri was supposed to have met them nearly forty-five minutes earlier but hadn't shown. Instead, he was busy cavorting with the foreigner.

Saki was growing weary of the constant tension between him, Terry, Akiko, and Yuri. Moreover, he was growing even more tired of the constant pressure from the Jonin. He felt as though he was being blamed for Yuri's actions. And for Yuri's part, he had totally abandoned that which was righteous and just.

And just as Saki was feeling as though his patience had reached the breaking point, Yuri jogged up the walking path wearing a wool cap, sweatshirt, jogging pants, and cross-training boots, with his harness and ninjatō slung over his back.

"Ladies," Yuri greeted matter-of-factly, placing his hands on his hips and bending at the waist to catch his breath after his five-hundred-foot ascent.

"**Nice of you to finally show up**." Terry focused on his gloves as he adjusted them. "**It's not like we have a schedule to keep**."

Yuri ignored him. "**What's the plan?**" he asked.

"**You are really pushing the limits**," Saki said.

Yuri snorted, unmoved, and stuffed his hands in the pocket of his sweatshirt. "**What're you trying to say, Saki?**"

Terry looked up finally. "**He's saying that we're all being more tolerant of your behavior than you rightfully deserve**."

"**Don't start**," Yuri growled.

"**No, you are going to listen—and listen well**." Saki spoke with his lips and never opened his jaw, trying to maintain his cool. "**You would do well to remember who you are and your place. You are Shinobi, and forgetting that will cost you your life**."

"**Are you threatening me? Because it sounds to me like you're threatening me, and I don't like being threatened**."

Terry pushed himself off of the tree, using his back. "**We're telling you to get it together. What you're doing is wrong, and you know it.**"

"**Terry**"—Yuri clenched his fists in his pocket—"**you better remember whose team you're on. If you want to threaten me, I'll take you out just the same.**"

Terry's expression was dubious. "**Nobody's threatening you. Stop it.**"

"**I *am* threatening you.**" Saki yanked his ninjatō from its sheath and leveled it between them. Terry and Yuri both looked at him. Saki's eyes were as serious as death. "**In fact, I am going to end this now. I am going to return you to honor and deal with the kōchō's consequences; his consequences are better than the dishonor of not defending Ninpo.**"

"**We can both die today, Saki,**" Yuri growled, whipping his ninjatō from its sheath.

"**Stop!**" Terry yelled, jumping in between his comrades; he'd stirred the birds to chorus he had yelled so loud. "**Look at us! Look—look what we've become! When did we all become enemies? Huh? When? We don't even need to fight Momochi, because we'll just kill ourselves! Because that's what Ninpo demands, right? Saki, is that what it demands, that we kill our brothers?**"

Saki shook his head.

Terry swung his head back toward his brother and implored, "**Is that what it demands, Yuri?**"

Yuri responded only with the menace that had filled his eyes.

Yuri's body language wasn't enough for Terry, who posed the question again, "**Does it?**"

"**Fuck Ninpo,**" Yuri spat, "**and everyone who follows it.**"

Terry snatched a handful of his brother's sweatshirt and yanked him in close. "**I follow Ninpo. Are you turning your back on me? Are you going to threaten to kill me too?**"

Yuri's eyes grew rapacious, and he didn't pull away. "**I'm not scared of you. I'm not scared of anyone.**"

"**This isn't about fear; this is about what's right! Look at us! We can't tell friend from enemy! This is what we've become! This is what *you've* become! Aspirations of slaying your own kin!**"

242

"They're no kin to me!" Yuri belched, straining against Terry's grip. "My only kin are my dead parents and you! Although I think you've forgotten that."

Terry exploded at the evocation of his parents, drilling Yuri in the cheekbone. "Do you think Mom and Dad would be proud of this, you fucking sociopath?"

Yuri toppled and rolled down the incline, his sword cartwheeling even further down.

"Do you think they'd be proud of you trying to hurt the only people who have ever loved you?"

Yuri, sliding a few feet down the hard-frozen incline, stopped on his knees and rubbed his face. Then he erupted. "They don't love me!" His eyes welled with tears. "They don't love us! They never have. We've always been outsiders. Kintake brought us here only to abuse us. We have the scars to prove it.

"They all just want us to play their stupid ninja game! And for what? They got along just fine without us! They never wondered how we were doing, if we were able to survive them abandoning us! Not even Saki, our so-called brother!

"I don't want to be here! I don't want to play their stupid game anymore! I just want to lead a normal life! I just want to be happy—like our parents were! I want their spirits to rest happily knowing that we made something of ourselves! I don't want to do this anymore—I don't want to be Shinobi! I don't want to kill anymore. You won't let me, though! You want to keep me trapped here with you!" Yuri clawed handfuls of frozen dirt from the ground and threw them at his brother. "Why don't you want me to be in love with Veronica? Is it because you're selfish and all you care about is your stupid code—your stupid honor?"

"Yuri, I—" Terry tried to say, but then he realized that he had nothing. He felt instantly small.

"No! Fuck your stupid code! I don't care anymore! Why can't I just be what I want to be? I want to be in love! I want to be a husband and a dad one day, just like our dad. But that's not okay is it? I have to be brainwashed just like you!"

"Yuri, you must not give up," Saki said, finally lowering his ninjatō. "I am not your enemy. I am—"

"Fuck you, Saki!" Yuri climbed to his feet. "Fuck both of you!" Yuri set off down the hill, back to the one thing that he felt was right in the world.

Terry started after his brother, but Saki grabbed a handful of Terry's harness.

"Let him go, Terry."

Terry threw his arms in the air. "What is happening?"

"I am not sure. There is something terribly wrong."

Terry sighed loudly.

"We should go speak with Omiyoshu Sensei," Saki said, returning his sword to its sheath. "Perhaps we can convince him that Yuri is no longer fit to fight. Perhaps we can convince him that Akiko should take his place."

Terry shook his head. "I don't want to involve Omiyoshu Sensei anymore. He's going to have us killed if we can't get it together."

"Do we have another choice?"

"Not if Yuri doesn't come to his senses. But I'm not ready to take my brother's life, nor am I ready to take my own."

*   *   *

Yuri didn't sleep well. He lay on his mat, inside his sleeping bag, and stared at Veronica as she slept. When he had returned, he hadn't cared about anything Fujibayashi, but as the night had pressed on, he'd started to question with whom he was so angry and so resentful and why. There was no dispute that he didn't want to be part of Ninpo, but he didn't want to be at odds with Terry—or Saki for that matter. They were important to him. His anger and disillusionment were causing him to lash out at them. Terry and Saki couldn't help that they were unable to see Yuri's perspective, and Yuri felt terrible about his reaction even if he meant every word of it.

What really played havoc on his mind was Terry's comments about their parents. Would they be unhappy with him and his choices? Would they disagree with his desire to choose Veronica over Ninpo? He doubted it, but he had no doubt that his parents would be disappointed if he abandoned his brother.

He couldn't abandon Terry. He was his brother's keeper.

Yuri got up and crept out of the cottage.

Terry stretched on the floor of his cottage with his legs spread to either side. He reached for his toes, stretching his hamstrings and the muscles around his ribs at the same time. Then there was a knock at the door. He jumped; he wasn't expecting anybody. Saki, who was on the opposite side of the room cleaning his weapons, rose to meet their visitor.

"Terry?" Yuri whispered through the crack of the door as he opened it.

Terry didn't get up. "**I don't want to argue anymore, Yuri. You win.**"

Yuri came through the threshold and shut the cold out behind him. "**I'm not here to argue with you. I just came to talk.**"

"**Oh yeah?**" Terry chortled, unamused. "**Are you here to draw your sword and threaten me too? You going to call me selfish?**"

"**No—I just came to talk.**"

"**To be sure, by all rights, we should have killed you**—Terry paused for effect—"*and* **Veronica two days ago. We didn't do that. You don't respect that you are jeopardizing our core values. All you care about is this new crusade that you're on. Which is news to me, because when we were in Rio a year ago, you showed no signs of turmoil. So, what is it you could** *possibly* **have to talk about, because I don't love you if my memory serves me correctly?**"

"**Terry, calm yourself,**" said Saki.

Yuri put a conceding hand in the air. "**No, Saki, I deserve that. I just came to tell you that I'm going to fight.**"

Terry shot up. "**My God, Yuri! Why? So you can change your mind and threaten everybody again tomorrow when you whimsically decide that it's not convenient to your love life?**"

"**Mom and Dad wouldn't want that. They wouldn't want me to let you put your life on the line alone. I'm going to finish this...and then move on.**"

"I'm not *alone*. I have Saki."

"**You have me too.**"

"What about Veronica?"

"I told you. I'm going to *end* this and then move on."

                              *   *   *

The three warriors waited outside the central cabin to speak to Kintake before a Jonin came out to address them. **"Omiyoshu Sensei will see you now."**

"So good of him to clear his busy schedule," Yuri growled.

The elder half-turned and threw Yuri a sidelong glance before guiding the three men indoors.

Saki, Terry, and Yuri had been waiting outside to speak with Kintake for the better part of two hours. It was cold, and the wind was blowing harshly, making being outside unforgiving. The gray and brown fall-winter terminus of the Suzuka mountains wasn't merciful. Saki, Terry, and Yuri were visibly frustrated. Saki and Terry tried to hide it. Yuri didn't. Having to wait in harsh weather for an audience with Kintake or the elder council reminded them of their childhood. Rarely was a Shinobi called into Kintake's presence for sweet, nurturing conversation—especially not youths. More often than not, the three warriors, when they were Kodomo, Genin, and early Chunin, had left Kintake's presence bruised and bloodied. They were expecting similar treatment and readied themselves for it.

The three men followed the Jonin into Kintake's chamber, where he sat cross-legged on a mat with a modest serving of tea and snacks to his left. Several Jonin of the elder council attended him, sitting on their knees to either side. Two Chunin, older than the three warriors but junior to them in rank, knelt nearest the door through which Saki, Terry, and Yuri had entered with their guide. Lying on the floor in front of the two men were their tantos, wrapped in paper.

The three warriors paid them little attention beyond initial notice as they approached their kōchō and took positions on their knees in front of him, bowing until their foreheads touched the floor.

"Thank you for attending me," Kintake said.

"It is with great honor that we do so, Sensei," Saki replied, his voice muffled against the planks of the wooden floor.

"Of course."

"How may we be of service to the clan?"

246

Kintake bid them rise with the flick of his hand. A Jonin in the audience voiced Kintake's command, and the warriors sat up.

Kintake gave a half-cocked smile. "**Have you three ever witnessed seppuku?**"

Saki and Terry shook their heads. Yuri scowled.

Kintake sipped his tea. "**I thought not. It is quite unpleasant. Honorable. But unpleasant. You see, one must turn one's own tanto—a Shinobi's truest ally—against oneself. One holds the blade to his or her abdomen, and then, once the individual reconciles the finality of the action for which he or she must take and the excruciating pain that will accompany it, one must decide which method to use to ensure one's own death.**

"**Should one drive the blade straight through, injuring the internal organs? Or should one slice the gut open and spill one's innards onto the floor? Which method will hurt more? Which method will bring death the fastest? Will increased pain ensure a return of honor? Will decreased pain affect the return to honor? Does hoping for a painless death reveal one to be unworthy of honor? So many questions. The work of a Shinobi is never done. I digress.**

"**Next, comes the decapitation by one's chosen secondary—a swordsman who honors him or herself by decapitating the individual following the impalement or disembowelment. Now, imagine for a moment, if you will, that you have just mortally wounded your abdomen and all you want to do his lay down while you suffer the pain. But you cannot. Instead, you must remain on your knees while someone you know readies their strike. You hope that their strike is true and clean. But what if it is not? What if the strike is true but their blade is dull? Or what if their blade is so sharp that it could make the air bleed but the wielder's aim is off, and they strike somewhere other than the weak point on the neck?**

"**In either case, one's head is not cleaved off. No—one is then dying of multiple wounds. And one must be struck again to complete the ritual. How terrible.**"

A Jonin signaled to a Kodomo attendant dressed in muted robes and a boken in his belt to refill Kintake's cup. Kintake acknowledged the boy when he finished refilling it. The boy scurried back to the perimeter of the room.

"I am sure that you three are familiar with Kurotani Eichi and Motoki Kodama." Kintake indicated with his hand the two men who knelt near the door. **They are going to return themselves to honor today. Eichi, Sumimito Sensei tells me that you expressed to him that you are fearful of death.**"

"Omiyoshu Sensei, I—" Eichi started, but Kintake raised a silencing hand.

"**You need not explain your fear. There is no dishonor in fear. The dishonor is in the inability to complete tasks or not abiding the other mandates of Ninpo. I say this to you so that you understand that seppuku will see your sins forgiven. You will walk with the ancestors because your final performance will be one of sacrifice.**"

Kodama nodded. "**Omiyoshu Sensei, I would like to apologize for our failure. Oharu eluded us because we were careless, but he never saw us, nor was he ever aware of our presence.**"

"**Your sins will be forgiven with seppuku,**" Kintake said flatly. "**Let us get on with it.**"

Kintake snapped his fingers and then pointed in Eichi and Kodama's direction. The three warriors turned their heads to watch.

The two dishonored Shinobi pulled their arms inside their robes and slowly peeled away the tops, revealing bare chests, abdomens, and tattoos. Eichi had Mamushi's likeness tattooed on his left shoulder. Kodama had Mamushi tattooed along his left collarbone. Each of their secondaries, dressed in blue, approached with sponges, washed the depictions of Mamushi, and then dried them with rags. The secondaries handed the sponges and rags to other attendees and drew their swords in an elegantly choreographed routine, first honoring the kōchō and then the condemned. Two other Jonin approached the secondaries with pails of water. They poured the water over the blades and then wiped the blades dry with rags. The secondaries, standing to opposite sides of Eichi and Kodama, raised their blades and readied themselves to strike.

Eichi and Kodama picked up their tantos and raised them level with their abdomens. With their left hands, they kneaded their stomachs just below the waistline, inside the hip, looking for the perfect spot to pierce.

The room fell silent as Eichi and Kodama seemed to gather their thoughts one last time—Eichi with his eyes shut and Kodama with an emotional stare.

"**Honor is the soul of the Shinobi**," they said in unison.

All in attendance replied solemnly, "**Shadow is their blood.**"

Both men plunged the tantos into their guts. Eichi's face did not change; he remained dignified. Kodama's face was pruned with determination.

Eichi drove the blade even further, giving the slightest whimper before stretching out his neck. Kodama's face never changed as he yanked the blade to the right and then up.

Then there was lightning, and both men slumped emptily to the floor with heads severed. The secondaries had precisely cut such that Eichi's and Kodama's heads remained attached by a sliver of flesh to prevent an undignified rolling of their heads. Blood gushed onto the floor like a punctured milk jug. But several Jonin were prepared to stop the flow of blood by capturing it with rags.

Attendees not assisting with the laboring returned their attention to Kintake.

"**Do not mind Eichi and Kodama**," Kintake said, taking a sip of tea. "**They were paying a debt for not living up to the code.**" Kintake took another sip. "**Their headless corpses do not bother you, do they?**"

"**Corpses are a commonplace for me**," Yuri said equally flat.

"**Indeed—which reminds me. It would appear that we have an unexpected visitor. How is it that this stranger has come to grace us with her presence?**"

Terry swallowed hard and opened his mouth to speak, but Yuri beat him to it. "**She came with me.**"

"**Would you, Yuri, care to explain why you have brought a stranger into Togakure Ryu?**"

Yuri's face was stone. Saki's carotid pulsed. Terry's forehead beaded with sweat.

"**Indeed. Yuri, Yuri, Yuri. Defiant as always. You have caused quite the buzz. Saki, you are the most senior warrior. Are you unable to control your Shinobi?**"

"**I am capable, Sensei.**"

"**I am not sure if I share your confidence.**"

249

A nervous exhale from Saki was heard by the contents of the room.

"**What was the colloquial phrase your father said to me years ago? Ah, yes, I remember.**" Kintake's eyes fixed on Yuri. "*I will level with you, Yuri.* **It is by my will that the Fujibayashi have not executed you.**"

Yuri's blood started to run hot. "**I don't fear—**"

"**Yes, yes. You do not fear death,**" Kintake said, cutting him off. "**I have heard that plenty. The problem is that you are missing the forest for the trees. If I finally command the clan to abide by the code, the clan will execute you. They will execute Terry and Saki for being accomplices to your transgressions. Then the clan will execute that lovely, innocent woman. What is her name?**"

Yuri's eyes burned icy hot.

"**Never mind. Her name does not matter. What does matter is that you, and everyone associated with you, is alive because I will it so. And do not assume that I am naïve either. I already know you are contemplating jumping to your feet to attack me, Yuri. But even if you manage to defeat me this time, it will not stop a sword from being plunged through the woman's ribcage. You are welcome to try, though.**"

Yuri stared hard, but remained silent.

Kintake shrugged. "**No? Excellent. Well, then, I have one last test for you three to prove your worthiness to the ritual combat.**"

"**If it involves drinking more venom,**" Yuri said, "**you can just kill me now because I'm not doing it again.**"

"Yuri, shut the fuck up," Terry whispered.

Kintake's eyes found Terry and then returned to Yuri. A smile materialized on Kintake's face. "**Since Eichi and Kodama were unable to eliminate Oharu, you will find him and eliminate him. Do not fail me like Eichi and Kodama.**

"**Oh, and Yuri, there is only one way the woman leaves here alive. You have to participate in the ritual. And if you survive, I will allow you to leave Togakure Ryu alive with her. But this is only if you comply. Mark my words, I will command the Fujibayashi to execute the three of you, the woman, and anyone else who so much as vexes me if you make one more open display of defiance. Am I clear?**"

"**Yes, Sensei**," Saki and Terry replied in stereo.

"**Yuri**?" Kintake's inflection was menacing.

"**Yes, Sensei**," he said finally.

"**Good**." Kintake turned his attention to the cup of tea on the floor, and his smile melted into a contemptuous sneer. "**Now, get out of my sight**."

Chapter Fifteen: So Many Questions

Toba. Mie Prefecture, Japan. Today.

"**I've never seen this man before**," Saki asserted, quite believing himself. He was crouched over the bloody corpse of a target given them by Kintake.

"**Why's that a problem**?" Yuri said smugly.

"**If Saki's never seen this man before**," Terry interjected, "**then he's not Fujibayashi**." Terry looked back in the direction from which they had come. Everything seemed to have gone as planned. Had they missed something crucial, or was Saki mistaken somehow?

Their surveillance and approach had met no obstacles:

Darkness—it was to the Shinobi as a blanket was to an infant asleep in a lonely crib. It comforted Saki as his meandered down the spacious street of the affluent Japanese neighborhood in which Oharu resided. To an unlikely onlooker, Saki was a simple pedestrian out for an evening stroll to stretch his legs. Saki didn't dawdle, however. If Oharu was a deserter, then he was surely aware that the Fujibayashi would come for him eventually, and strangers might alert him.

Saki crossed the street, walking along the perimeter wall of Oharu's residence to a point heavily shaded by trees. Then he gave the signal.

A shadow came to life and sprinted across the street, zipping past Saki and rolling into a ball as it neared the wall. It tumbled and then unfolded itself, landing in a crouch with its back against the wall—its menacing blue eyes scanning the street.

Another shadow beamed across the boulevard, accelerating towards Yuri. Yuri interlocked his fingers, forming a cup—a step—that Terry could stuff a foot in. Terry's eyes locked on Yuri's hands and then the edge of the wall twelve feet above. The jump was going to take some heave, but all he needed was to get his fingers on the edge.

Terry, at full speed, slammed his foot into Yuri's makeshift step, and together, they drove Terry upwards like a rocket. He soared up with outstretched arms until his hands made contact with the edge, and he grabbed hold.

In the split second that Terry went airborne, Saki sprinted towards Yuri in the same way. Saki's foot went into Yuri's hands, and together, they heaved Saki up. Once Saki reached the apex, he latched on to Terry and used Terry as an anchor to scuttle over the wall.

Yuri hopped up, backed away from the wall, and then sprinted up the side until he got handfuls of Terry's harness. Yuri used his brother as a rope to swiftly scale the wall. As he neared the top, Saki snatched Yuri's harness and helped him up. Once Saki and Yuri were both up, they grabbed hold of Terry and heaved him over.

Their timing was perfect. In all of six seconds, the three Shinobi had bounded over a twelve-foot wall, and nobody had seen a thing—even the people sitting in Oharu's living room.

They'd sneaked passed Oharu's visitors and eliminated him with no problem.

The garage door was open. It was an invitation to the Shinobi—please come in, my friends, and make yourselves at home.

The Fujibayashi slipped in without the lights coming on. Terry blinded the motion sensor with a laser pointer while the other two ducked behind the snugly parked vehicles. He then followed when they signaled that the coast was clear.

Saki went to the door leading into the house and checked it—locked. No matter. The best way to get someone to answer the door was to knock.

Rap, rap, rap! Saki banged on the door firmly before disappearing into a shadow.

A moment later, there was a hollow, mechanical click of the door's lock, and then it opened. An Asian man, aged perhaps thirty years and wearing slacks with a leather vest, with tattoo-covered arms and fluffy raven hair, emerged, looking about suspiciously. Half of the man's body peeked through the door; Saki seized the opportunity to strike like a viper from the shadows.

He yanked the man into the garage and coiled around him to dampen the struggle and surprise. Terry emerged for the assist while Yuri watched their backs. Once the man was unconscious, Saki and Terry dragged him to the far side of the garage and stuffed him a corner. Then they slithered back to the door and entered; Yuri took up the rear as they disappeared through the doorway.

The three Fujibayashi tiptoed down the hallway to the sitting room, where the last two visitors—two laughing, inebriated women— were sitting on the couch. Saki and Terry came up behind them and snatched them into vice grips, restricting their blood flow. Within seconds, both women were asleep and laid back onto the furniture.

From there, the Fujibayashi slithered through the residence, looking for Oharu.

They found him in his study. He was preparing lines of cocaine when they entered—three shadowed hunters brandishing hatefully professional blades.

Oharu's eyes widened.

But something hadn't been right.

"Are you sure, Saki?" Terry asked

Saki was sure that he wasn't sure. He knew everyone in the village but was practically sure he'd never seen this man before, much less heard of him. **"If he was Fujibayashi, he hasn't been in the village as far back as I can remember. I have been considering this whole time that I was not familiar with the name Oharu. I did not feel it was worth bringing up, however."**

Yuri pursed his lips beneath his balaclava. "**You sure you aren't making a mistake? His name could be an alias.**"

"**I am certain.**"

Terry was by the door, watching for anyone unlucky enough to arrive, be they new visitors or the unconscious ones downstairs. He waved a hand at Yuri. "**Cut his shirt off. See if he has a tattoo of Mamushi.**"

Yuri whipped his tanto across the corpse's shirt and pants, pulling them open like a cadaver in a vivisection to reveal a mural of colors.

"**Those are not Fujibayashi tattoos,**" said Saki after helping Yuri roll the corpse over so they could inspect it.

The man's upper body was covered in elaborate tattoos of dragons, koi, tigers, and skulls. There was even a snake, but none had any likeness to Mamushi.

Yuri shook his head. "**What difference does it make? We were instructed to eliminate him.**" He looked up at Saki. "**The flowchart says, '***If dead, move on.***' Well, he's dead. Let's move on.**"

"**But Yuri, those aren't Fujibayashi tattoos. I know those tattoos. They look the tattoos of a Yakuza soldier.**"

"**Saki, I don't really care. This guy deserted the clan. We eliminated him. Done.**"

"**He doesn't have Fujibayashi tattoos.**"

"**Maybe he got new ones. People get tattoos all the time, especially when they're rebelling against something.**"

"**Yuri's right,**" said Terry. "**These tattoos could have come after his departure. We don't know.**"

"**We should look around for more evidence, perhaps photos of his past.**"

"**You serious?**" Yuri chortled. "**You think he's going to have before-and-after selfies of his Fujibayashi tattoos?**"

"**We're spinning our wheels,**" Terry asserted finally. "**We'll discuss this later.**"

Yuri tossed a hand in the air. "**Thank you.**"

"What if this is a test, Terry? What if Omiyoshu Sensei is questioning our scrutiny?"

Yuri cleared his throat. "In case anyone hasn't noticed, I don't care what Kintake thinks."

"Yuri, can it," Terry demanded, making a cutting signal with his hand.

Yuri threw both hands up with resignation before standing to his feet.

"Let's assume for the moment that this was, in fact, a test, Saki. If there is an obscure clue we are supposed to find but we don't, what are the implications?"

"The implication is that this kill was not honorable; therefore, we will depart without honor. We are not able to perform the ritual combat without honor."

Terry looked around the room—at its walls, the desk, the bookshelves—and then fixed his eyes on their target's still corpse. The situation was vexing. Saki's point was strong, but Terry was more inclined to support Yuri.

Surveillance did not yield an objection to the hit. A major part of surveillance was to confirm a target and then double-check that the confirmation was valid. If Saki had doubts, he should have voiced them long before they'd plunged a knife into Oharu's back—or whoever he was. Now that the target was dead, going back wasn't an option. If this was the wrong target, then the consequences were a matter of *when* not *if*. Besides, if they set out to find an obscure clue and managed to find it, Terry reasoned that dishonor wouldn't be lifted on a technicality. And they weren't on the proving ground anymore. They weren't initiates; they were the initiated. Kintake had no reason to question their dedication to Ninpo; they'd proved that years ago.

Yuri started sorting through documents on and inside the desk. Saki followed Yuri's lead while Terry maintained watch over the door.

"Looks like Oharu to me," Yuri said, lifting documents and mail from a drawer. "Reads: Oharu Shinji. We got the right guy. Now that that's solved, let's disappear."

"That does not solve the question of why I do not know this man."

Everyone was quiet.

Yuri rapped his knuckles on the cage of thoughtful silence. "Look, Kintake instructed us to kill plenty of people in our teenage years. We never asked questions. Why are we suddenly overanalyzing this?"

"We were teenagers then, Yuri."

"So, we weren't expected to behave like proper Shinobi? What clan did you grow up in? Because the clan I grew up in didn't seem to show much leniency regardless of age."

"The kills we made as teenagers were different. They were different because—"

Saki cut him off. "What are you talking about? Who did you kill as teenagers?"

"Fuck, dude, I don't know. Plenty of people. Ten—twelve maybe." Yuri shrugged and then whipped a hand at Terry to continue.

Saki's inquiry, however, had derailed Terry's original point. "Why do you look so alarmed?"

"Omiyoshu Sensei instructed the two of you to kill people?"

Yuri's eyes became tight slits. "If this is one of those 'you shouldn't be allowed because you're not Japanese' comments, I swear I'll leave your body right here next to this stiff."

"No, Yuri, I would never say such a thing. But you have to understand that no one was ever sent to kill a person...that I am aware of."

Even through their balaclavas, Saki could see their faces twist with skepticism. Terry started before Yuri could, "They were part of our final trials. You had to do them too."

"I swear to you that I was never sent to kill anyone. This is the first human life I have ever been responsible for taking."

Terry and Yuri locked eyes. Their brotherly skepticism instantly became suspicion. How was this possible? Part of the initiation rites was to return with proof that a Shinobi could exercise their mandate in

257

accordance with the code. To prove his dedication to Ninpo, Terry had returned with a photo that a target had held dear; Yuri had returned with his first target's severed finger. They each had made their first human kill alone, but after that, Kintake had dispatched them together for successive trials. How was it that Saki had never done the same?

"How many times have you done this?"

"Like Yuri said, ten—maybe twelve—for the Fujibayashi that is. Countless away from the clan. I'm confused, though. Why would every initiate be required to perform a kill to cross over except you?"

"No other Kodomo or Genin has. Not me. Not Akiko. No one."

"That makes no sense." Terry shook his head.

"I find myself suddenly full of questions," Saki replied.

"Me too."

"Admittedly, my curiosity is piqued, but not enough to continue this conversation here," Yuri said. "It's only a matter of time before someone shows up and finds us standing over this body."

"Why would Omiyoshu Sensei send us to eliminate a criminal soldier?"

"For the same reason anyone would: He was probably a rival. What difference does that make?"

"Maybe he didn't," Terry said reluctantly. "Maybe we hit the wrong target. He could have been a decoy. If the real target was Fujibayashi, he knew that we'd come for him someday."

"Even if that was the case, why would an organized soldier be here and Oharu not?" Saki said.

Yuri gestured. "I'll say it again: It's possible that this guy was a rival. Kintake has always done business outside of the clan. Remember that Hattori Hanzo and he were always at odds. Maybe this guy was a loose end that Kintake wanted tied up. Tonight alone proves that the rabbit hole is deeper than we thought."

"Now, can we go?"

"Yeah, Yuri." Terry nodded. "We're moving."

"Wait," Saki said, thumbing through a massive photo album. "Look at this."

258

"What now?" Yuri said, hovering on the edge of irritation.

"There are myriad pictures of him in his youth. He is still covered in tattoos. He even took pictures of all the people he killed. Does the code prohibit that?"

Terry shrugged. "I'm not sure. I think it would. A picture would be evidence of presence, right?"

"Here is a photo with he and Omiyoshu Sensei—dated sixteen years ago," said Saki, pointing at the picture where both men were surround by middle-aged men in tuxedos. "Here is another."

"Hold up. Go back a page, Saki," Yuri said as he made a beeline to Saki's side. "What the hell?"

"What's the matter, Yuri?"

Yuri snatched two pictures out of the book and held them up. One was a picture of Oharu and an American man. The other was the American man with his wife and children. One child was a different color than other.

"These are our parents."

Chapter Sixteen: For Honor, To The Death

The time will come when Shinobi-no-mono—Hattori Hanzo—will be recalled to the heavens by the ancestor spirits. At such a time, three warriors from each of the Kato, Fuma, Momochi, Ishikawa, Fujibayashi, and Kirigakure clans will assemble on the site of the first Shinobi-no-mono's death. There, they will do battle until only one clan remains. From the ashes of the most honorable sacrifice, a new Shinobi-no-mono will ascend, and the victorious clan will be held in Shogun's favor.
The Ninth Mandate, translated from Ninpo.

Suzuka Mountains. Mie Prefecture, Japan. Today.

The time had finally come. Saki, Terry, and Yuri marched through snow-blanketed forest dressed in leather armor and snow camouflage towards the border.

All of Togakure Ryu—nearly every man, woman, and child—marched in a long column, three abreast, dressed in their most pristine vestments and ornate ceremonial weapons through the wooded hills that ascended to the sacred battleground. Men carried banners, women carried infants, children carried their excitement, and the elderly carried their piety. The Fujibayashi were a train of tradition and honor, puffing conviction into the air and pounding a trench through the snow as they followed Saki, Terry, and Yuri, and Kintake and his Jonin Council just ahead of them.

Togakure Ryu walked as a congregation, as a community, as an army to show support and solidarity to their fighters. They marched to the border of the sacred battleground to see their prized fighters off, hoping—knowing—that they would fight with honor, brilliance, and aggression and return to the village alive. If not alive, however, at least with honor.

The overall tone of the community was focused, but everyone had their own demeanor. Kintake was stoic, distant even. The Jonin were resigned. Saki's face was washed with consternation, even though he tried to hide it. Terry was tense. Yuri was a mix of turmoil and tenacity. Akiko felt repugnance.

Each member of Togakure Ryu had different expectations of the ritual. Saki had dreamed of this moment his whole life. When he was a child, he would sneak onto the sacred ground and look for signs and relics of bygone eras. He had always hoped to find a signal that he would one day be worthy to be a vessel by which Ninpo was venerated. He'd never found a sign as a child, but he was still so honored to find that it would be through his blood that Ninpo would be uplifted. If he were to die tonight, it would be with great honor.

From the border, Saki, Terry, and Yuri would cross, leaving the Fujibayashi behind to await the results. When it was all over, either Kintake or the Momochi kōchō would ascend to the holy office of Shinobi-no-Mono and the six chosen warriors between both clans would be commemorated for all time, like so many Shinobi generations before them.

*   *   *

The air was thick with tension. Saki couldn't feel the cold with Yuri burning a hole in his face. Yuri looked down only long enough to check his footing in the snow and then returned his gaze to boring a hole in Saki.

When the train of Fujibayashi stopped finally, Saki took advantage of the moment to address Kintake. Terry and Yuri followed.

"**Omiyoshu Sensei, I must speak with you,**" Saki said humbly.

Kintake barely turned, peering at Saki from the corner of his eye.

"**Omiyoshu Sensei, we uncovered troubling information last night, and I really must seek your counsel.**"

"**What is it, Saki?**"

"**I have reason to doubt Oharu's affiliation to the Fujibayashi.**"

Saki's suggestion caused several of the elderly Jonin to perk up. Kintake signaled them with a finger to place their attention elsewhere while he attended the three warriors.

Kintake folded his arms. "Saki, I understand it may have been difficult for you. But you must not allow anxiety to cloud your mind. Oharu was an errant Fujibayashi. He had evaded us for long enough."

"He did not have a tattoo of Mamushi. He had the tattoos of another affiliation—perhaps a criminal element. Pictures that we found provide chronological evidence that he lived in a city as a youth, and his tattoos came from somewhere not of Fujibayashi origin."

"Furthermore, Sensei," Terry chimed in, "we found pictures of our parents. How did he know our parents?"

Kintake's lips twisted as he stared hard at Terry, then Saki, and then Yuri. Then his gazed softened. "It's really quite simple, actually. You see, Oharu was an acquaintance of your parents, and he recommended them to my school."

Terry's eyes found the snow-covered ground. Something still didn't feel right. Something was off about this. There was still the issue of Saki's claim that no other Fujibayashi had ever conducted an assassination. "Sensei, Saki says that he never killed anyone before Oharu—"

"That is enough. You must focus. Beyond the border lies the most challenging event you will ever take part in. For the sake of the Fujibayashi, you must be focused and serious. You cannot trouble yourself with perceived deceptions and conspiracies. Death awaits you if you cannot focus."

"I'm looking at the forest, and something is wrong with the trees," said Yuri.

A single eyebrow rose on Kintake's forehead. He drew in a deep breath and exhaled slowly. "When you return from this battle—those of you that do, anyway—I will answer all of your questions."

"Sensei—" Terry attempted but was cut off.

"Honor is the soul of the Shinobi!" Kintake shouted before walking to the rear of the column. "You really should get going."

All in attendance, including the three warriors, who lagged behind the group slightly, made steeples of their hands in salute and replied: "Shadow is their blood!"

In the spring and summer, the sacred battleground—nestled in a shallow valley with the temple from the warriors' youth cradled at the center—was breathtaking, like a painting of a land in a fairy tale—at least that was the way Terry remembered it from the last time he'd been here. In the winter, however, it was not so endearing; in the winter, it looked haunted.

The trees looked like thousands of ghostly arms trying to drag the black sky down. The gradual slopes to either side evoked a sense of claustrophobia and blocked the moon unless it was directly overhead, heightening the anxiety of the forthcoming conflict. The anxiety was compounded by the layer of snow crunching beneath Saki, Terry, and Yuri's feet as they snuck down the eastern incline and into the shambling forest toward the temple single file, giving it their all to be as inconspicuous as possible. They weren't exactly sure where they needed to go; they just knew that they needed to engage the Momochi warriors, and the best way to do that was to remain invisible, spot them, track them, and then ambush them.

Yuri led, keeping a low profile and occasionally stopping behind a tree to scan the gray-blue horizon for movement. Saki let out a low, breathy whistle, and Yuri took cover, looking back.

Saki was in cover too, looking at Terry between them. Terry squatted, looking into the distance where light turned into darkness, holding his naginata across his thighs.

"**What's the matter?**" Yuri whispered, adjusting his insulation beneath his leather breastplate. "**What do you see?**"

"**A memory that I haven't thought about since I was a kid.**"

Yuri was incensed, puffing steam into the air through his white-gray balaclava. "**Can you find a better time to reminisce? We're right in the middle of something.**"

Terry looked at his brother. "**There may not be a later.**"

"**Well,**" Yuri said, raising an indignant hand, "**in that case.**"

"**Terry, we have to keep moving,**" said Saki, trying to appeal to Terry's better judgment.

"No, no, Saki," Yuri said, trying not to bubble over a whisper into audible inflections, "**let him have his moment. Memories are worth dying for.**"

Terry took cover. He alternated looking at his brother and Saki. "*This memory is important.*"

"It *better* be important," Yuri said sourly, "**because if we get ambushed while you're telling your campfire horror story, I'm going to scalp you in the afterlife as payback.**"

"**Saki**," Terry said, turning toward him, "**remember when you brought me here the first time?**"

Saki nodded.

"**Well, you said that the worthy can hear the ancestor Shinobi fighting. On the night my parents were killed, I came here. This was quite nearly the same path I followed to the temple. As I was running, I rolled my ankle and fell just over there.**" Terry pointed off to their right. "**I was face down in the mud, and I swear I heard the strangest sounds. Distant metal-on-metal sounds. Like swords clashing in a battle. At first, I thought it was just the thunder, but the more I heard it, the more I was sure of what I was hearing. It was the ancient Shinobi that I heard.**"

"Do you know what that means?" Saki asked.

"**It means while you're sitting here telling fairy tales, we're sitting ducks,**" Yuri retorted caustically. "**Or it means you're schizophrenic. Either way, wrap it up.**"

Terry nodded. "**It means that we're worthy. We were destined for this moment. Kintake said we weren't worthy and banished us, but here we are. Not even he can stop destiny.**" Terry signaled Yuri forward.

Yuri started to move, hurling a comment over his shoulder as he brushed past a tree: "**Maybe *he* can't, but the Momochi *can* if we get caught camping.**"

Just then, he saw something move out of the corner of his eye, and his body reacted, his head whipping to the left and jerking his body behind the tree. An arrow whizzed by his eyebrow so close that the fletching tickled his flesh, barely missing its mark in his eye socket. Yuri fell into the tree and slid to the ground.

Terry and Saki did the same.

264

"**Sniper**!" Terry whispered loudly.

THWACK! Another arrow struck Yuri's tree. He gritted his teeth and bore down.

"**Are you okay**?" Saki asked, unable to lift his head out of cover to see how badly injured Yuri was if he wasn't.

Yuri gave an insincere thumbs up despite his face being creased with pain. "Peachy." He sat forward, lifting his back off of the trunk just enough to reveal that the second arrow had penetrated the tree and its point had dug into the leather armor on Yuri's shoulder—the point had scratched him and drawn a little blood. *The sniper shouldn't have missed me*, Yuri thought. He was going to make him eat that arrow.

Terry checked both sides frantically, looking past Yuri on his right about five feet and Saki on his left nearly double that. He edged an eye around the thin trunk. His camouflage would hold up if the sniper hadn't seen him, but if he had, he'd spot Terry's movement. Terry got a fix downrange and then jerked back into cover.

THWACK! An arrow zipped past his tree and landed next to his leg. The sniper had seen Terry after all.

"**There's only one**," Terry said calmly. "**He's in a tree about one hundred yards off my left shoulder.**"

Saki looked at him. "**We must move. They are going to flank us if we do not.**"

Terry nodded and swung his head toward his brother. "**Yuri, you good**?"

Yuri's eyes were lupine. "**I'm good. Can't say the same for that Momochi son of a bitch**," he said, pulling a grappling hook from his belt and coiling the rope into tight circles.

"**I'm going to make a break for that next tree. When he fires, Saki, you close-in on the sniper's left. Yuri, you close in on the right. He'll have to choose one of us to fire at. Once we get too close, he'll have to come out of that tree.**"

Saki nodded.

Yuri did too as he stuffed his grappling hook back into his belt.

Terry tossed his naginata forward and lunged out of cover on his hands and feet—THWACK! Another arrow whizzed over his back and struck a few feet downrange—and Terry barreled up to the next tree, snagging the end of his weapon and snuggling up to it.

Yuri and Saki charged for the next cover, staying low.

THWACK! An arrow hit near Saki. Terry and Yuri were on the move the second they heard it and were into cover again a split second before the next one hit.

The Fujibayashi staggered their movement across the field, leapfrogging from cover to cover, barely escaping the bite of the sniper's arrows as they closed on his position. They taxed the sniper's aim as they got nearer; downrange, they appeared closer together, but they forced him to increase his azimuth as their relative distanced changed.

Yuri and Saki skidded into new cover, flinging snow and grass, Yuri on his stomach and Saki on his side. Yuri whipped out his ninjatō and flashed it at Terry and Saki to say that he was okay. Saki responded by drawing his ninjatō.

Yuri checked the left flank for movement—the sniper's right. THWACK! He heard an arrow strike on his left. He checked it. The arrow was lodged in a tree three feet away. He rolled out of cover and dug in with his feet, sprinting for the next point. He managed a glance uprange before he went airborne into cover ten feet ahead of his last position. He could make out the archer, perched on a limb, nocking another arrow. Then Yuri was heads down as he collapsed into cover, skidding through the snow again. He slumped against the new tree trunk, absorbing the impact with a forceful exhale. He lifted his head to see what progress his brother and Saki were making.

Terry was already in a new position, with his back against a tree and looking over his left shoulder towards the sniper. The sniper loosed an arrow at Saki, who was in mid-dive for new cover. THWACK! The arrow struck Saki's side. He hit the ground and skidded into the tree.

Terry and Yuri's heads snapped in Saki's direction. They held their breaths. They could feel their heartbeats in their heads.

Saki, leaving his ninjatō in the snow, scrambled to his knees behind the tree, using it for support with one arm and checking his side with the other. He drew the arrow from where it was lodged in between his backplate and his bag. He didn't feel any pain, nor was there blood.

He looked at Terry and Yuri, whose eyes were full moons with anticipation encircled by balaclavas. Saki raised a hand that said he was okay. Terry exhaled finally. Yuri was instantly out of cover, rushing forward.

THWACK! THWACK! THWACK! Downrange, the sniper was unable to land a clean shot; now the sniper was firing repeatedly, trying to increase his chances of hitting the Fujibayashi when the distance between him and them had become desperate. He was sacrificing his accuracy to increase his rate of fire, firing as quickly as possible to pin one of his targets down so he could flush out the other two and hopefully catch one as he was running for cover.

The sniper swung wide to get a shot off, and then he saw Terry leave cover for the next tree. Terry threw his naginata and dove as the arrow came loose and zipped beneath him, missing him by a hair's length—so close, in fact, that Terry felt the shaft graze his thigh. Terry crumbled into a ball and rolled end over end to the next tree, getting snow in his mouth, ears, and tunic. Terry hugged the tree and checked the right and left flank, waiting for Yuri and Saki to move before exposing a body part to grab the naginata. This close, the sniper's slant angle was much steeper, giving him an improved vantage even if his ability to hit arrayed targets had been diminished.

Saki hustled out of cover with his ninjatō in hand and slid to his next position like a baseball player sliding into home. Two successive arrows landed around him. He too scanned his flank.

Nothing.

Something wasn't right.

The other Momochi weren't pressing the flanks while their sniper had the range advantage. And with the Fujibayashi closing on the sniper's position, now was the time. Where were they? Were they waiting further uprange? Were they planning to snipe the Fujibayashi from even further away when they closed and flushed out the sniper, using one of their own as bait? Were they in cover near the sniper, waiting for the Fujibayashi to come close so they could launch a trap?

One question rang inside Saki's head louder than the others: how had the Momochi arrived on this side of the temple before the Fujibayashi had? The Momochi's approach to the temple was far more treacherous and shear, which nearly doubled their transit time. How was it then that they had covered the distance up their side of the peaks and the field of trees to set their ambush on this side of the temple before the Fujibayashi could even cross the boundary? Suspicion sloshed in Saki's stomach as he rolled over to see what progress Terry and Yuri were making in the seconds that his attention was elsewhere.

Terry was ahead of Saki, standing sideways against a tree, trying to draw the sniper's fire with his naginata. Yuri, overflowing with adrenaline, was even further ahead, situated at the far-left corner—the sniper's right—of the lazy rectangle the Fujibayashi had transcribed in the snow as they'd leapfrogged in and out of concealment. Yuri was perpendicular to the sniper, waiting for him to commit to firing at Terry. When the sniper did, Yuri hoped to rush the twenty yards to the sniper's position.

The sniper, with a ready arrow, swung his head back and forth to all three of the Fujibayashi, trying not to let them get the drop on him,

Terry glanced at Yuri, who was dug in like a sprinter. Terry intended to throw his naginata at the sniper, and he signaled Saki with his chin. Saki acknowledged and then check the flank again.

Terry wasn't certain that he could land the weapon, trying to throw from a defensive position, but it would at least give Yuri time to close in. Terry wasn't certain he could avoid getting shot either. It was the best chance they had, though.

Terry snapped the naginata to his shoulder, readying it. The sniper saw the weapon move and committed to firing a near-point-blank-range shot. THWACK! Terry winced as the arrow struck the tree trunk; the arrowhead created a steeple with the bark as it punched through the other side with a *crunch*.

Saki and Yuri held their position.

Terry tried again, but the sniper shut Terry down again with another near hit.

Yuri didn't wait any longer. He was out of cover, accelerating despite the snow's protest.

The sniper threaded his bow around a branch, struggling to nock another arrow whilst attempting to settle into a firing position—the nock was unsuccessful the first time, and he had to retry. Yuri was bearing down on him, and the sniper was desperate. He fired, but the arrow tumbled through the air when the sniper fired it without a proper nock. He hustled to reload.

Yuri yanked the grappling hook from his belt and hurled it into the tree at the sniper. One of the hook's flukes impacted the bow, causing the arrow to go wide and setting the sniper off balance.

The sniper caught himself and, realizing that he no longer had the high-ground advantage, drew his ninjatō and dismounted. Yuri rushed in, trying to catch the sniper as he came down, but Yuri was too late. The sniper landed, raised his sword, and swung it in a J-shape from above his head to waist level. Yuri slid beneath the blade as it hummed past his face, and turned to block the sniper's recovery slash; there was an angry metal-on-metal *clank*.

The sniper bounded backward, checking for the other two Fujibayashi—just in time too; the blade of Terry's naginata plunged for his ribcage. The sniper managed to deflect Terry's stab over his shoulder and then swapped feet to slash at Terry's waist. Terry, exposed from the sniper's parry, leaped backward to avoid being cleaved in half. The sniper pressed his attack, immediately turning the strike into a combination of blinding slashes, ending with a thrust that was meant to impale Terry. Terry gave ground and parried the slashes with both ends of his whirling naginata, driving the sniper's final thrust up and left.

Having the reach advantage by three feet, Terry used the distance to keep himself outside the lethal arcs of the sniper's ninjatō. Terry drove the blunt end of the naginata in a semi-circle at the sniper's shins. The sniper leaped backward. Terry finished the low swing and then changed course, bringing the blade around at shoulder level. The sniper continued to retreat backward, trying desperately not to slip in the snow nor get caught in between the Fujibayashi.

Terry reset and leveled the naginata at his waist as Saki came abreast with his ninjatō held in a high guard. Yuri was on his feet, pacing on the sniper's right flank. The sniper backed away cautiously, ensuring not to cross his feet as he stepped. All four men puffed steam into the twilight from beneath their masks.

Yuri kicked snow, and the sniper flinched. Terry took the opening and drove in with his blade. The sniper retreated at an angle, with Terry following and slicing a figure eight through the air. Saki moved left behind Terry, trying to corral the sniper.

Yuri rushed in. His ninjatō swung high, and the sniper met him with a parry. Yuri swung, changed direction, and swung again. His blade crashed into the sniper's sword repeatedly, driving him back. The sniper—his attention divided between the Fujibayashi, their weapons, the snow, and the trees—intercepted Yuri's strikes a fraction of a second later each time; it was beginning to add up. Yuri didn't let up, sensing that the sniper was falling behind.

Terry feinted with the naginata. The sniper's attention and weapon snapped in the direction from which Terry's strike never came. At that moment, the sniper knew he'd been had. The sniper buckled as Yuri sliced into the sniper's side. There was some resistance when the blade hit the sniper's ribs, but otherwise, the cut was clean.

The sniper retched, lowering his ninjatō, staggering to the side. Yuri swapped feet to change the dynamic of his next strike and brought his ninjatō down on the sniper's arm, severing it just below the elbow. The man howled. Yuri stabbed him through the neck, silencing him. The sniper collapsed onto his face, spraying a fan of blood into the mangled layer of snow.

"Dammit," Yuri panted, watching the steam rise from the sniper's blood.

"What?" Terry asked, taking cover behind a nearby tree.

Yuri and Saki followed his lead.

"I wanted to gore that asshole with my grappling hook really bad. Only thing I hit was his bow."

"Well, you got him out of the tree."

"There *is* that, I suppose."

"He is dead; that is all that matters," Saki said, returning his ninjatō to its sheath. "His death was honorable, if not premature."

"Hey, Saki," Yuri said bitterly, "any reason why you decided to hang out in the audience while me and Terry fought it out with this douchebag?"

"Easy there, kemosabe," said Terry, jumping to Saki's defense. "Someone had to watch our flanks. There are still two other Shinobi out there. Why don't you remember whose team you're on, huh?" It wasn't a question.

Yuri nodded. "**I guess that makes sense.**"

"**Where are the other two? Why did they not support their sniper?**" Saki said, scanning the expanse of trees and gray.

"**That's a good question,**" Terry replied.

"**Something is not right. Either they are waiting to ambush us somewhere, or they used him as bait, and they plan to attack us here.**"

"**Yeah.**" Terry pointed at the bloodied corpse of the sniper. "**And by doing so, they wasted a man. If they had flanked us while he was shooting, they'd have had us on the back foot.**"

"**Agreed.**" Saki nodded. "**What should we do now?**"

Terry pulled his mask down and wiped his mouth thoughtfully. The Momochi's tactics just didn't quite add up. Why sacrifice a man in vain? Terry looked at his brother.

"**Let's push on to the temple,**" Yuri said. "**It's going to be warmer there than here. If the other two are out here, my bet is they're there waiting for us. And if they're not, we can ambush them there.**"

"**Sounds effective enough.**" Terry turned to his comrade. "**Saki?**"

"**I support Yuri's rationale.**"

"**Alright, let's move.**"

*   *   *

The three Fujibayashi came up to the *torii*. Terry took cover behind one of the stone lanterns—*tōrō*—and Saki and Yuri stacked up behind the other. In light of the sniper's attack, their minds were racing as they tried to crack the Momochi strategy—granted, asymmetric warfare was the forte of Shinobi, but this went beyond the realm of making sense. In the thirty minutes it had taken them to trek from the sniper's position to the temple, the Fujibayashi hadn't seen so much as a trace of the Momochi—only the sniper's footprints leading away from the temple.

Saki poked the air in the direction of the torii with his index finger. Terry came out from behind the lantern and sprinted through the gate, angling right into the thick grouping of trees that sat just inside the temple walls and bordered the steps of the main approach—the sandō—from the torii through the temple grounds.

Yuri shot out from behind Saki and followed his brother into the pocket of trees. Saki waited a moment to see if the Momochi would make a move. When they didn't, he sprinted to Terry and Yuri.

The Fujibayashi crept through the gaunt trees to the wood's edge. They stacked one behind the other and surveyed the snow-covered grounds from the far right of the sandō to the honden. Not being populated by thousands of trees like outside the temple walls, a sliver of the moon was able to splatter silver over the blacks, browns, and grays of the nighttime temple, offering more visibility than they'd had earlier.

On the other side of the sandō, about twenty yards or more, were three tool-shed-sized structures that had at one time been dedicated to physical purification and worshipful expression. Just inside that were tombs numbering thirty or so that lined either side of the sandō. And directly in front of them, on the same side as the Fujibayashi but across a thirty-yard stretch of undisturbed snow, was the second largest building, known as the shamuso; in the shrine's heyday, the shamuso was its administrative node. Just beyond, and obscured by the shamuso, were the haiden and the honden. The Fujibayashi looked for signs of additional snipers or lookouts on the rooves but saw none. There was a single set of tracks along the sandō, leading through the torii and off the temple grounds toward the sniper's position. Other than that, the snow was undisturbed and pristine.

"**Where are these assholes?**" Yuri said out loud to himself.

"**If they are on the grounds, I am willing to bet they are either in the shamuso or the honden,**" Saki said just a hair above a whisper.

Terry agreed. The haiden was open to the elements and not large enough to stage an ambush. And with the shamuso and the honden as viable options, staging an ambush from the haiden made no sense.

"**This is their blindspot,**" Terry whispered over his shoulder. "**There are no windows on the wall across the way. If they're in the shamuso, they won't be able to see us coming. If they are in the honden, the shamuso blocks their view.**"

272

Saki leaned forward and placed his hand on Yuri's shoulder. "**Yuri, you move straight ahead to the shamuso and clear its far-right corner. Disregard those buildings on the other side of the sandō. They are not large enough to be great cover for the Momochi. If the Momochi are hiding in them, we will see them exit to attempt an attack.**"

Yuri nodded.

Saki continued, "**Terry, you follow after Yuri is set. I will cover our rear.**"

Terry nodded too.

"**Go.**"

Yuri crept up beside his brother, scanned the grounds one last time, and then sprinted thirty yards through shin-deep snow to the shamuso. As he neared the building, he went onto his belly and turned sideways so that he slid parallel into the wall. The snow broke his fall, slowed him down, and silenced his impact. Then he was on his feet and creeping toward his assigned corner.

Yuri kept his left shoulder in contact with the wall as he the neared edge. He pressed himself into the wall and gave a quick check of the space between the shamuso and the perimeter wall; it was clear. Yuri waved his arm.

Terry looked back at Saki, knowing that as soon as he made a break for the building, Saki would be vulnerable to attack from the rear with twenty yards separating him from the others if the Momochi had been there waiting the whole time. Saki drew his ninjatō just in case and nodded. Terry shot out of the woods and did a replay of Yuri's maneuver, just to the corner closer to the sandō—clear. He waved his arm.

Saki shot out of the woods with his ninjatō in a reverse grip, replaying the brothers' maneuver. The Fujibayashi were arrayed against the eastern wall of the shamuso: Yuri on the right, Terry on the left, and Saki between the two.

Saki tapped Terry on the shoulder to let him know to back up, without taking his eyes off their left flank, along the wall with Saki until they had reached Yuri. Once Saki and Terry were stacked on Yuri, Saki tapped him on the shoulder. Yuri turned the corner and approached the next one to check it the same way. The route to the honden was clear, and so was the space between the perimeter wall and the honden. Yuri waved his hand.

Saki tapped Yuri when Saki and Terry were stacked on him again. Yuri shot from behind the shamuso and up to the raised patio of the honden, ducking beneath it. He popped his head up and checked for movement on the other side of the sandō—still nothing. Yuri waved his hand. Saki ran up to him. Then Terry followed.

Saki tapped Yuri's shoulder again. Yuri slithered through the rail of the patio and crawled on his hands and feet to the door, pressing his ear against it—again, nothing. He sat up on his knees and glanced back at Saki and Terry, who were now coming through the rails themselves. Yuri indicated the door with his head and then drew his ninjato. Saki and Terry nodded. Yuri slid the door open a crack, tuned out the ambient noise, and listened. He heard what he surmised were birds rustling, dreaming in their nests and beating their wings occasionally in their sleep. He heard the breeze whistling through windows or vents in the structure. Otherwise, nothing, so he slid the door open just enough for him to fit through and rounded the door jamb so that his back was against the wall. After a moment, he rapped his fingers on the jam, and his brother and Saki followed, closing the door behind them.

The honden was a nearly pitch-black, large, singular room that was populated by kanji-inscribed pillars that supported the massive roof, numbering perhaps twenty. Each pillar had a candleholder on each cardinal side. The far side sported an altar that housed the shrine's cami, and there were two doors to either side. On the far right and far left of the honden were enormous wooden tablets situated like dominoes along either wall.

The Fujibayashi fanned out to clear the hiding places and then met up in the middle on the far side, in front of the altar. The coast was clear.

"Yuri," Terry said, "can you see if there's enough candle in any of those candle holders to light?"

"Is that wise?"

"I don't really care at this point. Do you?"

"Naw," said Yuri, walking off to check the candles. "I don't care in the slightest."

Yuri fumbled with the first candle holder and lit it with a lighter he pulled from his harness.

"Seriously?" Terry asked grimly.

Yuri shrugged. "What?"

"You brought a lighter?"

"The rules demanded traditional weapons; they didn't say anything about lighters. Besides, we're wearing poly-cotton balaclavas. Last I checked, poly-cotton wasn't a thing in the sixteenth century."

Terry shook his head and began to shake the water off of his gear. Saki did the same, and Yuri lit a few more candles before returning to the other two.

Just then, he heard something that didn't sound like a bird rustling. **"Did you hear that?"** Yuri whispered.

Saki shook his head, his hand gripping his sword tighter.

"Something's not right. We're not alone."

Then there was a strange voice. **"What's not right is that the Fujibayashi have allowed gaijin to pervert our culture."** The voice came from above them; all three looked up. **"Is that true? Are you gaijin?"**

The last two Momochi were standing on the rafters above them. They had set their ambush in here, but they had waited too long. They no longer had the element of surprise. The Momochi had given it up to inquire on the ethnic makeup of the Fujibayashi.

Amateurs.

"Why don't you come down here and look?" Yuri barked. **"I'd gladly oblige your curiosity."**

Just then, the two doors opened, and a handful of people dressed warmly in jeans, boots, and winter jackets poured in, armed to the teeth with guns and melee weapons. The Fujibayashi watched blankly, not quite sure what to think. There was no way this was happening.

"What is the meaning of this?" Saki demanded. **"This violates the Ninth Mandate of Ninpo! Never in four hundred years has the ritual combat been so corrupted!"**

"Do not seek to lecture me, Takejiro Saki," the Momochi cautioned from above. **"Your clan has violated the Third Mandate of**

Ninpo by assimilating foreigners and allowing them to soil this sacred ground."

"And these outsiders you have brought with you don't soil the ground?" Terry said, waving his naginata at them. "I may be a foreigner, but I *am* Shinobi. These insects have no place within these walls, and Mamushi would see you all to a slow, painful death just for insulting the ancestor spirits."

An impeccably dressed man of average height and slender build, with a rapidly receding hairline and crooked teeth, wearing a long designer winter coat, stood near the rear of the congregation. He said, "Actually, our presence on these grounds—which I am not sure if I would define them as sacred—is mandated, unlike your own, gaijin."

"Who the hell are you?" Yuri said, sounding territorial.

"My name is Itsuki Kawaguchi, and it's a pleasure to make your acquaintances."

"I can't say that I feel the same," Terry replied without pause.

"Indeed." Kawaguchi rubbed his hands, trying to warm them, and then stuffed them into the pockets of his jacket. "You see—we are all family here—minus you three, of course, and the two up there. We are Yakuza. We are the descendants of the Samurai. We are the vanguard against foreign invasion. The honor guard of the Shogunate. And therefore, we are here by order of the Shogun himself."

The Fujibayashi laughed.

"This guy," Yuri said, looking at Terry and indicating Kawaguchi with a hand.

"You got to be kidding me," Terry replied to his brother.

"I do not kid, gaijin," Kawaguchi said in English with a heavy accent. "You are here because the Shogun deemed it so. Shinobi, historically, were like draft animals, little better than livestock. To keep you from killing each other, Shogun Tokugawa and Hattori Hanzo wrote the Ninth Mandate. Better that the Shogun choose who lives and dies—can't have the livestock killing each other on a whim. After all, the Shogun was elected to his position by the gods themselves—not by some ridiculous cult belief like Ninpo. So—here you are again, Shinobi, doing a draft animal's work."

"Momochi take orders from criminals now?" Saki asked venomously. "Where is your honor?"

"Shogun's favor is changing, Saki," the other hovering Momochi said. "Do not chastise us because Omiyoshu Sensei failed to teach his Shinobi the true history of Ninpo and its allegiances."

"Some thug calls himself a Shogun, and the Momochi heel when he says so?" Yuri asked, looking up at the Momochi and tapping his ninjatō agitatedly against his leg. "How much are they paying you?"

One of the Momochi began to reply, but Kawaguchi interrupted, saying, "Come now, there is no reason to bicker like children over dead philosophy. Do you think this is all about some ancient Bushi code?" Kawaguchi smiled and shrugged his shoulders. "Do not be so blind."

"It's the Momochi that are blind," responded Terry. "They are without honor and morals, and they consort with the same."

"I have a remedy for dishonor," Saki assured.

Kawaguchi snorted. "Stop it, please. You all sound so ridiculous. Now I understand why the Shogun Nobunaga wanted to exterminate your kind. We'll correct that mistake, though. And the Shogun has sent me to ensure that the job was completed."

Saki's voice dropped. "The Shogun?"

"Yeah—you keep mentioning him," Terry said, backing Saki up. "Sounds like you have an egomaniac for a friend."

"Ah, I have said too much already. I have a reputation for talking too much." Kawaguchi smiled pleasantly raising a hand that had only four fingers. "You've never heard of the Shogun because only kōchō are worthy of speaking to him. I digress..." He pointed at one of the men in winter jackets nearest the Fujibayashi. "Take their masks off. I want to see their faces. I want to see these gaijin with whom the Fujibayashi have damned themselves."

One of the men walked up to each of the Fujibayashi and pulled down the cotton that covered their faces—each face a different color than the next. Kawaguchi approached and regarded them closely. He had wondered if he'd recognize any of them. He didn't, especially those that weren't Asian. He was a bit disappointed by that. Knowing them would have made killing them so much sweeter. Either way, the Shogun would be pleased once they were dead and the Fujibayashi were cast low.

Kawaguchi said, "**You should know that the Shogun is horribly displeased with the Fujibayashi's transgressions against our country— our history—by allowing gaijin to live amongst them. Hattori Hanzo was a fool for thinking it acceptable. The punishment is disfavor— disfavor for the entire clan—and the disfavor of the Shogun only brings death. Sadly, I have other engagements, so I will not be able to attend your deaths. The Shogun is a busy man, and he requires me to be in many places.**" Kawaguchi raised the same hand and snapped his fingers. "**Let's go,**" he said and left with five of his men in tow, leaving ten plus the Momochi.

The Momochi, with the grace of gymnasts, came down from the rafters and joined their Yakuza counterparts on the main floor. They were dressed similarly to the Fujibayashi except that their colors were a shade lighter and the headdress that went over their hoods were of slightly different design and sported a symbol of yamainu—mountain wolf—instead of Mamushi on the Fujibayashi headdress.

The silence among the Fujibayashi and the Momochi was tense; this was not so much the case with the Yakuza. Their instincts were not the same as the five Shinobi, which were born of years of harsh training and conditioning. The Momochi would not feel settled until the Fujibayashi were dead. The Yakuza talked incessantly among each other, not regarding the threat that living Fujibayashi could pose. The Momochi knew better, though, and urged the Yakuza to finish them. "**You shouldn't wait any longer. Kill them, and let's be done with it.**"

"**Don't rush me, *peasant*,**" the highest-ranking Yakuza said. "**I'd just as soon kill Momochi too.**" The Momochi didn't respond. The Yakuza returned to their mismatched conversations about how they intended to kill the Fujibayashi as painfully as possible.

Yuri's blood ran hot.

Sweat beaded on Terry's forehead as he considered his options.

Saki did the same.

They processed the situation as fast as they could. What they needed was an exit strategy, but they were outnumbered and outgunned. They individually surveyed the crowd: They were loosely surrounded by Yakuza, most of whom had handguns, though one had a submachine gun and another a katana. The Momochi were standing in between the altar and the Yakuza. Terry figured he could take out two of the Yakuza before he was shot and killed if the Fujibayashi could space the thugs out and attack them all at the same time. Saki had a chain whip and could use it to space them out; he just needed a split-second diversion to give him a moment to get the chain up to speed and out to its full length. Yuri could be the diversion.

Terry looked at Saki and Yuri to his right and mouthed, *Chain whip*. Saki scanned the room with his eyes. Yuri was a wolf on a leash.

"Go," Terry said.

Yuri exploded. He struck with the malice of a cornered pit viper, planting a kick squarely in the chest the closest thug, audibly crushing his ribs and sending him sprawling.

Saki snatched the chain whip from his belt, snapping it out to its full length and setting it whistling through the air.

Then everything was slow motion.

Yuri went beneath the chain and rolled right. Terry withdrew his naginata and ducked left. Saki increased the speed—increased the revolutions.

The chain was indiscriminate. Hateful. Its scythe-like blade carved deep, jagged wounds into the unprepared circle of Yakuza, painting the muted earth tones of the honden with radical spatterings of red. The Yakuza stumbled or fell, clutching the mangled body parts flayed by the chain; those that didn't stumble were struck again by the lightning strike of the chain, which carved even deeper wounds.

Saki stirred a shrieking tornado overhead, whirling the chain whip so fast that the blade looked like an orange-silver ring reflecting the candlelight. He drew in its length through his control hand. The pitch of the chain's wail climbed as Saki shortened its length. Then, like a dancer changing the direction of his or her sequence, Saki spun his shoulders and brought the chain crashing meteorically onto the floor, buckling the wooden planks.

Yuri uncoiled and found his feet, lunging at the first thug in his path—one that was helpless to fight back while he was trying desperately to keep his jaw connected where the chain whip had struck him. Yuri slashed the thug's gun arm with his ninjatō, severing his hand just above the wrist. And then he buried the sword's edge into where the shoulder and the neck meet.

A nearby second thug opened fire, shooting wildly. Yuri ripped his blade from the first thug and disappeared behind a pillar.

When Yuri went right, Terry split to the left, working counterclockwise. When Saki's chain came down, Terry sprinted toward the nearest goon and swung the naginata in a deep arc, hacking off the man's leg at the knee. Terry didn't seem to notice the grisly splash as the goon hit the floor separately from his limb, which tumbled end over end a few times as Terry rushed at the second goon further to the left. This one was injured from the chain whip clipping his neck.

Terry painted a wide arc from the floor into the air, spinning concentric circles above his head and then behind his back before leaving the ground acrobatically. The injured goon squeezed a shot off—*BLAM!*—but hit the far wall when Terry's athleticism and the injury made it impossible to aim. Terry came out of a spin, landed, and followed the blade around, slicing a bowl shape from the goon's skull.

BLAM! BLAM! Terry heard two gunshots from a thug firing at his brother, who had ducked into cover behind a pillar. Terry needed to get over there to help. He turned sharply and hurled his naginata at the next goon in the circle, trying to spear him. The second goon managed to avoid it—barely—but the third wasn't as lucky. The blade plunged deep into his thigh, punching through the bone and out the other side.

Terry rushed the second goon, who was trying to level his gun through a bloody veil of the laceration that Saki's chain had left on the goon's brow. Terry slapped the gun to the side and pounced on the goon, spinning him around and getting his arm around the goon's neck. In a flash of light, Terry drew his tanto, plunged it into the goon's ribs, and then used the man's own gun to open fire on third goon, who was sprawled on the floor with the naginata jutting out of his femur. Terry scored two out of five hits to center mass, ending him.

When Yuri went right and Terry split to the left, Saki kept the chain whip howling overhead for another couple of seconds to keep the Yakuza back—injured fighters were still dangerous. Then Saki repositioned his upper body and collapsed the chain onto the floor thunderously. Yuri was after thugs to the right. Terry rushed the goons to the left. And Saki darted straight ahead, after the gangsters at the top of the circle and the Momochi just behind them.

Saki attacked an uninjured gangster holding a katana in a high guard standing next to a gangster staggering with *v-shape* chopped into the bridge of his nose by the chain. Saki slung the weighted end of his chain at the sword, ensnaring it, and yanked the gangster off balance. Saki slipped inside, pushed the man's arms aside, and drove the sharp end of the chain into the thug's ribs just beneath the armpit. The thug's eyes opened like umbrellas in the rain as the blade pushed through his left lung and stopped at his heart.

Saki tossed him aside, scooped up his katana, and rushed over to the gangster with the bridge of his nose missing. The katana went up and came down at an angle, taking an entire portion of the gangster's head, just above the eye, with it. Saki whipped his back leg around and planted his foot in the man's gut, flinging the man off his feet and onto the ground like cold meat.

BLAM! BLAM! There were gunshots behind him, but Saki was unfazed.

Saki pulled his mask over his face so that the Momochi could only see his eyes. Then he drew his ninjatō and pointed the tips of both blades at the Momochi. They readied themselves for his advance. They had planned to hold their ground if the gangsters couldn't dispatch the Fujibayashi. Diving into the fray with the undisciplined, untrained Yakuza would have been disastrous. Now they could dispatch Saki while the other two Fujibayashi were occupied.

Saki charged between them, slashing in both directions with hell-bent precision. The Momochi parried and moved. Saki and the two Momochi became a ball of clashing metal, with Saki showing unprecedented swordsmanship as he struck and parried simultaneously.

Yuri was pinned down behind the pillar as the Yakuza thug emptied his magazine into it. Yuri hoped that the pillar would hold up, but the way it was showering splitters, Yuri was sure that the thug would score a hit eventually. Yuri had to do something.

Terry, still holding a human shield, leveled his barrel on the goon between himself and the thug shooting at Yuri. The goon, missing an eye from a chain whip strike, pointed his gun at Terry. BLAM! BLAM! Terry and the goon cracked off several shots. Terry felt his shield shutter. The goon fell. Terry felt an intense heat in his gut, and then pain radiated through his side. He gritted his teeth and aimed at the thug—BAM! BAM! BAM!—and put three rounds in him.

Yuri raced out of cover to help Saki. Terry dropped his shield and clutched his side.

Saki, the Fujibayashi's pinnacle swordsman, relentlessly assaulted the Momochi. He slashed, parried, spun to face the other, slashed, and then parried. One after the other, with crisp precision and calculation, he struck where his eyes had once been, meeting Momochi parries, and then blocked where he had never actually looked, intercepting Momochi strikes. Up, down, left, right, and at angles, their blades soared, cutting ribbons and circles in the air as they danced lethal concentric rings around each other, their feet landing in seemingly choreographed positions.

Saki's left blade slashed at shoulder level, and the smaller Momochi ducked. The right blade followed vertically, and the smaller Momochi rolled to his left, the blade missing him by inches. Saki parried with a high arc, driving a Momochi blade up and around as he spun to meet the next the sword strike. But it didn't come where he anticipated.

It happened so quickly.

Saki was spinning to catch the next strike as Yuri was covering the few yards from the pillar to the fight when the point of the Momochi's ninjatō sunk into Saki's spine. Saki aspirated and collapsed.

Yuri flew with his foot outstretched, aiming for the larger Momochi's head. He ducked, and Yuri sailed over the top of him, landing two or three feet away. Yuri rushed the Momochi, pounding his guard furiously with his ninjatō. Hate fueled Yuri's strikes as he chipped away at the Momochi's defense, forcing him back. The smaller Momochi came at Yuri, and Yuri leaped off of the larger and onto the smaller with twice the ferocity.

282

The Momochi chose their strikes, trying to corral Yuri in the same manner Yuri and the Fujibayashi had corralled the sniper. Yuri would have none of it. He blitzed repeatedly with a furious assault, slashing, stabbing, kicking, and striking. The Momochi knew that it wouldn't last for long, though. Pretty soon, the adrenaline would reach its limit, fatigue would take over, and the Momochi would score another Fujibayashi kill. They just had to wait Yuri out.

The pain was tremendous, but Terry had to help his brother. Terry aimed around Yuri, who was stirring a hurricane with his attacks, zeroing in on the Momochi furthest from Yuri. When he had a clear shot, he depressed the trigger twice and dropped the larger Momochi. The Momochi's sword hit the ground first. Yuri didn't even notice; he kept his fight on.

Yuri and his opponent were fairly matched now that fatigue was starting to catch up. They slashed, parried, thrust, and dodged, circled, and then slashed again. The Momochi danced and spun, catching and entangling Yuri's weapon. Yuri tried to keep hold, but the Momochi wrenched it free, slinging it to the ground.

Terry saw Yuri's sword tumble. Terry lined up the final Momochi and pulled the trigger, but the weapon was empty. Terry tossed it aside and staggered to another weapon that was lying on the floor.

The Momochi raised his ninjatō parallel to the floor, the tip pointing at Yuri's left eye. "**Death is your punishment, Fujibayashi. The Shogun wills it.**"

Yuri grimaced.

"**The ancestor spirits have decreed the Momochi victorious,**" said the Momochi before thrusting his blade into Yuri's chest.

Yuri had timed it. He slid beneath the blade and whipped around, drawing an arc on the floor with his back foot. His leg caught the Momochi's heels and swept him off of his feet. The Momochi came down hard onto his shoulder blades. Yuri rushed in for the kill, but the Momochi slinked back up to his feet as if going over a wave. This offered the Momochi the initiative, and he snuck a punch into Yuri's ribs and a hook to his face. Yuri fell back two steps, and the Momochi came with lightning-fast kicks to the head and body, one after the other. Yuri blocked high and low, giving ground and letting the Momochi close.

Yuri unleashed a torrent of blows, spinning to build momentum in between combinations. The Momochi was a profound fighter, but he didn't measure up to Yuri's raw talent. And Yuri's power alone was beginning to wear down the Momochi's guard. He'd need an ace up his sleeve if he were to beat the Fujibayashi warrior and kill the one that was hobbling in their direction.

Yuri lashed out with a roundhouse that whizzed by the Momochi's chin—the Momochi felt the wind as it passed. Then the Momochi rushed in behind Yuri's kick, trying to snatch him off his feet. Yuri hopped clear, pushing aside the Momochi's attempt at grappling. The Momochi found his feet as Yuri stepped wide to the left and launched another roundhouse from the right as cover for a sharp left-right-left with his fists. The kick smashed the Momochi's guard, and all three punches landed, drawing blood.

The Momochi retaliated, but Yuri parried and redirected, refusing to give ground this time. They exchanged back and forth and danced. The Momochi bounded backward with a backhand spring to put distance between them and to put himself in the range of his ninjatō. Yuri, in the heat of it, didn't realize it until the Shinobi had the sword in his hand.

The Momochi didn't make a show of it; he returned Yuri's aggression with the blade. He slashed at angles, repeatedly trying to etch lines into Yuri's torso that would connect his shoulders with the opposite hip. Yuri bounced backward, angling his body and arms away from the Momochi's strikes. He felt the sword graze his armor, shaving the top layer off. Yuri did a backhand spring too, trying to open some distance. The Momochi rushed in, swinging aggressively, trying to catch Yuri off balance. Yuri kept moving, feet-to-hands-to-feet-to-hands, as the sword slashed for any part of his body it could catch. Finally, the blade landed, cutting deep into the meat of Yuri's arm. He howled and collapsed onto his head, the wound vomiting blood onto the floor.

The Momochi took up a position at Yuri's head to gloat. **"The Shogun has made his decision. The Momochi are in favor. I am the**

new Momochi kōchō, and our former kōchō is now Hattori Hanzo. The Fujibayashi are defeated, and you...are dead, gaijin." He raised the sword above his head, point down.

Yuri's arm throbbed and squirted blood, but his combat wits were still about him. He wasn't going down so easily. Yuri snatched his tanto from its sheath and slammed it through the Momochi's knee; the point exploded through the inside. The Momochi screamed and dropped the sword. Yuri coiled himself around his opponent's impaled leg and wrenched it in an unnatural direction; the Momochi toppled. Yuri rolled over him, wrapped around him like a constrictor coiling its prey, and squeezed. The Momochi wrestled and bucked, trying to break Yuri's grip.

Yuri snaked his good arm around his opponent's neck and clasped his legs around the damaged leg. The Momochi pulled on Yuri's good arm, trying to relieve the pressure. Both men gritted and strained, trying to overpower the other.

Yuri released the Momochi's neck for a split second and drilled him twice in the side of the head before resuming the lock. The Momochi's resistance was beginning to weaken as his endurance was diminished with his airflow being restricted, and he became desperate. He reached out to Yuri's injured arm and dug his fingers into the laceration, spurring more blood flow. Yuri roared in pain and then bit down on the Momochi's ear. The Momochi writhed as Yuri tore his ear free with his teeth, spitting gore onto the floor.

Yuri was like an animal now—all fury. He clamped down like a vice and yanked at the Momochi's head. Yuri exhaled, inhaled, and yanked again. Then he did it again. He yanked and yanked, like an angry predator mauling its prey. The Momochi's eyes bulged. Yuri yanked harder each time, trying to pull his opponent's head off his shoulders. Finally, there was a wet pop, and Yuri heard the Momochi give a limp exhale. Yuri gritted his teeth and yanked has hard as he could, getting his whole body into it. There was a loud pop as the Momochi's spine disconnected from his skull. The Momochi slumped and didn't move again.

Yuri rolled off the dead fighter and flopped to the ground, gasping. The adrenaline was draining from his body, and he suddenly could feel the wound on his arm. He looked for his brother and found him hunched over Saki.

Yuri climbed to his feet and rushed over to them. "**Saki! Talk to me, buddy.**" That's when he noticed the twisted pain on his brother's face and the blood. "Terry, are you hurt bad?"

"I—I'm not sure."

"**Yuri,**" Saki whispered, his voice trembling.

"**I'm here, brother. You're going to be okay.**"

"I—I can't feel my legs."

"**We're going to get you back home. I just need you to sit tight for a moment.**"

Yuri looked about the shrine at all the corpses floating in a thin layer of blood. He couldn't believe they were still alive—he really could not. It was a miracle. They hadn't just been outnumbered; they had also been outgunned, and they'd survived it. They'd won.

Just then, the room shifted. He was dizzy from the blood loss. Yuri had to take care of himself before he could take care of Saki.

He pulled Saki's tanto free of its sheath, climbed to his feet, walked over to the nearest body, and cut enough fabric from its clothes to fasten a dressing on his laceration. He dabbed the wound with the fabric first, looking the wound over. It was deep—so deep, in fact, that Yuri could see bone; he'd need stitches. He'd have to worry about that once he got back to the village, though. In the meantime, he had to get his brother and Saki out of here. He tied the piece of material tightly over the wound.

He hurried back to Saki, who was having his wounds inspected by Terry. "**It's not looking good.**" Terry looked up and shook his head. "**He's losing a lot of blood.**"

"**That's not a problem we can worry about right now, Terry. We got to get him out of here.**"

Saki inhaled sharply. "**Just leave me.**"

"**Saki,**" Yuri said flatly, tugging at Saki's clothes to sit him up, "**shut up while grown folks talk. Terry, help me carry him.**"

"I don't know if I can. I think I've been shot."

"What? Where?"

Terry's eyes were glossy. "In my side."

"Fuck. Let me see." Yuri leaned across Saki, holding him up by his harness with his good hand, and used the hand of his injured arm to inspect Terry's right flank.

"Ow, goddammit."

"Shut up," Yuri said, pulling on the tunic and feeling around his brother's torso. "You've definitely been shot, but I don't see exit wounds, and the two bullet holes don't look that deep—looks mostly like shrapnel. I think I could dig it out. It's going to have to wait, though."

"Yeah. I'm in enough pain as it is. Are you okay?"

"I'll live if that's what you mean. The cut is pretty deep. I'm lucky that asshole didn't cut my arm off."

Doubt was breeding with the pain in Terry's side. They still had a long walk back to the Togakure Ryu over unforgiving terrain in the snow. He was always prepared to die, but he didn't know how to feel. "Yuri, I don't think we're going to make it."

"Don't you start." Yuri's survival instinct didn't have time for defeatism. "If you can't help me carry Saki, then at least help me get him on my back. I'll carry him back to the village; I just need you to walk. Can you do that?"

"Yeah—I think so."

"C'mon, we're going home."

Chapter Seventeen: The Code Less Followed

Suzuka Mountains. Mie Prefecture, Japan. Today.

The trek to Togakure Ryu was grueling. The snow and the topography conspired against the Fujibayashi as they painted three red dashed lines in the snow, trying to outpace frostbite and hypothermia. Their lungs burned. Their faces stung. Their fingers and toes ached. But they were galvanized. They hadn't given up yet.

Yuri plodded along with Saki tied into Yuri's harness, back to back. Terry carried Saki's legs, helping with the weight. Saki sagged like an overflowing rucksack, his arms at his side.

They often stopped when the pain became overwhelming. They would take a moment for Terry to pause and breathe and relieve a fraction of the burning misery in his side. Then Yuri would encourage him to keep moving. Terry listened.

Yuri's arm was throbbing too; he could feel his heartbeat in his forearm, and the dressing he had tied over the wound was soaking through. The cold, the pain, and the stress whispered conspiratorially in his ear to give up. And when he considered it, the thought of Veronica's alabaster smile reenergized him. For the first time in life, he felt that he had something to live for. That's what he had been missing all these years. That's why he'd never been able to dismiss Ninpo: because he'd had nothing else beyond it. Ninpo only gave him something to die for; love gave him a reason to live.

Yuri would feel Terry starting to lag and would say, "Come on, Terenzio. Stay with me." And Terry would.

They offered each other encouragement to push through the pain and the bitter, unforgiving cold.

After four hours of inching through the mountains, stopping for rest, negotiating the best route, hoisting Saki again, and inching some more, the three injured Fujibayashi came down the final slope that constrained Togakure Ryu.

A villager gathering firewood before sunrise in the rear of a cottage spotted them. He was at first surprised to see them—alive. His surprise evaporated, and he tossed the firewood to the ground and rushed to help them, imploring for assistance from anyone who could hear him. A handful of Fujibayashi burst from their cottages and ran to the three warriors.

Amidst praise and pious glee, the Fujibayashi relieved Terry and Yuri of Saki's weight and carried Saki into a cluster of cottages. Several assisted Terry to a nearby cottage; another coterie of Shinobi implored Yuri to follow them down the muddy walkway towards another. Two Shinobi tried to aid Yuri in walking, but he shrugged their help away. He followed them through a snow-covered pen of a border cottage across another muddy pathway and onto the porch of another. He looked over his shoulder towards the village center, noticing that it had come to life once the Fujibayashi warriors had returned.

Once inside, several villagers removed Yuri's dressing and stripped his cold, soaked clothing. While they'd been training for the ritual, the warriors hadn't been allowed to do anything by themselves, except perhaps to use the bathroom. The Fujibayashi had cooked for them, fed them, woken them, put them to bed, tended to their wounds, and dressed them. In the beginning, it had irritated Yuri, but now he was used to it; it had become routine. He just stood in the middle of the room and allowed the Shinobi to do their duty.

A Shinobi emptied a bucket over Yuri's head; a mountain range of goosebumps erupted all over his skin. The villagers began scrubbing his body with rough sponges and tending to his myriad scrapes and injuries—the spot where the arrowhead had dug in as well as bruises and scratches he hadn't even registered.

The Shinobi poured several pots of water onto his arm to ensure that the wound was sufficiently irrigated. One picked at the flesh, digging out particles and debris and dabbing it with a rag. Yuri squeezed his face and fists. Then the Shinobi began stitching without anesthetic.

Yuri tried to set his mind to other things, thinking first about Terry, then the fight, the arrows, the chain-whip's howl, Kawaguchi's face, the sound and feeling of the Momochi's head separating from his spine, and Saki collapsing after he'd been stabbed in the back.

Then a wicked feeling bubbled in Yuri's gut.

He looked at the Kunoichi cleaning the scrape on his knee. "**Where's Saki**?" Yuri asked.

"**Being tended to in another household,**" she replied.

"**Which one**?"

She shrugged.

Yuri looked at a man who was drying Yuri's shoulders with a blanket. "**Where is my brother?**"

"**He was guided to another household, but I am not sure which one.**"

"**Get off me,**" Yuri demanded, yanking his nearly-stitched arm from the older Shinobi doing the sutures. Yuri snatched the clean tunic and trousers that the Fujibayashi had prepared for him and pulled them on. He grabbed his harness with his ninjatō and threw them over his shoulder as he ran out into the snow barefoot.

"**Terry!**" Yuri yelled as he weaved through the squat buildings. He snagged a Shinobi by his tunic. "**Where's my brother?**"

The man pointed at a nearby cottage.

Yuri rushed for the building and barged through the rice-paper door, practically taking it off the rail.

Terry was lying on the floor, groaning as two kneeling Shinobi extracted the slugs and fragments from Terry's abdomen with nothing to kill the pain; several other Shinobi brought clean rags, removed the bloody ones, and assisted when needed.

Yuri pushed through the huddle. "Terry, get up," he demanded. "We have to find Saki. Quickly."

"Yuri—" Terry started to ask, but Yuri cut him off.

"Don't ask questions. We don't have time. Get up."

Terry raised a hand. "Help me up."

Yuri got a firm grasp and heaved. Terry grunted when his injured abdominals engaged as he found his feet. He exhaled audibly.

"C'mon," Yuri said, snatching clean clothes from a Shinobi and tossing them at Terry. "Get dressed. We have got to find Saki."

"What's the problem?"

"He can't walk." Yuri's face had never been so serious.

*   *   *

Saki lay on a feathered mattress, staring at the grain in the wood of the ceiling, contemplating.

Now that this generation's ritual combat was complete, what would Togakure Ryu be like? What would it be like on the other side? How long would the journey be? Would he still be able to speak to those he was closest to? Would he have to earn his place in the ancestral heavens as he did on earth? What would the ancestral realm look like?

Akiko's face appeared in his view, and she reached down and rubbed his face. Saki spoke, but his voice was so weak that Akiko had to bend and get her face close to his.

"**Hello, old friend,**" she said tenderly, wearing burgundy robes and a messy bun.

"**Hello, old friend.**"

"**You have returned and raised the clan up.**"

Saki smiled weakly. "**It was not me alone, Akiko. Terry and Yuri are equally responsible. They, after all, carried me when I could not walk.**"

"**Yes, surely we must not forget them. But you, Saki, are our most honorable. It was you that took the field undisputed. It will be you that goes with honor. Would it have only been Terry and Yuri that fell on the battlefield and not you. They—**"

Saki grabbed her hand. "**No, Akiko. The Momochi were not three,**" he said weakly. "**They brought others.**"

"What?"

"**There were more than three Momochi on the battlefield. They brought reinforcements. A man calling himself the Shogun sent fighters to ambush us, and we defeated them. Terry and Yuri fought valiantly for the Fujibayashi when the odds were against us.**"

"Saki," she said, a disappointed smile materializing, "**you were delirious from your injury. There were no others. It is okay, my old friend. All will be well soon.**"

"No, Akiko, you must listen. There are things Omiyoshu Sensei is not telling us. Something is afoot; Terry and Yuri must uncover it."

"Maintaining secrets is the prerogative of the kōchō."

"You must believe me. Terry, Yuri, and I uncovered information that has shaken my trust and left me confused."

"Saki, they have turned their backs on Ninpo. They—"

"Akiko, you must help them, since I will not be here to do so."

"I cannot do it, Saki. They are too far removed."

"Then help them return, Akiko. Help them be Fujibayashi again in peace as they have been in battle."

"Saki, you must not forget the Fourth Mandate. You have a duty to trust the clan and its leaders."

"What if the clan or its leaders have done something to violate our trust? What then, Akiko? I do not know who else has the answers to the questions we posed to Omiyoshu Sensei. But I need you to help them find those answers."

Her expression was a mixture of doubt and discomfort.

"I regret to say that somehow I think the secrets that Terry, Yuri, and I have come to witness are somehow connected to the events with the Momochi."

"Why are you telling me? Have you told the Jonin?" she asked, looking about at the handful of Jonin that knelt quietly against the walls in attendance of Saki.

"No," he rasped softly. "You, Terry, and Yuri are the only ones that I can trust."

"How can you trust them after all that has happened?"

"That is why I trust them. They are not our enemy. They never were. I have fought with them—I can trust them. You must too. This, Akiko, is my final request. Will you do this?" He gripped her hand firmly. "Will you help Terry and Yuri uncover these secrets, old friend, for I will be gone?"

She nodded, but her eyes were discordant.

Just then, the door slid open, and the elder council and a matronly woman—Saki's mother—filed in, spreading to fill the room. Akiko and the present Jonin bowed. The elder council took positions on their knees next to Saki's bedding.

"Takejiro Saki," a withered-faced elder began in a gravelly, aged voice, "**first warrior among chosen brethren, hunter without peer, shadow that stalks even in the light of day. You have given of yourself selflessly to the Fujibayashi and proved your honor and prowess to the ancestor spirits**." He drew a tanto wrapped in white paper from the sleeve of his robe and held it out.

Everyone bowed their head.

Saki stared at the ceiling.

The withered-faced elder lifted his head and spoke, "**Mamushi, Takejiro Saki, son of Takejiro Tsurimi, grandson of Takejiro Kentaro, has fought gallantly for Ninpo in honorable combat. We ask that if it pleases you, you accept the sacrifice that he has made and guide him to the court of the ancestor spirits**."

Akiko's mind raced as she knelt with her eyes closed and processed what was said—not what the elder was reciting, but what Saki had told her. She didn't know what to believe. Was Saki telling the truth, or was he delirious from his wounds? Could the Momochi have cheated to achieve favor in the face of the ancestor spirits—would they have allowed such deceit?

"**You have brought great honor to your clansmen, Saki**," the withered-faced elder said, laying the tanto on the floor next to Saki. "**The ancestor spirits wait in anticipation of your arrival. This is an exciting time for Ninpo, indeed. How do you wish to proceed?**"

Akiko leaned over so she could hear Saki. Then she straightened. "**Saki requests that I hold him in a sitting position and that Terry be his secondary if Terry is well enough to swing his sword**."

"**Honor is the soul of the Shinobi**," the withered-faced elder said with a nod.

All in attendance replied, "**Shadow is their blood**."

The withered-faced elder signaled for other attendees to clean Saki for the final time and signaled for a messenger to seek out Terry.

Several minutes later, the door to the cottage slammed open, startling all present. Yuri was first through the threshold—his face swollen, cut, and bruised. Terry was behind him, walking stiffly, circles of blood spreading on his tunic.

Yuri scanned the room; then his swollen eyes became serpentine once he noticed the tanto on the floor next to Saki, who was lying disrobed with two Jonin washing his trunk. "**Having a party without me?**" Yuri asked.

Terry's face was equally suspicious, immediately sensing threat when he too noticed the knife. He implored Saki with his eyes.

The room was full of silence.

Saki lifted a grateful hand towards the brothers and smiled solemnly.

"**Terry,**" Akiko said, "**Saki requests that you do him the honor of being his secondary. Are you well enough to swing your sword? Will you present your ninjatō for cleansing, please?**"

"**Saki, no,**" Terry replied curtly. "**You can't do this.**"

The room was a sea of stares.

The withered-faced elder grumbled and coughed before managing to say, "**How dare you refuse such a solemn rite? Have you no honor?**"

"**Sensei, I would never refuse something so honored and so sacred unless a situation were so dire. You must understand that Saki lies before you now not because he was defeated in battle against the Momochi, but rather because he was gravely injured defending Ninpo from treachery.**"

"**What treachery?**" another Jonin asked.

"**The Momochi fielded more than three warriors. In fact, the Momochi weren't even in command of them; a group claiming to be Yakuza and claiming to be under the control of** *the Shogun* **was,**" said Yuri.

"**That is preposterous,**" a toothless Jonin replied. "**There is no such thing. The last Shogun, Tokugawa Yoshinobu, died in 1913.**"

"**Fighting for the favor of the Shogun,**" a silver-haired one began, "**is ceremonial. Although such is recounted in the Ninth Mandate. Now our only audience are the ancestor spirits.**"

Terry appealed to them with his palm. "**I'm telling you, a group of Yakuza—claiming to descend from the Samurai—attacked us with the Momochi; and they claim they work for the Shogun.**"

A bald Jonin was indignant. "**You would lie to us?**"

"**Why would we lie about this?**" Yuri asked.

"**Because you are defiant of the code,**" another Jonin said.

"I am not fooled by your deceit," the withered-faced elder said. "How dare you come in here and spin such tales to confuse Takejiro Saki—our first senior of warriors and most worthy—before he must commit seppuku. How dare you try to confuse fellow Shinobi."

"You're not listening to what we're telling you, you old fossil," Yuri snapped, wiping blood from his weeping, half-stitched injury on his tunic. "The Momochi—our rival—has allied with another group and attacked us five to one. We don't even think the Momochi were in control."

"We need to dedicate our resources to striking back at the Momochi," said Terry, "not wasting our resources by having Saki kill himself."

"No—Takejiro Saki must take his own life," said the withered-faced elder. "The code demands seppuku if a Shinobi becomes a burden to the clan. He cannot walk; he is no longer capable of being Shinobi. He is a liability."

"I know what the code says," Terry fired back. "Saki is not a burden. He just fought in the clan's most sacred ritual and won. The Fujibayashi are favored, and our kōchō has ascended to the holy seat of Shinobi-no-mono, bearing the title of Hattori Hanzo." Terry pointed at Saki. "The Fujibayashi owe him, not the other way around."

Another Jonin barked, "The Fujibayashi owe no one—"

"Simon says: raise your hand if you've ever killed for Ninpo or the clan." Nobody moved, so Yuri continued, "Well, Saki has. The way I see it, the Fujibayashi do owe him."

"If our enemies invade the village," said the withered-faced elder, "Takejiro Saki will not be able to mount a defense. The Fujibayashi—"

"Are you hearing yourself?" Yuri cut in. "What year do you live in? The Tokugawa Shogunate isn't going to cross the ridge into the valley."

"Our enemies are never dead!" a Jonin said.

Another interjected, "Saki must do his duty! Ninpo must be upheld!"

"Saki did his duty," Yuri said. "He upheld Ninpo by representing the clan in combat. If seppuku needs to be performed so desperately, then why don't you offer up your own worthless life?"

The withered-faced elder rose to his feet finally. "**It is he that must commit seppuku, or he will dishonor the entire clan. It is his duty.**"

"**It's an antiquated duty,**" Terry replied, "**under an antiquated mandate.**"

"**You do not decide such things.**"

"**I'm taking Saki out of here,**" Yuri said. "**I'm going to find the best doctors money can buy. He'll walk again. There's no dishonor in that.**"

"**Absolutely not!**" the withered-face elder yelled. "**I will not allow it!**"

Yuri arched his neck towards the elder. "**Or what?**" he asked, unconvinced.

The withered-faced elder's expression hardened. "**I have had enough of this! You will no longer hinder our sacred rite nor heckle our Shinobi with your tales of treachery, Samurai descendants, and Shoguns! I will bring this clan honor if none of you will!**"

The rest of the elder council and Jonin—even Saki's mother—rose as well. The cabal of Jonin drew their ninjatōs and their tantos.

Yuri raised his sword into a high guard, blood swirling down his arm.

Terry drew his tanto. "**Please, you must listen to us,**" Terry said. "**This is what the Momochi want.**"

"**Stop!**" Akiko yelled over the emotional crescendo. "**It is true what they speak. Saki affirms the Momochi's treachery. Let there be no more bloodshed. The Momochi have turned their back against Ninpo.**"

"**You claim that they defied Ninpo?**" a Jonin asked Saki.

Yuri's face twisted. "**That's what *cheated* implies.**"

"**How is this possible?**" the withered-faced elder asked. "**They too are Shinobi. They would do no such thing.**"

Terry threw open his tunic and pointed at the grisly craters in his side. "**These are gunshot wounds. How do you all suspect that I received them if the Momochi didn't cheat?**"

The Jonin stared at Terry and Yuri as if they were speaking Greek.

"The code says that a Shinobi incapable of fighting should commit seppuku, true enough," Terry continued. "However, the code offers us no guidance in how to handle treachery during ritual combat, and I'm not willing to allow another Fujibayashi to give his life without clear direction."

"You do not have authority to interpret Ninpo. Only the Shinobi-no-mono has such authority."

Akiko appealed to the entire group. "We should, then, seek out his wisdom instead of resorting to fratricide. Where is Omiyoshu Sensei—Hattori Hanzo?"

"Hattori Hanzo has not be seen for hours," a Jonin with crooked teeth said. "He demanded that he not be disturbed until he addresses us, regardless of the outcome of the ritual combat. He left the conclusion of the ritual to council leadership, as he often does when he is not present in Iga."

"That's not a problem," Yuri interjected. "The leadership of the Fujibayashi doesn't rest on the shoulders of Hattori Hanzo anyway. It falls to the kōchō—and the new kōchō is Takejiro Saki—Takejiro Sensei. He's the first senior and assumes leadership after the ritual combat."

Terry looked at Yuri—*well played*.

Yuri acknowledged with his eyes.

The Fujibayashi were now the favored clan, positioning Kintake as the spiritual leader of Ninpo, Hattori Hanzo. Saki was the first senior, and that made him Kintake's successor as the kōchō.

"I recognize no such authority," an elder barked. "Takejiro Saki is impotent and is unfit to be the kōchō. The elder council assumes control in the absence of a kōchō."

"The line of succession, then," said Akiko, "grants Terry the title of kōchō, as the second senior, like my father during his generation and the previous Shinobi-no-mono during his. My father was the third senior and the only survivor of the ritual combat."

Terry's mouth was dry. Never in a million years had he seen himself in command of the Fujibayashi. He'd become Fujibayashi as an orphan without a past and now found himself the minister of a village of Shinobi. Part of him had always felt like an outsider, and he'd never seen himself propelled to the top. It was the greatest of honors, but he suddenly felt tremendous weight as centuries of responsibility poured onto his shoulders.

Questions rushed into his mind. What was he to do next? How was he going to handle the Momochi? How he was going to handle the code? How was he going to go forward? He had some thinking to do. He still had to deal with more immediate problems, though. He needed to get Saki out of the Togakure Ryu and into Tokyo so that they could fly him back to the United States to begin treatment for his paraplegia—carrying him on the trek to Tokyo was going to be brutal to say the least.

"**Put away your weapons. All of you,**" Terry demanded.

Nobody moved.

Akiko said, "**The kōchō, Ciccone Sensei, has made a demand of you. Who among you will defy him?**"

Yuri was the first to relax and restore his weapon. The Jonin followed.

"**Despite his orders, I need to speak with Hattori Hanzo. Elder Council, you will accompany me,**" Terry ordered. "**Akiko, please remain with Saki. Yuri, assemble a team of five Chunin and have them ready when I call on them.**"

Yuri nodded. Then his head snapped over his shoulder, looking toward the door as if he had heard something. Terry looked at him suspiciously, but Yuri's mind was elsewhere. Yuri remembered Veronica; he had forgotten about her in all commotion. He rushed out of the cottage find her.

The village was alive with movement. Veronica was treading water in the sea of Fujibayashi, an ignored guest, an apparition that didn't deserve their attention. Not that they could pay much attention to her with their warriors returning so recently and their anticipation to hear of the results of the ritual.

Yuri ran through the muddy snow in his bare feet to Veronica, who was standing on the porch of a cottage. Her faced twisted with confusion at his appearance: the bandaged yet weeping suture on his arm, the odd tunic and trousers, cuts and bruises from the fight, and the weapon harness and sword.

Yuri scooped her up in his arms—she was trembling.

"What's going on?" Veronica asked. "What happened to your face? Omigod, Yuri, what on earth happened to your arm?"

He looked over his shoulder and saw Terry leading a storm of Shinobi to the central hall to address Hattori Hanzo. Everything had changed; everything was different.

This was his moment, his time to be honest with the woman he loved. He had practiced this speech in the mirror repeatedly. He had prepared for this moment for several years; he knew exactly what he wanted say. It was like a marriage proposal, where he would humble himself to her and tell her everything—every gory detail.

It was now or never.

"I've been keeping secrets from you. I have been keeping secrets from everyone. I'm not who I say I am. But I don't want to keep secrets anymore."

"What are you talking about, Yuri?" she asked, grabbing his arm and looking at the wound. "What secrets?"

But right now, right at this very crucial juncture, he could not remember a thing. He tried to recall just some of the points that he had made to his reflection, but he could find nothing.

"Yuri?"

Yuri gazed deeply into her. "I'm Shinobi," he said, blurting out the first thing that came to his head.

"What?"

"I—I'm Shinobi."

"What does that mean?"

"My parents were killed in a plane crash when I was very young, and the people in this village—the Fujibayashi—adopted me and my brother. We were raised and trained as one of them...but I was always an outsider. We left here when I was a teenager because I was banished for fighting the headmaster for my brother. I've been killing ever since. This is why I've always been so secretive. I had to hide. Ninpo demanded it."

Yuri was rattling off whatever came to mind as he searched for an explanation that didn't make him sound like a lunatic.

"Nin-what?" Veronica's face was incredulous.

"Ninpo is my religion—it *was* my religion. It is the code of the Shinobi."

Veronica's face had gone from confusion to abject bewilderment.

Yuri's shoulders slumped. "I'm an assassin. I kill for a living. I don't write books. I never have."

Her face flushed. "What?"

The lies were coming apart.

"I was raised in this village to be a killer. I'm an assassin—Shinobi. Everyone here is. The farmers, the masons, cooks, everyone. Even the women and the children."

"Yuri, this isn't funny."

She made sounds, babbled, but nothing coherent. It was all too much for her; she burst into tears.

He wrapped her in his arms. "I know this is a lot to take in. I know it's all hard to believe, but you must know that I've killed for the last time. This isn't who I want to be."

"Yuri, this isn't funny," she said, pushing away from him. "This isn't funny at all."

"None of this is a joke. I've never been so honest in my life."

"You said you were an author," she sobbed, the color red filling her face from her neck.

"I lied. I was never an author. I was an assassin."

"Most men lie about women or their whereabouts. You lie about writing to cover up killing people?"

"Yes—I had to."

"Oh God." Tears streamed down Veronica's face. She was inclined towards disbelief, but the blood Yuri dripped onto the floor said otherwise. "I—I want to go home."

"Veronica, I love you."

"Send me home," she said.

"Veronica..."

"Please, just send me home. I want to go home."

Yuri conceded to her demand. He didn't want to hold her hostage; that wasn't why she was here. She was here because he needed her, but his secrets had consequences. He wasn't naïve; he'd known this wouldn't go in his favor, but he'd been hopeful. He'd been hopeful that love would light the path away from a life of hollowness into a life of fulfillment. Love, after all, was built on hope. But perhaps love wasn't an option for a killer. Perhaps love was an option one gave up when one chose to kill for the first time.

Yuri felt hopeless, and he hated Ninpo for it.

*   *   *

"So, what's the plan?" Yuri asked his brother, leaning against the fence of the pigpens. "How are we going to strike back at the Momochi?"

"I haven't thought it all the way through yet. I have mostly fragmented ideas. There is still some resistance from the elder council. Some are with me, some are against me, and some haven't made up their minds. Hattori Hanzo's absence isn't helping."

"It's hard for me to call him that."

"It's even harder for me to call myself the kōchō."

"Things feel different," Yuri said, adjusting his arm in its sling.

"Yeah, there's a lot to be done. And to be honest, I don't even know where to start. I went to talk to Saki about it, but he's just not himself right now. I'll get it figured out."

"We will. We need to act quickly, though. No telling what the Momochi will do next."

Terry shook his head. "No—*we* don't."

Yuri's eyes became thin slits. "What's that supposed to mean?"

"Yuri, you have to leave. You've defied Ninpo, and I don't know how long I'll be able to protect you from the more pious Shinobi."

"C'mon, Terry, you know that they won't do shit."

"I can't take that risk, little brother. Kintake ordered them to stay their weapons so that you could fight. And if we won, they were to let you leave. I can't speak of your safety if you stay."

"I'm not scared of them. I never have been."

"Yuri, you wanted out. You're out. You said that you were going to fight for me, and when it was over, you were going to move on. Do just that."

"I'm not going to leave you here to figure this shit out on your own."

"I'm a big boy, Yuri."

"You know what I mean."

"Yuri, I need you to lead that team of Chunin out of Iga to get Saki back to Tokyo. You need to get him on the first flight back to the U.S. That is your number one priority. Then, of course, there's Veronica." Terry patted his brother's good shoulder. "You have to get her back home and build that future you've always wanted."

"No point in even factoring that into the equation. That future is a pipe dream. This is who I am. She's done with me. I told her who I was, and she is disgusted with me."

"Are you giving up?"

"What am I supposed to do?"

Terry sighed. "You know, Francesca wasn't the easiest woman to love—at least that's what Dad told me—but Pat never gave up. He gave everything he had to love our mother. We both were young when they passed, but I think I was old enough to learn the lessons they taught us. And I think you should do what Pat did."

"I suppose." Yuri's face was sour. "I can't just leave here, though. What would our parents say if I left you behind?"

"Yuri, you're the culmination of the hopes and dreams of two headstrong, hardworking kids from Jersey City who loved each other more than words could express. You're all they ever wanted in life. Don't squander that dream here in Iga. Go make that dream a reality for them."

"Terry—"

"I've got to figure where Hattori Hanzo has run off to. I have a lot of work to do. So go do right by Mom and Dad, and go do right by Veronica. I really do want a niece or nephew," Terry said as he started back for the central hall. "I love you, little brother. Best of luck. Until we meet again."

"I love you too, Ciccone Sensei."

Terry threw up an acknowledging hand as he staggered back into the village center.

Yuri looked over his shoulder at the terrain in between him and Tokyo. He exhaled steam.

Chapter Eighteen: Divided They Fall

The prudent Shinobi retreats when disadvantaged or overwhelmed. Leave the battlefield and strike where the enemy least expects.
The Tenth Mandate, translated from Ninpo.

The Ciccone Residence. National Harbor, Oxen Hill, Maryland. Today.

Life didn't return to normal when Yuri returned home. Yuri navigated each day without any real sense of direction, spending most of his time working out, getting Saki to his medical appointments, and sulking. He couldn't get Veronica out of his mind. He wanted to talk to her so badly, but she refused his calls and communication.

Yuri wasn't sure what to do. He'd given up Ninpo for himself, sure, but Veronica was the prime mover. Now, with her ignoring him, Yuri wasn't sure why he'd left Togakure Ryu. His defiance and rejection of the code had divorced him from the clan. The worst part was the separation from his brother. Yuri never realized how much he relied on his brother for support. Now was a time that he could use Terry's counsel.

Saki had been seeing a neurology specialist in Germantown for his paraplegia and had sunk into a terrible depression. His depression didn't only affect him; it also affected Yuri. It made the atmosphere in their penthouse septic. So much so that Yuri had to leave often, leaving Saki's care to his nurse. Saki was on the edge of suicide, his feeling of dishonor weighing him down heavily. Unlike Terry and Yuri, he had scarcely ever been beyond the Suzuka Mountains, and his new residence was a tremendous culture shock. Saki was not accustomed to the technology, and he didn't speak English. He felt that he was burdening Yuri. It was a terrible feeling, and he was questioning why he hadn't committed seppuku. He understood why the ancestor Shinobi had written the mandate. If he had followed it, he wouldn't be choking on despair.

Yuri did what he could to support his old friend, but his struggle with Veronica didn't leave him much energy. He constantly thought of ways to get through to her—some mundane and some drastic. She was ignoring the mundane, however, and he was considering the drastic.

*   *   *

Work was relentless. Veronica just didn't have much time for Veronica since she'd come back from Japan. Relentless work was good for one thing: smothering depression. But depression was like a houseguest that overstayed his welcome and waited for the depressed to return home. Her houseguest kept her up late nights and bothered her when she was working in the courtroom.

Admittedly, she was just as confused as she was hurt and depressed. How had she ended up in this situation? She'd always wanted that movie-esque, fairytale-type relationship—what girl didn't?—but she hadn't bargained on a man who lied to cover up his killing.

She had always known that there was something that Yuri wasn't telling her, but she could never have predicted that he was an assassin. Yuri didn't look like a killer, not at all. She always expected an assassin to look dangerous, to be smooth, suave, manipulative, and physically perfect. Yuri was none of the above. He wasn't tall, he wasn't dark, he didn't look at all dangerous, and he was too quiet to be smooth. But to find out that the arms that she had been falling into for comfort had been used to take lives messed with her head. It scared her.

Yuri made several attempts to contact her. He called her, sent her emails, came to her home, and came by her job. She refused to speak to him. She was paranoid. What happened if he became desperate? Would he hurt her—kill her? What if he felt that she knew too much? What if she was a loose end he needed to tie up? Who could she tell? Who would believe her? But there was the part of her that questioned whether she was overreacting. If Yuri had been a soldier, would she be able to accept him then? It was stressful to think about, and she used work to try to mute it.

It was hard to mute the thoughts of the man she loved.

"No, Mom, I don't have time. I'm right in the middle of a case," Veronica said, pushing through the door into the lightless parlor of her condominium. She grunted, dropping two handfuls of bags on the floor, and made for the nearest lamp. "I'll see what I can do, but don't get your hopes up. I talked—"

"Can we talk?" asked a disembodied—yet familiar—voice from the darkness.

Veronica yelped, knocking over the lamp and practically jumping onto the side table. "Yuri?" She saw movement near a window on the far side.

"I'm sorry for startling you."

"No, I'm fine, Mom," she said into the phone, her mother suddenly alarmed. "My shadow startled me. I'll call you back. No, Mom, I have to go. I'll call you back." Veronica felt around for the lamp and turned it on when she found it. "How'd you get in here?"

"Don't ask me questions you don't want answers to."

She looked up, and he was barely an arm's length away—and she yelped again.

As if she wasn't already a bit creeped out to find Yuri in her locked apartment with an armed security system, he was dressed in all black, wearing an odd harness with a plethora of straps. Wait, why didn't the alarm system beep when she came through the door?

"I would like to know how a prowler gets into my home."

"I'm no prowler," Yuri deadpanned.

"Well then, what are you? Because it looks like you broke into my house."

His icy stare searched her. "Just a man that's in love with you."

Her eyes filled instantly with tears and suspicion. "You love me so much that you lie to me?"

"Veronica, I didn't come to argue with you. I didn't come to convince you to accept the terrible things I've done, either. I came because I love you. I came because I can't bear the thought of being without you." He paused, trying to keep his emotions together. "I can't breathe without you. Can you see my pain?"

"Your pain?" she scoffed. "Please, Yuri, tell me about your pain."

For the first time, she saw vulnerability in Yuri's eyes. He didn't seem so hardened, so unreachable. It was terribly disorienting.

"I've been hiding from you, and it hurts. I've wanted to open up to you, be the real me, but I couldn't."

"Couldn't or wouldn't?"

He shrugged. "Both. I'm an emotional person, Veronica. I've always been hot-tempered, passionate, and intense. I wear my emotions on my sleeve. But I hide it. Intense emotions were frowned upon where I grew up, so I became good at hiding them."

"But why, Yuri? Why hide from me? Why hide it from anybody?"

"You have to understand the way I was raised."

She cut the air with her hand. "I don't know anything about the way you were raised."

"Veronica, I know you're angry and hurt—"

She put an acrimonious hand in the air. "*Angry* and *hurt* don't even begin to explain how I feel, Yuri."

Yuri didn't have a reply; he just watched her.

In the caustic silence, Veronica replaced the lamp and sat down on the ottoman, placing her face in her hands. How had it come to this? How had she ended up in this situation—in this drama? Revelations like this only happened in the movies.

"You better talk while you have the opportunity, Yuri. Because this is more than you deserve."

Yuri swallowed hard. "I was raised under a code called Ninpo— it's really more like a religion than a code. Ninpo demands silence and deception. It demands adherence to its mandates, and failure to do so is punishable by death and death only. I couldn't tell you, not just for my safety, but yours as well."

"So, if you told me, were a bunch of people just going to show up and kill me?"

"Perhaps. Perhaps not." He approached her and sat on the corner of the ottoman opposite her. "More to the point, I believed in Ninpo the same way you believe in Christianity."

Her response was ice. "Christianity doesn't compel me to murder others."

"I could argue that, but again, that's not why I'm here."

"So, Ninpo makes you a ninja or something?"

"In a manner of speaking, yes."

"In a manner of speaking, is Terry a ninja too?"

"Yes."

"Is he going to kill me now that you've told me?"

"No."

"How do you know, if Ninpo demands silence or death?"

Yuri rubbed the side of his head. "Because Terry remained in Japan. And before I left, he told me that he wanted me to walk away from Ninpo and pursue the woman I love."

"If he told you to kill me, you would do that too, wouldn't you?" she snapped.

"That hurts, Veronica."

"Well, good," she spat, whipping her head in his direction. "You deserve to hurt a little, considering the people you've killed."

Yuri shook his head. "I've lived this way since I was a child. I've never known anything different...until I met you. You showed me that there's life beyond Ninpo. It's the same type of life my parents had, and it's the same type of life that they would've wanted for me if they were still alive."

"So, that's it? Am I your one hope for a normal life? Trade killing for me?"

Yuri didn't reply immediately; he swished his answer around in his mouth for a moment. "You're my one hope at true, unconditional love. I've wanted to give Ninpo up for years; I just didn't know how. You've shown me that I can be without it."

"And you'll give it all up if I love you in return, huh? Then what?"

"I don't know. I haven't thought that far ahead. I just know that I don't want to be part of Ninpo anymore. I've followed it faithfully—defiantly—since I was seven years old, and now I want to do something else; I want to be something else. I don't want to be bound to a code."

"Can you be *something* else, Yuri?"

"My father told me I could *be* anything I set my heart to," Yuri said, his determined demeanor returning instantly. "It probably sounds cliché, but his death doesn't allow me to take life for granted. Well, I want to *be* with you, Veronica. I've never known love until you. Tell me you don't feel the same way."

Her eyes were misty, but her face was sharp. "I don't."

"You're lying."

A tear ran down her face. "No, I'm not. I can't love someone who lies to me."

"Veronica, I've been conducting espionage for the better part of a decade. I read people well, and I can see it in your face that you're not being honest."

A tear ran down the other side. "I don't want to be honest with you, Yuri. It hurts too much." She sniffed, trying to hold back more tears. "I miss you terribly, but what am I supposed to do? How am I supposed to feel? You come to me covered in blood with your arm practically cut off. Then you matter-of-factly tell me you're an assassin, when, all this time, you've had me convinced that you were a foreign writer." Tears began streaming down her face. "What am I supposed to do, huh? Just say, *Fuck it. Lie to me. It'll be cool*? Am I not allowed a little dignity?"

He felt horrible, like scum, but the honest fact was: "I had no other choice. By breaking the silence, I've dishonored myself in the eyes of my clan. To them, I'm no better than the criminals that you prosecute. I gave up the life I knew the moment I brought you to the village. I've banished myself from the only life I've ever known."

"So, what happens now?"

"I—I really don't know."

"What'd you hope to accomplish by coming here?" she asked, wiping her face—a futile endeavor.

Yuri touched her hand. "I hoped to ask for your forgiveness. I hoped to ask that you continue to love me. I hoped to ask that you'll still be my lady. I love you, Veronica, more than I can put into words. Please, don't give up on me. Please."

"I don't know what to say."

"Say you haven't given up on me. Say we can go forward."

She sniffled and brushed rogue locks of hair from her salt-stained face. "I don't want you to lie to me, Yuri. You have to be honest with me."

His tender touch became a devoted grip. "I will."

"You'll have to earn my trust again."

"I'll do that, too."

"It won't happen overnight."

"I have the rest of my life to prove it to you—to prove that I'm worth loving."

Chapter Nineteen: Fanning The Flames

The Peninsula Hotel. Tokyo, Japan. Today.

Akiko was filled with anxiety—not because she was alone in enemy territory, but rather because she felt the entire weight of the Fujibayashi on her shoulders. Her heart gonged like a church bell as she tiptoed down the plush carpeted hallway toward the moment she would prove her worth to the clan. She had been unable to prove her worth when her father had forbidden her from fighting in the ritual combat, but tonight she would make up for it with a vengeance.

Two days ago, Terry had approached her during morning chores. "**Akiko**," he'd said, "**Hattori Hanzo contacted my satellite phone. He requests that you meet with him at the Izumo Ryu temple.**" The temple was an hour's walk north of Togakure Ryu. She was elated to know that her father was okay. While she was used to him being away from Togakure Ryu for long stretches of time, the events of the ritual combat caused her to fear for her father's life. Terry, however, did not share her elation. While he was relieved to hear from Kintake finally, he was suspicious. He wasn't going to let Akiko go alone, despite Kintake's instructions. Something told him that it was a Momochi trap—they, possibly, were trying to use Akiko as a means of retaliating against Kintake for their loss despite their treachery.

Terry departed with Akiko shortly after noon, leaving the elder council to place the finishing touches on their retaliatory plans.

Terry and Akiko were early to Izumo Ryu, staking it out for the better part of an hour, before entering the temple. There, they waited for nearly three hours; Kintake never showed. If they hadn't been originally concerned for Kintake before, they were after never receiving him at the temple; and Terry intended to order the elder council to plan a search for the Shinobi-no-mono once Terry had returned to Togakure Ryu.

Terry and Akiko hustled back. As they ascended a butte nearing Togakure Ryu, they were confounded by two phantasmal columns

310

cutting the gibbous moon into pieces the same way curtains cut a window. They pondered them individually as they climbed, noting that the columns moved like curtains in the wind. Then it hit them: those were columns of smoke. Terry and Akiko quickened their pace to the top, through the adjacent saddle, and then hustled up the next incline. Their fears were truly realized when they crested the final northern ridge to see towers of black smoke rising out of the skeletal canopy of Togakure Ryu and fire devouring five hundred years of history.

Terry and Akiko sprinted down the slope as fast as their legs would take them, their desperation erasing the stabbing pain of exertion. They hustled through the periphery, screaming to their clansmen, calling every name they knew. Inside a wintered garden was the answer to their calls: the body of a Chunin lying in a heap, surrounded by a horseshoe of darkened snow.

They drew their ninjatō and crept through the first cluster of cottages, spotting more bodies. It was a scene so horrible that they could have only imagined it in fiction. What started as a cautious slither, became a brisk walk, and then a hurried sprint. Terry went one way, checking for survivors; Akiko went the other.

Terry was in and out of cottages, one after the other, hoping that he could find someone alive. Most of the residences were empty or burning, and corpses lay in the snow and on the porches and draped the rails.

He bounded off a porch, into a rock garden, and was hurrying to an adjacent cottage when he noticed several children arrayed in a bloody fan, with two matronly Kunoichi sprawled behind them in the garden. He approached to inspect them. The two women had attempted to spirit the Kodomo to safety, but they'd all been machine-gunned as they ran. Just beyond them were the pigpens filled with bullet-riddled, freezing animal carcasses.

Terry shivered. It wasn't the cold; it was the emotions that were flooding him. He closed his eyes and breathed loudly, trying to calm the rising tide he felt on the inside. How could this have happened? Who had done this? Who dared? Could everyone truly be dead? Had no one escaped? Terry had witnessed massacres when he'd been a mercenary, so they were questions to which he already had answers.

Akiko initially went from body to body, which were strewn about the snow and buildings like leaves blown from tree branches in the harsh autumn wind, checking for signs of life, but she eventually resolved to move faster to look for survivors instead of the barely living since there seemed to be none. The deeper she got into the village, the bleaker things looked. Never had she seen death on such a scale. The snow in the village was equally as red as it was white, and the smolder of the cottages crackled and popped and sizzled when red coals and embers fell into the snow.

Then she heard a whimper. It was coming from the direction of the river. She felt a sudden glimmer of hope. "**Terry!**" she screamed as she hustled in the direction of the cries. Frantically, Akiko darted between the cottages, trying to close the distance to the sound, calling to it, saying she was there to help. She narrowed its origin to two cottages facing the bank of the river. It sounded as though it was coming from beneath the buildings.

She hustled down the walkways and was looking beneath the structures when she heard the cries from an opening into a cottage's crawl space. Akiko went on her hands and knees into the opening and then onto her belly. Then she saw movement. She low-crawled through the frigid, wet dirt to the survivor, leaving her sword behind and digging in with her fingers. Akiko reached the individual. It was a little girl, aged eleven years. She had beautiful jet hair and angular features, but now she was a charred, melted mess like a plastic doll left unattended way too close to a hearth. She had only a sliver of hair left, the cartilage of her ears was cooked to the side of her head, and her eyes were clouded from heat damage. It was a miracle, though, she was still alive.

"**Terry!**" Akiko yelled, getting her arms around the girl and starting to drag her from the crawl space, accepting there was no painless way to extract her.

The girl shrieked in abject pain.

Terry dove through the opening and crawled to Akiko, getting a hold on the girl as well and doubling Akiko's effort. They reached the opening and extracted her, carrying her into an otherwise undamaged cottage. They laid her on the floor, and Terry went searching for blankets to warm her. He returned minutes later with a single half-burnt blanket. Damaged as it was, it was better than nothing.

"**We must help her,**" Akiko said in between singing a song to soothe the young girl, who was crying and sobbing.

"**We're not doctors.**"

Akiko looked at him. "**We must do something. You know the way to a hospital. You know Tokyo well.**"

"**Akiko,**" Terry said, shaking his head, "**she won't survive the trek.**"

Akiko stopped singing and lowered her head, placing a hand on the girl's forehead.

"**I'm sorry,**" Terry said.

Akiko nodded, tears stinging her eyes.

Terry drew his tanto and sidled up to the girl. He was going to end her suffering. Then Akiko reached out and touched his hand.

"**I'll do it,**" she said.

He relinquished the knife to her.

Akiko resumed her song, not fighting tears but trying desperately to hold back sobs. The tune was a tranquil melody recounting the bravery of a flower withstanding a monsoon. *See how it blossoms, little flower, in the face of danger. Sweet little flower, none braver.* Then she jammed the blade into the girl's weak heart. The girl squeaked, her little hands twitching. Then she let out a *hic* before expiring. It was quick. Humane.

The flood of emotions had no words. Terry anguished audibly through gritted teeth. He hadn't felt such terrible pain in decades. This resurrected the empty pain of the loss of his parents and stirred the grief over the death of the children in Israel. It was a mix, a miasma of emotional torment, that came to life like reanimated corpses in a horror flick walking about inside him.

Akiko's grief shook the peaks of the Suzuka Mountains. She couldn't hold it in. It was like she was drowning in a pool of glass shards. She'd wanted desperately to save the girl's life, but she hadn't been able to. The one life that had managed to survive the carnage in Togakure Ryu, and Akiko had been able to do nothing except see it to its bittersweet end. She had never taken a human life until now, and her first kill had been the act of euthanasia of a beloved Kodomo. A terrible duty, indeed.

Terry and Akiko anguished over the girl's body, Terry blaming himself for not acting fast enough, Akiko angry that she had not been there to fight and die with her people. What next? Where would they go from here? They couldn't just leave their people to litter the ground like trash spilled in a neglected alley, left behind to be scavenged by animals and vermin. They'd build a pyre and burn the bodies, then; there was no way the two of them would be able to dig a suitable grave for seventy people in frozen earth.

Terry and Akiko toiled for hours, well into the morning light, cleaning the corpses of their clansmen and dragging them to their fiery resting place atop the pyre they'd labored to build. It wasn't the way any Shinobi wanted to be honored, but what other choice did they have?

Terry and Akiko did their dismal, melancholic duty. The first couple of hours were white hot and scalpel sharp. As the hours passed, though, the voltaic emotions dulled and the pain numbed. They felt hopeless and dejected as they stood there in front of the pyre's charnel heat and smell. All was lost.

Something caught Akiko's attention through the licking flames— the only unburned stanchion on the central hall. The *kanji* carved into it translated to read: *Allow Not Dishonor To Go Silently.* She read it to herself first. Then she mouthed the words. Then she said it aloud; Terry looked at her. Then Akiko said it loudly, and it was as if the pyre's blaze leaped into her, filling her veins. Vengeance was her only recourse—

their only recourse. They had to return the clan to honor since they could not return the Fujibayashi to life.

Terry and Akiko found their strength and decided to pursue the murderers, using the information they had uncovered when they had searched the village and when they had tended to their clansmen's remains. Among the dead, Terry and Akiko had found six bodies not of Fujibayashi origin, no doubt stabbed to death by Fujibayashi fighting back. In fact, four had tattoos like Oharu. In addition to the six strangers, three additional clues put Terry and Akiko on the track of those responsible: tracks leading into and out of Togakure to the southwest, bullet wounds riddling the bodies of the Fujibayashi, and bullet casings beneath a layer of fallen snow.

Unfortunately for those responsible, years of freelance espionage had made Terry a peerless tracker. He pooled his resources and skills, connecting the clues to find affiliations and eventually names. Two names interested him most: Itsuki Kawaguchi and Takehito Kato—the man in command of the attack during the ritual and the man calling himself the Shogun.

Terry tracked the Shogun, who appeared to be a bureaucrat that was well insulated by the underworld, to the Peninsula Hotel, where he was attending a political conference with a small security detail. Terry ordered Akiko to eliminate the so-called Shogun while Terry dedicated himself to finding Kintake and addressing the Momochi.

Now she came to the door of the Shogun's security chief's suite, just down the hall from the penthouse suite that the Shogun occupied during the week-long event. She needed access to the penthouse; the Shogun's security detail had access. *Tap, tap, tap.* She lightly rapped the door with her hand and checked that she was in order before returning it to her side.

The door opened, and a man wearing a dark blue suit—minus the coat—answered. His eyes bulged out of his head when he saw Akiko—her lustful eyes, rosy cheeks, ruby lips, slender, muscular frame, and porcelain skin. She wore her ebony hair in a messy bun held in place by a crisscross of chopsticks; she was dressed in a sheer pair of black panties and red satin robe that barely reached the middle of her thigh. It was tied loosely, and a sliver of her almond nipple showed. The man hooked the neck of his shirt with his finger and vented the steam of his instant boil.

Her lips curled into a fiendish smile. "**I was instructed to ensure that you have settled in well**," Akiko said. "**Is there anything you need?**"

The man sized her up with his eyes. "**What do you mean by anything?**" the man asked, sounding almost occupied.

"**Anything**," she deadpanned.

The man chortled, taking another moment to regard her. "**Well, come in, then**," he said, opening the door fully. "**I suppose I have some things that I need.**"

Akiko entered, walking straight through the sitting room toward the bedroom. Her eyes touched every inch of the room as she sashayed—she was mapping the environment and looking for weapons. She noticed two pistols, one on the counter of the kitchenette and one on the coffee table. There was also a fork in the sink as she passed it. The windows were large, but all the curtains were drawn. The TV was on, and there was a box of cigars on the coffee table next to the pistol, with a suit jacket draped over a seat. There was also only one way in and one way out.

She flung the door to the bedroom open, startling a skinny man sitting on the bed and browsing the internet. Akiko slid her robe off her shoulders, letting it flutter to the ground. The man on the bed didn't blink. The first man approached her from behind and stroked the tattoo of a wrathful serpent that ran the length of her spine.

"**Look what I found**," the larger man said to the skinny man, urging Akiko onto the bed with his hand.

She slithered onto the bed and rolled over, sitting up on her elbows and inviting him with her legs. The larger man chortled again and, with a hand, offered her to his companion while the larger man went into the bathroom, closing the door behind him.

The skinny man surveyed Akiko's curves. Akiko wrapped her fingers around his wrist and pulled his hand towards her, cupping her

316

breast with his hand. He swallowed hard, hovering there for a moment before mustering the courage to explore her body. His hand reached for her panties and stalled. She impressed him further, her rib cage expanding and her back arching. Akiko tugged at the man's shirt, drawing him towards her. The man rolled over finally, setting himself between her legs and grasping at her underwear. He pulled them from her supple curves. Akiko lifted her head just as the underwear reached her ankles and found the man's face hovering at the base of the v that her legs made. She could feel the humidity of his breath against her womanhood. Not bothering to take her panties off completely, he descended his face into her sex, her thigh muscles pressing into his face. She crossed a leg behind his head, driving his face deeper. Akiko grasped the ankle with the opposite hand and pulled it tight, closing the vice that her thighs created. The pressure, at first, didn't bother the skinny man, until it became difficult to breathe. He cracked the seal that his face made and drew in a raspy, labored breath. They made eye contact, and he didn't see the same woman he'd seen just a moment ago. He saw the conflagration that blazed inside her, and he realized that he was in terrible danger.

Akiko squeezed with every ounce of power she had in her small frame. The skinny man struggled in her grip like a coyote caught in a trap, becoming more violent as he struggled more and more for air. Akiko's years of ground fighting kept her in control, using her weight to prevent him from standing, and overpowering his arms with the strength of her legs.

The skinny man swung wildly, pounding her sides and buttocks; she blocked and absorbed the majority of his desperate strikes. Despite her effort, he was beginning to slip free of her grip. Akiko grabbed hold of her underwear, still attached to her ankles, and stretched them, wrapping them around his neck like a spider spinning a web around its prey. Now she had a leash to aid in controlling him. If he tried to pull away, he'd strangle himself just the same.

The toilet flushed.

She renewed her devotion and pulled as hard as she could on her noose. The skinny man shook and retched, his eyes turning the color of ripe tomatoes. He tried several times to hit her in the face, but she batted away his attempts.

The sink's faucet began to run.

Akiko bore down, trying to finish him, a shiny layer of sweat appearing all over her skin. The skinny man's arms flailed and then dropped. Akiko quickly rolled over his body.

The heavier man opened the door and entered the room, smiling. Akiko straddled his partner's head, clawing at the ceiling and moaning. The heavier man stroked her again and then climbed on the bed, aiming his face for her breasts. Akiko guided him into her chest, where she cradled his head in her arms while he began unbuckling his pants.

Akiko extracted a chopstick that was holding her bun, allowing a lock of hair to fall down her back. The man opened his eyes and gazed up at Akiko, and she slammed the chopstick into the heavier man's eye, hitting the back of the socket with a *thump*. He shrieked, spurting blood onto her face. She leaped upon him, driving him onto his back with her weight, and brought the second chopstick down in a merciless arc, burying it in the man's neck. His arms shot out to his side. She pulled the red-painted utensil from his throat and stabbed him repeatedly with it, showering the bed in blood until he didn't move.

Akiko hopped off the bed and grabbed ahold of the heavier man's pant legs, yanking at them to straighten him. He gurgled and hacked, but she paid no attention. She dug in his front pockets and rolled him over to check his back pockets. Nothing. She crawled to the skinny man and did the same. Still nothing.

She slid off the bed and went over to the chair where the skinny man's cashmere jacket hung. She checked every pocket but came out empty handed. Her mouth became a straight line. Akiko went back into the parlor and checked the heavier man's jacket. She found two card-keys in the inside pocket. As she was preparing to make her way to the front door, she noticed the trail of red footprints she was leaving on the carpet.

Akiko scurried to the bathroom. She started the shower running and stood back for a moment to allow it to warm, taking the opportunity to regard herself in the mirror: she was covered in blood. She had made her first two kills and had baptized herself in their blood—a crimson Picasso. This was what she was meant for, like her

318

father before her. Her father would be proud of the Shinobi she had become, and she was only getting started.

After a second, Akiko climbed in the shower and rinsed the blood from her skin and hair. She exited, slicked her hair back, and went to the front door without drying. She opened the door and checked the hallway in both directions—it was clear, so she sidled up to the penthouse door, pressing her ear into it. She could hear voices inside but couldn't make out the conversations nor the number of occupants, but there was no one immediately near the door, nearest she could tell. Akiko inserted the first card-key, and the lock replied with a red light. She swapped to the second key; it yielded a green light and a mechanical buzz as the jam unlocked.

She held her breath and pushed the door open slowly. The greeting room was clear, and so was the hallway leading the parlor. The voices sounded amused. She counted three distinct ones. When the door was open just enough for her to fit, she squeezed through it and eased it shut behind her, ensuring that she didn't close the door completely so as not to alert anyone with the sound. Then she slithered toward the parlor.

To her right was a side table with a tray full of liquor bottles, shot glasses, and a bowl with a nugget of ice and an icepick. She picked up the icepick as she passed the table and hid it behind her forearm before emerging in the parlor opening. She stood at the throat of the hallway, scanning the room. The first man looked up, and his mouth dropped open. The other three—there were four, though she'd only heard three—did the same when they realized what he was looking at. There was a tense silence as the four Japanese men—two middle-aged, wearing business suits, one balding and one with glasses; a young man in a leather jacket, a shirt, and denim pants; and another young man covered in tattoos, wearing slacks and dress shoes—stared in disbelief from their individual seats of the parlor, which held a couch, a coffee table, and a single seat.

"**Who are you?**" asked the balding middle-aged man, who was nearest. "**How did you get in here?**"

The tattooed man jumped to his feet and drew a gold-plated pistol from his waist.

"**I was sent here as a gift for the Shogun,**" she said, her eyes touching everything in the room. "**Are you the Shogun?**" She noted that two of the men were armed. There was also a leather bag on the counter in the kitchen and a knife and a set of nunchaku next to it—and only one way in and out.

The leather-jacketed man looked over his shoulder at the furthest man, the one wearing glasses.

"**You didn't answer the question,**" said the tattooed man, drawing nearer.

Her eyes found him.

He came close and looked Akiko over from head to toe, gently probing her right breast with the barrel of his gun. The tattooed man glanced over his shoulder and grinned. "**She is built well.**"

The men were all a mix of emotions. The leather-jacketed man smiled. The balding man's face was a mix of entertained and perplexed. The man with glasses was suspicious. The latter signaled to the tattooed man to bring Akiko to him.

The tattooed man nodded and aggressively snatched Akiko's elbow. That's when he noticed the icepick tucked behind her forearm. Before he could register it, Akiko seized his wrist and wrenched it, forcing him over at the waist. Then she slammed the icepick through his shoulder blade and into his chest cavity.

"**It is a hit!**" the man with glasses shrieked over the tattooed man's pained screams. She wasn't the delicate sex object nor the sweet, mysterious seductress that she had appeared to be just moments earlier. She was a hornet that they had mistaken for a butterfly.

The balding man shot to his feet, reaching into his coat for his gun. Akiko rushed him, planting a fierce blow against his knee with her leg. The man's knee buckled, and she caught him on the way down with a second kick, driving him through the coffee table. She leaped on him, driving her heel through his face with a ghastly *crunch*. The contents of his skull spilled onto the floor.

The leather-jacketed man attacked. His strikes were wild and undisciplined. Akiko ducked and slipped with ease as she watched the man with glasses retreat across the parlor toward the kitchen. She gave ground in his direction.

320

The leather-jacketed man threw in telegraphed arcs. She drew him in before shooting the gap and hitting with a furious combination that ended with an uppercut to his jaw and a reciprocal elbow to his brow. He stumbled back as blood began to run down his face.

The man with glasses lunged for the bag on the counter, scrambling for the pistol inside. Akiko made the distance between them, scooped up the nunchaku, and batted the pistol from his hand before he could level it. He flopped against the wall, holding his forearm where the nunchaku's free handle had struck bone; it was definitely fractured.

The leather-jacketed man attacked again, with an aerial kick this time. Akiko dodged and then swung the nunchaku in kinetic sequences. The free handle punished the leather-jacketed man's head, face, and shoulders, the chain of the weapon clanking with each strike. He tried to block, but she changed directions each time with blinding speed, going around his arms and coming from a different angle with different timing. She drew translucent circles and ellipses in the air around her head and shoulders with the nunchaku, generating more power for each hit. He went one direction to escape, only to be slammed in the face by the whooshing free handle. Then he tried the other direction, but another strike came. He couldn't even back up without being hit.

The tattooed man came into the melee, the icepick still protruding, offering the leather-jacketed man a moment of reprieve. Akiko, in mid-sequence, shifted to him, belting him repeatedly across the head from opposing directions, even cracking him in the teeth. The tattooed man stumbled back, holding his mouth.

The leather-jacketed man staggered in and swung a pathetic kick. Akiko slipped inside, holding both handles of her weapon, lassoed his head with the chain, and yanked him forward, driving her knee into his face. He crumpled in a bloody mess onto the floor.

Akiko turned to the man with glasses, the nunchaku spinning a circle off to her side. "**I did not take you for a coward, Takehito Kato. I assumed the Shogun would be a better warrior since he claims to be of Samurai descent.**"

"**Do you know what I can do to you?**" he brayed. "**I can have your family killed! I will have them tortured before they die!**"

"You have already killed my family," she said. "I am Fujibayashi. I am death. And as long as one of us lives, we are legion."

The tattooed man staggered toward her again. She fired a sidekick into his gut, sending him sprawling onto the icepick.

The Shogun lunged for the pistol again while he thought her attention was elsewhere, and Akiko dove on him, wresting the gun from his hand and drilling him in the face twice with the nunchaku like a billy club. She grabbed a handful of his hair and yanked him to his feet.

"You are the Shogun, right, Kato?" she asked, tossing the nunchaku aside and grabbing the knife from the counter.

"Yes!" he screamed.

"My name is Omiyoshu Akiko. I am the daughter of Hattori Hanzo—hallowed be his name. I am here to return my clan to honor and find my father."

"What?" he said, his voice strangled by pain. "Wait—I know you."

"If you refuse to tell me Hattori Hanzo's whereabouts, I will make your death slow and agonizing." It was a threat; she had no intention of prolonging this. There had been enough noise; someone was going to come find out the reason for the commotion.

"You are Omiyoshu Kintake's daughter? I let you live!" he bellowed. "It was *my* word that honored your father's request!"

"Where is he? Tell me!" she demanded, plunging the knife into the meat of his back.

The Shogun screamed.

"Where is he?" she yelled again.

"He is here! He is here!"

She looked around. "Where here?"

"I do not know," he cried. "He left some time ago."

Then she heard movement.

She looked toward the center of the parlor. The leather-jacketed man was still alive—barely conscious—but alive. She would see him to his death shortly. The tattooed man was dying a slow, agonizing death nearby. The balding man had assuredly expired.

"Please, you have to believe me. This was his plan. He asked me for help."

She returned her attention to the Shogun. "**My kōchō and I will see your co-conspirators to their graves.**" Then, with all the power she could muster from the fire that raged inside of her, Akiko slammed the Shogun's head into the corner of the counter with a terrible crack, splitting his head like a dropped melon. She slung his body to the ground contemptuously.

She heard movement again. Akiko snatched the knife from his back and readied herself.

A figure emerged from the hallway's throat into the parlor, with a sword held in a high guard. She recognized his face. "**Father**?"

And he recognized hers. "**Akiko? Daughter?**" he asked in disbelief, his guard relaxing.

"**You are alive. Oh, thank the ancestor spirits!**"

"**What have you done?**" he asked solemnly, scanning the room.

"**Ciccone Sensei ordered me to find and kill the Shogun. I have avenged the clan, father.**"

Kintake's eyes found her, his expression turbulent. "**Terry is alive?**"

"**Yes!**"

"**Still?**"

"**Yes, father. We must go.**"

He swallowed hard and stood there for a moment, staring at the floor.

"**Father, we do not have much time.**"

Kintake raised his guard again.

Her heart fell into her stomach. "**Father?**"

"**I am sorry, daughter. Truly I am.**"

*   *   *

The Ciccone Residence. Oxen Hill, Maryland. Today.

Yuri felt liberated soaking in his Jacuzzi with Veronica as himself, not the character he had created. It was the best feeling in the world. No code, no stealth, no limitations. Just him and her and what lay ahead. For the first time in his life, he had options—and options made him feel alive. He was practically in a meditative state, cuddled against her warm skin, making his senses hyper-sharp. He could feel eddies in the water generated by the rise and fall of Veronica's ribcage. He could smell the faint oil in her evening fragrance. He could taste the brilliance of her hair. She filled him with passion and with love.

Liberation wasn't all sweet, though. There were some sour points. Sometimes Yuri had to answer questions that he knew Veronica wouldn't like. But he was done lying. If she wanted to know the darker points in his life, he would tell her. This is what he wanted. A life that had meaning. Not one where only death had meaning.

Veronica lounged against Yuri like a beach chair as she stroked his leg with a sponge. "What was it like?"

Yuri lifted his head. "What was *what* like?"

"Growing up the way you did?"

"It was humbling. We didn't have the same utilities that we take for granted here. You saw what Togakure Ryu was like."

"I'm more referring to growing up, you know, a ninja."

"Shinobi."

"That's what I meant."

"It was tough. Ninpo is not easy for children. It's demanding. But it was all I knew."

"You said you lived with your parents, though. Didn't that have any impression?"

"Sure—but I was seven when my parents died. So my most formidable years were in Iga."

"Did you miss them?"

"No."

"Really?" she asked, half-turning.

"I don't really care for the Fujibayashi, anymore. You can thank Kintake for that."

"I was referring to your parents."

"Oh," Yuri snickered. "Well, yes, I did miss *them*."

"What were your parents like?"

Yuri chewed his lip for a moment as he tried to remember their faces. "My mother was a beautiful woman with long black hair and icy-blue eyes. I remember her being a passionate woman."

"You got her eyes."

Yuri smiled. "Terry says I got more than her eyes."

Veronica smiled back. "I guess you got her looks too, huh?"

"No, I look like my father. He was a rugged man, and I guess a good soldier. He was a boxer in his youth, but Terry always said that Dad hated talking about it."

"How did they die?"

Yuri sighed. This wasn't a conversation he enjoyed. It brought back feelings of emptiness that he would much rather leave buried. He and Terry didn't even talk about their parents' death that often—not that Terry was one to talk about his feelings in the first place. It was something they tried their best to leave in the past. But Veronica deserved answers even if they stirred demons that he'd tried to forget.

"They died in a plane crash while we were at summer camp in Togakure Ryu with Kintake."

"How did you find out?"

"Hattori Hanzo—the grandmaster at the time—told us. I'll never forget it. The rain." In his mind, he could see the hateful storm and the torrent and the disbelief on Terry's face.

"That's awful." She shook her head. "No one ever came to get you guys?"

"I dunno." Yuri shrugged. "You know, I never really thought about it. I suppose the grief kind of overshadowed that. So did my youth."

"I mean, your grandparents or aunts and uncles never tried to find you?"

"I'm not sure."

"Did you try to reach out to them?"

"No."

"Why not?"

"I don't—I don't have a good answer. I suppose it was the effect of Ninpo."

"Wow," she said, straightening herself.

They were silent for almost a minute; then Veronica started again. "How long did it take you to get over it?"

"I don't think I ever did. I think I just learned to cope with it."

Veronica half-turned again. "Do you remember the feeling?

Yuri remembered retching because he couldn't keep food in his stomach. He remembered the emptiness. He remembered wanting his mother to hug him one last time. "Yes, it was white-hot. It was suffocating. The days ran together. I didn't sleep much."

"How did you deal with it?"

"I screamed a lot—a whole lot."

"How about Terry? Did he help you?"

Yuri sighed. "The best he could. I mean, he was just a kid then too, barely older than twelve. He had to deal with his own pain. Regardless, no one could ask for a better brother."

"How did he deal with it?"

Yuri rubbed his mouth with his hand. Part of him felt like he was going to betray Terry's most intimate secrets. It was bound to happen, though. Terry was a major part of his life, and there would be points where the lines between Yuri and Terry blurred. Yuri needed to tell her.

He swallowed his apprehension. "Terry bottles things up. He distances himself when he's confused or in pain. He stops talking. When my parents died, he just stopped talking altogether."

"He just bottled the *whole* thing up?"

"I suppose you could say that, but it was more serious. He stopped talking until I was about twelve. Guess that made him seventeen or so."

"Are you serious?" she asked him in complete disbelief.

Yuri nodded.

"Omigod, that's so horrible. That must've been so difficult for you."

"For the longest time, I thought he was angry at me."

"I can imagine. How did the—um—what exactly do you call the people in the village?"

"Which people?"

"The people who raised you."

"Jonin and Chunin—high-ranking Shinobi and middle-ranking Shinobi."

"How did they take it? How did they respond to Terry not speaking? Did they help?"

"His refusal to speak was often seen as defiance in the eyes of our headmaster, Kintake, and the Jonin. They punished Terry for refusing to speak."

326

"They used to punish Terry because of his reaction to psychological trauma?" she asked, her face painted with disgust. "Your parents died. Did they not realize how that may have affected you guys psychologically and emotionally?"

"They punished me for his refusal when punishing Terry wouldn't work."

"Why on earth would they do that?" Veronica asked, becoming visibly disturbed.

"Kintake was abusive, even by Shinobi standards. He advocated harsh treatment. And grief isn't widely accepted by Ninpo. It's understood that some grief will exist, but you're expected to get over it quickly."

"That doesn't make sense. You were just children."

"No, we were Shinobi."

"Can I ask you a personal question?"

Yuri laughed. "You haven't already?"

"Well...I suppose I have, but this is kind of off the topic of your parents."

"I'm *totally* okay with that."

Veronica turned fully, situating herself Indian-style between Yuri's legs. She reached up and touched his face, her expression sincere and concerned. "I'm sorry if this is difficult for you, Yuri. We can stop if you want."

"No, let's get this out now so we can be done with it." He inhaled sharply, held it, then let it out. "I'm sorry. I didn't mean it the way it sounded."

"It's okay. This isn't easy for you. I can see that."

Yuri gave a flimsy smile. "What were you going to ask?"

Veronica shook her head. "Never mind. I don't think I want to know."

"Ask the freaking question," Yuri said, splashing her.

"Okay," she sighed, unconvinced that she should even open the can of worms. She did anyway. "How old were you when you killed for the first time?"

"Oh jeez, I don't know." Yuri looked at the ceiling as he went through his mental archive. "Ten. Eleven, perhaps? I think eleven. I killed a pig. I didn't kill a person until I was fourteen."

Veronica's eyes searched him. She still couldn't see it—the killer. She had met killers before, and he looked nothing like them. Then Yuri made eye contact with her, and she could finally see the predator.

"So, you weren't sent on missions when you were a kid?"

"Veronica," Yuri said, furrowing his brow, "that only happens in Hollywood."

"Well, how am I supposed to know? I figured you were like those ninjas in the movies."

"Shinobi. And not even close," Yuri chortled, shaking his head. "The Shinobi are a lot like the Native Americans in the sense that they have practices and customs that have been passed down through generations and have evolved into traditions to preserve a culture rather than a protocol."

Yuri wasn't being fully honest. He realized that at Oharu's residence, he had been, in fact, sent on missions. Though at the time, he'd thought they were rites of passage that all Kodomos had to complete. Yuri didn't feel a need to get into it. The fact was, he was still trying to sort it all out in his head.

"Oh." She felt suddenly small. She knew better than to make pop-cultural assumptions, but she fell into the prejudiced trap of ignorance on occasion like everyone did from time to time. "Okay—so, Shinobi didn't run all over the countryside killing people in their sleep."

"No, the *Fujibayashi* didn't. Not since before the Meiji Restoration." That much was true.

"So, when did you leave?"

"When I was about sixteen. Terry and I had a falling out with Kintake—more so me than Terry. We didn't have anywhere to go. Long story short, we became mercenaries."

"Mercenaries?" That's not at all what she expected. "You mean you were paid to fight wars?"

"We were paid to *fight*."

"What kind of fighting?"

"Insurgency and wetworks mostly. The stuff we were skilled to do. Shinobi aren't the mystical swordsmen that the movies make them out to be. Shinobi are espionage agents, similar to the CIA or something. So, we went where the money was."

Veronica's face was cross. "Who did you work for?"

"Militant Islamic group that fought against Israel."

"What?" Veronica said, sitting up straight. "You mean you were a Jihadists?"

"No—we were *mercenaries*. We were paid to do a job; we did the job. It paid fairly well, and we thought it aligned with Ninpo. We later decided that it didn't. As Terry put it, '*It made us no better than animals, killing indiscriminately for another man's delusions.*' It was a tough time for us."

"What changed your minds?"

Yuri grumbled in the back of his throat, trying to clear his sinuses. "I'd rather you didn't know those specifics. That's not a proud time in my life. Some memories are better left where they occurred."

"Okay—well, we never finished with my original point."

"Fine."

"You seem edgy."

"Nope," Yuri said distantly, running more water. "Just ask the question."

"Are you mad at me now?"

"No—this just isn't easy. I'm recalling memories that I don't necessarily want to remember. If you want answers to your questions, ask. Just don't be offended if I seem a little off keel."

"Okay then—what did it feel like the first time you killed?"

"The first time I killed or the first time I killed *someone*?"

"Um." She didn't quite know how to respond to that. "Both, I guess."

"The first time I killed, I was eleven, and I killed a pig."

"Why did you kill a *pig*?"

"It was part of an exercise; a pig simulates human flesh pretty well. Anyway, we used the dead pig—as well as the others that were killed that night—to feed the village."

"How did it make you feel?"

"Accomplished," Yuri said, wiping his forehead. "I was praised for how cleanly I had cut its throat. The pig barely made a sound as it died."

"That's horrible, Yuri. You don't even seem affected by it."

"Should I be?" Yuri's brows raised. "Killing is basic; it's fundamental to who we are as humans. Ninpo simply justified my natural inclination towards killing."

"But you were just a kid. You don't think that affected your development?"

"Perhaps it did; perhaps it didn't. But one thing was for sure, I *wasn't* just a kid. I was Shinobi. Killing is a part of who we are."

"Who you are?" Her eyes were suspicious.

"Who I was," Yuri replied, correcting himself.

"Did you ever feel anything other than accomplishment?"

"Sure. I remember feeling *nothing* the first time I killed a person."

"You didn't feel anything?"

"Well, there was the thrill."

Goosebumps erupted all over Veronica's body. "You found it *thrilling*?"

"Relax," Yuri said, sensing her uneasiness; it was the uneasiness that a deer radiated when it sensed the wolves stalking out of sight. "I'm not a serial killer or anything. I felt thrill in a manner that I don't think you quite understand."

"Then how? Because it sounds a lot like a serial killer to me."

"I suppose," Yuri started, licking his lips as he searched for the right metaphor, "in the same manner a boxer or a mixed martial artist is thrilled by a fistfight. Imagine spending several hours a day training and conditioning to fight. Fighting is what you do. Now imagine yourself being in the grocery store and some random individual picks a fight with you. There's a thrill that envelopes you as you stand on the precipice of a confrontation with an opponent who allowed their pride to escalate a fight that they have no chance in winning. That's the thrill."

Veronica lowered her head; this was big—*huge* big. She felt weight on her shoulders. "I knew I shouldn't have asked. You know, I kept telling myself that I couldn't see the killer, but I feel like I see it now."

Yuri didn't know what to say after that. Resolving himself, he said, "I'm a good person, Veronica. I want to be something new."

"Are you sure?"

"Yes."

She wasn't positive that he was, though. "How many people have you killed?"

"Not sure."

"That many?"

"Perhaps."

"Do you think you're going to hell?"

Yuri looked deeply into her. "I don't believe in hell. Not as you know it, anyway."

"Do you believe in God?" Veronica asked, suddenly feeling very insecure.

"You mean the Christian God?"

"Yes."

"No."

Yuri seemed very alien to her, and for the first time, she wished she had the character back that Yuri played all this time. "What do you believe in?"

"I don't know. I don't know what I believe in anymore."

Yuri's eyes snapped in the direction of the door, five yards away, leading into his bedroom. The wall of the bathtub blocked its view, but the door drew his attention no less. Yuri lifted himself from the basin and leaned over the side.

"What're you doing?" Veronica asked. "What's the matter?"

"Shhh," Yuri demanded.

Trained ears focused on the sounds in the house. There was the harmonic warble of disturbed bathwater, the static thrum of the lighting fixture over the sink, the breathy aspiration of the ventilation, the faint creeks from support structures, distant traffic outside, and something out of place.

"Yuri, what? You're scaring me."

He didn't answer; he focused on the sound. Then he realized what the sound was: footsteps.

Terry was in Japan.

And Saki was crippled.

*   *   *

The doorknob rattled.

Veronica had locked it behind them when they'd come in to bathe. She always did. She claimed it was a habit of living alone. Yuri never appreciated it more than now.

Rationality told him that it was his brother, who had simply returned home from Japan and never let Yuri know. His better judgment, however, told him that there were intruders in his house. Yuri didn't much care for the details; he had an assortment of weapons in the walk-in closet opposite the door.

He planted a finger against his lips, gesturing for Veronica to remain quiet. Then he patted the air, instructing her to lay down in the tub and remain there. Confusion covered her face, but Yuri ignored it and climbed out of the tub. She grabbed his wrist, but he shook free and moved to the shower—between the entrance and the tub—starting the flow on hot and leaving its door open. Then he continued to the closet, passing the sink on his left, pointing at the tub and silently, deliberately mouthing the words, "Stay there." Yuri disappeared into the closet.

He pulled a hardened case from a shelf, popped its latches, and pulled a silenced pistol from it. He kept his eye on the door and felt around the top shelf until he found his ninjatō. Yuri placed it on the floor next to his feet.

The doorknob rattled more. Veronica's head popped up, and she whispered something, but Yuri ignored her; he watched the door intently.

The door collapsed inward from a foot, and a shotgun leveled. Yuri opened fire first, hammering the doorway with the hushed claps of his pistol. Yuri's first shot shattered the corner of the marble counter; his second struck the gunman in the leg. The gunman's weapon barked harshly, but the wounding of his leg forced him off his mark. The roar of the shotgun forced Yuri back into the cover of the closet.

Veronica covered her ears, screaming.

The shower was filling the far end of the bathroom with steam. When the shower door was left open as it was, it filled the bathroom with thick vapor in less than a minute. The reduced visibility would aid Yuri greatly.

The shotgun barked several times consecutively, showering Yuri with splinters of drywall and wood. Yuri slid his pistol around the corner and fired blindly. He let off six rounds, and then he was back in cover, pulling a flashbang from the open case. He yanked the pin out with his teeth and chucked the canister across the bathroom floor. The canister *click-clack-clacked* to a halt against the far wall and then—*BOOM*—there was thunder. Yuri took the split second to reload.

The intruders protested loudly in Japanese.

Japanese.

Hitmen for the Yakuza. They'd come to finish the job.

Yuri snatched up the ninjatō in his right hand and leaped out, firing with this left. He sprinted into the fog, catching the gunman center-mass with the first two shots. Yuri dropped to his knees on the rug in front of the sink and slid on it across the bathroom floor, catching the gunman across the chest with his sword. Yuri banged into the wall to the immediate left of the door frame and saw a second gunman trying to get a bead on Yuri.

Yuri swept his sword in an upward arc, setting the gun off target when its muzzle reported. Yuri dove through the doorway, going bodily into the second gunman, driving him hard into the wall. Yuri scrambled over the gunman and found his feet. A third intruder—another Asian man like the first two—slashed at Yuri with a katana. Yuri batted the strike away and gave ground. The swordsman assumed a low stance, holding the katana parallel to the floor. His stance wasn't a traditional sword stance; it was a stance exclusive to taijutsu. The swordsman was Momochi.

Yuri lunged, hurling combinations with his ninjatō. The swordsman intercepted Yuri's strikes, angling the blade away from his body. Yuri snuck a kick through and drove the swordsman onto and over the bed. The swordsman bounced and recovered over his shoulders, diving clear and rolling to safety as Yuri hurtled the bed and brought the ninjatō down in a punishing arc, carving a chasmal line in the wall.

The swordsman was on his feet again, and the two men were exchanging blows, intercepting, reposting, and dancing for the advantage. Then Yuri heard the second gunman—who had found his feet during the fray—advance on him. Yuri retreated two steps from the swordsman and spun a wicked arc with his blade at the gunman's waist. The gunman let out a sickening *hic* as wriggling snakes fell from his stomach and plopped onto the floor in front of him.

The swordsman was on Yuri before he could fully reset. Yuri did what he could to defend himself, but he wasn't able to stop a strike that cleaved a chuck of flesh from his shoulder. Yuri yelled. Fortunately, the swordsman overcommitted and Yuri was able to crowd him and grapple. The two men fell into the wall, trampling the second gunman's entrails. Yuri gritted his teeth, trying to gain the advantage despite the bloody pain in his shoulder. The katana was pinned between them and the swordsman was inching its bitter edge toward Yuri's neck.

The men growled and strained as they spun and rolled along the wall to the door leading into the hallway, like a top bumping against a vertical surface, trying desperately to overpower each other. The blade began to press into Yuri's neck, slowly slicing his flesh. Yuri raged, trying to muster every bit of strength to stop the katana from severing his carotid.

Then the intruder's eye shot open; his mouth tightened in an O-shape, and he let out a pained aspiration. Then he slumped against Yuri, the sword falling limp. Yuri pushed his lifeless body to the floor and gulped air, panting, and looked through the doorway. Saki was on his hands like an angered viper, with the handle of a blood-tipped ninjatō beneath him. The two Shinobi exchanged looks; even paraplegic, a Shinobi could strike. Yuri helped Saki to the bed and then went to comfort a hysterical Veronica.

*　　*　　*

"Terry," Yuri practically yelled into the phone. "They sent a hit squad after me. I'm coming back."

"They're all dead."

"Who's dead?" Yuri asked, gritting his teeth at the pain in his shoulder.

"Everyone. The women. The children. The entire clan."

They were silent for a moment.

"How?" Yuri asked finally.

"They sent shooters. Akiko and I were the only survivors. Weren't in the village at the time. I also believe that the Momochi and the Yakuza have taken Hattori Hanzo. I've sent Akiko after a lead I had on the Shogun."

"Everyone is dead?" Yuri couldn't believe it.

"Yes."

"Sit tight. I'll be there in twenty-four hours."

"I know this isn't what you wanted—"

"It's over. I had a vision of what I could be, but that's not what I am. I'm a killer, Terry, and she's seen me for who I really am. The universe won't have it any other way."

"Yuri."

"Yeah?"

"I'm sorry."

"It's not you that should be sorry."

Chapter Twenty: Blood On My Eyes

Accept an honorable surrender, but never show mercy. Your enemy will not.
The Eleventh Mandate, translated from Ninpo.

Kitashirakawa, Kyoto, Japan. Today.

VERONICA MARTIN: Yuri why won't u answer me? **Sent 9:43 PM**

VERONICA MARTIN: The cops r treating me like a criminal...like I killed all those people. What am I supposed to do? **Sent 9:44 PM**

VERONICA MARTIN: Yuri!! **Sent 9:45 PM**

VERONICA MARTIN: U said u love me and this is how u treat me! Ur a monster! **Sent 11:06 PM**

VERONICA MARTIN: Saki is dead too?! Did u kill him?! **Sent 11:13 PM**

VERONICA MARTIN: Im under suspicion 4 his death 2. **Sent 11:14 PM**

VERONICA MARTIN: ANSWER ME!! **Sent 11:27 PM**

VERONICA MARTIN: Told the cops it was u. U left me no other choice. **Sent 12:02 AM**

VERONICA MARTIN: I loved u once. Now im in hell. **Sent 12:11 AM**

*   *   *

After Terry had sent Akiko to kill the Shogun, he went to work planning his revenge against the remaining leaders of the Yakuza and the Momochi that he could link to the massacre. He wanted to act immediately, but he knew patience was of the utmost importance. Akiko's attack on the Shogun was an action that he could orchestrate while the window of opportunity was open. He would finish the job once his brother arrived.

The plan was to go after the Yakuza—the easier of the two targets—first. Then they would attack the Momochi. The Yakuza—no doubt on high alert in the wake of the death of their Shogun—were formidable, but a divide-and-eliminate plan would pull them apart. The Momochi, however, unlike the Yakuza, were hardened against wetworks and would be far more difficult to hit. Once a single Momochi turned up on their back, the clan would close ranks and start enacting counter-espionage protocols; Terry and Yuri would them find themselves at a serious numerical disadvantage. Granted, the Yakuza outnumbered Terry and Yuri as well, but the Yakuza weren't as homogenously trained as the Momochi. To that end, Terry surmised that he would use the Momochi's own tactic against them: he and Yuri would attack the Momochi leadership all at once, the same way the Momochi and Yakuza had attacked and overwhelmed the unsuspecting Fujibayashi of Togakure Ryu.

The first target was a Japanese entrepreneur of Taiwanese descent who'd laundered millions of dollars for the Yakuza.

Yuri was contemptuous. He sat on the passenger side of an unassuming jalopy, playing a game on his cellular. He was trying to forget Veronica by occupying his mind with a mindless activity while he and Terry awaited their target.

"You going to answer those?" Terry asked, watching intently out of the driver window for their target and hearing Yuri's text prompt chime periodically.

"No point. There's nothing to be said except her telling me how I deceived her."

"The target is on the move."

Yuri nodded, disinterested.

"You know, I'm proud of you." Terry looked at Yuri. "Mom and Dad would've been happy to see how you glowed when you were with her. You really gave it your all."

Yuri scoffed. "Can we just let it go? I'm trying not to think about it."

"Okay."

Yuri let out a deep sigh, venting the anxiety poisoning his insides.

"You good?"

"Revenge doesn't require me to feel good," Yuri deadpanned.

The target strutted down the walkway to his car, talking on the phone. He unlocked the car as he approached, opened the back door, threw a bag in the backseat, and then opened the driver door and sat in the front seat, closing the door behind him.

Terry watched intently. Any moment now.

The engine turned over, coughed, and spat. Then there was a *boom* followed by repeated *pops*. The car billowed smoke, and tongues of fire licked the sky. Then the door flew open, and the target dove from the driver's seat half in flames.

"Shit!" Terry said. "Gimme your sword."

Yuri looked up at Terry and saw the flames of the blast reflected in the lens of his sunglasses. "What?"

"The bomb didn't detonate properly. He survived. He's rolling around in the grass. Gimme your sword."

Yuri threw his phone onto the dash and unbuckled. "I'll handle it," he said, drawing his ninjatō. Yuri hopped out of the jalopy and galloped across the street onto the lawn where the target rolled around screaming. Yuri came over top of him and turned the point down. The target, skin melting on his neck and arms, outstretched a pleading hand. Yuri's eyes burned blue with hate. Then he slammed the point through the target's chest, hitting the ground on the other side. Yuri torqued the weapon counterclockwise while burning a hole through the target's face with his eyes.

BLAM! BLAM!

There were gunshots.

Yuri, startled, looked up to his left and bristled. Another man holding a pistol flopped to the ground, face down. Yuri looked back and saw his brother standing on the street with his gun raised, the barrel smoking.

Yuri recovered his weapon and ran back to the jalopy.

*   *   *

Shinbashi, Tokyo, Japan. Today.

Yuri slithered through a sea of faces, tailing Itsuki Kawaguchi as he weaved through the busy Shinbashi rush-hour crowd. Kawaguchi was the same lanky Asian man who'd commanded the ambush at the shrine and was also the second-highest-ranked Yakuza Terry had connected to the massacre next to the late Shogun. Kawaguchi claimed to be the Shogun's major domo, and Terry and Yuri were going to make sure that he was buried right next to his boss.

"Terry, can you see me?" Yuri whispered into the throat mic buried below the neck of his black jacket.

"Yeah," Terry replied into Yuri's earpiece.

"Kawaguchi's ten feet ahead of me in the navy-blue suit, sunglasses, and a briefcase in his right hand."

"Contact."

"Where are you?" Yuri asked.

"I'm at the bus stop across the way."

Yuri looked left, across the congested street, and spotted Terry leaning against a *no parking* sign within an arm's reach of the cellphone-crazed mass transit patrons mobbing the bus stop. Terry was wearing a loud designer t-shirt and designer jeans, with a hipster-style bag over his shoulder. Both stood out in the homogenous sea of Asians, but no one noticed Americans in Tokyo. Kawaguchi sure hadn't, and Yuri had been following him from his place of business for nearly thirty minutes. Kawaguchi stopped at a vendor near the corner of the block and browsed some goods as Yuri passed him, drawing his phone and pretending to search the contacts.

Yuri walked to the corner and turned so that he could keep out of Kawaguchi's view. Terry kept a solid watch on Kawaguchi and gave Yuri updates. After several minutes, the target was on the move again, approaching Yuri's position. Terry told him and started walking ahead

339

of Kawaguchi but at a slower pace. Kawaguchi overtook Yuri on the crosswalk, swimming through waves of pedestrians. He reached into his pocket when his phone rang, rattling on in his nasal Japanese, and then he turned around sharply. He and Yuri made eye contact. Kawaguchi briefly showed a sign of being startled, but then he turned back around just as quickly and marched away, stuffing his phone into his pocket.

Yuri boiled, stirred by frustration. "Terry, I think he noticed me."

"Are you sure? How do you know?"

"We made eye contact?"

"You did what?" Terry's pitch climbed an octave. "Are you new at this?"

"I didn't mean it."

"What's he doing now? I'm having a hard time seeing him."

"He's walking at his normal pace..."

Kawaguchi took off, rocketing down the sidewalk and bulldozing anyone unlucky enough to get in his path.

"Terry, he's making a break for it!" Yuri yelled as he sprinted after his target.

Terry cursed as he tried to keep his brother and Kawaguchi in sight over the cars and the numberless heads. He could barely keep a bead on them; he needed to get to higher ground. Terry hurried to the bus stop's bench, launched himself onto the back of it, pushing several patrons away, drew his pistol, and aimed it at the bouncing head of Kawaguchi. Terry chopped off several rounds, the spent casings hitting several panicked patrons ducking for cover, but he was too far and too hurried to manage clean shots. The gun's reports, however, stirred chaos at the intersection, pedestrians scattering in every which direction. Terry paid them no attention; he focused on Kawaguchi, attempting to land a few more shots, until the gun's slide slammed open when the magazine ran dry.

Terry leaped off the bench and ran into the parking lot that the street had become, reloading simultaneously. "Yuri, keep eyes on him. I'll be there in a moment," Terry huffed into his throat mic as he sprinted over to a motorcyclist. He brandished his gun, urging the cyclist from the vehicle. The cyclist didn't argue, and Terry mounted the bike, stuffing the gun down his pants. Terry held the front brake and mashed the throttle. The motorcycle shrieked, burning an arc into the

340

pavement until it was facing the opposite direction. Terry released the brake, and the front wheel peeled off the ground as the motorcycle rocketed through the packed rows of cars. Then he whipped the bike around the next turn to follow.

"Terry, he's heading for the train station," Yuri said as he zigzagged through the stampeding crowd.

Terry didn't have time to answer; he could see Kawaguchi, and Terry drew the pistol from his belt, opening fire with his off hand through the crowd of people and cars. He couldn't score a hit, though, with the maneuvering of the bike and his off hand degrading his aim. Terry stuffed the gun back into his belt, saving the rest of his ammunition, and poured on speed. He could see Kawaguchi sprinting for the stairs to the underground terrace. A second later, he was out of sight. On the one hand, that was bad—a target they couldn't see was the same as a target who'd escaped. On the other hand, that was good—he wasn't going anywhere; the next train wasn't going to show for the next seven minutes.

Terry shot past Yuri, weaving through cars to cross the street. He jumped the curb and hurtled down the sidewalk, coming up hard on the terrace entrance. Terry hunkered down against the bike's tank, rolled the throttle back, and went headlong down the stairs. Pedestrians dove out of the way of the plunging motorcycle, the bike bucking angrily from end to end with Terry in the saddle as he dropped three stories into the cavernous, postmodern edifice.

Kawaguchi looked over his shoulder at the roar he heard coming down the stairs. Then he saw Terry hit bottom and gun the throttle. Panic filled Kawaguchi's stomach, and his veins filled with adrenaline as he sprinted for the stairs on the far side of the terrace, weaving between stanchions for cover. He dug into his briefcase as he ran, struggling to extract his gun.

Terry split the distance between the rows of stanchions and rammed the throttle to its limit. The engine screamed as the bike devoured the space between Terry and Kawaguchi. Terry got close and realized that Kawaguchi had a pistol in his hand and he was trying to level it as he ran. Terry jerked the bike over, laying it on its side. Terry separated from the bike as it slid, scraping and howling, across the tile toward Kawaguchi. Kawaguchi couldn't get away from it; the bike

341

clipped his heels, pulled him to the ground, climbed over him, and drove him an easy twenty feet. Terry clambered to his feet, despite the pain of his power slide, and rushed over to Kawaguchi, following the trail of scratches and blood.

Terry hopped up onto the overturned motorcycle that pinned Kawaguchi's legs; Terry aimed the barrel of his gun at Kawaguchi's eyes, who cried when the additional weight came down on his smashed shinbones. **"Don't run,"** Terry said smugly. **"You'll just die tired."**

There were sirens on the surface.

Kawaguchi begged for his life. He pleaded and sobbed while he fought against the bike's weight with his hands. Terry didn't regard anything that bubbled from Kawaguchi's mouth until Terry heard "Kintake."

Terry's eye peeked out from behind the barrel. **"What did you say?"**

"It was not me; I am not responsible! Omiyoshu Kintake is responsible!"

"What're you talking about? Where is he? What'd you do with my Shinobi-no-mono?"

"I didn't kill your clansmen!" Kawaguchi cried. **"It was Omiyoshu Kintake who did it!"**

"You're saying my Shinobi-no-mono killed my people?"

"Yes, he ordered the attack! It wasn't me!"

"Where is my Shinobi-no-mono?" Terry growled.

"He left for Dubai!"

That didn't make any sense. **"Why is he in Dubai?"**

"To start his new life—a new life that he asked us to help him make."

The sirens grew louder.

"Terry," Yuri yelled as he hustled down the stairs, "we got to go! The cops are coming!"

Terry looked over his shoulder at Yuri, and then his head snapped back to Kawaguchi. A sneer stretched Terry's face, and he smashed Kawaguchi's face with the receiver of the pistol. **"You piss-ants will say anything to keep me from killing you all."** Terry stomped on the bike and yelled, **"Where the fuck is my Shinobi-no-mono?"**

Kawaguchi cried, gurgling blood and spitting out tooth fragments. "I swear! My assistant arranged a six-month work visa for him through a contact at the embassy! Omiyoshu Kintake set up a business in Al Barsha outside Jebel Ali! I swear!"

"We'll see. I don't believe a fucking thing you say. I'm going to find my Shinobi-no-mono—you can't hide him from me forever—and I'm going to send as many your associates to early graves as I can while there's still air in my lungs."

"Terry!" Yuri yelled. "Put a bullet in him! We got to go!"

Terry pulled the trigger.

*　　*　　*

Suzuka Mountains. Mie Prefecture, Japan. Today.

The forest of the Suzuka Mountains was the somber auburn-gray that accompanied dusk, causing the forest of the Momochi territory to feel more alien than Terry and Yuri had remembered. They weren't familiar with these forests; they'd had only a few prohibited incursions here when they were adolescents, incursions that had left them and Saki severely bruised and punished. This time, though, there was no one to stop them from invading and no one left to punish them.

The terrain of Momochi territory was at a considerably higher altitude and lacked the constant rise and fall of the hills around Togakure Ryu. Instead of being nestled into a natural formation along a river, the Momochi village—Tomo Ryu—was set into hand-carved flats just beneath the summit of a fierce peak crowned with white, centered in a range to the west of the Fujibayashi territory. The craggy terrain soared skyward at its highest and boiled up as cantankerous knuckles at its lowest, sporting less flora too. The trees were perhaps half as tall, and the low foliage was composed mostly of brown-green brush. Adding to the topographic violence were the harsh winds, whipping up one side of the peaks and hurling down the other. Walking a straight path through Momochi territory was next to impossible. Because of this, the Momochi were always hailed as better climbers than the Fujibayashi—and for that matter, the other clans before they disappeared—and the terrain was a testament to that reason.

Additionally, the Momochi were historically famed, and chastised, for being an obstinate, zealous clan—the most difficult to invade—without the good sense to employ tactical retreats. The Shinobi knew better, though; the Momochi were obstinate because their enemies had to fight uphill, and the terrain didn't favor tactical retreats from the Momochi, nor did the terrain encourage flanking massed enemies like the lands around Togakure Ryu, the Momochi preferring a Shinobi flavor of head-to-head attrition warfare. Terrain played a huge part in the history of Shinobi warfare and more often than not played a huge part in the past victories of the clans—the home-field advantage made enemies reconsider invasions. The brothers planned to neutralize the advantage with the element of surprise and a minefield of lethal force.

Yuri went ahead and scouted the terrain to look for a prime location from which to spring their ambush, while Terry kept persistent surveillance on Tomo Ryu. Yuri passed imagery back to his brother via phone as Yuri mapped the terrain, trying to familiarize himself with it the best he could to minimize the home-field advantage of their ancestral enemy.

Terry recalled Yuri after several hours when two scouts departed Tomo Ryu and ambled into a cutaway that led away from the village and into a tight crevasse constrained by sheer, towering walls. The two Genin scouts bounded past Terry's hiding place, unaware of intruders, and jogged off—hopped, really—into the belly of the crevasse. They did a complacent, routine survey of the grounds in advance of the main party, leaving Tomo Ryu for an equally complacent training session after dark. Terry watched them swagger out of sight. Then he dropped a pin on his location and pursued them, keeping his position updated for Yuri.

Terry followed them through the crevasse and into a depression in the slope that formed a natural cutout. Inside were a cave and a natural spring, around which the Momochi had erected a shrine in honor of a patron spirit. Terry was tempted to assail the scouts, but the Momochi would become suspicious when they didn't return. Instead, he allowed the Genin to continue their routine and gleaned from them that a Momochi party would arrive here sometime after sunset. According to the Genin's conversation, accompanying the party would be their kōchō. And if the kōchō were going to be in company, then several other high-ranking Momochi would be too. The leadership of the Momochi would be within a sword swing of each other. The downside would be that the Momochi's most experienced fighters would all be together. Terry and Yuri would have one shot to get it right. If they dropped the ball, they'd have one hell of a fight on their hands.

*　　*　　*

Terry was prone on the high ground, with his barrel trained along the pathway that led into the open-air shrine. Yuri was practically across from him, offset just to the right, on the far side. Terry would hit the targets from the front, and Yuri would hit them from behind. It was a sweet setup, like shooting fish in a barrel.

Two strapping Chunin crept down the pathway into the shrine and scanned it. Their movements and their subsequent survey looked choreographed, like it was a pattern—a ritual—that they were expected to perform. Once they finished their survey, they signaled down the pathway, and a group of Jonin, numbering five in total, strode into the shrine. Behind them was the kōchō, Daishi Nishida, under the escort of his newest first, second, and third senior Chunin—the previous three having been killed in combat against Saki, Terry, and Yuri—like a newly ascended king being attended by his knights. Just behind them were three more boyish-looking Genin, two of whom were the earlier scouts.

The Jonin in the lead stopped, regarded the shrine, and was opening his mouth to begin a speech when there was a crack of thunder that exploded the nearest Chunin's face, spraying gore all over the Jonin. The Momochi barely had time to react before another thunderclap blasted a dreadful hole in an elder's neck that squirted blood despite the owner attempting to stifle the flow with his hand.

The Momochi scattered for cover, feeling their way through the darkness, but not before two more reports left a Jonin lying on his side and clutching his chest. The darkness didn't aid the Momochi as much as they could have hoped, with Terry and Yuri aiming through nightvision. Then the thunderous reports became constant, with *whooshes* of heated metal, *twangs* of ricochets, clouds of stone shrapnel, and the cries of injured and dying Shinobi. Relentless sniper fire dropped Jonin and Chunin alike from headshots or shots to center mass.

The second senior hunkered down behind a boulder, having an internal argument whether to rush out of cover to assist a comrade or try to spot the ambushers. Then, through the panicked fog, he saw Nishida hobble through the carnage on a mangled leg and back into the crevasse. Nishida was nearly being carried by a considerably older Jonin who had Nishida's arm draped across his shoulder. There was a report, and the Jonin spilled to the ground, causing Nishida to topple. The second senior leaped from cover and sprinted toward Nishida.

The second senior came over top of his kōchō. **"Nishida Sensei, I have you!"** But a hole blown in the second senior's forehead caused him to tumble over Nishida and convulse against the rocks.

Nishida crawled to his feet and hobbled down the crevasse. An injured Jonin followed him; the two surviving Genin ran back up the crevasse toward Tomo Ryu.

Yuri dismounted and pursued the Genin. Terry went after Nishida.

The Genin ran as fast as their feet would take them up the tight vein, gasping for air in the burning cold and tingling from the panic. As they felt their way back up the scantily moonlit path, they glanced over their shoulders like paranoid antelope looking for lions. The crevasse seemed like a never-ending hallway in a horror movie: the danger was real and present, just unseen and unknowable.

There were suddenly two cracks of thunder from directly above, where Yuri stood atop a crevasse wall, and both Genin fell, one spilling the contents of his cranium and the other clutching a gaping hole in his chest. Yuri scanned the pile of bleeding Genin creating a small river in the crevasse. One wasn't moving, but the other rolled over, trying to catch his breath. Yuri hefted a rock of substantial weight, aimed it, and let if fall onto the still living Genin. Gravity did its job, leaving the Genin's right leg twitching.

Yuri checked for reinforcements coming from Tomo Ryu and for other survivors trying to escape. Nothing. So he ran off to find his brother.

Terry was into the crevasse and on Nishida's trail. The old man was gravely injured; he couldn't have gotten far. Terry paused and listened. He didn't hear anyone clawing their way up the steep igneous walls, nor did he hear the injured tempo of footfalls plodding along the pathway. The kōchō was surely hiding, probably hoping to catch Terry unawares as he passed by.

Terry slung his carbine and drew both his pistol and his ninjatō, supporting his gun hand with his sword arm as he vigilantly crept down the widening crevasse toward the terminus of a saddle. He eyed the rocks and boulders that pocked the serpentine path, watching for movement. The kōchō was here; just where *here* was he?

The question didn't remain unanswered for long. Two gunshots echoed down the crevasse from a point closer toward Tomo Ryu. Using the cacophony to cover their movement, the kōchō and his Jonin protector lunged from behind nearby boulders nearly simultaneously, with a near vertical slash from Nishida and an angled slash from the Jonin. Terry managed to get clear of Nishida, but he wasn't so fortunate where the Jonin was concerned. The angled slash bit into Terry's tricep, an unarmored portion of his ensemble that would have likely been completely severed from his body had Terry not bounced backward. Terry hissed from the pain and squeezed rapid shots into the Jonin's trunk, dropping him on the spot. Nishida hurled another slash that let out a metal-on-metal reply when it struck Terry's pistol, yanking it from his hand. Terry was lucky it wasn't his hand that flopped to the ground.

The kōchō showed no quarter, keeping up his assault by cutting ribbons in the air between them. Terry settled his defense, answering the swings of Nishida's sword with his own and backing up the crevasse to leverage the cramped space and Nishida's hindered mobility. A testament to the tenacity of Shinobi, Nishida's attacks continued, Terry intercepting them or opening the distance enough to avoid them. Terry continued to use distance to slowly move into an advantage.

Nishida committed one last time, trying to feint high and then drive the blade through Terry's heart. Nishida's injury, however, highlighted his intent, and Terry was able to anticipate the attack. As Nishida's blade came out from behind the feint, Terry intercepted it, locking it with his own blade, and drilled Nishida with a rock-solid fist. Nishida's head snapped back, but he didn't release the handle of his sword. Terry drilled him two more times before snatching the sword from Nishida's grip and slinging it over his head; the blade tumbled several times before it came to rest at Yuri's feet, who had since descended into the crevasse and was coming up behind his brother to help. Terry then impaled the inside of Nishida's thigh, the blade scraping the bone with its edge and bursting out the other side. Nishida crumbled to his knees, dripping blood in a pool. Terry hooked a shot to the side of Nishida's head, dropping him before Terry yanked the sword free. Nishida mewled from the pain on his hands and knees.

"**Sit up**," Terry demanded.

Nishida did, wincing.

Terry's blade was nose to nose with the Momochi kōchō now. "**I am Terry Ciccone, kōchō of the Fujibayashi. My brother and I are the survivors of your failed conspiracy. You know why I'm here**," Terry said coolly.

Yuri walked up behind Terry.

"I do," Nishida replied. There was dignity and defiance in his eyes, but there was also resignation.

"**Would it that I could exterminate the entirety of the Momochi and the Yakuza. I will settle for the lives of your leaders.**"

"**I am defeated, Ciccone Sensei. You have bested me, and I am bleeding out. Grant me seppuku, so that I may find honor.**"

"Fuck that," Yuri spat. "Let's chuck him off the ravine."

"No."

"Don't go soft on me, Terry. We're here to send a message."

"I can't do it. My arm is injured."

"What? Where?" Yuri checked his brother's arms, finding the open wound and the waterfall of blood. "Damn. You okay?"

"I'll live," Terry said over his shoulder. Then he returned his attention to the Momochi kōchō. "**Nishida Sensei, I grant you seppuku. Yuri Ciccone will be your secondary.**"

Nishida nodded, peeling off his tunic slowly and drawing his tanto from his belt.

Terry slid past Nishida and positioned himself opposite of his brother. Yuri stowed his pistol and drew his ninjatō as he approached to striking distance.

"**Do you have any final words, Nishida Sensei?**" Terry asked as he dug in his pack and extracted a glow stick.

"**Killing me and cadre will not return your clan to honor, Ciccone Sensei,**" Nishida said, his breathing labored from the pain and blood loss. "**It was your former *kōchō* that orchestrated these events. He approached me, not I him. As long as he lives, your clan will forever be dishonored. No amount of killing can change that.**"

Kawaguchi had said something similar, about Kintake, anyway. Terry mostly didn't believe Kawaguchi, but Nishida's words made Terry reconsider the possibility. One thing was for sure: Kintake was alive.

Terry cracked the glow stick, shook it, and placed it on Nishida's shoulder. "**Get it on with it, Nishida Sensei. We can't stay much longer, and if you delay us, we'll just kill you outright.**"

Nishida nodded and then sat up as straight as his injuries would allow. He kneaded his waistline just inside his hip, looking for the surest spot to drive the blade into this gut. He found it and positioned the tanto. "**Ciccone Sensei,**" Nishida aspirated, "**will you assist me? I don't have the strength. My injuries are too great.**"

"**You must think me stupid, Nishida Sensei. You won't have the luxury of ambushing me while I lean over you. Get on with it, or I'll oblige my brother's initial demand to heave you from the ravine.**"

Nishida sighed, closing his eyes and accepting that Terry was not as naïve as he had hoped. He'd wished to take one of their assailants with him. Truly defeated, Nishida resigned himself and drove his tanto into his abdomen with a continuous grunt. Then he jerked it upward twice.

Yuri sliced a line from his shoulder to Nishida's jaw, cleaving open his mouth and skull like a partially chopped tree. Yuri didn't feel that Nishida deserved a dignified death and had seen to it that he didn't receive one by maiming him instead and leaving him to die horribly against the stone.

Terry didn't take the time to argue.

Chapter Twenty-one: Die by the Sword

Al Barsha. Jebel Ali, Dubai, United Arab Emirates. Today.

The sand and the dust of the desert paradise were starkly different from the atmosphere in Honshu to which Kintake had been accustomed to over the past sixty years. He couldn't say that he loved sand, but sand was a symbol of something he had never felt until now: freedom. Here, just outside of downtown Dubai, near the industrial port of Jebel Ali and the Southwest Asian jewel of the Mall of the Emirates, Kintake maintained a martial arts school. His little piece of freedom for the first time. For that, he could love sand.

True that he operated the martial arts school in Tokyo, but that was an illusion of freedom. That school wasn't owned by him; the Yakuza owned it. Part of the deal was that Kintake would act as an assassin for the Shogun as well as train the Shogun's recruits—*shatei*. The illusion was strained by Kintake's responsibility to the Fujibayashi and the former Shinobi-no-mono—Saburo Moroi. And the more distance or more time Kintake put between himself and Togakure Ryu, the more Saburo Moroi increased the pressure for him to return; pressure that often erupted into heated arguments and threats. But even the illusion of freedom offered a much-needed reprieve from the suffocation of Ninpo. It paled, however, in comparison to the freedom he felt now.

Now, he had his own residence and his own school. He wasn't beholden to anyone's code, nor did he have to answer the call of a paymaster. His life as a Shinobi was over. His plan had worked, finally. The cost had been great, and it hadn't gone off exactly perfectly, but it had worked. And he was free. For the first time. Free.

Kintake's voice echoed as he barked a command. With impressive silence, arms and bodies jerked and snapped into position. He gave another, and their limbs swung and snapped again. Parents of myriad ethnicities, mostly Arab and Filipino, lined the perimeter of the training floor and watched with amazement the skill of their young students. Omiyoshu Sensei had disciplined the youngsters into fine athletes with an exclusive art.

Kintake was the only instructor in the region that taught little-known arts *daken-taijutsu* and *ju-taijutsu*. He informed newcomers that his art wasn't the commercialized, competitive styles that the vogue, boutique-style schools taught. His art was a special discipline that had been passed down for generations to only the most exclusive groups— only the most serious, focused minds. He even used a wicker basket filled with beads to teach potential students to pay attention to detail; it hooked them every time.

Kintake couldn't have asked for a more dedicated clientele. He even had a wait list of potential clients salivating to learn. Business was good and prosperous. Kintake had only been able to dream of a successful life of his own creation. Never did he think it would truly happen. But here he was, teaching a classful of hungry students a world away from Ninpo.

He barked another command.

They obeyed.

His clients were deeply fascinated with his charisma, expertise, and his background. Where was he from? Where did he learn *taijutsu*? What was his life like? And why did he choose to bring his art to Dubai? Kintake explained that he was from a rural, forgotten region of Japan that was leagues from the hustle of urban life.

He commanded. They obeyed. Arms and bodies snapped into a new position.

Kintake said that he came to teach a dying art and to mentor a new generation, to provide them with a legacy that connected them to a rich and ancient past.

He commanded again. They obeyed. Arms and bodies snapped into another position.

Kintake said that his family had moved on from his art, disapproving of Kintake's chosen path—a tragic loss but a necessary one.

He commanded one last time, and the youngsters concluded with a showy display that left their parents in awe. Kintake scanned the small crowd of parents—their eyes bright and faces so full of life. Then he saw *those* eyes. Two unmistakable, icy-blue, hateful orbs, like a predator's eyes glowing in rogue light.

Ice began to form in Kintake's stomach and began to climb his esophagus. He swallowed hard, trying to push the feeling back down. His eyes darted across the cascade of parents and found Terry further to the right. Kintake's eyes found Yuri again, who bored holes in Kintake's face with his eyes. Kintake never even saw them come in, nor had the parents, who were still completely oblivious to their presence.

They'd found him.

Of course they'd found him; finding targets was what they were trained to do—it was what *he* had trained them to do. Kintake tried to remain unfazed. Admittedly, it was hard when he could see the contemptuous hunger in Yuri's face and the cold menace in Terry's. Kintake had truly hoped that they'd be killed in their crusade when they weren't killed during the ritual combat. He'd been sure, at the very least, the Momochi would finally put the brothers down. But deep down inside, he'd known it would come to this: him versus them.

Terry and Yuri said nothing. The patrons did not suspect the threat lurking among them, but they could feel it. There was a sudden skittish tension in the room like deer watching dark tree lines for the movement of wolves.

The brothers could have drawn a gun and shot him by now; they hadn't, though. That meant that they had come with a parlay in mind. Perhaps Kintake could talk them down. It was an unlikely chance, but it offered better odds of survival—or at least a diversion until he could escape—than fighting both of them did.

A warm smile stretched across Kintake's face. "Ladies and gentlemen," he said, clasping his hands together, "I'm sorry, but I have to end our session early this evening."

The patrons were a sea of confusion. Kintake never ended early. He devoutly held to schedule, asserting that consistency was the mortar of discipline and that discipline couldn't be rushed.

"Please, I ask that you all excuse me. I have two out-of-town guests that have just arrived unexpectedly, and I really must attend to them. "

The emotions were mixed. Some immediately called to their children. Some scanned the room for the interruption, landing on the two strangers. Some were indignant.

Terry ignored them, staring hard at Kintake.

Yuri's patience with the suspicious occlusion of people wore thin. "I'll start killing everyone in here," Yuri said aloud, drawing his ninjatō and whipping it in a lazy display around his shoulders. "If any of you stay, or you choose to dilly-dally, it's your funeral."

The tension-humid air thickened, and a dose of malice was injected when Terry hefted a naginata from a rack, lifting it to eye level to check the weapon's shaft for warping and integrity. He gave the room a sinister look that rivaled his brother's. The patrons got the message—there was a real possibility of violence—and started filing out. One patron asked Kintake if he needed help, to which he answered, "No, I will be just fine. I must speak to these gentlemen about a family affair. Please, afford us the time. I am terribly sorry for this inconvenience."

One teenage student even claimed that if Kintake was feeling threatened that he and the other experienced students would defend him.

"Cute, kid," Terry said, cracking a grin and resting the shaft of the weapon against his shoulder. "We don't do karate. Now get out before you get hurt."

Kintake smiled warmly, nodded, and then indicated the door with his hand. Everyone drained out through the door. It was just Kintake, Terry, and Yuri now.

"I suspect," Kintake began, wringing has hands, "that you came to talk, since neither of you has attacked."

"I was advised to postpone decapitating you immediately," Yuri deadpanned. "Wait for it, though. It's coming."

"Indeed," Kintake replied, sounding almost amused.

"You owe us an explanation," said Terry.

Yuri jumped in. "You owe him an explanation. I could care less what you have to say."

Terry didn't miss a beat. "You owe us an explanation. You said that you would answer our questions if we survived the ritual. Now you have a lot to answer for."

"Fair enough." Kintake nodded. "May I ask how it is that you found me?"

They stared hard.

"I thought not."

Terry's hand shot up, presenting a picture of his parents found in the trophy book dedicated to Oharu's kills. "What is this?"

"Well, this is a bit awkward to say the least—"

Yuri cut him off. "Answer the fucking question, Kintake." That was the first time Yuri had ever addressed him by his first name.

"Why did Oharu have it?" Terry asked.

"Oharu was a lieutenant in the Yakuza—an ambitious one—and a hitman."

"Did he kill our parents?"

Kintake chewed his bottom lip as he considered his answer.

"Did you know the whole time?"

Kintake locked eyes with Terry and exhaled as he thought about what to say and how to say it.

"Did you betray the clan?"

Kintake held Terry's stare.

"If he isn't going to answer anything, Terry, I'm just going to gut him and be done with it," Yuri said.

"Listen, all is not what it seems. There have—"

"No more lies!" Terry roared. "Kawaguchi ratted you out before I splattered his brains all over a train terminal. And a week later, before Yuri hacked a slice out of Nishida's face, he corroborated the story. All this after *you* called to meet with Akiko at Izumo Ryu temple. And after you lied about Oharu being Fujibayashi."

Kintake shrugged. "Part of me knew it would end up this way. I always knew. I just hoped it wouldn't."

Yuri's brow furrowed. "You always knew betraying your clan— your people—would end this way? You make it sound like betrayal is something to aspire to."

"I have betrayed no one. I have wanted nothing save to be free. Surely, you, Yuri, understand that. You too wanted to be free."

Yuri's lip curled.

"Free?" asked Terry.

"Yes."

"Free from *what*?"

"From Ninpo. Just like Yuri wanted." Kintake indicated him with his chin.

The brothers looked at each other.

354

Kintake continued, "Ninpo is an undying slave ship with a captain who tells lies of honor and paradise. It sails without end with a rotting cargo of downtrodden souls. It cleaves to a tide of despair and throws its crew overboard to ensure that it remains seaworthy. Do you not see? We have been slaves to dead masters. We always have been. I freed you. I freed all of us."

Terry's face pruned. "On what planet does this make any sense? You didn't free us; you sent us to die in an ambush that the evidence claims you orchestrated."

"No, Ninpo sent you to die. I was under no obligation to stop you from doing what you thought was right."

"Don't give us that bullshit, Kintake. You made the decision. You chose the fighters. You negotiated the terms," Terry said, stabbing the air with his finger to each point. "*You* sent us to die, and then you had the Fujibayashi murdered—massacred."

"The Momochi and Yakuza did that."

A wave of anger washed over Terry's body at Kintake's denial of responsibility. "Convenient. A scapegoat for your actions. Plausible deniability. If you wanted freedom so badly, you could have taken to the battlefield yourself, and they'd have *happily* set you free."

Kintake showed them his hands. "Were it that easy. Do you think the Momochi would have sat by idly had we not abided the code? Do you think they would have hesitated in descending into Togakure Ryu to exact bloody retribution? There was never an end in sight. Lives have been thrown away for Ninpo since its inception, and there were going to be many more after you, just like there were many before you. I fought in the ritual a generation before you, and the loss was great, unbearably so. Both of my brothers were killed so that Saburo Moroi could ascend to Shinobi-no-mono. I bared the scars of my brothers' deaths," Kintake said, tracing his facial scar with his finger, "ever since. I even lost my mother to it. I, however, resolved to end the cycle."

"And that justifies betrayal?"

"Would you not kill for your parents?" Kintake paused to let them consider it.

There was silence except for the drumming of Terry's heart and the crackling fire inside Yuri.

Kintake continued, "Why then should I be different? Besides, you cannot betray that which you claim no affiliation with. That is why I would not allow your brethren to kill you, Yuri. Because you, like me, wanted nothing to do with Ninpo."

"Don't compare me to you," Yuri snapped. "I'm nothing like you."

"What makes you so certain?"

"Because I want to be free of Ninpo. I won't murder innocent people to achieve it."

"And that is why you are, and always will be, a slave. Freedom is not always clean. It so often requires blood."

Terry felt heat rising from his stomach. "Was Akiko's death part of your calculus? Was this self-perceived emancipation worth the life of your own daughter? Were you even aware that she's dead? Does that even matter to you?"

Kintake's jaw tensed, and he exhaled a sound of resignation through his nose. "Yes, on all counts. You, Terry, sent her...my daughter...to eliminate the Shogun. When she was done, I"—he paused—"took her life. I had to."

Terry bristled as anger began to boil his insides, and he lurched forward a step before regaining control. Now, knowing that she was murdered by the very man who gave her life, Terry considered foregoing the need for answers, for blood. He hung his head and tapped it with the shaft of the naginata as he figured out where to put his swelling emotions, his vision blurred from tears. As if the massacre wasn't bad enough to deal with, her death was one more weight added to the burden.

Yuri's breathing became labored watching his brother's anguish. Akiko's death was tough, but it was no more injurious for Yuri than the individual deaths of the Fujibayashi. He knew, though, it was one hell of a blow for Terry. Terry had always had something for her; in another life, he would have wanted to love her. Now there was no chance. Even the dream was shattered. Yuri's eyes found Kintake again and blazed hotter than before as he began to pace the edge of the room.

Kintake retreated a few steps and raised his hands in a display of quiescence. "It was a calculated risk. My daughter made her choice—to be a slave. I tried to free her in life. I had no other choice but to free her

356

in death. There was no reasoning with her. She was more like her mother than she was like me in that regard.

"Freedom comes at a terrible cost, indeed: my brothers, my mother, my daughter, and many that I called friend—Oharu among them."

"How did our parents factor into this cost equation?" Terry asked, hanging his head but composed.

"Oh, for goodness' sake," Kintake said, growing frustrated with the back and forth, "you are not the only victims here that lost parents. I told you that I lost my mother too."

"Kintake," Terry said sternly, imploring him to answer the question.

"How can one be free of a culture that murders its subjects for thinking differently? I couldn't just walk away. Saburo Moroi and his confederates would have never allowed it. We were forced to march to his music. My mother took her life because of it; her grief over the loss of her two eldest sons dishonored her, and Saburo Moroi ordered seppuku. I, the new kōchō at the time, had to watch helplessly as my mother spilled her intestines on the ground. I could not give my mother back the lives of my brothers no more than I could return her guts to her stomach. At that point, I decided that I wanted to be free of Ninpo, but I could not just walk out of Togakure Ryu. Like any slave, I needed a plan if I were to leave alive. You two were the key to freedom, my own personal warriors, free of Togakure Ryu's conditioning, that I would train to kill Saburo Moroi and aid me in a coup. He took you from me, though, just to spite me, to turn you against me."

Terry's eyes found the ground. "None of this makes sense. Why would you train us to kill him and then banish us? Why would you kill Akiko? Why did you side with the Momochi? Why with the Yakuza?"

"One plan wasn't enough. A man like Saburo Moroi does not remain in power because he is not cunning. All plans before this one had failed. You were a failed plan and a liability. But you were no good to me dead if a case arose in which I needed you to fight. You two and Saki were some of the most gifted Shinobi ever, and I could not afford your death until I was ready.

"As for my daughter, I tried to spare her life. But she gave me no other choice. She is a fierce fighter and an even fiercer enemy. She fought valiantly."

Kintake eyed the hallway that snaked to the door, looking for the flash of red and blue; he saw none yet. He was sure at least one patron had called the police, especially with Terry and Yuri brandishing weapons as they did. He just needed to keep their attention. Telling them lies, though, only threatened to force their hands early. He needed to keep his cool and stall them longer. "The Yakuza were my ticket out of Togakure Ryu. I had accrued tremendous credibility eliminating their enemies either by my own hand or by sending you two when you were teenagers."

"What?" Terry's face was creased with perplexity.

"I brokered the deal with the Shogun and Nishida. The Momochi had no investment in me save for Akiko's mother, so they were happy to accept the power of being the only clan left in existence. The Shogun supported it because he intended to use the last surviving clan as a means to extort federal monies from the government when the heritage committee leaped to preserve the existence of a dying jewel of Japanese history."

"They massacred Togakure Ryu," Terry said, emotion arcing in his voice.

"And they would have murdered me if I had left."

If everything that had transpired over the years were a wound, Kintake's words were salt.

"You speak of us like objects," said Terry. "Possessions you could just throw away when we had served our purpose."

"Kintake," said Yuri, who was reluctantly strangling his aggression because his brother had asked him to, just wanted the old man to answer their real question: "Did our parents die in a plane crash? Yes or no?"

Kintake looked hard at Yuri. He was tired of hearing them mewl over their parents after all these years. It was the same old story. He had always tried to spare their hearts. But if it were the truth that they really wanted, then he'd give them the truth. "They did not die in a plane crash."

Frankly, he'd hoped he could talk his way out of this, but he had resolved that they, like his daughter, didn't share his sensibilities, his vision, and his conviction. Now he'd give them the merciless truth that they *so* desired. Then he'd fight his way out.

"Oharu killed them after all, and you knew about it?" Terry asked. "You lied about it."

Kintake let out a mirthless laugh. "No—Oharu killed no one. No one of repute, anyway, that he didn't shoot in the back. Oharu was an awful assassin. He proved to be a coward and a strain. So no, he didn't kill your parents." Kintake's face darkened. "I did." There, he'd said it.

The boil began to spread from Terry's chest to his arms.

Yuri's grip on his ninjatō was so intense that his knuckles were white.

"Why?" Yuri asked harshly.

Kintake said, "An explanation won't change your mind, Yuri."

Anger was transforming into outrage inside Yuri. Electricity shot through him, and his ears filled with fog. It was doubtful that he would have even heard Kintake's explanation if he had given one. Now Yuri's need for answers had reached its end. There was only one thing he wanted.

"How can you be so impassioned about taking innocent lives?" asked Terry, his voice rising, belying his anger. "You destroyed our childhood and murdered our family! Have you no honor?"

Yuri was practically salivating.

"You are an assassin, Terry. As am I. Killing is our craft."

"I did it with honor!"

"It disappoints me that you believe in your own legend," Kintake said. "There is no honor. You murder, and you justify it with Ninpo. I figured your time away from Togakure Ryu would have opened your mind. Made you realize that Ninpo is a construct made to control you."

"We're going to kill you, and we're going to make sure it's painful."

Kintake had tried to talk them down. The chance of success had been small, but it had been worth a try. At the very least, he'd managed to stall long enough for him to hold them off in a fight before the police arrived. Better to fight them for ten minutes than for twenty if he could help it. He couldn't beat them both, but he could delay them. That was all he needed.

He sighed deeply and drew his ninjatō into a high guard. He couldn't stall them any longer.

Terry weaved his naginata through the air before snapping it horizontal and holding it like a spear. Yuri skipped across the salon floor, on cue, and arced a meteoric overhead strike at Kintake's forehead, venting anger with a roar. The blade shrieked through the air before finding the steel of Kintake's weapon. The metal-on-metal *clang* as the blades locked was a thunderous metaphor for years of stewing anger and contempt.

Yuri drove himself bodily into Kintake, the blades' edges scraping maliciously until his was face to face with Kintake. The men locked eyes. Here they were, finally, after all these years, this one inevitable moment in which they knew the end was not far off. In Kintake's eyes, Yuri could see frustration and desperation. In Yuri's, Kintake could see the anger and the mania that had germinated over the years.

Yuri exploded, letting out another roar as he drove Kintake back and plunged a killing stroke toward Kintake's heart. Kintake directed it over his shoulder and responded, trying to slice Yuri's head from his shoulders. Yuri channeled his momentum into a somersault, narrowly avoiding Kintake's blade as it hummed over his head. Kintake wanted desperately to follow him and finish the job, but Terry was not far behind. Kintake turned just in the nick of time to react to the blade of Terry's naginata stabbing for his head.

Kintake jerked his head to the side and then whipped his ninjatō up at repeated angles, deflecting the repeated stabs that followed. Kintake tried not to give ground into Yuri—who was surely on his feet by then.

Yuri launched another strike, this time at the back of Kintake's head. Kintake disengaged a parry with Terry and slung his sword behind his head to intercept. The blades clashed, but Yuri didn't relent—he pressed the attack, slicing at angles, spinning, and launching kicks to fill their latency.

Kintake etched polygons with his parries and blocks, looking for proper counters. Yuri wouldn't give in, responding to Kintake's unsuccessful counters with increased aggression. Kintake managed to time Yuri and slipped through his guard, forcing Yuri to give ground. Yuri, on the defense for the briefest of seconds, ducked Kintake's slash, and Terry leap-frogged over him in an acrobatic display, attempting to impale Kintake from above.

Kintake drove the naginata off target and countered by trying to bury his sword in Terry's ribs. Terry used his weapon like a staff and spun it to defend his trunk. He then turned the weapon's momentum into an offense, repeatedly attacking with both ends. Kintake mounted a defense walking a half-circle trying to keep Yuri in view. Terry ramped up the speed, pirouetting two full revolutions through the air, the spear merging with his vertical axis. Kintake saw the blade of the naginata beginning to level through the last turn—the threat of the weapon's length becoming realized—and launched a bone-shattering kick that purchased Terry's gut and folded him like a half-filled sack with a muffled *crunch*. Terry hit the ground and rolled clear, trying to catch his breath with the stabbing pain of broken ribs. Kintake barely had time to settle both feet onto the ground before Yuri was on him again, pouring the aggression on by the liter.

Yuri was relentless, hurling strike after strike and driving Kintake this way and that around the salon. Yuri's assault seemed to gain more energy as time pressed on. Kintake had always known Yuri to be a kinetic fighter, but he was surprised to see that Yuri had been able to increase that energy over the years. He thought surely that Yuri would have begun to slow as he approached his third decade, but that was clearly not the case, and Kintake wasn't sure how long he could keep up.

Yuri struck high and low, drawing arcs, circles, and zig-zags with the tip of his blade. Kintake drew perpendicular velocities, breaking even each time. Yuri corkscrewed towards the floor, arcing a lightning slash at Kintake's shin. At the last second, Kintake jerked his leg up and stomped down on the blade, grinding it to a halt. Yuri had time to look up and see Kintake's fist barreling at his face before it careened into his cheekbone with a *crack*. Yuri, his sword, and some of his teeth hit the ground at the same time. Kintake was readying a killing strike when Terry, from across the room, buried his tanto deep into the meat between Kintake's shoulder and chest.

Kintake barely had time to register the pain radiating out from the epicenter of the knife, as Terry was a half-second behind it. He had scooped up Yuri's ninjatō in a rearguard and spun and sliced fierce figure eights, attempting to lop off whatever unlucky appendage got into his line of fire. Kintake responded the same as he had done with Yuri, except that he had to will himself to be even faster—Terry was a better swordsman than Yuri. Terry was a busy swordfighter like his brother, but he had Saki's speed and precision; Terry pressed his attacks craftily and with grace. Kintake was at a disadvantage for more reasons than just a knife jutting out of his body: Terry was, in fact, a better swordsman than Kintake himself. The only chance Kintake had was to crowd him; Terry didn't handle crowding as well as Yuri.

Speaking of Yuri...

Kintake leaped clear of a sweeping slash from Yuri who was holding Terry's naginata. The brothers advanced, alternating blows and corralling Kintake. Kintake redoubled his efforts the best he could; his entire left side felt like he had shattered glass in his veins from having to use his arm in spite of its injury. He was struggling to keep up, losing ground piece by piece. Terry arced a cleave over his head. Kintake's block couldn't drain the strike fully of its kinetic energy when they met, and the blade bit into his face, reopening his facial scar from forehead to chin and revealing white meat and bone; blood splattered onto a nearby wall. Just a second behind it, Yuri smashed the blunt end of the naginata into Kintake's face, turning his nose to powder and spraying blood and mucous in a pink mist.

Kintake crumpled, and Yuri leaped on him in a frenzy. Despite being tactically blind and racked with pain, Kintake drew and stabbed his tanto in the meat of Yuri's thigh. Yuri howled, and Terry yanked his brother off Kintake by his shirt, preventing Kintake's retaliatory slash from opening Yuri's throat. It didn't prevent a slash across Yuri's chest. Lucky for him, he was wearing a flak vest beneath his shirt.

Kintake was instantly back on his feet, his face an endless stream of blood. He drew the knife from his shoulder and slung it to the side. "I have had enough," he said, spitting blood defiantly. "Ninpo took everything from me: my brothers, my mother, my daughter. You will not take what I have left."

362

Yuri gritted his teeth as he thumped the wound on his thigh with his fist.

Terry pressed the attack again, slicing at Kintake in circles. Kintake backed away and sidestepped as quickly as he could. His vision was blurry, and his head was cloudy. Kintake snatched a staff from a nearby rack, planted his feet, and whirled it, blocking Terry's strikes. Kintake was looking for a counter as Terry pounded his guard.

Kintake fired a roundhouse, missing Terry but setting up for a sweeping attack with the staff. Terry sensed it and bounded backward, tossing Yuri's sword over his shoulder. Yuri was airborne as if choreographed, seamlessly grasping the handle of the blade and bringing it crashing down on Kintake's staff, the blade biting a huge angular chunk from the treated wood. Yuri followed with a second overhead strike, which split Kintake's block in half. Right behind it, Yuri's foot battered Kintake's chest. He coughed and fell back.

The brothers changed tactics. Terry—his naginata back in hand—fought linear, stabbing and spearing straight ahead and chopping overhead, using both ends to defend. Yuri rushed in at angles, zipping in from the flanks, slashing and kicking, never staying still long enough for Kintake to get a fix on him. The tactic effectively neutralized Kintake's counters and his deathlike patience. He was forced to fight at their pace, blocking and striking with the two halves of his defunct staff, having no choice but to fight Terry at a distance he preferred and Yuri with the energy he craved.

Terry drove forward with the naginata, trying first to impale Kintake's chest, his stomach, his face, and his groin before attempting to chop a bowl-shape from his skull. Kintake parried and dodged, keeping his guard close for when Yuri leaped in.

Like clockwork, Yuri charged in from the flank like an angry rhino. He slashed twice and then did an aerial cartwheel over Kintake's horizontal counter. Yuri landed on his feet and continued into a somersault to outpace Kintake's second response, who then turned to answer Terry's renewed volleys. When Yuri was on his feet again, he snatched a small nearby table and bashed it against Kintake's kidneys, staggering him, but he managed to stay on his feet and parry and dodge the strikes from both brothers.

The old man was a hell of a fighter, to say the least.

The three men gave it their all in spite of bumps, bruises, broken ribs, lacerations, stab wounds, and blood. They were a ball of whirling and clashing steel and wood, controlled chaos, a light-speed game of chess, a game of poker with the highest possible stakes. The pain and the fatigue were intensifying, so was the desperation on both sides of the fight. Kintake was losing; he couldn't keep this up anymore—he had to escape if he was going to survive. It was the only chance he had.

Just then, he saw red and blue light reflecting off the walls in the hallway.

Kintake caught Yuri and staggered him with a backbreaking elbow counter that split his eyebrow open. The strike tactically placed Yuri in between Kintake and Terry. Kintake jumped back, grabbed hold of a heavy shelf near the doorway, and pulled it over. Yuri and Terry leaped clear as they watched Kintake disappear through the door. They hurtled the shelf and sprinted after Kintake. They hit the door just in time to see the sand-colored service uniforms of the Dubai police moving towards the door amid red and blue flashing lights. Both men ducked back inside.

"Fuck!" Yuri hissed.

"There's a back door," said Terry, throwing his thumb over his shoulder. "Come on."

"You go," Yuri said, wiping the blood that dripped down his face with the back of his hand. "I'm going to hold here."

Terry shot him a look. "What?"

Yuri pulled a Katana from the wall near a painting. He had his ninjatō in one hand and the Katana in the other. "I'll keep them busy."

Terry's face was painted with mild confusion, then disappointment, and then resignation.

"C'mon, Ter—it'll be fun. Ninpo and all that jazz." Yuri gave Terry a weak smile, wiping more blood from his face. His eyes had that look that said *I'm going to do something stupid just to say I did.* Then he rapped the wound on his thigh again.

Terry searched his brother one last time, the bloodied, bruised constant in his life. Terry didn't know what to say. Yuri didn't either; he just looked at the door and readied himself. Terry pushed back into the salon, hurtled the shelf, and ran for the back door.

Yuri waited by the door with one sword raised and the other held low like a pair of opened scissors. Once the first officer came through the door, Yuri sliced a half-moon with the high sword that severed the officer's gun hand. The officer shrieked and recoiled. Yuri caught the next officer unawares while he watched blood squirt from his partner's freshly cleaved wrist. Yuri popped out, jabbed the low sword in and out of the man's chest, leaving two growing read ovals on either side of the uniform, and withdrew back inside the door.

Then there were gunshots and screaming.

Yuri stayed low in the small hallway as bullets punched holes in the stucco all around him. He couldn't make out what they were saying, but they surely were going to come in after him. The longer he kept them here, the more time Terry had.

Yuri retreated into the atrium and stood to the side of the doorway separating it and the hallway. He waited for the police to make their move.

It seemed like forever before a tactical team of six stormed the front door. They led with a flashbang that half-tumbled and half-rolled down the hallway toward the atrium doorway. Yuri, still pressed against the wall, swatted it with his sword like a hockey puck back down the hallway and caught the team as they were breaching. Their panicked screams were shrill when the canister exploded in brief thunder, brief sunlight, and translucent smoke.

Yuri was out of cover and into the hallway with the katana leveled. He impaled the first officer and hacked the next with the ninjatō, bulldozing them back into their comrades with his shoulder. The third officer attempted to raise his carbine, but Yuri slashed the weapon's sling, forcing the officer off target, the bullets going into the floor. Yuri unzipped the man's face with another slash before sending the fourth officer into the wall with a bone-crushing elbow. The fifth officer struck Yuri in the cheek with the butt of his weapon, staggering Yuri enough that the fifth and sixth officers could rush him. Yuri had awareness enough to recover and shoot the gap, cutting an angle and getting both arms around the fifth officer's hips, taking him to the ground. The sixth officer leaped on Yuri's back and locked both arms around his neck. Yuri struggled backward to shake him, but the man's grip bracketed as he tried to squeeze Yuri into unconsciousness. Yuri bucked wildly, and the sixth officer hung on desperately. The fifth officer, back on his feet, cracked Yuri in the cheek with his weapon. Yuri didn't go down; the hit only galvanized him. Yuri struck back, planting his heel in the man's chest, toppling him over a fallen comrade.

Yuri yanked and maneuvered inside the sixth officer's hold, repeatedly slamming the man's back in the wall. The officer's lock wasn't fully settled, but he wouldn't let go. Yuri managed to position himself just right and climbed the wall with his feet, flipping over the officer's shoulders—the tables had turned. Yuri drilled the officer in the kidneys with his knee until the man's legs buckled. Then Yuri obliterated the officer's head with the most devastating roundhouse he could muster, knocking the man's still-buckled helmet clean off.

BAM! BAM!

A volcano erupted in Yuri's side, and he collapsed face first into a wall. His breath left a spray paint mark of red on the cream-colored stucco, and his ears gonged like church bells.

"Fuck you, Kintake," Yuri aspirated into the wall.

He could feel a mob of police filling the hallway. He just needed to get to his sword and cut down as many as he could.

"Get that bastard, Terry," Yuri said, the whisper becoming a growl. He launched himself from the wall to his ninjatō as if he had never been shot. Yuri lunged below waist level and slashed a vicious sweep, slicing deeply into an officer's thigh at a terrible angle. The officer shrieked and hit the ground, but not before Yuri was on another, burying his sword to the hilt in the man's gut.

BAM! BAM!

Yuri slumped against a wall and slid to the ground, smearing a portion of the wall with blood. Yuri lay on the ground amidst a field of injured and dead, the side of his face pressed into the floor, blood dripping in a pool around him.

The policed leaped on him like wolves to restrain him.

The room was spinning, and the edges of his vision were darkening. His body felt cold against the hot, Middle Eastern floor. Yuri, though, was somewhere else, sometime else. A final whisper left his lips, "Veronica."

*　　*　　*

Terry hurtled through the back door, slamming thunderously against the stucco wall. He skidded to a halt in the loading area of the lonely commercial strip and scanned it. Then he beamed out to the street and looked both ways frantically. To his left, around the corner were the police—and failure. To his right, the vast expanse of the lower Dubai urban sprawl crawled towards its skyscrapers and a vast desert brownness turned gray with the setting sun. The sidewalks and street weren't busily flowing.

Terry's eyes darted as he looked for a clue as to which direction Kintake had made his escape. He was bleeding; he'd leave a trail. That was when Terry's eyes spotted a trail of crimson that led diagonally across the street. He sprinted after it, angling down a dusty cream-walled alley between an aging food market and a row of janky-looking tailors. The blood trail led to the right, down a three-way between the buildings. Terry raced down, keeping up his speed.

Within two blocks, Terry found himself in a souk, swimming with residents and shoppers dressed in veils and thobes as well as Western wear. His speed slowed with the increase in volume, but his conviction didn't. His eyes made a parallelogram, darting side to side, down at the sporadic drops of blood, and then downrange. He knew Kintake couldn't be far; Kintake was injured, and outrunning Terry on foot was out of the question. Then the trail went cold.

Terry pushed a little further into the souk, investigating patrons' clothes for blood spatter from Kintake pushing by. Terry also looked for rogue drips near doorways of shops in which Kintake could be hiding. Nothing. Nor did anyone seem alarmed.

Terry pushed back toward the trail's end, anxiety beginning to strangle his stomach. A vision shot through his mind of Yuri looking Terry in the face with an expression that said, "Don't let me down. Get that bastard," before Yuri darted out the door with a sword in both hands to greet the police.

The trail couldn't have just ended. Kintake was bleeding profusely, so someone had to have seen him. And if the blood trail stopped, that meant Kintake had to have stopped the bleeding, which

367

also meant that *someone* had to have seen him. Terry didn't have much time to deliberate; the police were going to expand their perimeter very soon looking for him. Anxiety was holding hands with desperation, and Terry decided to start shaking down the vendors and patrons.

Terry approached a media vendor in a hijab and said harshly in his crude Arabic, "Have you seen a bleeding Asian man come through here?"

She gave Terry a sheepish look, and the patrons to either side of him stirred.

"I know someone here as seen him. He has a bleeding wound on his face." Terry traced a line on his face with his finger.

The vendor's expression was still sheepish but suddenly morphed into one of alarm. Terry whipped around just in time to get an arm up to protect his neck from being impaled with a screwdriver by a woman in a black niqab; it dug a crevasse in his forearm instead. Terry clasped his arm and growled. The patrons in the thoroughfare peeled away from the assailant and Terry.

She came again, and Terry darted backward, the screwdriver just missing his face. The woman didn't let up, stabbing at him again. Terry bounded sideways, out of her reach, and then leaped onto a vendor's table to escape the next attack. Then the woman turned and ran—limped quickly, really.

Terry, crouched in a three-point stance, noticed that she was wearing the same shoes beneath her abaya that Kintake had been wearing. And for a second there, Terry had thought the old shinobi had enlisted a bodyguard. The man was old, but he was still full of tricks. Terry gave chase, ignoring the bystanders that had watched the violence. He kept his eyes on Kintake, who was moving as fast as an injured man aged sixty years could.

Kintake hobbled across a tight thoroughfare lined with two- and three-story buildings and packed densely with slow-moving traffic. A driver barked hotly at him when he darted in front, forcing the driver to stop short. Kintake didn't even look back.

Terry was two rungs below a sprint, zig-zagging through indignant patrons; they were getting more numerous now. He looked like a football player dodging tackles as he swam over them, side-stepped, and spun. Once he reached the same thoroughfare, he leaped over, getting both feet above the hood of the same car that had almost hit Kintake and slid across it on his rear, landing in full stride. He saw Kintake make a right past an incense stand just fifty feet away.

Terry slowed to make the turn and then accelerated again towards Kintake, who was straight ahead and going through a gate with windows just above and to either side. Kintake checked for Terry over his shoulder and then pulled the gate shut, barring it with its lock and jetting deeper into the covered hall to look for an exit on the opposite side. Terry didn't slow. He assessed the size of the window and determined that he could get through if he went feet first and sideways. He just needed to get up to it.

In a seamless display, Terry bounded up a dumpster and vaulted up the wall, getting ahold of the trimming above the window's frame with both hands, tucking his legs, and sling-shotting them through the orifice like a snake slithering through a crack after its prey. He dropped down and rolled to disperse the impact, found his feet, and accelerated after Kintake again.

Kintake reached the opposite gate that led out to the main road and mass transit rail just on the other side. He went into the gate with his shoulder, but it didn't budge. Then he pulled it—nothing. It was locked.

End of the line.

Kintake ducked and cut an angle as Terry's foot crashed into the gate where Kintake's head had been. Kintake hobbled backward with his guard up, the screwdriver in his left hand. He shot a glance over his shoulder back down the way he had entered—it was behind him now.

"Don't run, sensei. Don't make me have to stab an old man in the back."

"Terry, I refused to die a slave. I wasn't going to be a slave to Ninpo, the Fujibayashi, nor the Shogun."

"You can't be a slave to the dead."

Terry led with his feet, firing several shots at center mass. Kintake blocked and countered with repeat punches, landing two against Terry's face, and then with the screwdriver. Terry slipped it and drilled Kintake in the ribs with a volley of punches before changing directions and slamming him in the jaw.

Kintake spun and struck the outside of Terry with a double-shot, one to the lower leg and one to the thigh. Then he swapped sides, trying to catch Terry in the ribs. Terry collapsed his guard, drawing his knee and elbow together to absorb the impact. Kintake launched another flurry, this time with the screwdriver, catching Terry across the chest and ripping open his shirt, revealing the flak vest. Terry responded with another burst of punches and kicks, going first up the middle and then spinning circles as he looked for an opening in Kintake's desperate parries.

Becoming overwhelmed, Kintake snatched Terry's shirt and pushed him back, dropping the screwdriver in the process. Terry reciprocated, meeting force with force. They pushed back and forth until Terry planted his knee against Kintake's mangled nose, prompting a release. Kintake retreated, holding his face.

Terry pressed the attack again, leading with his feet once more, repeatedly kicking, allowing his momentum to generate more power with each swing. Kintake ducked and dodged where he could, and rolled with the impact of the blows where he could not. Terry wheeled his heel around, missing Kintake's head by a hair's breadth, instead smashing through a clay pipe that climbed a wall. Terry lunged back in with a right and left, but Kintake slipped both and countered with a spinning elbow to the side of Terry's head, immediately following with a spinning hook kick and a reciprocal set of punches that planted Terry against a wall, spitting blood from his mouth.

The two men attacked at the same time, Terry kicking low and Kintake kicking high. Terry caught Kintake cleanly in the knee while Kintake caught Terry cleanly on the side of his head, knocking both men back again.

They took a moment to regain posture and their faculties. Terry wiped blood from his nose and mouth and blinked his swelling eye. Kintake yanked off the niqab to reveal his mangled, swollen face, letting blood stream freely as he leaned against the wall trying to catch his breath.

You go, Ter. I'll hold here. Ninpo and all that jazz. Terry could see his brother's face—the raw determination. Then he could see the anguished face of a teenage Yuri as he hobbled over forested mountains on a broken, mangled foot. Then he saw the face of Akiko and Saki. He saw his parents—the last smiles they'd ever give him. He saw Yuri as a child, screaming for his parents. He saw the expression on Kintake's face as he abused them. He saw the expressionless face as he beat Yuri for Terry's silence. He could see the ghastly faces of the Fujibayashi as they lay rotting in the snow. He saw Veronica's terror as attackers stormed his house. He heard Yuri's voice once more: *I'm your family! I'm the only family you've ever had!*

No.

Terry's blood turned to fire.

NO!

He thrust himself off the wall, lunging with an airborne punch, slamming into Kintake's guard. Terry fired in succession: high, low, high, low, spinning and changing directions, choosing different targets and purchasing whatever he could. Kintake ramped up his defense and used the length of the hall to retreat step by step, stopping most of what Terry dished out and allowing only a couple through. Terry grabbed hold of Kintake's thobe to stop his continual retreat, but Kintake peeled out of it like a snake shedding his skin.

Kintake was covered in a checkerboard of scars. And he had a faint shadow of a serpent tattoo over his heart—it looked as though Kintake had undergone procedures to have it removed.

Terry came again. Kick followed punch, punch followed kick, and kick followed spin. Kintake painted shapes in the air with his arms and legs, redirecting attacks where he could and absorbing impacts with his elbows and legs where he couldn't. Kintake was nothing if not resilient; his defense was solid. Tactics changed: Terry was going to punish Kintake's guard until he couldn't hold it up anymore.

Terry shifted directions by bounding off the wall, and he drove his knee into Kintake. Kintake absorbed it with his arms, going into the opposite wall for support. Terry snapped three kicks at him—low, middle, high—then switched legs and repeated—low, middle, high. Kintake mirrored him with his guard, so Terry feinted right and hooked left, *crunch,* planting a grueling punch against the bone of Kintake's forearm. Kintake cut an angle and zipped out into the open, shaking the pain from his arm. Terry, taking a page out of his brother's playbook, didn't let up. He closed the distance and launched more attacks at Kintake's arms and legs, mauling them with bone-crunching intensity.

Kintake tried to hold his guard, but the pain was too great, and he had to retreat. He backed away, continuing to block and parry until he saw an opening. Kintake timed Terry and slipped his injured leg through Terry's defense, planting his shin against Terry's injured ribs. Terry immediately recoiled, allowing Kintake the advantage for the first time.

Kintake went on the offense, hurling every variation of hand strike that he could muster. Terry kept his parries tight, zoning out Kintake's punches, knife hands, and elbows. Kintake tried to bait Terry into spacing out his guard with feints, but Terry wasn't going to be fooled. Every shot Kintake made for Terry's ribs, he defended jealously.

Despite sensing Terry's vulnerability, Kintake picked his shots carefully, not wanting to overcommit against his larger, stronger, and younger opponent. He kept working the sides of Terry's knees and kept working at trying to get through Terry's guard, slowly backing Terry up until Kintake was in range of the screwdriver again.

The pain in Terry's side was stabbing, and it made swinging agonizing—he just needed another moment to get it together. He kept his guard tight and worked angles around Kintake to continue to zone out Kintake's strikes. The shots to the outside of his knees didn't hurt too badly, but they were beginning to add up, surely in the way the repeated attacks Terry had brutalized Kintake's guard had added up. Terry just needed another moment, just one more. That's when he realized Kintake's play.

Kintake lunged for the screwdriver, and Terry responded with a roundhouse aimed for Kintake's face. Kintake tucked and rolled, barely escaping as Terry's leg howled past his head. Kintake scooped the tool up and turned, only to catch a gutful of a retaliatory sidekick that sent Kintake sprawling on his back.

The pain suddenly muted, and Terry was alive again and on top of Kintake, attempting to wrest control of the screwdriver. Terry pinned Kintake's weapon arm down with one hand and bludgeoned him with the other, using his arm as if it were a club. Kintake fought back with his free arm and bucked his body and legs, trying to erase any leverage Terry was gaining.

In a lightning-strike movement, Terry wrapped himself around the shoulder of Kintake's weapon arm and leveraged his weight against the joint. Kintake groaned and grimaced as Terry applied more and more pressure to it. Kintake squeezed the muscles to keep the joint from separating. Terry jerked, attempting to compel Kintake to let go of the screwdriver. Kintake wouldn't—he couldn't. There was only one way out of this hold, though.

Kintake jerked hard—*pop*—the shoulder painfully came out of its socket. Kintake, grinding his teeth, now unconstrained by the joint, rolled over and pounded his free fist against Terry's undefended face. Terry released him, rolled backward, and hopped to his feet. Kintake tried to stand, but he was just too injured to do it fast enough to defend against Terry's next chain of attacks.

Terry laid into Kintake with utter malice, driving him onto his back and beating him until Terry's knuckles were covered in Kintake's blood. Terry mounted Kintake and grabbed his throat in both hands. Terry looked Kintake in his haggard, swollen eyes—into his blackened soul—and then started to squeeze, not all at once either, but slowly.

Kintake reared, trying desperately to dismount Terry, but Terry's weight was settled in, and he was in complete control. Kintake battered Terry with his unseparated arm. After a few hits, though, Terry slammed a fist into that shoulder's stab wound. Then Terry resumed his grasp on Kintake's throat.

Terry stared his former mentor in the face. Beneath the blood and the torn and lacerated flesh was a man he'd once looked up to— he'd once idolized. The man had been his father figure, had taught him to fight and to kill in the name of honor, had given him a path and a higher calling, had given him life when all seemed lost, had given him a family when his family had been taken from him, and had given him purpose. And all of that was a lie.

Terry was going to make it right as he looked his former mentor in the eye while he choked the life out of him. He was going to do it for all the lies and the lives that had been destroyed because of them. He was going to make right everything that had gone wrong. He was going to find retribution for the path he had been set on. And he was going to finish what his brother started many years ago.

Terry watched as Kintake's face flushed red and his eyes became bloodshot and bulged. Terry listened as Kintake gurgled through a desperate O-shaped mouth, his tongue wagging as he fought for air. Terry watched his former mentor seize and spasm like a beheaded viper, his hands becoming hooks, until there wasn't a drop of life left in him, just a faint aspiration as the air left his lungs and a small twitch in his foot.

Terry sat up finally. "Yuri," he said, "it's over. Tell Mom and Dad I love them wherever you are."

Epilogue

Al Wathba Prison. Al Wathba, Abu Dhabi, United Arab Emirates. Today.

"Prisoner," said a correctional officer in Arabic at the bars of the claustrophobic, dingy brown cell.

Terry's eyes and head turned slowly, his expression empty beneath a wild beard and a full head of neglected, coarse hair.

"You have an envelope," the man said, passing it through.

Terry climbed to his feet and approached the man. They made eye contact for a brief moment, and then Terry took the parcel and returned to his spot on the floor.

He turned the dirty envelope over in his hands and read the return address: Veronica Martin, 4200 Massachusetts Ave NW, APT 504, Washington, DC.

Terry stared at her name for a bit, deep in thought, reflecting on the months of pain and struggle, the ritual, the massacre, the pyre, the killings, his arrest, his trial, and his confinement. It had been all over the news. Now, he was here, wasting away.

Terry slid his finger into the crease and tore the flap. HE pulled a letter out and unfurled it:

Terry,

Where do I start? Never in a million years did I ever foresee myself caught up in such an awful situation, involved with killers and criminals. My life has been thrown into complete disarray. I have been investigated by the police and the FBI in connection with you and Yuri. I've been vilified. And, for what? What did I know? I was just a stupid girl who was deceived by you and your brother.

I loved Yuri. I was so ready to be a wife. I was so ready for the next step. You have no idea how devastated I am to know he was a monster. For goodness sake, I watched him kill. I still can't sleep at night. I can't believe that his soft hands were so capable of such violence. And the nightmare only grew when I saw your faces on the news—the subjects of an international manhunt.

I just want you to know how much damage you did. Would that I could only tell Yuri himself. I also want you to know that I'm eight months pregnant. I'm having a girl. What should I tell her about her father...about her uncle? Should I tell an innocent little girl that they were murderers—monsters? How will she feel knowing that she will have family members she will never see?

This is what you created. I'm so terribly hurt, and there just aren't enough words to express it. I just wanted you to know that while you sit in jail. I wish there were something you could say that would make it all go away, but you can't.

Sincerely,
Veronica

Terry folded the letter and placed it on the floor next to him. He lifted his head and rested it against the wall, exhaling a sigh. What could he say to make it all go away? Nothing. He had nothing to say.

Death Before Dishonor

Printed in Great Britain
by Amazon